THE KING'S COMMISSAR

The King's Commissar

DUNCAN KYLE

St. Martin's Press
New York

Library of Congress Cataloging in Publication Data

Kyle, Duncan.
    The king's commissar.

    1. Soviet Union—History—Revolution, 1917-1921—
Fiction. I. Title.
PR6061.Y4K5   1984   823'.914   83-26992
ISBN 0-312-45584-4

First Published in Great Britain in 1983 by William Collins Sons & Co. Ltd.

In memory of
DESMOND BAGLEY
storyteller
and friend

*Extract from the diaries of
the late Capt. J. R. A. Walters, DSC, RN,
Captain (1917–21) of HMS* Airedale.
Entry for April 19, 1918:–

During the night the man came up on my bridge and
asked permission to remain a while. The sea was high
that night, for we were bucking into a strong nor'eas-
ter. For two hours or so he stood quietly by the bridge
wing door, watching *Airedale*'s bow lift and fall, half a
smile on his lips and an odd look on his face. He was a
handsome fellow, too – what one could see of him
behind the black whiskers, for he had a full set – and I
judged from his stance and bearing he must be Royal
Navy, and twenty-six years of age or thereabouts. He
stood easily on the canting deck, back straight as a gun
barrel. A sailor, beyond a doubt.

The man who must have been Walters's passenger was
born in 1892, and he lived to be seventy-eight, but that is
the only description of him in youth anyone was able to
find, though his history was later investigated with great
vigour by squads of Treasury men. So many of his tracks
had been covered by time or by events or, more often, with
intent, that hardly anything remained.

The foregoing passage of Captain Walter's diary entry is
also not without interest:

Ordered aboard flagship and went, all a-tremble,
wondering what offence I had committed, only to be
greeted, on saluting the quarter-deck, by Beatty's
glossy flag lieutenant *in person*! Given orders: *Airedale* to be made ready at once for sea. She would be
temporarily detached from the fleet and would await,

5

with steam up, the arrival of an unnamed man who would be brought to her in Admiral Beatty's own barge. When the man was aboard, *Airedale* was to sail at once. Only after clearing Scapa was I to open the sealed envelope containing sailing orders. And there was more of this, all said in a low and mysterious tone: our passenger was not to be engaged in conversation by myself or anyone else! How our masters love their mysteries!

Well, the fellow arrived and with him came a goodish amount of baggage for a man alone. I gave him Number One's cabin, which didn't please Porky much . . .

The diary entry concluded:

Put him off at Bergen in Norway, where he was met at the quayside, and then without waste of time I put back to Scapa to rejoin the Fleet.

Captain Walters's daughter, who now owns the diaries, said her father had wondered to the end of his life about the identity of his passenger and that there had been an occasion, some time in the late 1920s, when Walters, introduced to Admiral Beatty at a fleet reunion, had asked Beatty direct about the incident. Ten years had gone by, after all, and it could hardly still be a great secret. Walters afterwards told his daughter that Beatty only gave his celebrated grin and said he could recall nothing of the incident.

One final picture of the man from life was unearthed in Sainte-Maxime in the south of France. The last housekeeper, Anne-Marie Frey, a Frenchwoman by now in her ninetieth year, was able to furnish a word picture of sorts, of him as an old man. He was bald. He wore spectacles. He had a white beard and a white moustache. He sounded, and probably looked, like thousands of other elderly gentlemen. She remembered him well but said there was so little to describe. He had no particular interests, or close friends.

6

He was just an old man who lived alone. But there was one thing. He slept always with a photograph on the table by his bed.

Where is it now?

Alas, m'sieu, destroyed with his other trifles; there was so little and his instructions were perfectly clear.

This photograph – was it of a man or of a woman?

Oh, a woman, m'sieu!

Do you know her name?

I cannot be certain though I believe so. The photograph was destroyed before I could compare.

Compare?

With a picture I saw in a book, later.

Of the same person?

Oui.

The name?

It is a great sadness, m'sieu, if I am right. She was a princess, the daughter of the Russian Tsar. I see her picture in a book and at once I recognize her. She was Maria, but they called her Marie . . .

CHAPTER ONE

———◆———

His Debt goes Marching on

The car park, at thousands of pounds a square foot, was worth a fortune to any developer. In theory, it offered room for four large cars or half a dozen smaller ones to enter and turn, but in fact it contained only two regal spaces. The rest of the area had been made into a garden, blooms appropriate to the season being tended throughout the year by an elderly gardener with a green thumb and a very substantial appropriation of funds. An office building could easily have been constructed upon the site, and in the opinion of a great many people in the City of London should have been erected long ago. Such people were given to talk of assets unused, money going to waste, and ostentation. Car park and garden could be put to better, profitable purpose and in a City of London densely-packed with expensive office space the argument had its point. But this cavilling, though outwardly rational, though founded upon sound calculation and good husbandry, was in truth more emotional, its roots in envy. Proprietors, chairmen, senior partners, those men of substance who controlled great enterprises, were simply jealous.

The car park belonged to, and adjoined, the private banking house of Hillyard, Cleef, at 6 Athelsgate. Its two celebrated parking spaces were used by the two most senior partners; and by no one else, *ever*. It was even rumoured in the City that when, at the time of some Royal Occasion at St Paul's Cathedral, close by, an informal request had been made from Buckingham Palace, a deaf ear had been turned. But then, rumours about Hillyard, Cleef had long abounded.

9

On that spring morning, as most mornings, the royal blue Bentley belonging to Sir Horace Malory halted for a moment in the street outside and his chauffeur got out to unlock the gold-painted chain which guarded the two parking spaces. The car was then driven through, and took its place beside an immense black Lincoln. Malory got out, grunting a little. 'You're to pick up Lady Malory at eleven, Horsfall,' he said. 'She's going to Harrods, I understand, then Burlington House.'

'Yes, Sir Horace. At five, here?'

'Not a minute later.' Sir Horace, at seventy-eight, liked to be back in Wilton Place, whisky in hand, by five-twenty, 'Daffodils are coming up well, are they not?'

'Wish mine were as good, sir.' Horsfall climbed back into the Bentley, turned and drove out, pausing to refasten the chain.

Sir Horace lingered a minute or two, looking at the immaculate flower-beds. Snowdrops were fading, crocuses aglow, daffodils high and ready to burst, and tulips were marshalled to follow. He was no gardener, but appreciation of handsome surroundings came naturally to him. He gave a little sigh, surprising himself, and wondered for how many more years the flowers would be there. Young Pilgrim wouldn't actually override him, but at seventy-eight there couldn't be many more years left, and then Pilgrim wouldn't hesitate: there'd be builders stamping past the chain before the first spadeful of earth rattled on his coffin lid. Of course it wasn't the flowers themselves, no, no; he knew himself too well to believe that. Rather it was *having* the garden, here, in this place. The flowers were a symbol of eminence. Like the gold.

Swinging his stick a little, he walked out of the car park and round the corner, and stopped. Workmen were busy at the front door of Hillyard, Cleef.

To the man who appeared to be in charge, Malory said, 'What's all this?'

The man turned. 'What's it to you, mate?'

10

Mate, Malory thought. *Mate*! Still, there was not much to be done about workmen's manners. He said mildly, 'I work here. Even sign some of the bills. Tell me.'

'You ought to know, then,' the man said aggressively.

My father, Malory thought with regret, would have broken his stick across this oaf's back. He looked at the opening and saw the old mahogany door was being taken from its hinges; and leaning against the wall a few feet away was a door-sized rectangle, wrapped in corrugated paper.

'Ah,' he said, 'I see. We're to have a new door.'

'Good morning, Sir Horace,' a girl he recognized as a secretary said, nipping past him in embarrassment, an hour late and as aware of it as he was.

''Morning.' He touched his bowler hat to her, and found the workman looking hard at him.

'You the boss, then?'

'In a manner of speaking. Tell me about the door.'

'Thought you was an accounts clerk. Well, guv, that old door's coming out, that and the fanlight, and this one goes in.'

'Handsome, is it?' He moved towards the thing and ripped at the covering. Something shiny and coppery gleamed at him.

'Reflecting glass, that is, guv. Three-quarters of an inch thick. Weighs a bleedin' ton, I'll tell you.'

'It would, yes. But what takes the place of the fanlight?' Like the old door, the fanlight was Georgian and exquisite.

'Door's curved at the top, see. Takes up the whole space. Smashing thing it is, all copper. You can see out, but no nosey bleeder can see in. *And* it's reinforced.'

'Charming,' said Malory gently. 'A fine match for the name-plate, there.' He glanced at the plate with distaste. For seventy years nothing but a small, silver square had indicated that this was the home of Hillyard, Cleef. Generations of women had worked on it with silver polish until the copperplate inscription had been worn almost away.

Pilgrim, typically, had moved at once to change it. The new one, in stainless steel, was inscribed in a modern lettering:

HILLYARD
+CLEEF

And that, Malory thought, since there hadn't been a genuine Hillyard in the bank for a hundred years, or a Cleef either, was unnecessary and even misleading.

'And that's coming off, too, guv.'

'The plate – changing it again?'

'Yer. We got another. Want to see it?' The man fished out a small package from behind the new door, and slid out the new plate. 'Brushed stainless, guv.' The man held it for Malory's inspection. 'Somebody don't like that one there.'

Malory's distaste deepened. The lettering this time was modern-barbaric. It now read

HILLYARD
& CLEEF

and reminded him of the figures spewed out by their various computers.

'Like it, guv? I reckon it's great. Just like a record cover.'

Malory said, 'Certainly your description is apt. Thank you for showing me. Good morning.'

'S'okay. 'Ere, guv. You couldn't organize us some coffee, could you?'

Malory smiled bleakly. 'I expect so.'

He stepped past the old door, which now hung drunkenly from a single hinge, and paused for a moment, looking at the door's familiar numeral: the slender, cursive, brass figure six which for decades had been the colophon on the bank's stationery. A smaller version, finer and in gold, hung from Malory's watch-chain. He was thinking that the Almighty sometimes handed out talents in a seriously unbalanced way. Pilgrim was superlatively well-equipped as a

12

banker: sensitive antennae, rapid mind, a good eye for the possible and an even better eye for the impracticable; toughness, skill in negotiation, the ability to think well on his feet. All that: yet in matters of taste Master Pilgrim would have made a very fine Goth.

Slowly, thinking about Laurence Pilgrim, Sir Horace Malory ascended the stairs to the first floor. The day had already provided its first surprise, and there would be others. Pilgrim, six months in London after a meteoric rise in New York, was still engaged in a process he called 'getting acquainted with the total landscape'. When Malory once enquired what he meant, Pilgrim explained: 'I like to know all the flowers by name.' It meant Pilgrim was working a sixteen-hour day, prodding sticks into every corner.

'Oh, Sir Horace,' Mrs Frobisher said, 'I'm so glad you're here. Mr Pilgrim has called a meeting at eleven.' She stood waiting for his hat, coat and stick, and put them away in a wardrobe that was part of the furnishing of her office.

'Be surprised if he hadn't,' Malory said.

'Just time for some coffee, though.'

He sat at his desk, a little heavily. For a man his age, Malory was, and knew he was, quite unusually spry. The stairs took it out of him a bit nowadays, but it was a private point of honour to avoid the lift.

'Oh, Mrs Frobisher, that reminds me,' he said as she came in with the tray, set with two silver pots and a Crown Derby cup and saucer. 'There's a party of men downstairs. One of them asked me, now let me see: yes, he wanted to know could I *organize* some coffee?'

She gave her little laugh. Mrs Frobisher had been Malory's private secretary for two decades, and the laugh was her only real fault. 'You mean the workmen?'

'That what they are? I took them for Vandals.'

She missed the reference, and the laugh came again. 'I'll see to it, Sir Horace. It *is* a pity to move that door, though. So elegant, wasn't it?'

13

Sir Horace poured his own coffee, as he preferred to do, black this morning, glanced at his watch, and busied himself with his morning cigar, a Romeo No.3. He made a small ceremony of cutting and lighting, and settled himself to ten minutes of civilized enjoyment. Life, these days, he reflected, appeared to consist entirely of meetings, and damned dull a lot of them were.

An hour and a half later, the morning's meeting having proved quite as tedious as usual, he was allowing the discussion to pass by him, and considering lunch. The food served in the partners' room was moderately good, but he knew from much recent sad experience that the meeting was certain to continue across the luncheon table. On the other hand, if he went to his club – well, things there weren't too inviting nowadays. The beef was usually all right, but beef wasn't on the menu every day . . .

He realized Pilgrim was addressing him.

'I do beg your pardon, Laurence. What was that again?'

'There's this payment here, Horace. Fifty thousand pounds on the seventeenth of July every year to Zürichsbank. You know anything about that?'

He was instantly awake. 'I think I might.'

'Care to explain? This has been going on for years. Started nineteen-twenty, for God's sake! That's a heck of a time –'

Gently Malory interrupted. 'I'll have a word afterwards, Laurence.'

Laurence Pilgrim's evident exasperation did not surprise Malory. 'Look, Horace, we ought to get this thing out in the sunlight.'

Malory said mildly, 'A point or two for your private ear, no more. Better, I think.'

'Well, okay.'

With the meeting at an end, or at any rate adjourned while the participants washed prior to resumption over food, Malory followed Pilgrim through to the rosewood-

14

and-chrome of the newly-furnished office. 'Have you the file, or just a note of the payment?'

'The file. Right here.' Pilgrim held it up. 'Fifty thousand for sixty years, Horace. That's three million before we even *start* computing interest. What in hell's going on?'

'May I see?' Malory opened the folder. It contained merely a single typed sheet of paper, on which were set out instructions for payment. At the bottom were a few hand-written words. 'It says, "See Senior Partner's note,"' Malory said. 'Did you check up on that?'

'No.'

'Then perhaps you should.'

Pilgrim said, 'What's a Senior Partner's note?'

'Well, when things last a long time, like *this*,' Malory said, 'sometimes they go on well beyond the lifetimes of the people originally concerned. And sometimes matters of discretion are involved also. You see?'

'I suppose. But sixty *years*!'

'I'll have the Senior Partner's Notes sent up.' Malory picked up the telephone and gave instructions to Mrs Frobisher. 'They're kept for safety in the basement safe,' he explained to Pilgrim. 'Most remiss of me not to have mentioned it to you before. Supposed to be my job to introduce you to our curious ways, after all –'

'Horace.'

'Er, yes.' Malory stopped burbling.

'We're talking about fifty thousand pounds a year, right? For sixty years, right? Horace, how *long* were you Senior Partner?'

'Thirty years, or so, I think. Yes, thirty-two.'

'You never questioned a sum like that – *never*?'

'Not me, no.'

A tap on the door heralded Mrs Frobisher, accompanied by a member of the security staff carrying an old, oaken, brass-bound box.

'M'key's on my watch-chain,' Malory said. 'The other's in your safe, I do believe.'

15

They fumbled with the keys, finally lifting the lid. 'It's like Captain Kidd's treasure's in this thing,' Pilgrim said. 'Why the melodramatics? What's wrong with a security file in a strong safe? No, don't say it – it's traditional.'

'There'll be a number on the paper,' said Malory.

Pilgrim looked. 'Twenty-eight.'

'Ah. Just a moment. Yes, here we are.' He extracted an envelope, glanced at it. 'Addressed to the Senior Partner. That's you now, old chap.'

Pilgrim took a stainless steel paper-knife from his desk, slit the envelope and removed a sheet of paper. He read it, then laughed sharply.

'Humorous, is it,' Malory said. 'That's unusual.'

'Don't know about that. It sure is melodramatic.' Pilgrim handed him the paper.

Malory took his half-lens spectacles from the top pocket of his jacket. 'Well, now, let me see.' He read the note and handed it back. 'Clear enough, I should have thought.' He removed his spectacles.

'Clear?' Pilgrim looked at Malory as though he might be mad. 'Let's have it again –'

He read aloud: '"At no time must this payment be missed. Nor is it to be questioned at any time, for any reason. Whatever the future circumstances of the bank, the payment must have priority. Failure to follow this instruction would have extremely severe consequences." Initialled with two Zs,' said Pilgrim, 'and undated. Who was that with the Zs?'

'Sir Basil,' said Malory.

'Who?'

'Zaharoff.'

Pilgrim's fingers drummed for a moment on the red leather of his blotter. 'Look, Horace, I've heard of him. Sure I have. I know he was important and able and tricky and mysterious and all that, but hell – he's been dead fifty years!'

'Forty-four,' Malory corrected. 'The twenty-seventh of

November, nineteen-thirty-six. And do you know, Laurence, sometimes I still find it rather hard to believe. His soul, such as it was, goes marching on.'

'Sure does, and damned costly it is! Horace, *why* did he leave that instruction?'

Malory shrugged. He looked benign and unconcerned. 'There must have been a good reason. A *very* good reason.'

'And we –' Pilgrim's exasperation was mounting – 'aren't even allowed to know about it. Not permitted to – look what it says: "Nor is it to be questioned at any time, for any reason." Horace, it makes no sense at all! Even you must –'

'*Even* me?' Malory enquired with soft malevolence.

Pilgrim at once raised an apologetic hand. 'I'm sorry, Horace. You worked for the guy, I know that. But it's the hell of a legacy, you'll allow, to commit your heirs and successors to payments like this without any explanation *at all*!'

Malory had strolled to the window and was looking out towards the dome of St Paul's. After a moment he said, 'I suppose I can appreciate your feelings. But then you didn't know him.'

'He died six years before I was even born!'

'Quite. But I did, you see. And he was a most remarkable man. Oh, *most* remarkable. He was gifted with extraordinary foresight, you know, among many other things. Almost never wrong.' He turned. 'I tell you, Laurence, even now it would never cross my mind to countermand one of his instructions.'

Pilgrim was staring at Malory in clear puzzlement. 'Not after forty-four *years*?'

'No.'

'I'm sorry, Horace, but it certainly does occur to me.'

'So I see.' Malory pursed his lips. 'I can only advise against it. That's my role now, is it not, to advise? Well, I would suggest this sleeping dog be allowed to lie.'

But Pilgrim had the bone between his teeth. Everything in him: the poverty of his youth, the *summa cum laude* from

17

the Harvard Business School, the years on Wall Street, dictated that no sum of this magnitude, indeed of *any* magnitude, or for that matter any sum at all, should be paid over to anyone without explanation. Not on anybody's say-so, and certainly not on the instructions of some long-dead mystery man.

'I'm sorry, Horace, but that way I can't work. We have to find out *something*.'

'I remind you,' Malory said with the utmost seriousness, 'of Sir Basil's instruction.'

'And I hear you. But the decision has to be mine, now.' Pilgrim paused. 'Look, Horace, I'll meet you half way. We'll keep it close and quiet, right?' He pressed the intercom button. 'Get Graves in here, will you, please.'

With a sigh, Malory sank into a chair. They waited in silence for a few moments. A tap came on the door, and Jacques Graves entered.

'Just once more,' Malory said. 'Don't.'

Pilgrim ignored him. 'Sit down, Jacques. We have a little problem here.'

Graves sat obediently. He was a man of a little over forty, dark-haired, lightly-tanned, and he moved with easy, athletic grace. He had fluent command of several languages, and a wide understanding of finance and of people. Pilgrim, introducing him into Hillyard, Cleef, had described him as 'a high-grade troubleshooter'. Graves came originally from New Orleans French stock, but he was, in another of Pilgrim's phrases, 'International Man'.

He nodded to Malory. 'Sir Horace.' Even the accent was neutral.

'We have a payment situation here,' Pilgrim said, 'which makes no sense, at least to me. For sixty years Hillyard, Cleef has been paying fifty thousand pounds a year to a bank in Switzerland. There is no explanation. All there is – well, we have a kind of hereditary note to the Senior Partner that the payment must continue. Further, Jacques, it must not be queried.'

18

'Ouch,' said Jacques Graves.

'Ouch is right. Now, the instruction was given by Sir Basil Zaharoff one hell of a long time back – *he* died in 1936. Sir Horace has continued to, well, to honour that instruction. That was his privilege. I feel now, though, that maybe the time has come to ask a few discreet questions.'

'Three million paid,' Graves said.

'Right. So what we'll do is this. You're going to Switzerland, Jacques, first available plane. And what you do there is you go to the bank in question, the Zürichsbank, and you ask them, very discreetly, whose account this goddam money goes into. Maybe they won't tell you, we all know it's against Swiss law to let these things out. But you do your best, Jacques. Understand?'

'Yes.'

'Your best best.'

'Sure.'

'But don't stir up any mud. I mean it. The word here is discretion. If the bank won't play, maybe there's some guy works there likes champagne or girls or motor-cars.'

'I'll be there in the morning. First thing,' Graves said.

When he'd gone, Malory tried once more. 'I really do wish you wouldn't.'

'Sure,' said Pilgrim. 'I appreciate that. But –' he shrugged – 'different people take different views. You coming in to lunch?'

Malory took the gold hunter from his waistcoat pocket. 'I think perhaps not. There's a man I must see at my club.'

In fact he ate alone, chewing lengthily at some over-roasted saddle of mutton, and afterward sat for an hour with a half-bottle of claret. He was filled with foreboding.

Jacques Graves took the afternoon plane. That night he stayed at The Palace Hotel in Zürich. The following morning at ten o'clock he telephoned the Zürichsbank and spoke first to a telephonist, and then briefly to a Mr Kleiber. He introduced himself as a representative of

19

Hillyard, Cleef, and arranged an appointment with Kleiber for eleven-thirty. By eleven-forty his conversation with Kleiber was ended, and he was waiting, in a room with a locked door, for 'something we have for you'.

Kleiber had been unforthcoming. Graves's first sight of him had not been encouraging: Kleiber was in his thirties, fair hair cut *en brosse*, a man of medium height whose forehead, above heavy-framed glasses, still bore the residual marks left by ancient pustules of adolescent acne. He was dressed in grey, and it matched his eyes. He was a grey-looking man altogether, who did not offer to shake hands, merely gesturing to the chair which stood on Graves's side of the table. He then waited for his visitor to speak.

Graves looked at him for a moment, familiar with the ploy. Without the lubrication of conventional politeness, any opening acquired a harsh quality. So he began with deliberate triteness.

He said, 'You know Hillyard, Cleef, of course.'

The Swiss nodded once.

'We have not had many dealings with Zürichsbank over the years.'

'Please show proof of your identity.'

Patiently Graves showed him a letter which said, on Hillyard, Cleef stationery, 'Mr Jacques Graves is acting in my name and with my full authority.' Pilgrim had signed it. Kleiber examined it with ostentatious care, thumbnail picking at the embossed letters of the bank's name. 'Go on, please.'

Graves said, 'We have something of a mystery. You will be aware that every year on the seventeenth of July the sum of fifty thousand pounds is paid by Hillyard, Cleef into an account here.'

'Yes.'

Did this bastard speak only in monosyllables, Graves wondered. Kleiber was as opaque and uncommunicative as a concrete block.

20

'You may also know that these payments have been made every year since nineteen-twenty.'

Kleiber nodded.

'The mystery,' Graves said, 'is that the original authorization for these payments was made by a man now dead. At some point the record of their purpose has been mislaid. We continue to pay, naturally, because that is our obligation, but we would now like to know –' He stopped.

A tiny smile twitched Kleiber's lips before he said, 'Unfortunate.'

'And expensive,' Graves agreed.

'Also careless.'

'As I say, we would simply like to know to whom the money is being paid, whether to the bank, or to an individual, or to a company. In complete confidence, of course.'

'Wait.' Kleiber rose and left the room. A lock clicked as the door closed. Graves, familiar with Swiss caution and precaution, was unsurprised.

A minute later Kleiber was back, resuming his seat across the table. He said, 'The payment goes into a numbered account.'

'Yes, I know. The number –'

Kleiber shook his head. 'It is a matter of law. I can give you no information.'

Graves said, 'We hoped you might be disposed to help us.'

'No. The law is specific, as are the bank's own regulations.'

Graves dangled his feeble carrot. 'It would be nice to think our two banks could find other ways to co-operate.'

Kleiber's face was stony. 'Mr Graves, it is impossible. You knew that before you came here.'

Graves shrugged. 'All right, Mr Kleiber.' He rose. 'The door's locked?'

Kleiber nodded, looking at Graves with pebbly eyes. Then he said, 'It is not unknown that people seeking illicit

21

information about numbered accounts approach the staff of the bank. I should warn you that such approaches are pointless.'

'I have no intention –' Graves began.

He was interrupted a second time. 'Only a very few people here have access to numbered accounts,' Kleiber said, 'and all of them, I promise you, will at once report any such approach to the police. The police would prosecute. The man who made the approach would go to prison. It is the law.'

'I understand. Perhaps you'll unlock the door now.'

'In a moment,' said Kleiber. Again came that twitching and superior smile. Briefly Graves wanted to hit the pudding face. 'You will not leave empty-handed, Mr Graves. There is something we have for you.'

'What?'

'Wait, please.'

Kleiber left the room; once more the lock clicked. He returned almost immediately holding an envelope, which he laid on the table. 'For your principal.'

'What is it?'

Kleiber's twitchy smile now became a small smirk. 'My bank holds an instruction that should any enquiry be made about deposits made in the account, that packet is to go to your principal.'

'*My* principal?'

'The principal of the company, or other organization making the enquiry, Mr Graves. In this case Mr Laurence Pilgrim, since we are aware Sir Horace Malory is now standing aside.'

Graves picked up the envelope. It was not addressed.

'Follow instructions,' Kleiber said. 'It is for your principal. Do not be tempted to open it.'

Behind Graves the other door clicked open. He said, a little sardonically, 'Well, at least you're letting me out.'

'Good day, Mr Graves.'

He stood for a moment in the corridor outside the secure

22

interview chamber, turning the bulky envelope in his hands. It was manilla, sealed with red wax, in an image which appeared to be that of an eagle. A guard, in a grey uniform watched him from a desk at the end of the corridor. It occurred to Graves that the envelope was far from new: the shine from the paper-maker's calender rollers had gone, though the strong paper remained pristine. How long, he wondered, had the envelope been here, in the Zürichsbank, awaiting the question?

Briefly Graves debated what he should do. He had been well aware, before Kleiber told him, of the hazards of tampering with the employees of Swiss banks, but he had tampered before and would again, so Kleiber's clear threat didn't discourage him. But the envelope *was* unexpected; and since it was for his principal, it should be delivered at once. He could always come back.

He collected his document case from the guard, placed the envelope inside it, and entered the lift. In the street outside he had to wait two or three minutes for a taxi.

At the airport a disappointment awaited him: the British Airways flight had left and there was an engine fault on the Swissair flight to Heathrow. It was two hours before the jet took off. When he arrived by taxi at Hillyard, Cleef, he was unable to deliver the envelope to his principal. Pilgrim, was, by now, on the M4, being driven to Gloucestershire, and dinner with some Nigerians interested in the funding of a steel mill.

The envelope must wait until morning.

Sir Horace was counting. Two, three, four of the daffodils were showing yellow; a good many more seemed about to burst their buds. Even the tulips were swelling. Early, he thought. But then, the garden was well sheltered.

He strolled round the corner, wondering about Jacques Graves and when he would return. There was no doubt Graves was efficient, but something about the man put him off. Seemed to wear some kind of scent: one of those

23

concoctions advertised for after a shave. Standing too near him once, Malory had caught a whiff of it and was instantly reminded of the interior of his new Bentley. Leather and wood, some such nonsense. Malory had not liked that smell, and he did not like the scent in his nostrils now. It was clear and he recognized it: the smell of danger.

He had quite forgotten the door. When he reached it he halted, appalled. In some way it caught the spring sunshine and reflected it back in dazzling, coppery sheen. God, he thought.

'Oh, Sir Horace, Mr Pilgrim was asking for you,' said Mrs Frobisher.

'Hardly unusual,' he murmured, easing off his coat.

'Yes, sir. He did say –'

'I'm sure he did. Is Mr Graves back?'

'Yes, Sir Horace.'

'Mm. Coffee first, I think.' It was more self-discipline than self-indulgence. Horace Malory, sipping his coffee and removing the hand from the Romeo No.3, positively burned to know how Graves had fared with the unforgiving Swiss. But he had learned long ago that violent curiosity was best allowed to subdue itself. He therefore drank a second cup.

There was a curious expression on Pilgrim's face when Malory entered the modernistic office: an expression he tried to analyse and couldn't quite place.

'Horace, I wanted to see you.' Excitement, perhaps?

'I hear Graves is back. How did he fare with the clock-work neutrals?'

'They wouldn't talk.'

'Hardly unexpected. Still, I must say I'm rather relieved.'

'But he did bring something back.'

'Significant, is it?' The scent was back in Malory's nostrils, stronger now.

'Like something out of a bad B-movie.' Briefly Pilgrim recounted what had occurred at the Zürichsbank.

24

'What was in the envelope?'

Pilgrim picked up a folder which lay beside his hand. 'Why don't you read it, Horace? We can talk about it later.'

'Very well.' He still found Pilgrim's expression elusive. 'Is it of vast import, Laurence?'

'I don't know,' Pilgrim said. 'Probably not.'

As he spoke, Malory suddenly divined the look that Pilgrim wore. He had not seen it before, on that confident face.

It was doubt.

The top sheet was a letter. Paperclipped behind it were a good many sheets of typescript. Malory polished his spectacles, and started on the letter. It was signed with a set of initials: H.G.D.

'Sir Basil would have known better than to approach Zürichsbank. Tempted, as he must have been, he would have thought long and hard, and then put temptation from him.

You, whoever you may be, have not. The annual and presumably unexplained payment must have struck you as requiring an explanation, and since you demand it, it is forthcoming.

Let me tell you how.

Attached to this letter, you will find the first page of a narrative. I assume you will read it, but in case your inclination is to throw it away before you reach the end, I must advise you not to do so.

You will find that the first part of the narrative contains instructions for obtaining the second, the second for the third, and so on. There are seven parts altogether.

I believe you should find the narrative interesting, and I hope interest alone will direct you to pursue the other parts, even if, as you will, you find difficulties in your way. But I must add a warning. If, within three months, you have not obtained parts one to six, part seven will be directed into other hands. The arrange-

25

ments are made, and there is no way in which you can alter or affect them.

Should part seven fall into those other hands, I confidently predict that the consequences will be catastrophic. I choose the word with care. It is in no sense an overstatement.'

Sir Horace removed his spectacles, laid them on his blotter, and stared for a while at the wall opposite. The letter frightened him, though less for what it said than for what he knew of Basil Zaharoff. A secret had been buried, long ago and at great cost. Sir Basil, who never undervalued a halfpenny in his calculations, would only have entered into such an agreement for the most pressing of reasons, and in extreme need. That was why he had advised letting the sleeping dog lie: because Malory's knowledge of Zaharoff made him wary of the consequence of other action. I should have insisted, he thought angrily. I should have *prevented* Pilgrim's asking.

But he hadn't. And this narrative, Malory now felt horribly sure, constituted an opening of Pandora's Box.

He came out of his chair, walked sharply to Pilgrim's office, and pushed the door open. Pilgrim stood by the window with two men, pointing out at something. One of the men held an elaborate camera and had a second hanging from his neck.

'Laurence, if I *could* have a word?'

Pilgrim turned, 'Horace, these two gentlemen are from *Fortune* magazine. Gentlemen, Sir Horace Malory.'

''Morning.' Malory nodded briefly.

'They're here,' Pilgrim said, 'to do a piece about the gold showing.'

The man without the cameras introduced himself. 'Jim Coverton, Sir Horace. And, say, we'd very much like you in the picture. Will that be okay?'

Malory glanced at him. 'Perhaps. But Laurence, I've just read –'

'They're doing some kind of profile on me,' Pilgrim said, with well-contrived modesty. 'Won't take too long for the pictures. You want to come down with us, Horace?'

Malory did not, but he went, walking fuming down the stairs, leaving the lift to the others, and wondering where Pilgrim got his extraordinary sense of priorities.

He succeeded in grasping Pilgrim's arm while they waited to enter the viewing room, far down in the basement. 'Laurence, I'm anxious about that letter. I think we have –'

Pilgrim said, 'Did you read the stuff that came with it?'

'Not yet.'

'Crap,' Pilgrim said decisively. 'Ancient history. No contemporary relevance at all. Stop worrying, Horace. Come and have your picture taken.'

Malory followed them inside. It was two minutes to eleven. On the hour, lighting appeared behind a blank glass wall, and a soft humming began. Through the glass an immense strong-room door became visible, opening slowly on a time clock. 'This vault,' Pilgrim was saying, 'is as safe as Fort Knox. And has to be. Gentlemen, the Hillyard, Cleef gold. Take your pictures, Mr Bauer. Quite a sight, isn't it?'

A huge pile of gold bars stood glowing in the middle of the vault.

'Jesus.' The photographer looked in awe for a moment, then took several pictures swiftly. Then: 'Could you stand right there, Mr Pilgrim. And you, sir.' He was excited, as visitors always were.

Malory posed obediently.

'Now,' said Pilgrim, 'here's the second act. Just watch closely.' He sounded, Malory thought irritably, like a guide at some museum.

Inside the vault a mechanical hand rose from the floor behind the gold stack. Pilgrim said, 'The gold price dipped last week. We have to add a little more.' The mechanical hand dipped and reappeared with a bar of gleaming gold gripped securely in metal pincers coated with rubber; the gold bar was deposited on top of the stack. 'There'll be three this week, gentlemen,' Pilgrim said as the camera clicked frantically. 'The aim is that we have one hundred million in bullion here at the weekly showing.'

'That's dollars?' asked Coverton, his voice a trifle hoarse.

'We're in London,' Pilgrim said. 'It's pounds.'

The hand was depositing a second bar, returning for the third.

'Where's the new gold come from?'

'Sorry, gentlemen.'

'Okay, where's it go?'

'Same sorry. That's our secret.'

'Anybody ever try to bust the vault?'

Pilgrim turned to Malory. 'Have they, Horace?'

'Mmm?' Malory's attention was elsewhere. He'd seen the gold many times before and the letter drummed in his mind.

'Anybody ever try to steal it, sir?'

'Once I believe. Sometime in the 'forties,' Malory said.

'What happened?'

'It is protected in many ways,' Malory said. 'They died, if I remember, of electrocution. Two of them. Very foolish.'

Now the third bar was in position. Pilgrim regarded the stack with pleasure. 'It was a little short just a couple of minutes back. Now it's right up to par again. Take a look at a *full* hundred million.'

They looked reverently for long, silent moments, until the hum sounded and the strong-room door began to close. Pilgrim touched the glass. 'Glass can't be broken,' he said. 'Not with a hammer, not even with a jack-hammer. Too thick to cut. Any explosion strong enough to break it would bring the whole building down.' Silently, behind him, the great door closed. Wheels turned automatically on its face. It sat there, massive and invulnerable, its tungsten steel face gleaming, until abruptly the lights went off.

Malory had watched Pilgrim play the confident show-
man. Where, he wondered, was the doubt he'd seen earlier?

Pilgrim was saying, 'It's been there a long time. We've
been showing it once a week since nineteen-twenty-five.
School kids come, students, politicians looking for reassurance.' He laughed. 'That, gentlemen, is what made
Hillyard, Cleef pre-eminent, and keeps us up there with
Rothschild's and Lazard's. People have faith in a stack of
gold. Not a bad hedge against inflation, either. Now come
and have some coffee.'

'Before you do,' Malory said crisply, 'would you mind if I
had a word with Mr Pilgrim?'

'Not at all, sir,' Coverton said politely. He thought
Malory looked a nice old guy, veddy British, veddy British
indeed. Kind of a relic, maybe.

As they left the viewing room, Malory seized Pilgrim's
arm. 'I warned you,' he said. 'But you chose to ignore it.
Do you realize what you've done? This is something that
was buried; a thing Zaharoff himself intended should *stay*
buried. And now it has been released!'

'Zaharoff himself?' Pilgrim said. 'Listen, Horace, you
have to read that stuff. Some old guy's reminiscences –
what harm can they do? Horace, the worms had Zaharoff
forty-four years back.'

Malory shivered.

'You cold, Horace? The air-conditioning –'

'Not cold,' Malory said. 'But I have a feeling those
worms you spoke of will soon be turning their attention to
Number Six, Athelsgate.'

Pilgrim touched his shoulder. 'We just saw a hundred
million. What can touch us?'

Malory stared at him. 'Something will, I'm sure of it. We
must find out what it is.'

'So find out.'

Malory turned abruptly. 'I'll do that,' he said. 'If I can –
before the catastrophe.'

Back in his own office, Malory poured himself a substantial bracer of Glenfiddich and sank into his chair with a thoughtful grunt.

Pilgrim, he thought. This fella Pilgrim . . .

Malory's senses, all five of them, remained sharp. Plenty of men in the City of London would have sworn he possessed a remarkable sixth, for business, and that it also was finely-honed. Conspicuously missing from his armoury, however, was anything resembling a sense of fair play. His willingness to look at a problem from different viewpoints sprang out of a determination never to overlook possible advantage, rather than from attachment to abstract concepts of justice.

But he was aware of the lack. When necessary, he took remedial steps; and with young Pilgrim, such steps were undoubtedly needed.

For he did not like Pilgrim. Malory was Edwardian by birth, Wykehamist by education; he was deeply conservative, a traditionalist, and massively self-confident. He liked to be surrounded by men of like background and attitude, men whose neck-ties he recognized and whose family ties he also knew, or knew about.

A few days earlier, paying a weekend visit to a crony, he had been put rather uncomfortably in mind of Pilgrim. At the time he was watching an aristocratic litter of three-month-old golden Labrador pups romping with a mongrel terrier which was appreciably quicker, more intelligent and more vital than any of them. Put the thing in canine terms, and yes, Pilgrim was the mongrel terrier, no question of it; Crufts wouldn't look at him above a moment, but quick and vital he certainly was. Yet if Hillyard, Cleef was, in its own way, a *kind* of Crufts, the mongrel was already in.

Forced on him, Malory reflected. Well, not *forced* exactly: but all the same, Pilgrim was a product of change. Hillyard, Cleef had followed Lazard's and Rothschild's into Wall Street rather late, but the American offspring, fattening rapidly, had quickly become the dominant part of the enterprise. On Wall Street, the partners felt that in Pilgrim they had what one described as 'a colt set to win the Derby' and the suggestion had been made that Pilgrim come to London and do a few hard exercise gallops beneath Malory's gaze, before he grew too big and hard-mouthed, and Malory too old, for the experience to be beneficial.

And so here he was: a youngish man who had learned much, learned fast and learned well. Pilgrim was smart. To Malory's mind, he might be a little too smart, inclined to parade his gifts under the noses of men too old and too successful to enjoy it. A lifetime of manœuvre had developed in Malory the conviction that a banker, like an overcoat, should be comfortable and warming. And Pilgrim tended towards the prickly and chill.

What, Malory wondered, would Zaharoff have made of Pilgrim? Or Pilgrim of Zaharoff? It would be fascinating to see what Pilgrim did *now* in the face of events. Real and major danger threatened. Could Pilgrim handle it? It might well be the perfect test of his judgment. But he'd have to be watched carefully, by George! He'd made one bad blunder already.

Malory picked up the typescript. It began:

My name entire is Henry George Dikeston. In the early spring of 1918 I undertook a journey . . .

CHAPTER TWO

An account, written by Lt-Cdr H. G. Dikeston, RN,
of events which took place on, and subsequent to,
the evening of Saturday, March 30th, 1918.

My name entire is Henry George Dikeston. In the early spring of the year 1918 I undertook a journey. Even as it began there could be no doubt of the high responsibility of the tasks entrusted to me. As time passed it became ever clearer that in my hands lay the only means to resolve great matters. By the end . . .

But there is much to tell and care must be taken that the end does not precede the beginning. Were it to do so, much thought and planning would be brought to naught; so that the answer I have devised for those who subsequently misused me would lose its merit. I shall therefore tell my story straightforwardly, save that the end, when it is reached, will not be an end at all, not *finis* in any conventional sense, because yet further events will have been set in train. It now seems I shall not live to see them, but I take satisfaction in knowing they are inevitable.

I hope that you, Sir, whoever you may be, reading this account for the first time, have already experienced what the French describe as a *frisson*: one of doubt or uncertainty or fear.

On the night of Saturday, March 30th, 1918, I was on leave in London, having served for some months in His Majesty's Monitor *Makesure* on coastal bombardment duties, mainly off the Heligoland Bight. I had few friends in London; they, such as they were, comprised in the main serving officers of the Royal Navy, and so were away at sea. Accordingly I was faced with dining alone. Normally I would have sought out a quiet restaurant, perhaps in

Soho, but on that evening I felt some need for entertainment.

I decided, therefore, to attend a performance at the Gaiety Theatre, and to take a quiet supper afterwards. But as so often when one seeks to have one's spirits lifted, the reverse happens. Amid the colour, the music, the elaborate good cheer, my spirits refused to rise and I took myself off to the bar at the first opportunity. I had been standing there for only a few minutes, increasingly conscious, in that cheerful throng, of my own solitude, when a hand fell on my shoulder. I turned to see a brother officer, one Jameson.

'Enjoying yourself, Dikeston?'

'Not particularly,' I said.

'Neither am I. It's too big a change, all this.'

We stood for a moment, looking at the swirling silks and the lights, both of us filled with the knowledge that while all this empty gaiety pranced and thudded before us, men were fighting and dying, and this night upon the North Sea was cold and perilous.

'What would you say,' Jameson asked me, 'to a quiet drink and some supper at my club?'

I agreed at once. Far better to spend the evening with one who could comprehend one's mood than to persevere in the search for elusive and temporary pleasure.

We collected our greatcoats and caps, turned into the thronged Strand, and began to walk westward. The Strand was lively that evening, full of soldiers and girls, all filled with the same kind of somewhat spurious high humour which had so affected my spirits at the theatre.

We turned in at last through a gate marked 'Out'. Jameson's club was the Naval and Military in Piccadilly, whose premises were the late Lord Palmerston's old house; the club was known throughout London as the 'In and Out' because those words, in white lettering, appeared upon its stone gateposts as directions for cabbies and other drivers.

After about an hour of quiet companionship, during

33

which we sat relaxed with our drinks in deep armchairs, exchanging little but the occasional word, one of the stewards approached Jameson. Thinking he was seeking our supper order, Jameson waved the man away, but the steward persisted.

'Beg pardon, sir, but I see your guest is Mr Dikeston.' His eyes were on the braid at my cuff, two wide bands and one narrow. 'Would he be Commander Dikeston, sir?'

'I would,' I said.

'Commander H.G. Dikeston, sir?'

'The same.'

'Then, sir, there is a gentleman at the porter's desk asking for you.'

'Who is he?'

'Didn't give his name, sir. Said he was from the Admiralty.'

I excused myself to Jameson and made my way to where the man stood. He wore mufti; a dark tweed Ulster and a somewhat rakish billycock hat. I approached and stood before him. 'My name is Stott,' he said. 'From the Admiralty. Will you collect your coat and hat, please, Commander, and come with me?'

I remember that I stood regarding him for a moment, and not liking what I saw. It may well have been a premonition of some description, for truly I liked nothing of what came afterwards. 'Can you prove who you are?'

He flung back the cape of his Ulster in an irritated way and produced a card: it was nothing I had seen before, but bore the Admiralty crest and his name and some signature I do not recall. 'Very well. I must tell my host –'

But he interrupted me. 'No time for that. The porter will tell him you have been called away. Your coat, please, Commander. I have a car waiting.'

Shortly afterwards I descended the steps with him and we entered a Daimler car which stood waiting, its engine running. The car at once moved off, without any instruction being passed to the driver.

34

'What's all this about?' I asked the man Stott.

His sole reply: 'You know better than to ask, Commander.'

Naturally I was puzzled. *Makesure*, my ship, was being fuelled and munitioned at Harwich, and could not sail until Monday's morning tide – though it's true her remarkably shallow draught rendered her less dependent upon tides than other vessels. Still, she would be all of two days making ready for sea. I could not therefore see why my forty-eight-hour leave was being interrupted.

Stott next said, rather querulously it seemed to me. 'You had notified your captain that you were to stay at the Hotel Russell.'

'I have a room.'

'But you were not there. We have been looking for you, Commander Dikeston.'

I confess I did not bother to reply. Did the fool imagine that officers on leave sat alone in hotel rooms, eating off trays? Looking out of the Daimler's window, I was curious to know our destination. The car stood halted at the head of St James's Street and was awaiting a break in the oncoming ranks of cars, buses and horse-drawn vehicles, to turn. The street down there was naught but clubs, anyway: had I been prised out of one to be taken to another?

The turn accomplished, we proceeded down St James's and my curiosity diminished. Pall Mall and then the Admiralty: I had guessed by now where I was bound. Still, it was odd on a Saturday night, when I knew my ship would not yet be half-loaded. But the Daimler halted again at the foot of the street instead of turning left into Pall Mall: looking out of the window, I saw, and pitied, for it was a night of sharp winds, the khaki-clad guardsmen standing their duty at the entrance to St James's Palace. Then we were turning again, and turning *right*, and the car was passing the guard, actually entering the confines of the Palace!

'Follow me,' Stott snapped, climbing quickly from the car. He made his way across the yard to a door and rapped

35

upon it sharply. The door was opened by a footman in livery and I had barely come to Stott's shoulder before he was setting his foot across the threshold. He glanced impatiently at me over his shoulder, said, 'Hurry, please!' and began to mount a stair.

We entered an old and ornate ante-room, dominated by pictures of the Hanoverian Georges, I remember, each uglier than the last.

'Wait here, Commander Dikeston,' snapped Stott. Then he wheeled back to the stair and left me.

Now, of course, I was curious indeed: not every day is one hustled in so mysterious a way first into a closed car and then into a royal palace! Instinct led me to inspect the shine on my boots and the creases in the doeskin of my trousers. These first were satisfactory, for I had an excellent naval servant, but even he was unable to persuade doeskin to accept and retain a good crease, and there was some bagginess at my knees. I therefore spent a moment or two nervously straightening myself, brushing at my tunic and so on. But before I had time to think beyond that, a door opened and a four-ring naval captain appeared. 'This way, Commander.'

He stood back to let me pass, and closed the door, himself remaining in the ante-room, though it was a short while before I realized he had left. Other matters now clamoured for my attention, for as I entered the room a dark-suited man who stood before a table on the far side of the drawing-room in which I now stood, turned to face me.

'Dikeston?' he enquired.

I was rigid at once. 'Yes, Your Majesty!'

* * *

Malory pinched the bridge of his nose, where his spectacles pressed indentations into the flesh, and thought about Pilgrim's dismissive words. 'Some old guy's reminiscences' indeed! A few pages of the narrative, and this Dikeston, whoever he was, had already been taken in secret to meet

36

the King! Didn't Pilgrim understand that such a thing was unheard of – especially in 1918, when a remote God of a King-Emperor ruled a quarter of the earth . . .

The *frisson* was in him now, right enough, and hardening into a nasty little knob of unpleasant anticipation somewhere in his chest. Sighing, Malory replaced the spectacles, took a mouthful of whisky, and resumed reading.

*   *   *

The King took two or three paces towards me. 'Thank you for coming,' he said gravely. Now, looking at him, I could see he was grave altogether, his brow lined, his eyes weary, and there were white flecks in his beard. The war, I thought, is taking its toll of him, as it is of all of us. I remained rigid.

The King then drew my attention to two other men in the room, stretching his hand out towards, first, a tall man with piercing, dominant eyes, and a small white moustache and beard cut in an old-fashioned French manner. 'Mr Zaharoff,' the King said, 'is a director of Vickers, Maxim and Company.' I made a small bow, knowing the man's name and something of his curious and menacing reputation. Zaharoff looked imperious enough to be Sovereign himself: commanding, and cold and steely as the armaments he produced. He did not return my bow, though some small motion of eyes or brow gave acknowledgment. Now the King's hand indicated the other man present. 'Mr Clark,' he said. There had been no need to explain Zaharoff, but His Majesty clearly felt Mr Clark required further introduction; and *that* was hardly surprising, for Clark was a most unimpressive individual, obviously wearing his Sunday suit. He was small, stooped and, I judged, in his seventies. He looked like a rather shabby clerk, and it struck me that his name was remarkably apropos. 'Mr Clark,' said the King, 'is employed in the library of the British Museum, and has been so for –?' The royal eyebrows rose enquiringly.

37

The old man's voice cracked a little as he answered. He was evidently greatly overawed and had to begin his answer a second time. 'For fifty-seven years, Your Majesty. Since 1861. I should have retired . . .' The old voice wavered and fell away uncertainly.

The King nodded and took a seat. 'Sit down, please, gentlemen.'

We were grouped round a low table, the King in an armchair, the rest of us on small, high-backed and rather flimsy and uncomfortable chairs of gilt.

'Tell me about yourself, Commander,' the King instructed me.

I cleared my throat. 'In what respect, Your –'

'No Majesties,' he said. 'Sir will suffice! I want a brief summary of your life.'

It is not an easy thing to give. 'From birth?'

He nodded.

'I was born,' I said, 'in St Petersburg in Russia, in 1893. My late father was a merchant in the fur and timber trades, and my late mother the daughter of an officer of the Royal Navy.'

'You have brothers and sisters?'

'No, Sir.'

He nodded and I went on. 'When I was a child, my family moved from St Petersburg to the town of Perm where my father was for some years the British Consul. I was educated there, in the main by private tutors, until the time came for me to return to Great Britain and enter the Royal Naval College at Osborne as a cadet.'

The King smiled a little at that. Osborne, as was well-known, was always close to the Royal heart.

'I became a midshipman in 1909, Sir. Sub-Lieutenant the following year, and Lieutenant –'

He raised a hand to stop my discourse. 'How good is your Russian?'

'It is a second tongue, Sir.'

'Good as your English?'

'If anything,' I ventured, 'it is better.' And wondered: where the devil is *this* leading? Already I was beginning to harbour premonitions.

'Have you visited Russia since?'

'Yes, Sir. For two years I was on the staff of the naval attaché in St Petersburg.'

He was looking at me in a speculative way. Then he asked suddenly, his voice gruff, 'You know of the plight of my cousin?'

'I do.' As who did not, I thought.

'And where they are – the Imperial Family?'

'What I read, Sir – in the newspapers.'

George the Fifth sighed heavily. 'The reports are all too correct. We ourselves know little more. Tell me this, Commander: have you at any time, in St Petersburg or elsewhere, come into contact with any one of the leaders of these – Bolsheviks?' He spoke the word as though it were a vile expletive, as well he might.

'I have not, Sir.'

He brooded for a time and I glanced briefly at the other two. Zaharoff sat still, and watchful as an eagle, the startling eyes half-hooded. Poor little Clark, on the other hand, appeared entirely preoccupied with the handle of his stick, twisting it this way and that, prey to extreme nervousness.

At length the King said, 'I can trust you, Commander?'

'My life, Sir, is at your service.'

'Good.' He became abruptly brisker in manner. 'You will know, since the newspapers have discussed the matter at length, that the imprisonment of my Imperial Cousin is not merely a matter of personal injustice, but also a high affair of State. The Bolshevik leadership is even now treating with the Germans, thus freeing German armies to fight against ours on the Western Front.'

'Yes.'

'Forgive me, Sir,' Zaharoff cut in, speaking for the first time since I had entered the room. Since he had not been addressed, the interruption showed a measure of the man's nerve. 'There are sufficient German troops still on Russian soil to menace the Bolsheviks. That, you will recall, Sir, is the basis –'

The King raised his hand, himself interrupting the interrupter. 'I was about to say to the Commander that strictly political and military considerations enter further than one could wish into the question of negotiating the release of the Imperial Family.'

Zaharoff bowed his head a little. I had the distinct impression such a movement did not come easily to him. Perhaps the King felt it, too, for he at once went on. 'I cannot and must not interfere with the deliberations and decisions of the War Cabinet, though I am certain you will understand my anxiety for the safety of the Tsar, the Tsarina and their family. But the possibility appears to exist of a private negotiation which has a chance of achieving their release. Before I tell you more, have I your word that nothing of this will be spoken beyond these walls?'

'I swear, Sir.'

(I am solemnly aware that I am now breaking that oath sworn to my Sovereign, but I do so in the knowledge that no harm can now come from my personal treachery. In any case, I was to have so much of treachery and so soon that I could legitimately regard any oath as void. Except one: and that, an oath to myself, I am keeping as I write.)

'Very well,' said the King, continuing, 'It appears that if the Imperial Family is to be rescued and brought to safety, it is necessary, however distasteful it may prove, to treat with this Bolshevik, this Lenin. And to do so privately.'

I stared in astonishment. The notion of the King of England himself engaged in clandestine negotiation with the bloodstained leader of a revolutionary mob, was so unlikely I could scarce believe my ears.

'Fortunately,' he continued, 'the means to communicate informally with this Lenin is to hand. And also, it seems,

40

the possibility that there exists something to be offered –'
He broke off, quite abruptly, and it was apparent that King George was under deep emotional stress. When he continued, his voice was very low, not much more than a whisper, '– to be offered to Lenin, in exchange for the persons and the safe conduct of the Imperial Family.' He coughed and his voice strengthened as he asked me: 'You will do all you can to further this?'

'Of course, Sir.'

He rose then, and all of us rose also. 'It would be entirely improper,' the King then said, 'for me to know what is to happen. I can only give my blessing to the brave and generous men who may yet save the Imperial Family.'

He walked to the door. 'I thank you, gentlemen. And wish you Godspeed.'

The door was no sooner closed than Zaharoff took instant command. From beside his chair he took up a small attaché case and carried it across the room to the table at which, earlier, the King had stood. He pulled out a chair and then, from the case, produced stationery, pen and ink.

'Sit down, Clark,' he said, 'and write as I dictate. This letter –'

'But I really don't see that I can,' Clark protested, his voice high and even squeaky with trepidation.

Zaharoff ignored him and turned to me. 'Clark is about to write a letter to his *friend* Lenin, which you will –'

'*His* friend?'

Zaharoff said evenly, 'During his half-century in the Reading Room at the British Museum, Clark befriended and served first the German Jew, Marx, and his jackal Engels, the men who wrote the creed, and then their follower Ulyanov, now named Lenin, who is putting it into practice.'

'I *can't*, don't you see?' The little man protested again, with some vehemence, and I could see the tears start in his eyes.

41

'For the last time, Clark,' Zaharoff said, 'think of your *wife!*'

Clark shivered. And to tell the truth, so did I, for in Zaharoff's quiet voice lay such a wealth of command, of threat, of power, that it is impossible to describe. He then said mildly to me, 'Clark is entirely persuaded by these men. But he has a wife, and she is ill and I am able to help her. Still, he appears to have difficulty in reconciling his wife's great need with his own loyalty to the Bolshevik cause. But he *will* write the letter – won't you, Clark? – and you, Dikeston, will deliver it to Lenin in Russia!'

I felt as though I had been sandbagged. First the introduction to His Majesty's presence, then the grave courtesy of his conversation, and now this blatant brutality, and the King barely out of the room! Not to mention the news that *I* was to be sent as emissary to Lenin! I had suspected for some minutes that I was bound, willy-nilly, for Russia, but hardly for *that* purpose.

'Now, Clark,' Zaharoff went on, his voice soft but still instinct with menace. 'You use the patronymic form, I expect?'

Clark nodded.

'You're quite certain?'

Clark nodded again. I watched him with a certain pity. Bolshevik though he might be, I was certain that this abundantly fearful old man was at that moment incapable of deception. But Zaharoff was taking a paper from the case. 'Yes,' he said, 'I see that you do. So begin, "Dear Vladimir Ilyich," yes, that's right.' He was peering over the wretch's shoulder. '"This is to introduce Lieutenant-Commander H. G. Dikeston, RN, who comes to you with my full knowledge and approval."' He waited while the poor fellow's pen scratched across the paper. 'Now – "I know how busy you must be with great affairs, but I beg you, for the sake of our friendship, to consent to receive Commander Dikeston. He bears a document of the

42

greatest importance which I am certain you would not wish to pass into hands other than your own.

'"My wife has been ill recently, but there is promise now of better treatment for her. She sends you her warmest greetings and we join to congratulate you yet again on the first steps to the achievement of all our dreams."

'Now, let me see, how do you sign yourself. Ah, yes. "In affectionate brotherhood". Very suitable. Write it, Clark, and sign it.'

Clark did as he was told; he wrote a fine old-fashioned copperplate. Altogether the letter was of a neatness which belied the strain under which it had been written.

'Now the envelope,' said Zaharoff. 'Your name in the top corner, Clark. "From William Clark, British Museum, London." And now, just "V. I. Lenin." Yes, that will do nicely.'

Zaharoff blotted the letter and its envelope carefully. 'Now you may go, Clark. Your bag is in the car, is it not?'

'Yes.' Clark rose from the chair looking beaten, and Zaharoff picked up a small bell and rang it. A footman appeared at once, and it occurred to me that this imperious old man was making himself quite remarkably free of the Palace. 'Escort Mr Clark to my car,' he said.

When the door closed, I said, 'Where are you taking him?'

'Spain,' said Zaharoff. 'To my house there. His wife will benefit from seclusion in the sunshine. So will he, though he doesn't believe it. And so –' here something like amusement seemed to pass momentarily across those strange eyes – 'and so will we, I fancy.'

Basil Zaharoff then produced from his attaché case two envelopes. 'You will deliver these *unopened*, you understand, to the men to whom they are addressed. Here is your passport. Here are the documents.'

He handed them to me: two heavy envelopes, each sealed with red wax. The first, not surprisingly, in view of earlier talk, was addressed to Lenin. But the sight of the name on the second envelope rattled me to my toes.

43

'But how –' and I am certain I stammered – 'am I to deliver this?'

'*You* must persuade Lenin to permit its delivery,' said Zaharoff bleakly. 'It *must* be handed over unopened – and then brought back to my hands duly signed.'

I stared at it in utter incredulity. On the envelope appeared the words: 'To His Imperial Majesty Nicholas II, Tsar of all the Russias.'

Those eyes of his were on me as I stood there. I could feel them and his attention, as certainly as a man feels the warmth of sunlight. But no warmth emanated from Zaharoff: the reverse indeed, for across my shoulders passed that shudder attributed to the passing shadow of a grey goose's wing. I heard a rustle and looked up to find he was holding out a sheet of paper. 'Your route,' he said.

Again I felt the shiver. The October Revolution in Russia was about six months past and the great spaces of that vast country were a prey to warring factions, into which I was to be plunged at this man's will. For already I sensed that Zaharoff, the great salesman of war and death, was truly the hand behind my mission. I had pledged my life to my Sovereign, but it was now to be at Zaharoff's disposal.

'Go at once,' he said urgently, 'and you *may* save the life of the Tsar and his Family. I can put it no higher. When His Imperial Majesty signs the document, and only then, will the opportunity come to us.'

'Yes, sir,' I said, though I did not understand, and turned and left the room.

When, long afterwards, I returned to England, he had been knighted—by a grateful King, one must suppose, though I know now that it was that devious Celt, David Lloyd George, who conferred honour upon him. Behind every man, it seems, there stands another, strings in his hands, to pull by means of some deeper knowledge.

But all that was far ahead. The paper in my hand already had me on the midnight train to Thurso in the far North of

44

Scotland; yet first I had to outfit myself for the journey. I had no clothing suitable for Russia; indeed, I had access to little more than a weekend's changes of socks and under-clothing lodged at the Russell Hotel. Now, in the next few minutes, I was to have a foretaste of Zaharoff's ways. The Daimler still stood in the courtyard, and though the odious Stott had vanished, the driver clearly had instructions.

'Gieves, first,' he said to me. 'Be quick, sir, if you please. We haven't much time.'

So it was *up* St James's this time, with my wristwatch now showing twenty minutes to eleven o'clock. Gieves would surely be shuttered long ago! But as the car stopped a minute or two later at 27 New Bond Street, lights blazed inside and a man in shirtsleeves stood in the doorway, tape-measure round his neck. Inside, to my amazement, there appeared to be an entire workroom staff!

The outfitting, I swear, took only minutes. A big suitcase was produced, and into it there tumbled a torrent of socks, underclothes, handkerchiefs, all of the choicest. Shirts of wool taffeta, fine as linen, yet of wonderful warmth. Three suits came. 'From the peg,' said the tailor regretfully, 'but you may rely on us, sir, to do our best.' I slipped on the jackets, watched him make his swift chalk hieroglyphs, and then they were whisked away as I tried trousers, whose length was adjusted with equal speed. From a long rack of ties I chose six in silk foulard, then collars to my size and taste. How many people laboured at stitching behind the mahogany I cannot know. But the jackets were quickly back for further fitting only seconds, it seemed, after they were taken away. And meanwhile I was being fitted with a thick topcoat of soft wool, the material from Crombie, the cut unmistakably Guardee, and of ankle length. Finally there were boots, soft leather and in the Russian style.

Dazed, I asked the tailor whence they came. He only smiled and said, 'We carry a large stock, sir. Our gentle-men come in many sizes and we try to meet both taste and need.'

45

By a quarter past the hour I was out of the shop, I swear it, and with a full kit in my case and not a bill to sign. It struck me, as we bowled away down the 'Dilly, that not Admiral Beatty, nor Jellicoe himself for that matter, could have commanded such service, even at Gieves.

At the Russell Hotel a man waited in the entrance. At first sight of the Daimler he started forward, opened the door as the car stopped, and handed me my toilet valise. 'The rest will be looked after, sir, unless there is something you need.'

'The bill?' I asked.

'Attended to. Don't concern yourself.' He held out the receipt for examination, and while I satisfied myself that it had indeed been paid, he passed a wicker hamper into the car. 'In case you feel peckish on the train, sir.'

And by Jove, but I *was* peckish. Stott had robbed me of my supper and in the press of events there had not been a moment to think of the inner man. Now hunger was growling inside me.

Again the Daimler moved off, quick beyond appearances, along Guilford Street, into Grays Inn Road, then towards King's Cross Station.

The terminus, and the night train too, seethed with people, but the Daimler was met by a detachment of military police who cut a way for me and my baggage through teeming masses of soldiers and sailors of all ranks who were bidding farewell to wives, sweethearts and children. Any man who travelled on the wartime trains will recall how dense the crowds were and how uncomfortable the conditions. Already, as I proceeded along the platform, I could see that even the corridors were crowded.

'Here, sir,' the Daimler's driver said, laying a hand upon my arm; our small party halted beside a first-class carriage two back from the engine. A door was opened for me, and I found myself entering what, in a ship, might be described as a small stateroom: possessed of bed, two comfortable seats and a tiny bathroom-cum-lavatory. The driver, entering behind me, drew down blinds on the corridor windows. 'No one will disturb you now.'

'But this is unfair!' I protested. There were many brother officers on the train, men bound for Scapa Flow and the hardship of duty at sea, who now faced a night and a day of discomfort in this jammed train, while I travelled in comfort.

'You are to have privacy, sir,' said he, shaking his head. 'Those are my orders.'

'From Mr Zaharoff?'

He did not answer, and was already backing out of the compartment. 'Safe journey, sir,' he said, touching his cap, and was gone.

A minute or two later I heard a whistle, followed by a great belch of steam and the sound of the wheels skidding for grip upon the rails. The train was moving, and I was off. I divested myself of hat and overcoat, hung them in the wardrobe, and flung myself into one of the two seats. So much had happened in so short a space that my mind was in turmoil, and I wanted only to sit quietly and seek to unravel the astounding events which, in a single evening had turned me from an officer on leave, with nothing before him but a day or so of rest, into the Emissary of my King, sent to encounter the bloodiest revolutionary alive and thence to the rescue of the once-mighty monarch of all the vast lands of Russia! In an attempt to focus my kaleidoscopic thoughts and fancies, I put my hand to my pocket for cigarettes, and then swore, for the pocket was empty. I could recollect, on considering the matter, that the packet had lain on the table at Jameson's club when I was called to see Stott. A night without tobacco, when so much was swirling through my head, was unpleasant to contemplate.

* * *

Mention of tobacco drew Horace Malory's attention to the fact that his own cigar was out. He, too, swore—though mildly and under his breath. Disliking both waste and relit cigars, he tossed the stub irritably into the large silver ashtray on his desk, an ashtray which commemorated the victory of his first racehorse, Sir Basil, over a long-ago mile at Newbury, and busied himself extracting another Romeo No.3 from its aluminium tube. When it was lighted, he closed his eyes for a minute or so to rest them, and then resumed reading.

*   *   *

How they knew, I cannot tell, but when, in search of refreshment, I opened the hamper, its wickerwork branded with the name of the provision merchants Fortrum & Mason, I found that it contained a plentiful supply of cigarettes, all of them Player's Navy Cut, the make I favoured. Also there were several boxes of lucifers. I lit up with a feeling of relief, and unwrapped one of the several napkins within the hamper to find cold chicken legs therein. Two bottles of a chilled Bernkasteler Mosel of excellent quality lay invitingly in the hamper. I would make my supper, I decided, and consider my position afterwards.

Twenty minutes later, having disposed of a dish of the most delicate strawberries (and where could *they* have come from, in the month of March?) I lit another cigarette and looked again at the papers in my pocket. The passport, the first I had possessed, (since up to the outbreak of hostilities no Englishman abroad had need of such frivolities) contained my photograph. Whence had *that* been obtained? From the Navy, no doubt, though I could not recall being photographed for years except for snapshots taken by the occasional friend. Still, there it was: 'We, Arthur Balfour, His Majesty's Principal Secretary for Foreign Affairs, command . . .' I wondered to myself how far Balfour's writ might run in a Russia crowded with armies: the Whites, the Czech Legions, the Reds themselves, and the Germans, too! The letters I placed to one side; my orders were to bear them unopened, and though even then I had misgivings, if King George believed that they might save his cousin's family then who was a mere Navy commander to question such matters?

I concentrated my attention on the paper Zaharoff had handed to me as 'Your route'. Nothing written there was in any way surprising, save the final words: 'Proceed henceforward at, and with, discretion.'

Finally, having finished my bottle of Mosel, I undressed and slept.

Late the following afternoon, in darkness, the train came to Thurso and I reported, as instructed, to the Navy Transport office, and thence aboard the transport vessel which was to make a bitter, stormy crossing of the Pentland Firth. Of that short journey I remember little, spending most of it green with sickness at the ship's rail ridding myself of chicken legs, strawberries, wine and much else as the small vessel plunged and heaved its way across that vile and narrow Pentland channel between the north coast of Scotland and the Isles of Orkney.

Fortunately for me, the crossing was accomplished in little more than a cheerless two hours. At Scapa Flow I again presented myself to a Movements Officer, and was at once ordered into a barge – an admiral's barge, no less – for immediate transportation aboard the destroyer HMS *Airedale*, which I could see already had steam up. No sooner was I aboard than I was shown to the First Lieutenant's cabin and the low, fast warship weighed anchor.

Next day I landed at Bergen, and proceeded by train to Oslo on what must be the most exquisitely beautiful rail journey on earth, and thence, again by train, to Stockholm. In Stockholm I had time only for a good dinner, which I took at the Grand Hotel in the belief that it might be some time before I could enjoy another such, and then boarded the ferry for Helsinki. Now my mood was beginning to change, as every mile brought me closer to a land I had loved since childhood, but a land whose mood could likewise change, in a second's caprice, from warm good nature to sullen, cold and cruel brutality.

From Helsinki I again took train. And now my ears were filled with the accents of the Baltic and of Northern Russia. The time of Mosel and chicken legs, of private compartments and deference, though only a day or two behind me, might never have existed. On that journey I slept cramped on a wooden bench, dined off black bread, a little cheese and tea from a samovar, without lemon, and woke as the train rolled in to the Finland station in St Petersburg to find that name had been erased from the station platforms. Nothing, I think, could have so emphasized that the Russian world would now be unfamiliar to me, as those painted boards bearing the word *Petrograd*.

The city was filled with activity, doubt and confusion. I went first, and on foot because I deemed it wise to avoid unnecessary contact, to the Smolny Institute, which in my St Petersburg days had been the finest of girls' schools, but was now, since October, the headquarters of the new Soviet of Peoples' Commissaries. Its gracious, pillared entrance now stood decorated with machine-guns and a ferocious-looking but clearly dispirited band of revolutionaries.

In several discreet conversations I gradually learned the reasons. The Government had taken itself off to Moscow so St Petersburg, as the cradle of the Revolution, now felt spurned. There was little love lost, then as later, between the two cities. And now even Trotsky, who had remained two weeks and more after the rest, had departed. The guards at the Smolny had nothing left to guard. 'Except our backs!' I was told sourly.

For me this was hardly the best of news, for it meant I must somehow contrive to journey to Moscow, and I had learned by now that the trains were crowded and permission to board them almost impossible to obtain. In the old days a little bribery would have achieved it in an instant, but I felt strongly here that a bribe proffered in the wrong place would lead to a beating, or worse.

I then thought of the British Embassy, and took myself and my heavy suitcase there, and sat outside on the case for a time, hoping for the sight of a familiar face. I wanted at all cost to avoid entering and thus placing myself or my name on any official basis, but it seemed to me that members of the staff might well be knowledgeable about the best means of proceeding.

But no one came, or at any rate no British face I recognized. Then, as evening was drawing on, with the cold deepening, I felt a sudden hard thwack between my shoulder-blades and rose, half-turning, to see Vorozhin. His mouth was open wide, his face alight, his arms spread.

'I thought so – Dikeston!'

I laughed too, delighted to see the old reprobate. 'Vassily Alexandrovitch!' He had been supplier of fodder for the Embassy horses for many years, a great cheerful Cossack and himself a horseman of enormous daring.

'Why are you sitting so sadly –' he kicked the suitcase – 'on *that*?'

'Because I have nowhere else.'

'No? And *they* –' he gestured scornfully at the Embassy building – 'so busy looking after themselves they have no time for you. Eh?'

'True enough,' I lied. 'I need to get to Moscow, and it seems –'

He gave a great laugh. 'Difficult? Yes, my friend, it is difficult. What is not difficult?' Then he bent his shaggy head close to mine. 'But *nothing* is impossible, eh?' And laughed hugely.

'You can help me?'

He picked up my case in his enormous paw and took my arm. 'A drink, my friend. A little talk, some food. And then we see!'

He now had only a third of his fine house, but it was more than enough, for he lived alone. More important, he saw himself as in my debt because, years earlier when he had been in England, I had been able to arrange for him to visit

51

a Newmarket trainer of my acquaintance, whom I suspect he had startled greatly with his vaults and side-riding and other Cossack tricks.

Like everyone else in the aftermath of the Revolution, Vorozhin was waiting. Horses had always been needed, were needed now and would always be needed, and he was patient, waiting to discover how his eye and his skills could best be employed by new masters. That and maintaining his friendships. We ate frugally: bread and a little fish and some tough horsemeat ('The old ones die, my friend, and keep us alive. A last service, eh?') and talked over old times, and drank some vodka, and my difficulties began to disappear. There was a former corporal of cavalry, it seemed, now employed in the railway station, with apparently unlimited authority over the movement of people. 'We'll see him in the morning, Dikeston, old friend. First, more vodka, then sleep, eh?' He loved using my surname, thus, and also teasing me by converting my Christian names into a bastard Russian patronymic form: Henry Georgevitch. A wonderful man and a fine friend. True to his word, he had me on the Moscow train early next morning.

By nightfall, suitcase still in hand, I wished he again stood beside me as I faced a levelled machine-gun at the entrance to the tunnel arch that led through the Kremlin wall beneath the Spassky Tower, with the musical clock chiming high above. The same clock which once had played 'God Save the Tsar' now ground out the sober notes of the *Internationale*.

The gun barrel was levelled at my chest. Thumbs rested on the firing buttons. Several pairs of eyes stared at me, examining from head to foot. At last one of the men, a black-bearded giant with fierce and angry eyes, jerked his head to indicate I should approach.

'Your business?'

'I have a letter for V. I. Lenin.'

'*Comrade* Lenin.'

52

'Yes, for Comrade Lenin.'

'Who's it from?'

'An old friend.'

The giant stuck out his hand. 'Give it to me.'

I shook my head. 'Only to his secretary.'

His manner became more menacing. 'Give.'

Again I shook my head.

'Do you imagine,' he grated, 'that Comrade Lenin has time to waste with —' and his eyes ranged over my clothing — 'bourgeois postmen?'

'I imagine,' I said levelly, 'that he might be angry if this letter were not delivered.'

He stared at me wrathfully, a jack-in-office faced with a situation of which he was uncertain. This examination, like the first, went on for some moments, but at last he jerked his head again, this time to indicate I might pass beneath the arch. 'Present yourself at the Kavalersky Building and wait.'

I proceeded through, suitcase still in my hand, and found that the Kavalersky Building stood, as described, opposite the Potyeshny Palace. Again I was stopped and asked my buisness. Again I explained about the letter. Again I was examined closely by hostile eyes. Finally I was allowed to enter and found myself at the end of a long corridor. A guard sat at a table with his pistol before him. He did nothing: did not rise, did not ask what I wanted, did not invite me to be seated. He did not even answer when I spoke. I had been given instructions to wait, however, and that is what I did, turning my back upon the guard and fixing my attention upon an icon over the main door. It has always seemed to me that one of the advantages conferred upon a young man by service training is the ability to stand still for extended periods, without impatience and without the need for such distractions as magazines and newspapers. So I stood properly at ease, hands behind my back and kept my gaze upon the icon.

How long I stood so I do not know, but after a time there

came the sound of swiftly approaching footsteps, and a youthful voice demanded, 'You have a letter for Comrade Lenin?'

Turning, I saw a sailor in uniform, in his early twenties, scrubbed and red-faced. 'You are his secretary?'

'No, Comrade, I am not. But I am privileged to assist him.'

'I will deliver the letter only to Comrade Lenin's secretary.'

We stared at each other for a moment, he a little impatient of this stranger who sought to impose his will, I guessing that my only hope of achieving my goal was to be entirely firm. Behind him the corridor was busy, men crossing from room to room with pieces of paper in their hands. For a moment one of them looked familiar, a medium-sized man in a tunic with a shock of hair, a small goatee and wearing pince-nez. 'Is that Trotsky?' I demanded.

'It may be *Comrade* Trotsky.' The sailor did not look round. I was again instructed to wait, and resumed my contemplation of the icon. That sight of the revolutionary leader, however, had had its effect upon me. It was like a sight of an enemy warship, with the knowledge than an encounter was to begin: I was suddenly aware that here, in the Kavalersky, I stood only steps away from the determined crew of Bolsheviks who had seized power so ruthlessly and triumphantly a few short months ago! These were the men who had wiped away a Romanov Dynasty which had held in autocratic thrall the largest nation on earth for more than three hundred years! I felt my heart begin to thud within me more powerfully even than it had at St James's Palace; King George was but a constitutional Sovereign, for all his dignity, and these men were, or aimed to be, the power in all the Russias.

The footsteps came again. 'Follow me.'

I walked after the sailor down the long corridor, steps clicking on the tiled floor, but having to pause once or twice as somebody emerged hurrying from a room and crossed in front, heedless.

The sailor stopped and gestured with his hand. I entered a room equipped entirely, and in unlikely fashion in this place, with light birchwood furniture, perhaps from Kare-lia. A man in a dark suit sat behind a desk and he too wore pince-nez from which a black ribbon fell to his neck.

'This letter,' he said. 'You must give it to me. We must have an end to these childish mysteries!'

'You are Comrade Lenin's –'

'Secretary?' He sighed. 'Yes.' And held out his hand commandingly. 'From whom does it come?'

'From Mr William Clark, at the British Museum in London.' I took the envelope from the inside pocket of my jacket and handed it to him.

'I will ensure that it reaches Comrade –'

He was interrupted by the abrupt appearance through another door of Lenin himself! Though for a brief moment I did not recognize him: for his head was shaved and his celebrated beard gone and thus he was of altogether more Asiatic appearance than I had imagined.

He looked at me sharply. 'From *Clark*?'

I stood to attention. 'Yes, Comrade Lenin.'

'Who are you?'

'Commander Dikeston, Royal Navy.'

He laughed, quite gaily. 'So – now Clark has naval officers delivering his messages, eh? You've seen him? Is he well?'

I thought of the poor wretch sitting and writing at Zaharoff's cold command. He'd been old, and almost terrified out of his wits, but his health had seemed good. 'Yes, he's well.'

'Good, good!' Lenin ripped open the envelope, saying, 'He's a splendid man. From Marx onward, who knows where we'd all have been without –' And then he stopped, the laughter shut off, and gave me a hard, sideways look. 'This other document he speaks of. You have it?'

'Yes, Comrade Lenin.'

'Come in here.'

I reached into my pocket for Zaharoff's missive, and followed him into his office. He went behind his desk and stood there like a Lord of Creation, hand outstretched.

'Give it to me.'

In removing the single sheet of paper, Lenin did not slit open the envelope, though a paperknife lay upon his desk. He tore it, and there was plain impatience on his face. The thick foolscap crackled as it was unfolded. I could not see what was written, nor did Comrade Lenin offer to show me, but I had an impression of a few handwritten lines, no more.

Then Lenin was shouting: 'Comrade Secretary!'

The man bustled through from his own outer office. 'Yes, Comrade Lenin?'

'Please ask Comrade Trotsky and Comrade Sverdlov to join me for a moment.'

'Yes, Comrade Lenin.'

This repeated use of the word comrade, once, twice, three times in every spoken sentence, struck me as both excessive and amusing. I must have smiled, for Lenin snapped at me: 'Something is funny?'

I dipped my head. 'Your pardon, sir. I am simply much taken at the thought of the imminent presence of men whose names are so widely known.' He shot me a warning look. I straightened my face and resolved to smile no more and nor indeed, in the ensuing weeks, was I to do so.

A minute passed, no more, before they arrived, and they were hurrying. I found it interesting that Lenin was so evidently master, for, nominally at any rate, Yankel Sverdlov was Head of State; and there could be no doubting Trotsky's power. The fact remains that they came trotting in like a pair of terriers, and when Lenin said, 'Sit,' and pointed to chairs, the pair of them sat and looked up at him, all but wagging tails.

Lenin's finger now stabbed towards me. 'This man brings

56

a message.' He looked from one face to the other, from Sverdlov to Trotsky, and back again. 'He is British.'

Two pairs of eyes turned, regarded me for a moment, then returned their attention to Lenin.

'The message –?' Trotsky began.

Lenin flung the paper down on the desk before him. He radiated a pleasure that was almost triumphant. 'Vickers,' he said. 'And Zaharoff.'

Trotsky swung to face me. 'Zaharoff's emissary?'

Since I was in reality nothing of the kind, I shook my head. 'I merely brought his letter, sir.'

'Not "sir". Address me, please, as comrade.' Trotsky snatched up the letter, read it quickly, then handed it at once to Sverdlov. While it was read a third time the others remained silent, though it was clear they ached to speak.

It was, in any event, no more than a moment before Sverdlov looked up and said softly, 'Fifty *million*?' It was as though he could scarcely believe what he was saying.

Trotsky, in the same instant, cried, 'But can he be trusted?'

Lenin pursed his lips, his head tilted a little, his hand turned over to finish palm up; it was a curiously Gallic gesture. 'As a gift?' he said. 'In arms? It's worth far more than the lot of *them*.'

Trotsky blinked several times. '*They* put their trust in Zaharoff. What happened? Nothing was delivered.' He said it again, with a bitter edge to his voice. 'Russia paid Vickers. Zaharoff had the money. Nothing was delivered.'

'Fifty million in arms,' Lenin said. 'We need them, Lev Davidovitch. Yesterday in this room you said that without –' He stopped and looked at me. 'Leave us. Wait outside. I will send for you.'

I took a seat in the secretary's office, wondering who 'they' were. 'They' who had put trust in Zaharoff; 'they' who seemed equated with Russia. I wondered, also, in my innocent way how anybody, having met Zaharoff as I had, could possibly trust him. In my mind's eye I could picture that eagle face, those compelling eyes. It was a face to be watched, to be examined, a gaze to be avoided—but hardly to be trusted. Yet clearly the King himself was placing faith . . .

Sverdlov came bustling out of Lenin's room. He did not stop; he merely crooked the finger of authority at me and continued walking out into the corridor. I scrambled to my feet and followed him. A few doors along he turned into an office, closed the door after me and gestured me to chair. I sat obediently, as he had done earlier.

'How well do you speak Russian?' he demanded.

I said, 'Perfectly.'

'With what accent?'

'I grew up in Perm, but there is barely a trace. Usually I am thought to be from St Petersburg.'

'Petrograd,' he growled at me.

'Of course. I beg your pardon.'

He glared at me. 'Your profession?'

'I am an officer of the Royal Navy.'

'Accustomed to command, eh?'

'Yes.'

He was silent then, staring hard at me. It is an old trick, to disconcert a man in that way. I simply stared back. At last he said, 'You have other languages?'

'Some French. Fair German. English, naturally.'

He nodded. 'And the language of the Revolution – can you speak that?'

'Imperfectly, Comrade Commissar, but I am not wholly unfamiliar with the modes of expression. I have read Marx and Engels, and Comrade Lenin. And I learn quickly, when necessary.'

'Then take my advice,' Sverdlov said, 'and do so. They are hotheads in the Urals Soviet. Do you know the name Yakovlev?'

'No.'

He favoured me with a look that was almost a smile, though in it there was a certain contempt, perhaps even pity. 'Familiarize yourself with the name Vassily Vassilievitch Yakovlev. And report back here tomorrow morning. Nine o'clock.'

When I did so, I quickly learned why it had been so necessary to remember the mysterious name of Yakovlev. I also found myself arbitrarily placed in command of a force of one hundred and fifty horsemen.

* * *

'The man must be mad,' Malory murmured. His ears heard the sound of his own voice and he grimaced. Talking to himself: softening of the brain. But by Jove, he wasn't the only sufferer! Extraordinary fellow, Pilgrim. Read something Sir Basil wanted buried, found it referred to Zaharoff himself, to the King, to Lenin, Sverdlov and Trotsky; read all *that* – and then took no notice! The document even mentioned fifty millions in arms and Pilgrim ignored it. Ancient history, indeed!

The trouble was, of course, that Pilgrim had never met Zaharoff. Accordingly Pilgrim had no experience of the certitude which had characterized all Zaharoff's actions and dealings. Malory, knowing that certitude well, could feel it now, reaching to him across the years. Fifty of them, now, since the old man had stood here in this room – yet Malory could still sense his presence, could sense the will and even the words 'Find out. It's dangerous –' of the message which had earlier insinuated itself into his brain and was becoming ever more urgent. The words seemed to vibrate in his mind as he looked at the envelope which was paper-clipped to the last sheet of Dikeston's manuscript. Pilgrim had opened it, and then had apparently replaced the paper inside it.

Malory took it out again.

CHAPTER THREE

---◆---

The House of Four Forks

In the maroon-carpeted corridor Malory stopped outside the door of Pilgrim's office, knocked faintly and entered. Pilgrim, talking on the telephone, glanced up and nodded. Malory helped himself to coffee from the ever-hot gadget on the side table, and stared out of the window. In a moment he heard the phone replaced and Pilgrim's 'Yes, Horace?'

He turned, Dikeston's narrative in his hand. 'We disagree, I think, about the importance of this.'

Pilgrim shook his head. 'Nope. It could be important, I see it.' He laughed ruefully. 'Fifty thousand a year and no questions isn't the kind of thing you dismiss. I just have a block.'

'A what?'

'A block, Horace. This guy, Dikeston, he's a joker. He gives us part one, then sets us chasing part two. There's a whole trail laid and he's going to have us running our butts off. And then at the end – nothing. I can smell it.'

'And the promised catastrophe?'

Pilgrim leaned back in his chair. 'I can't make myself believe in it. Tell you why. Let's say this guy Dikeston has a big grudge against us, let's say that we foreclosed on his widowed mother's mortgage way back when, okay? She was turned out in the snow. He hates us. He's spent years muttering into his whiskers and plotting vengeance. Now listen – in 1918 he's already lieutenant-commander so he's rising thirty *then*. What is he now, ninety? No, he's dead. Everybody's dead. Dikeston's dead, Lenin's dead, Zahar-

60

off's dead. Are you saying Dikeston spent half a century plotting a disaster he wouldn't live to *see*?'

Malory said, 'Zaharoff seems to have agreed a payment in perpetuity. Of fifty thousand a year. Have you any idea how much that was in about nineteen-twenty?'

'Sure. It was a crazy sum. So maybe Dikeston had something on Zaharoff. What else could this thing be but blackmail, anyway? Horace, think – Zaharoff died in nineteen-thirty-six.'

'You're saying, are you *not*,' Malory said, 'that Dikeston's grudge must have been against Sir Basil himself?'

'Well, why not, Horace! It couldn't be much more personal, could it? Annual payments on Zaharoff's say-so, Senior Partner's Notes, don't even query it or catastrophe follows. There was a two-man game here. Zaharoff lost and we keep on paying. But I reckon we're now paying Dikeston's ghost, we have to be. And a few pages of manuscript with dust on them don't convince me otherwise. God, Horace, it's too melodramatic to begin to be true!'

Malory looked at him steadily. 'There's one thing that isn't dead.'

'Okay, what?'

'Hillyard, Cleef.'

'You think he can wreck the bank? Now – from the graveyard?'

Malory shrugged. 'I don't know. Sir Basil seems to have feared something cataclysmic and he was not given to unnecessary panic, I do assure you. I feel we must find out – and quickly.'

'I tell you one thing, Horace – it's going to be costly. We won't find much, but we'll pay a hell of a lot.'

'Perhaps less costly than failing to find out?'

Pilgrim fingered his chin. He shaved twice daily and Malory's eyes caught the faint rasp of the stubble. 'Horace, we're in a strange position, you and I. You were boss man. I'm boss man now. We have an understanding of sorts. You don't like some of what I do and maybe I don't like some of your ways over here. We can both live with it. There are even advantages. But my whole instinct is to forget this thing and to cancel the next payment. Yours is not.'

'Most certainly it is not.'

'Based on what you know of Zaharoff?'

'Principally, yes.'

Pilgrim's fingers still rasped against his beard. 'That's what throws me, Horace. Somebody told me once you're a downy old bird – and you are! You're exactly that. Unsentimental, experienced, knowledgeable. Yet you're still hypnotized by that old man. Why?'

Malory smiled. 'Because I knew him. Because I watched him work. Because he never in his life wasted a ha'penny. Because I know that an arrangement such as this one to pay an annual fifty thousand would never have been made except under the most extreme pressure and would have ended the moment an ending became possible. Yet it had already been paid for sixteen years when Sir Basil died. I promise you this, Laurence: there would not have been a day during those years when he did not give intense thought to the means of ending the payments. Since he didn't end them, it can only be because he couldn't.'

'So you're saying we have no alternative but to follow Dikeston's trail?'

'Pretty well that.'

'No matter where it leads or what it costs?'

Malory nodded. 'On my say-so, perhaps? Old Malory must be crackers, you can say, but he's insisting.' He watched Pilgrim with some anxiety. Understanding of Pilgrim's reasoning had come to him, quite suddenly, as often happened while they talked. Pilgrim was Hungarian by birth, a child refugee in 1956, had been a brilliant student in America, had had a brilliant career very young on Wall Street in investment banking, and was head now of an important international house. *But terrified of looking a fool*. That was the clue of it.

62

'If it goes wrong, Laurence, you can blame me entirely,' Malory went on. 'And I'll keep you informed all along the line. That way, well, I stay right out of your way, don't I? And I'm not exactly known for throwing money about, would you say?'

Pilgrim frowned. 'Give me one more reason. If I'm not convinced I don't sleep nights.'

'All right. How do *you* know that Hillyard, Cleef was Zaharoff's bank?'

'How? You told me, I guess.'

Malory said, 'And Graves knows too, now. But there aren't six people in the City with that knowledge, now or any other time. Sir Basil moved very quietly.'

'So?'

'How did this man Dikeston know?'

'So many years,' Pilgrim said. 'I feel as though it's archæology I'm paying for.'

'Let's hope,' Malory offered, 'That we can keep the mummy's curse safely in its tomb.'

'Go ahead. Feel free. Use Graves, any time you want him.'

'I'll remember. Thank you, Laurence.'

Malory pottered back, satisfied at getting his own way, but feeling the burden of concern heavier on his shoulders. In his own room, where many times in making a decision he had said, 'What would you have done?' to the lurking shade of Basil Zaharoff, he now addressed the ghost another question. 'Why the payments?' Malory said aloud. 'Why?'

The shade gave no answer. It never did.

But as always, other voices clamoured. Busy departments at Hillyard, Cleef, accustomed to instant attention from the Partners, found that Malory in particular seemed distracted. Even to see him was difficult.

A partner named Huntly, whose present task it was to advise one seed and fertilizer corporation in its struggle to take over another – a matter of seven or eight million pounds was involved – threw customary deference out of the window, stormed past Mrs Frobisher's defensive protests, and barged into Malory's sanctum with a cry of, 'It's absolutely *vital*, Sir Horace!'

Malory gave him a longish look, but otherwise offered no comment. 'Sit down, Fergus.'

Huntly sat. He was in his early forties, with aristocratic if impoverished Scottish connections and a reputation for dourness. But he burst out: 'The offer will have to be increased again!'

'Then increase it,' Malory said. Huntly gaped at him. 'By how much?' Malory was renowned for fighting his takeover battles halfpenny by halfpenny.

'By what's necessary, for heaven's sake!' Then Malory abruptly took another tack. 'Fergus, do you do crossword puzzles?'

'Now and then, yes.'

'Then tell me what you make of this.' Malory reached for a slip of paper and read: 'In a cavity in The House of Four Forks, a mile from the meridian.'

'How many letters?' Huntly asked automatically, just as Mrs Frobisher opened the door to admit Graves.

'It is a clue, Fergus, but not to a crossword puzzle. Any ideas?'

'No. Can I think about it?' Huntly rose at Malory's nod. 'And I *am* to increase the bid price as I think necessary?'

Malory nodded.

At the door Huntly turned. 'The meridian has to be Greenwich, of course, house must be there, or in Blackheath. I'd get Mrs Frobisher to ask the local house agents.'

Malory turned to Graves. 'Better if you do it. Find me The House of Four Forks.'

With both men gone, Malory sat back in his chair. He could now pursue other thoughts along other paths. Who, exactly, had this fellow Dikeston *been*? And that Russian name – Yakovlev was it? – perhaps some trace of it existed somewhere. Who might know? The essence of banking, Horace Malory had always insisted to his juniors, lay in knowing how to find out that which you did not already know. He made two telephone calls: one to a retired admiral who held a couple of minor directorships under the Hillyard, Cleef umbrella; the second to the master of an Oxford College, who was a distant cousin of his wife's.

As Graves's taxi crawled along a crowded Old Kent Road, Fergus Huntly was instructing his own secretary to hawk the clue around the company finance department. Prize for the solution: a bottle of whisky.

The bottle was claimed within minutes by an infuriatingly smug young man named Nayland who grinned his way to Huntly's desk and said 'It's really just another advantage of Oxford, you know. We're talking derivations, of course. This one would be from the Latin *quadrifurcus*, which means four-forked, and became in Middle English *carfouk*. If I may write it down for you?'

'Please do.'

'*Carfouk* – like that!' said Nayland. 'But the word had to undergo further metamorphosis into. . . .' He paused like a conjuror.

'Into?' said Huntly with reluctance.

'Carfax.'

'Carfax? That's the place in the centre of . . .'

Nayland grinned again and nodded. 'Centre of *Oxford*, you were about to say.'

With a sense of relief, Huntly telephoned Malory and then retuned his attention to his fertilizer companies. 'Tell Mr Graves, when he telephones,' Malory told Mrs Frobisher, 'that he's looking for a house called Carfax.'

Now for a while, all the enquiries began to inch forward. A history fellow from Oxford telephoned Malory on the instructions of the Master of his College, to offer to Hillyard, Cleef his expert knowledge of the Russian Revolution – in which, as it later turned out, Yakovlev had played no part. The tame admiral, having consulted that fat rump of the old Admiralty bureaucracy surviving now within the Ministry of Defence, called to report that Admiralty Records pertaining to Lt-Cdr. Henry George Dikeston stopped abruptly with an entry in 1918 which read 'seconded to special duties.' Beyond that entry the file was blank.

In an hour Jacques Graves stood with one foot on either side of a narrow strip of steel embedded immovably in stone, thus straddling the Greenwich meridian. One foot, his left as it happened, stood in the Eastern hemisphere and the other, in the Western. The thought gave him obscure pleasure, which disappeared at once when a schoolboy took his place, yelling the same thought aloud. Graves coloured a little and thought –

Carfax. And one mile from here.

Up or down? Greenwich lay below him, with Wren's superb buildings grey-white in the noon light. Up the hill lay Blackheath.

For no good reason he walked down, and failed to find a convenient house agent. A policeman advised him to try Blackheath. 'Top of the hill, sir, then across the grass. That's where they are, sir. Where the money is.'

Prosperity there certainly seemed to be, Graves thought as he walked up the stiff hill of the park and out on to the Heath. This was spick-and-span suburbia: old houses expensively restored, well-dressed young women walking with children on the grass. Everything tarted-up. Boutiques with canopies, an old Bentley car, driven by a boy in his early twenties.

Finally: a house agent's premises.

A variety of experiences that afternoon convinced him that the English were ill-served by their house agents. One fat young man said disagreeably through a haze of beer fumes that if Graves were not interested in buying property he shouldn't be wasting time in the place. Outside the premises Graves stood still for a moment waiting for the red mist of fury to clear. When it did, he found he was looking at a poster. 'Protect your environment,' it read, 'by joining the Georgian Society.'

There was a telephone number. When he called, a steely female voice answered. The lady was, she said, Jessica Drummond, honorary secretary of the Society. Yes, he could call to see her that very afternoon – if he was quick about it.

She lived in a terrace just beyond the railway station. A fat cat dozed upon the bonnet of a car in the driveway. When Graves pressed the bell, the door was opened on the instant by a lady in a blue-and-white check skirt, white blouse, and blue cardigan. She had grey hair, and grey rims to her bifocals. She would be, he thought, about sixty-five.

'Mrs Drummond?'

'*Miss* Drummond. You telephoned about the Georgian Society?'

'I did.'

'Then come in. I haven't much time.' She marched him into an over-furnished sitting-room, pointed to a chair and said, 'You're resident, or new to the district, or what?'

He smiled. 'Well, neither of those.'

He took a visiting card from the pocket of his waistcoat and handed it to her. Miss Drummond pronounced his name aloud, with precision and in French. 'Oh, and you're a banker, Mr Graves? How may I help you?'

'It's an odd little matter,' Jacques Graves said, 'concerning a client of ours, very long-standing, but just a little, well – eccentric. It was a habit of his to set us little puzzles concerning his instructions.'

Miss Drummond looked disapproving. 'Rather foolish, surely. Was there not a danger of misunderstanding?'

Graves waved a hand deprecatingly. 'There was, but these things go on. However, unfortunately the client has died and left us an unsolved puzzle. Part of it may, we think, concern a house in this area.'

67

'Oh, really? How exciting!'

'Miss Drummond, do the words Four Forks mean anything to you?'

'Four *forks*, did you say?' He nodded. 'No, nothing. Four forks, how very odd!'

'What about Carfax?'

'Oh yes.'

'It does?'

'Oh certainly.'

'What does it mean?'

'Well, Carfax House, of course.'

Graves smiled at her. 'Here in Blackheath?'

'Not a quarter of a mile from this very spot!'

'That's convenient, Miss Drummond. Can you tell me anything about the place?'

'Oh, it's *such* a good thing you came to me. I mean, it hasn't been known by that name for years.' She was looking across at him, her face full of a rather girlish enthusiasm. Then suddenly her expression changed. Money, he knew it: 'I, er, suppose this is really quite important, is it, Mr Graves?'

'Hardly that, Miss Drummond. It's just to tidy things up.'

'Oh yes, but you're a frightfully well-known banking house, are you not – like Rothschild's?'

'Well, not exactly like –'

'And the Georgian Society is always chronically short of funds, d'you see. I mean, all the people who live in Blackheath, they love it, of course, but they're all mean and they won't *give*, and there's so much for the Society to do, and it's all so expensive nowadays. Even stamps, you know.' By now, she was looking at him implacably.

'Well, I'm sure a donation could be –'

'I was thinking,' said Miss Drummond, 'of five hundred guineas.'

'You were *what*?'

'Five hundred, I thought.' She gave an unlikely giggle. 'Only the other day, we had a bill for that very sum from a

68

firm of solicitors, and they'd done almost *nothing*, I assure you. When I protested they said we must pay for their knowledge. So I thought to myself, Mr Graves is wearing a beautiful suit, His shirt is from Jermyn Street and his shoes are hand-lasted – you can always tell, can't you? – and he must be really quite an important man. So, I thought –' she giggled once more, – 'that I could be like those solicitors and *sell* my knowledge.'

'I think,' Graves said seriously, 'that five hundred might be just a little high.'

Miss Drummond giggled yet again. 'Oh, I *am* enjoying this!'

'A reasonable sum might be –'

'Reasonable is what the market will bear, that's what my father always said.'

'And he –?'

'Dealt in Oriental carpets, Mr Graves. Look, why don't you do it this way. See if you can find out somewhere else. Then if you can't, and if it's important, you can always come back to me.'

Graves came to his feet. 'Well, five hundred *is* rather a lot. Maybe I will try –'

'Of course, you understand the price will go *up*, Mr Graves, if you have to return to me.'

He looked hard at her. 'How do I know it's worth the money?'

The giggle had subsided into a broad and very confident smile. 'You don't, Mr Graves. That's what's so delightful. Tell me something. Do you like dust?'

'Dust?' Graves repeated, perplexed.

'You'll be up to your neck in it, hunting through history for Carfax House.'

He blinked at her. 'Fifty pounds seems fair. Including support for a worthwhile cause.'

'Five hundred.'

Graves wriggled around miserably for a minute or two, but he was done and he knew it. And the money, after all,

69

was not his. He even thought for a moment that he might renege on the promise, but that was before she made him write it out.

Carfax House, she told him, once the paper was locked away, had been built in the 1790's and burned to the ground during World War One, when a passing Zeppelin dropped an incendiary on it. It was rebuilt after that war by a certain Mr Cavendish, who had made money out of army contracts for bully beef, and who liked it to be thought that he was related to the Dukes of Devonshire, whose family name, was Cavendish. Cavendish House it now became. It may be true of lightning that it rarely strikes twice in the same place; but the same cannot be said for German bombs, for in the autumn of 1941 a Heinkel 111 proceeding upon an attack on the Isle of Dogs was hit by anti-aircraft fire and turned for home, jettisoning a stick of bombs, one of which turned Cavendish House into a ruin. But once again, said Miss Drummond, it was rebuilt, still as Cavendish House. The man who rebuilt it – she had forgotten his name – was something of a recluse and had, in any case, eventually moved away.

'So who has it now?' Graves asked.

'Oh, some frightful people. He's something in popular music, or advertising is it? I forget which. She's just a tart. Well, a model anyway. I always think they're interchangeable, don't you?'

'Do you know the name?'

The name merely cost him a fiver, this time for the Lifeboats.

The house was not big. It stood two storeys high in a walled garden close to the grass of the Heath. It was painted a delicate shade of pale lemon, with white window-frames, and it was clearly in first-class order. Miss Drummond's view that 'There's precious little of the original fabric left, of course, but it's still one of the prettiest little Georgian houses in the village,' was obviously sound.

Graves lit a cigarette and paced across the grass, looking thoughtfully at Carfax/Cavendish House. Somewhere inside must lie the second part of Dikeston's story, no doubt carefully hidden. By whom – by Dikeston himself? It seemed at least possible that the recluse whose name Miss Drummond could not remember was in fact Dikeston.

Had he then moved away and left the packet of paper concealed? They'd have to be well concealed, Graves thought, or somebody who had no business to do so might find them.

The white front door, with its gleaming lion's head knocker, looked somehow forbidding in the sunshine. Graves, who would not normally have hesitated to approach the devil's own front door on Hillyard, Cleef business, found the thought of knocking on that door strangely daunting. How did one say it: 'Good afternoon, I'd like to search your house'? Graves felt himself agreeing with Pilgrim's stated view that Dikeston was a joker who was going to make all of them run their butts off.

His own butt first. He returned to 6 Athelsgate.

'Do next?' said Sir Horace Malory. 'Good Lord, isn't it obvious – you find the packet of papers, man! They're somewhere in the house – must be. Go and look! And get a move on!'

The white door, now lit from above by a bulb encased in a gleaming brass fixture, looked still less inviting as Graves crunched up the short gravel path towards it. His hand already on the lion's head knocker, he paused as laughter sounded from inside the house. Was it a dinner-party in there – or a television set? He knocked, and felt as he did so like an encyclopædia salesman.

It was a dinner-party. The door was opened by a man flushed with wine and carrying a napkin. Damn!

'Mr Abrahams?'

'Bit late, don't you think. Whatever you're selling, come

71

back another time.' Abrahams dabbed the napkin at his lips and made to close the door.

Graves thrust a visiting card at him. 'Please,' he said. 'It's quite important.'

'Oh?' Abrahams glanced at him with some suspicion, and then at the card. After a moment his thumbnail scraped at the embossed lettering. 'Hillyard, Cleef? Merchant bank, isn't it?'

'Yes.'

'First time I heard of a merchant bank going door-to-door,' Abrahams said, grinning. 'I know about the recession, but Christ!'

Graves, feeling the beginnings of fluster, now turned to dignity. He emitted a sombre laugh and said, 'We have a request, Mr Abrahams. You may see it as somewhat unusual, but we hope you may consider helping us in a small way.'

Abrahams's eye ran over him knowledgeably, pricing the suit, the haberdashery, the shoes. Miss Drummond had done the same, Graves thought. Blackheath and its denizens clearly judged the goods by the wrapper.

'Come in, Mr Graves,' Abrahams said abruptly. 'Have you eaten yet? We have a couple of friends in for a meal but I'm sure there'll be plenty.' He closed the door and led the way into the dining-room, where three slightly startled faces turned towards him.

Abrahams's initially suspicious manner had now become airy. 'Mr Graves is from a merchant bank. Just dropped in to see me about something they want.' He contrived to imply that nocturnal visits by City figures were commonplace events at Cavendish House. Abrahams was also, Graves shortly understood, trying to drum up business from the other male guest. Graves found himself being used, and disliking it.

But the evening ended, the guests departed, and at last Graves found himself making the nightmare request: 'We'd like to search your house!'

He had to repeat it, naturally, more than once. The eccentric client, now regrettably deceased, made a further appearance –

'Search the house?' screeched Mrs Abrahams. She was much as Miss Drummond had described her: half-tart, half-model. 'You mean, go poking into the cupboards, don't you?'

Graves explained, with all the smoothness he could muster, which was a good deal, that the Abrahams' own possessions would of course be inviolate. It was likely to be in the fabric of the house –

'You're going to lift the floorboards!' she yelled accusingly.

'There would,' Graves assured her, 'be a fee to cover any inconvenience.'

'A fee?' said Mrs Abrahams.

'Good one, I should hope,' said her husband.

Negotiations proceeded. The search, it was at last agreed, was to be in two stages. In the first of them, Graves accompanied by a man expert in building matters, and no doubt by Mrs Abrahams too, was to have complete access to loft and attics and cellars. The living-rooms could be examined but not disturbed. In the event that the search revealed nothing, Stage Two arrived. For that the removals department of Harrods would arrive, the entire contents of the house would be removed to store while the search took place. Mr and Mrs Abrahams would be accommodated in a suitable hotel, and the interior of Cavendish House would be redecorated pending the return of the owners and their possessions.

Mr Abrahams had ideas similar to, though grander than, Miss Drummond's. Stage One was a thousand. Stage Two was five thousand, plus all costs. Take it, or leave it.

Graves took it. He also required the deeds of the house, the plans, if any, from which the house had been rebuilt on the second occasion; also, before he began handing over money he needed corroboration of the statement by Miss

73

Drummond that Cavendish House *had* once borne the name of Carfax. Brief consultation with Hillyard, Cleef's solicitors gave Graves the welcome tidings that all the information could be obtained. The less happy news was that he would have to take trouble to get it.

This entailed first an easy trip to the Borough Records Office in nearby Lewisham, where a yellowish rate book for the year 1910 demonstrated Miss Drummond's veracity. At that time Carfax House had a rateable value of £125. Graves now telephoned Abrahams at the advertising agency of which he was a director, to ask the whereabouts of the deeds. Abrahams replied that, since the house was mortgaged, the deeds were lodged with the building society from which he had borrowed money, and would remain so until the mortgage was paid off in twenty years or so.

'Which building society?'

'The Leefield.'

'Which branch?'

Abrahams told him.

Graves set off by car armed with Abrahams's written permission to inspect the deeds, duly did so, and discovered what seemed to be shining gold. The bomb-damaged Cavendish House had been purchased in 1945 by one Henry George Dikeston. And sold by him some twenty years later to the Land Commissioners, who now held the freehold.

Carefully Graves noted the addresses: of the lawyers through whom the sales had been made, and of the Land Commissioners. There was not precisely a song in his heart at the prospect of tracking Dikeston down, for Dikeston at that stage was hardly the spectre he was later to become, but Graves was pleased. His pleasure increased when, later, at the offices of the Planning Department, he asked to inspect the plans of Cavendish House, and was given them.

The pleasure evaporated at once.

74

The bombs of 1941 wrecked Cavendish House. Its roof was destroyed: less than fifty per cent of the exterior walls remained standing. The architect's plans showed meticulous concern for the character of the house, and such of the original fabric as had been left standing was most carefully incorporated in the rebuilding. Turning the plan this way and that, looking for indications as to where the promised cavity might be, Graves found he was actually looking at that very word on the plan. In the architect's small, neat hand, appeared the phrase, 'Throughout in 9-inch cavity brickwork.' In the planning authority's office there was no shortage of people to explain the meaning: the walls of Cavendish House consisted of an outer and an inner skin of brick with a cavity between.

Graves swore under his breath. The second part of Dikeston's narrative was now somewhere in the hollow walls of the house, and there was no indication at all as to where. Easy to imagine the scene: scaffolding, bricklayers, the walls rising – and a packet, contained in some waterproof material, simply dropped down between the two skins of bricks, there to be safe for as long as the house stood.

'We need a consulting engineer,' Sir Horace Malory decided. Graves, surprised, thought he detected a trace of wry amusement in Malory's face. It was confirmed as Malory went on, 'This fella Dikeston's going to lead us the devil of a dance. I'm beginning to get a feeling about him.'

'What's that?' Graves asked.

'Remember the Cheshire cat, do you?' Malory asked ruminatively.

'Well, sure. I read *Alice* at school. Who didn't?'

'If you remember –' Malory was removing a Romeo No.3 from its tube – 'it vanished quite slowly, beginning with the end of the tail and ending with the grin, which remained some time after the rest of it had gone. Well, this

75

is just the beginning of the tale, d'you see. And the grin is still here with us.'

'I'll fix the engineer,' Graves said.

Sir Horace, wise as he undoubtedly was in the ways of man, might have been a little surprised at the broad distribution already achieved by news of Hillyard, Cleef's interest in a private house in Blackheath. An advertising agency is not a Trappist community, Denis Abrahams was more loquacious than most. When he heard, by telephone from his excitable wife, that no fewer than five people had spent the morning at his house, inspecting it according to the agreed terms for Stage One, and that one of them was a Knight (Sir Horace was in fact a baronet, but Mrs Abrahams didn't know that) Abrahams opened his mouth wider and spoke more loudly. Since he was in the bar of the Wig and Pen Club at the time, his story was heard by lawyers, who were only idly interested, and by one or two reporters, who began to show a professional attention.

Before Sir Horace returned to 6 Athelsgate, Mrs Frobisher, his secretary, had already twice denied knowledge of the matter to city-page reporters of two London newspapers.

'Keep doing so,' Malory instructed her. He had spent an annoying morning. Not only had careful examination of the roof and walls of Cavendish House failed to produce any indication of where the Dikeston papers might be concealed; but while Graves and Smithson (the consulting engineer) had carried out the inspection, Malory, unable to climb to the roof space and unwilling to rummage in cellars, had been exposed to a good hour and a half of Mrs Abrahams. She had clutched his arm and given him precise information about every stitch of curtain and carpet, every Wedgwood cigarette lighter and every mock-Adam fireplace. He was mildly surprised to find he had lived through it.

Now he must face Pilgrim, who would undoubtedly be amused, and probably patronizing. Pilgrim said, in fact, 'I told you this thing was going to get pricey and you ain't started yet. What's the next stage?'

Malory explained about the walls and watched crossly as Pilgrim controlled a laugh. 'It's not funny, Laurence!'

'It's not bad from where I'm sitting,' Pilgrim said. 'You're actually going to pull half of it *down*?'

'There's no alternative,' Malory said stiffly. 'You must see that.'

'How much is the place worth?'

'We have an estimate of about fifty-five thousand to rebuild.'

'A hundred thousand bucks!' Pilgrim said. The humour was ebbing fast from his face and voice. 'Better take care, Horace.'

Back in his own room, Malory instructed Graves to arrange as expeditiously as possible to transfer into Harrods' repository the Abrahams' furniture and effects; also the transfer of their persons to the Inter-Continental Hotel. He then made a neat little list of the visible difficulties. First, it would be necessary to inform, and indeed to persuade, the Abrahams of the necessity to pull down half of their beautiful house. Secondly, the local authority would have to be told and its consent probably have to be obtained before any work on the outside of Cavendish House could be carried out. Thirdly, the same must inevitably be true of the Land Commissioners, as ground landlords.

None of them would agree, and Malory knew it.

Then *what?* That the affair had its comic aspects was not lost on Malory. But his conviction that Dikeston's manuscript was of enormous importance was undiminished. His developing 'feeling' for Dikeston now told him that he was involved in a hunt and that like all good hunts it would be exciting and probably dangerous, and that there would be blood to be spilled at the finish.

They would just have to pull the walls down – knock 'em down and take the consequences. And what consequences they would be: suits for civil damages from the Abrahams; prosecution by the local authority. Etcetera, etcetera.

77

Horace Malory suddenly discovered he was holding his head in his hands, and frowning so hard that his forehead felt stiff. He sat up and looked around the room: that damned Cheshire cat grin was here somewhere.

He said aloud: 'Just have to face it, that's all. Just have to face it.'

A week later the furniture was expensively in store; so were Mr and Mrs Denis Abrahams; and the early morning calm of the leafy crossroads which had given Carfax House its original name was mildly disturbed by young mothers taking their offspring to school in French and German estate cars, and making way for a bulldozer which turned clumsily in at the side gate of Cavendish House, shoving the gatepost pillar aside.

Sir Horace Malory and Jacques Graves were there to meet it, with Smithson the consulting engineer, and a small gang of workmen.

As they stood watching they were joined by a neighbour whose presence had not been requested and who would certainly have been invited to leave had she not been an exceptionally handsome blonde in her mid-thirties. Malory tended to be gallant to handsome women.

'Of course it's very *pretty*,' she observed. 'But it's mani-cured half to *death*! In any case, hardly any of it's original. Why are you doing this, anyway?'

'Out of need, madam,' Malory muttered.

'Yes, well . . .' The woman looked round her with a critical eye. Graves guessed she could price everything in sight to within a pound or two. '. . . I wouldn't really want any of it, myself. Ours *is* authentic Georgian, of *course*.'

'Nice for you,' said Malory.

'Except the sundial. 'I'd *love* that. Done long before *they* came here, naturally. Have you seen it?'

'I believe not.' Malory's gallant habits were warring now with a growing dislike of her manner.

'It's in the garden at the rear. Beautiful thing. A cockatrice. Highly imaginative.'

Malory merely nodded, his attention on the now roaring bulldozer as it manœuvred; but Graves frowned as a little bell tinkled in his mind. He turned to her. 'Did you say cockatrice?'

She smiled. 'That's right. If you're interested, you should have a look.'

'Some kind of heraldic animal, right?' Graves said. And when she nodded, he asked her, 'Isn't there another name? Seems to me I've heard –'

'Oh yes,' she said. 'It was also called a basilisk. That's the other name. Do you know about it?'

But Graves, now with both arms held high in the air, was signalling the bulldozer driver to halt. As the diesel's noise subsided he said, 'Sir Horace, this lady says there's a kind of special sundial. A basilisk.'

'Interesting word,' Malory said. 'Tell me more, if you will, madam.'

It was all she needed. 'Come on, I'll show you.'

'By all means.'

She led them to it. It was a big sundial, on a massive wrought-iron base in the form of a cage with the animal in it. The morning sun was pale and the shadow faint, but later in the day that shadow would fall upon the wall.

'Evil, you see.' She pointed to the wrought-iron animal. 'The embodiment of evil.'

Malory looked as she rattled on: 'Its glance was fatal to any man – and to any animal except a weasel. Its breath was poisonous and killed all vegetation except the rue. It could only be killed by –'

Basilisk. Basil, Malory thought. Basilisk the embodiment of evil. Oh, Dikeston, Dikeston!

He held up his hand. 'We can start here, I think, where the shadow's on the wall. And I hardly think we'll need the bulldozer.'

CHAPTER FOUR

———————◆———————

Second instalment of the account, written by
Lt Cdr H. G. Dikeston, RN, of his journeyings
in Russia in the spring of 1918

So they had been promised weapons, these Bolsheviks, that much was plain! And what a figure: fifty million sterling, *in arms*! It was no wonder I had seen eyebrows raised in pleasure and surprise on those hard, determined faces. For Lenin, then trapped in a nutcracker between the White Russians and the Germans, it was the gift to save both his revolution and his Tartar hide. Trotsky, commissar for an army near empty-handed in the field, beamed like a child in a chocolate factory, and Yankel Sverdlov, Head of State to a tottering conspiracy, must on the instant have felt the ground grow firm beneath his feet. Not Zaharoff the war-monger now: Zaharoff the Saviour!

All haste was made at once to propel me along on my journey.

I was in Sverdlov's hands, and busy hands they were! No sooner had I been waved from his presence with the admonition that I must on no account be late next morning, than I was approached by a male secretary. I saw this man on that one occasion only, and for but a moment or two, yet I remember him, clear as can be, as though there were a camera in my brain. He had a tall, narrow head without a hair upon it anywhere, a white imperial beard upon his chin which reminded me of Zaharoff's own, and pince-nez upon his nose, attached to his lapel by a wide ribbon of brilliant crimson silk. If I waste time here upon the man, it is only because in Moscow it was the only item of striking personal adornment that I saw: in that great city, a mere two feet of silk ribbon! He called a man with a camera and my photograph was taken.

The man passed me on to a messenger: a sailor in uniform who said in a curt manner, 'Follow,' and set briskly off. Striding behind him, I left the Kavalersky Building and after some five or six minutes' brisk walking, was brought to another, the name of which I do not know. The sailor said only, 'Enter,' and left me there.

Inside I was greeted by what I judged to be some kind of petty officer in the Fleet. 'From Comrade Sverdlov's office?' he demanded.

I nodded.

'This way, then.' He pointed to a door. 'And help yourself. It's all there. Take what you need. Oh, and here – take this.' He handed me a valise and turned away.

I raised my hand. 'One moment. You have instructions about me?'

He looked round in surprise. 'Naturally.'

'What are they?'

The man took a paper from his pocket. There was handwriting on it, somewhat grubby and likely I guessed to be his own. He read slowly, 'Officer's uniform, winter journey east.'

I said, 'What rank?'

'No ranks in there, Comrade. Help yourself, I told you.'

I did as he bade me and passed through the door to which he had pointed. Inside, in a dim-lit chamber of some size, I was struck first by an overpowering smell of wool, sweat and human bodies. Great racks of dark clothes stood everywhere: and when I came to examine them it was at once apparent that all were naval officers' uniforms.

I wondered soberly, as my hands moved over the heavy, soft, navy-blue doeskin, where the men might be whose garments these were. It was hardly a thought to offer reassurance, for there were hundreds, perhaps thousands of them. I sniffed cautiously at one or two and without exception they had been much worn and little cleaned.

81

Still, it was my task here to outfit myself and I began to hunt among them for jackets and trousers of a size appropriate. I tried clothing on, then boots, for though my own were excellent, no man ever came to harm by equipping himself with good spare boots. And I know that I was struck, standing there in the gloom amid all this second-hand rag-merchant's stock, by the contrast between this dingy outfitting and that splendid efficiency at Gieves' the night before I left London. I did not trouble to seek out a greatcoat, for it was doubtful whether in this odorous hall there would be the equal of mine from Gieves, with the full Guardee cut. At last, my valise full of cast-offs, I left the hall.

The petty officer awaited me. 'Put them down on the table, Comrade.'

I did so and he went over the two tunics, the trousers, and the cap carefully. He was looking for something. I asked what.

'Making sure there are no rank badges, no stripes, no braid,' he said. 'Here, they're all right. You can take them.' He directed me back to the Kavalersky Building, where I collected my own suitcase and was told I had been allocated a bed for the night in the guard barracks. At mess I was given borsht and a kind of solyanka, which should be made with fine beef steak but was not. It was also cooked without wine, but I have had worse in RN wardrooms often enough, so all I had to complain of was that my bed had neither sheets nor blankets and that because of the cold I must perforce sleep in my clothes.

I fell asleep thinking of Vassily Yakovlev, the name that Sverdlov had told me to remember.

Who, I wondered, could he be?

I woke uncomfortable. Sleeping in day clothes is a habit perforce to be acquired in service at sea in time of war; so too is the hasty eating of half-prepared food. There was no way to wash more than face and hands, and that only in bitterly cold water. Breakfast was rough bread and a sliver of cheese washed down by sadly weak tea without lemon. We in Britain had heard much of the discomforts of the new Russia and it occurred to me then that discomforts is what they were. Certainly not hardships.

All the same, as I made my way to the Kavalersky and my morning appointment with the Head of the Soviet State, I felt far from fresh, less than clear-headed, and in truth somewhat dull of mind. I knew in general what might lie before me. The envelope containing Mr Basil Zaharoff's document lay safe in my travel case, and I had known from the beginning, of course, that it was Zaharoff's intention that I be sent to the Tsar. It seemed also, from the previous day's events, that I was indeed to be sent east. But that morning, with my creased clothes sticking to my unwashed body, it was difficult to care.

I presented myself ten minutes early, was kept waiting for fifteen and then was shown in to Sverdlov, who was breakfasting at his desk.

'I have been here since six,' he told me. 'It is the best of disciplines to wait for food.' He was peeling a hard-boiled egg as he spoke, and when it was done, inserted it whole in to his mouth. Accordingly further conversation was postponed for several moments. Then he said, 'The name – you remember the name?'

'Yakovlev,' I said. 'Vassily Vassilievitch Yakovlev.'

'Good, good.' He opened a drawer in his desk and extracted a large envelope of yellowish-brown paper. This he placed at the edge of the desk, close to where I stood. 'Open it.'

I took it up, and lifted back the flap. Naturally enough, the envelope contained papers, the first of which bore a photograph and a seal. I took it out. It was a combined *laissez-passer* and identity document. The photograph was of my own face, and could only be the one taken on the previous day. The paper bore the name Yakovlev, Vassily.

I looked at Sverdlov. 'I am to be Russian, then?'

He was busy with another egg.

'It is safer. Read while I eat. A man works up an appetite at a desk.'

The *laissez-passer* held further and surprising news. I was, it seemed, to be no ordinary Yakovlev, but *Commissar* Yakovlev! My eye travelled down the lines, making further discoveries as it went. I was on a mission of great importance for the Soviet Central Executive Committee, whose seal, in black wax, decorated the bottom of the paper, and whose chairman, Sverdlov himself, had signed it. I held in my hand a paper issued by the most powerful men in Russia demanding that my every requirement be met by whomever I encountered.

But there was more even than that. There was the threat – no, it was more than a threat – it was a plain statement: that summary execution awaited those who defied the wishes of Commissar Yakovlev!

I must have looked as astonished as I felt, for when I raised my eyes, Sverdlov was regarding me sardonically. 'We must hope that it works,' he said.

'I beg your pardon?'

'You are going to Tyumen, to Tobolsk,' he said. 'And both are a long way from this desk and from the Kremlin.'

'But surely, with such orders –?'

He raised a hand, amused. 'You think that suddenly the word of Comrade Lenin is law from the Ukraine to the Pacific? My friend, it all takes time. The regional soviets are made up of men who have never governed, who have spent their lives in secret activity and in fear of their lives. They are in the open now, but the old instincts remain. They fear and distrust the ruler in the distance, even when it is Comrade Lenin himself. *They* will govern the Urals, Georgia, the Ukraine.' He gave a low, rumbling laugh. 'Oh, they will listen. Or anyway they will *say* they are listening. Oh yes, Comrade Sverdlov, well naturally . . . oh yes, they say it all the time. When they are here. But let them get off the train and it's a different matter. In their own territories they are independent and mean to stay so. Word from Moscow will be considered, sometimes it will be accepted, but sometimes the order is destroyed and the messenger with it. You'll be in danger, Englishman, whatever papers you carry. Be in no doubt of it.'

I nodded. To be in danger would be no great novelty after three years of war.

'What am I to do?'

He considered me for a moment. 'What is your relationship to Zaharoff?'

'None, sir. I am a messenger only.'

He gave a little snort of disbelief. 'That fellow would not send anyone but his own man.'

I protested. 'I am a serving officer, sir. I have been three years with the Grand Fleet. A month ago I was patrolling the Heligoland Bight on coastal bombardment. I met Mr Zaharoff only on the night I left London!'

Sverdlov waved an arm dismissively. 'It doesn't even matter. You are Yakovlev now, and Zaharoff too is far away. The matter is simple. You must have understood at yesterday's meeting that you had brought with you his promise of arms. The price is Nicholas Romanov and his family.'

I nodded; it was likely enough.

'But –' Yankel Sverdlov wagged a finger. 'There is more. Nicholas Romanov himself will pay for the arms. He has a hidden fortune in London. He releases the money to Zaharoff, Zaharoff releases arms to us, we release Nicholas Romanov and his family to his cousin, the English King. The former Tsar must sign your paper, so you must reach him at Tobolsk. And there are people in that region, members of the Soviet at Ekaterinburg, for instance, who would want only to stop you. They want Romanov dead. They think it matters that an ex-Tsar lives on. It doesn't. Nicholas Romanov counts for nothing. Except –' and Sverdlov produced again that sardonic smile – 'in so far as he can be useful. That is why he lives.' He lit a cigarette and glared at me for a moment. '*He* lives and you live. But it would take very little to change that. Be very careful.' Then he gave me a sudden grin full of genial cunning. 'And give an increase in pay to the guards at Tobolsk, eh!'

And then, abruptly, his attention had switched to other things upon his desk. The interview was clearly at an end, and I was left standing with my papers. I bowed and withdrew and in the outer office stood in a corner and gave my own attention to the other papers in the envelope. They gave specific instructions to certain officials of the Trans-Siberian Railway; they gave me my command; they conferred upon me all the power and authority necessary to this strange mission of mine. When I had read them, nothing remained to be done except to depart. There was no car, no arranged transport, not even, I was told, the possibility of summoning a taxi.

So Commissar Yakovlev walked to the station with his valise and his new power of life and death.

It is needless, I believe, to describe the journey by rail eastward from Moscow, along the endless track of the Trans-Siberian. This account is not a travel journal and I kept no notes of the food nor of anything else. I had a soft seat in what had been a first-class carriage, but that was all. I sat on my documents for safety and remained in my seat, sleeping for much of the time. The journey was uneventful.

Tyumen, on the far side of the Ural Mountains was heralded by much snorting and clanking from engines and coaches. As the train drew in, I took papers and valise and, alighting, saw a heavy-set man, booted and spurred like a hussar, standing beside the track looking keenly round. From the top step of the carriage it was possible to see his troop of horsemen drawn up not far away, for the steaming breath of many close-ranged horses made a considerable mist in the cold air.

I made for him and introduced myself. 'I'm Yakovlev.'

He turned and saluted; he was a veteran by the look of him of twenty and more years as a cavalryman. He said, 'Welcome, Comrade Commissar,' but said it awkwardly as though, like myself, he would be more at home with a simple 'sir'. As I buttoned myself together I saw his eye resting doubtfully on the naval uniform and I laugh cheerfully and slapped his shoulder and said, 'Don't worry, Comrade. I can ride!' For now I must play a part, and confidence was of importance. 'You have a good horse for me?'

He smiled and I saw an imp of mischief in his eye.

'One of those, eh?' I said. 'A stallion, I'll bet!'

'A fine animal, Comrade.'

'You ride it,' I said. 'I'll take yours.'

He grinned in embarrassment, but he took it like a sportsman. He had spoken the truth: it was a fine stallion. But his was better, and with a long ride ahead I was glad not to have to battle a wayward beast.

We set off at once, he and I in the van, the rest strung two abreast behind: one hundred and fifty of the fine horsemen of the steppes – and under the command, now, of a naval officer. I could not help wondering what they would think had they known I was a *British* naval officer.

'You were sergeant?' I asked.

'Yes, Comrade Commissar.'

'Your name?'

'Koznov.'

'Good. How far to Tobolsk?'

'Two hundred versts.'

That is a distance of about one hundred and thirty miles, the Russian verst being approximately two-thirds of an English mile; and the saddle was hard, with wood in its construction. Also, it was years since I had spent even a day on horseback. I would be sore, and walk accordingly, by the time Tobolsk was reached. That was unfortunate, for upon arrival I would need all the dignity, authority and confidence I could muster, and few things are so irresistibly comic, especially in central Russia, as the man who is saddle-sore.

Again, there is no need to describe the journey. We rode, we ate, changed horses, slept briefly, and we rode again. And so, at mid-morning on April 22nd, we rode into Tobolsk. I made direct for the Governor's House, where the Imperial Family was held under guard. By the time the house was reached we were awaited, for even when the earth is snow-covered, a hundred and fifty horsemen do not travel quietly and our approach had been seen and heard.

I reined in at the gate and called to one of the two guards on duty to summon the officer in command, a Colonel Kobylinsky.

The man demanded my name and my business.

'Tell him Yakovlev,' I said, 'from Moscow. Commissar. On the business of the Soviet Central Executive Committee!'

I dismounted then and told Koznov to get his men settled and fed. A moment later Colonel Kobylinsky was before me. Knowing a little of his story, I looked at him with interest. He was a big man, healthy-looking, but with the white whiskers of an older man. Like his master the Tsar, the Colonel had assumed in recent months a far lower station in life than he was used to. Once he had commanded at Tsarskoe Selo, the great palace of the Tsars; but he too had been exiled by Kerensky, like his master, and was with him still. But the guards now were not the fine, shiny soldiers of more prosperous days. According to Sverdlov's situation papers, Kobylinsky now had two sets of men in his nominal charge: the first group was from Omsk, in western Siberia, the second group came from Ekaterinburg and it was these, the so-called 'Red Guards,' who presented the greatest threat to the Romanovs and, indeed, to me.

'Commissar Yakovlev,' I said loudly, and held out my *laissez-passer*. 'Here on the instructions of the Central Committee.'

'Kobylinsky.' He looked down his nose at me, clicked his

heels, then took the paper and held it at arm's length while he read it. As he was doing so a man came to stand and read at his shoulder, glancing at me several times.

'Who are you?' I demanded.

'People's Soviet of the Urals,' he said, 'That is who I am.' He said no more, and indeed a moment later he had turned and was moving away; but there was something in his manner I found disturbing.

'Come inside,' Kobylinsky said, taking my arm. 'Let us give you refreshment. Come – your men will be attended to.'

He gave me breakfast. The bread was warm and fresh, the coffee hot, and he did not force questions upon me. It would have been most pleasant had we not twice been interrupted by members of the rival guard factions intent upon inspecting my papers once again. One of them was the fellow from the gate, and having examined my pass once more, he said softly, 'You come direct from Comrade Sverdlov?'

'Yes.'

'You met him?'

'Yes.'

'Who else did you meet?'

'Comrade Lenin,' I said. 'And Comrade Trotsky.'

He gave a nod and a little smile. 'Remember you are beyond the Urals now, my friend.'

Again he sidled away. 'Who is that man?' I demanded of Kobylinsky.

'Ruzsky,' he replied. 'From Ekaterinburg. He is a member of the Urals Soviet. I can tell you no more, except that he sometimes calls himself Bronard.'

'You can tell me,' I said, 'of the former Tsar. He is well?'

'Yes.'

'And his family?'

'They, too, except the son. You will know, I imagine, that the boy is hæmophiliac, subject to bouts of severe

89

illness and only now beginning to recover from the most recent.'

This latest bout was hardly welcome news. 'The boy is in bed?'

'And will be for some days,' Kobylinsky said. 'He suffers great pain still.'

Kobylinsky had tobacco and paper and we made ourselves cigarettes in the Russian manner, but we were not even to finish them before the man Ruzsky returned. He did not knock, merely walked into the room, accompanied by others, and said, 'Your presence must be discussed, Comrade.'

And discussed it was. Largely by them. I informed them that my business must, for the moment, be of a confidential nature, that when the time came they would be informed of my purpose, and then said no more for a while.

The man Ruzsky was plainly still suspicious of me and he did not hesitate to say so. If, as Sverdlov had told me, the Bolsheviks of Ekaterinburg were more militant than most, it was clear that Ruzsky was among the most virulent of them. 'Papers can be forged,' he said, looking hard at me, and speaking in a quiet voice but with great emphasis. 'Who among us knows Comrade Sverdlov's signature?' The man was chronically suspicious and went on about plots to save the lives of the Romanovs, about lurking traitors to the Revolution, some of them there in the house, and many swarming in Tobolsk. As he talked, others came into the room and it became possible to sense dissension, Omsk against Ekaterinburg. Ruzsky's statements were received by some with head-shaking and pursed lips. He wanted the Tsar killed, and quickly, before somebody – the Whites, the Germans, or maybe the treacherous leadership in Moscow – liberated them. 'The family too. They must all be wiped out,' he insisted.

'The Revolution doesn't kill women and children,' he was promptly told by one of the Omsk men.

He came back at me then. 'Who is this supposed Commissar? He says he is here on Comrade Sverdlov's orders, but he will not tell us what they are!'

I judged it time to speak. 'There is such a thing,' I told him, 'as a telegraph. Send a telegram to Comrade Sverdlov.'

'No telegraphs here, Comrade,' he said. 'You're in the wilds here, not Moscow. The nearest is at Tyumen.'

'Good,' I said. 'Go there. We'll find you a horse.'

This observation, for some reason, was greeted with loud laughter from the Omsk men and when Ruzsky began again to speak they hissed at him. Soon, to my surprise, he withdrew from the room.

Since it was clear most of the men remaining were now fairly disposed toward me, I chose that moment to tell them of Sverdlov's authorization of an increase in their pay, and that I would like to address their committee. Five men then sat at the table with me. Kobylinsky tactfully went out. The rest withdrew.

I said, 'You are right that I am here because of Nicholas Romanov. Right, too, that I am to take him away.'

They frowned at me then, all of them, even the Omsk men.

I said, 'Has he any value to Russia now? Tell me!'

Heads were shaken. 'None, none.'

I said, 'You are right. But he has value to others. In exchange for his person we are to receive enough weapons to equip an army.'

'Yes,' demanded one of the remaining Ekaterinburg men sourly, 'but will it be an army to put him back on the throne?'

I shook my head. 'An army to smash the Whites. To defeat the Czech Legion. An army to win the revolutionary war! Once he's away, Russia will never see Nicholas Romanov again. He can safely be forgotten for ever!'

Somebody said, 'Where's he to go?'

'Omsk first,' I said.

'Why?' This was an Ekaterinburg man. 'He's ours. We have jurisdiction.'

'No, *we* have.'

I said, '*I* have. And *I* am under orders that I am powerless to alter. Comrade Lenin and Comrade Sverdlov want him moved. I'm to move him. And now I must *see* this enemy of the people who is to equip the people's army!'

There were smiles at that and they rose from the table. My mind went winging briefly to London, to Zaharoff, who, whatever one's thoughts about him, had so accurately divined the assorted wishes of different men and seen where they came together.

Much has been made of the hardships and gross indignities suffered after the abdication by the Imperial Family, and I for one can testify to the truth of such stories as the year 1918 drew on. But in the Governor's House at Tobolsk they were far from uncomfortable. They had wintered warm and well fed. Bored maybe but nothing worse.

Colonel Kobylinsky having gone upstairs to inform Nicholas Romanov of my presence and my requirement to meet him. I took up position in the hall of the house, near the foot of the stairs, and waited. Only a few moments passed before I heard footsteps and, looking up, beheld the former Tsar of all the Russias descending towards me. I did not at that moment see him clearly, for the hall was high and ill-lit, with coloured glass in small windows. Still, even in drab he was recognizable, and as he reached the foot of the stairs and came towards me, he was more than that: for this was the absolute double of the King George to whose presence I had had the honour to be summoned a mere three weeks before. The same eyes, the same hair, the same beard and moustache; it was the same face, even to expression, for the gravity of his eyes was identical with that of his royal cousin.

It was this, perhaps which affected my behaviour. I had

intended formal propriety, no more, addressing him as Comrade. But the words escaped me involuntarily, and I responded to his polite 'Commissar Yakovlev?' with:

'Your Majesty.'

I saw his quick frown, the surprise in his eyes, and thanked my Maker that, Kobylinsky's apart, there were no other listening ears. Those words, overheard by such as Ruzsky, might have had me shot!

I told Nicholas of the intention of the Central Executive Committee that he and his family be moved from Tobolsk within twenty-four hours.

His body stiffened. 'Moved? Where to?'

I said, 'The intention is ultimately to take you and your family into safety abroad.'

He shook his head. 'We go nowhere without prior knowledge of the means and conditions. I ask you again: where?'

I lowered my voice. 'Your Majesty. I am acting under orders from the highest. I am to remove you from the hands of these people here. My own life depends upon your safety.'

'I repeat: I can *not* go,' he said. 'My son is ill and cannot safely be moved and I will not abandon him.'

'It is important for you to understand,' I said, 'that my orders are that you must go from here. The preference is that you should go voluntarily, but it is only a preference. For go you must.'

'If it means force, Commissar Yakovlev?'

'Those are my orders.'

He looked at me thoughtfully. This, I suspected, must in all probability be the first threat of actual force against his person, and no doubt it was a shock. He said, 'Will you tell me what you know?'

I nodded. 'At Tyumen a train is to be waiting.'

'Where is it bound?'

'We shall not know that until we reach Tyumen. Further orders from Moscow will await me there.'

93

He closed his eyes. 'What is your guess, Commissar Yakovlev?'

'Probably a return to Moscow. It is my belief you are to be sent abroad quickly. I know such action to be the wish of Comrade Sverdlov.'

'Sverdlov? But if *he* wishes it –'

I nodded, and still keeping my voice low, said, 'Sir, there is a train. Whether it goes west to Moscow, or east to Omsk and beyond, I shall not know until I receive further orders. But I and my men are here to ensure your safety.'

'East to Shanghai, perhaps?'

'I cannot say, Sir. It is a possibility. I know only that Comrade Sverdlov wishes your family to leave the country in safety.'

Nicholas drew himself up. He had much simple dignity as he spoke. 'You leave *me* no alternative but I beg you not to move my son. To do so would be to inflict much needless agony upon a young boy.'

'He can remain here,' I said, 'and others of your family, if necessary, to be with him.'

'Thank you for that.' He made a little inclination of the head. 'I must discuss this, of course. There are family decisions . . .'

I nodded. 'We leave in the early morning – at four a.m.'

'At four? So early?'

'The train is scheduled.'

He left me then, and Kobylinsky with him, to talk with his family. I watched him walk heavily up the staircase and felt a deep regret that I was unable to tell him more. But what could I say that was true? Beyond Tyumen I knew nothing. Upon reaching the railway telegraph there I was to send a signal to Sverdlov and await his reply. The matter of Zaharoff's document now concerned me greatly, for in addition to getting it signed, I *must* get Nicholas away. If he read the document and knew as a consequence what he was being required to sign away, might he not suspect that in

94

doing so he was sealing his own fate? He might indeed – and then refuse to leave, and what then would I do?

I did not, in any case, have reason to believe anything was intended other than that the Imperial Family should leave Russia for England.

* * *

Sir Horace Malory, engrossed in Dikeston's narrative, did not at first hear the ring of the telephone on his desk. When it rang a second time he muttered at the interruption, picked it up and briskly instructed Mrs Frobisher that he would accept no calls.

'But it's the man from Oxford,' she said. 'You were most anxious –'

'Very well, put him on. What's his name?'

'Dr Felix Aston.'

It was a young voice with a jaunty note in it. Malory had a mild impulse to ask whether Aston were wearing jeans but forbore. 'You're an expert on the Russian Revolution, is that so?'

'It's a foolish man who pretends to expertise, Sir Horace,' the voice said cheerfully. 'I've made a study for some years. Written a book.'

'Name Yakovlev mean anything to you?' Malory asked.

There was a pause, then, 'Yes, it does – if it's Vassily Yakovlev. If he was a commissar.'

'That's the chappie. Tell me.'

'Well, it was post-Revolution, of course. But Yakovlev was the man who went off with the Tsar and all the jewels, then vanished.'

Malory said slowly. 'The jewels?'

'Trainload of stuff.' Aston's voice was positively chirpy. 'Tremendous mystery man, Commissar Yakovlev. Have you come across something about him?'

'Hmmm?' said Malory, with sudden caution. 'Oh no, no, no, nothing like that. Sorry if I raised a hare. But thank you, thank you.'

95

He put down the telephone, then pressed Pilgrim's button on the intercom. 'Laurence, anybody with you?'

'Just Graves.'

'Well, he'll be interested, too. Our man Dikeston went off with all the Romanov treasure.'

'All of it – what's that mean?' Pilgrim demanded.

'A trainload,' said Malory, and took his finger off the button.

*   *   *

I was far from idle as I waited while the Imperial Family made its decisions. My trusty hussar Koznov was set to scouring Tobolsk for the largest *koshevas* he could find and horses to draw them.

'Will the owners give them up?' he asked me. 'What do I do if –?'

'The threat of death should suffice,' I said grimly. 'If any man refuses, bring him to me.'

None did. The Commissar from Moscow was evidently to be obeyed. As the day went on, the courtyard of the Governor's House began to fill with sleds of many kinds. I sent for Kobylinsky, who had spent hours closeted upstairs with the Family, and instructed him to arrange the packing of all the Romanov possessions. Only the essentials of living were to remain in Tobolsk with those who stayed behind.

My work was interrupted many times, not least by the odious Ruzsky, who came smirking to me and said, 'I hear you're taking him away.' His expression surprised me. He seemed almost pleased. 'To Moscow, I believe?' he went on. He was half-drunk.

I told him I awaited further orders from the capital and the Central Executive Committee.

He smirked yet more. 'The way to Moscow lies through Ekaterinburg,' he said, and turned and sauntered off. That was his way, to deliver an unpleasant thrust and turn his back. As I watched that back retreating I wished more than anything that I could put a bullet in it.

He came again, later. It was dark and the room lit by candles. He stood before me, a bottle in his hand, and said, 'Keep a place for me.'

I said, 'What do you mean?'

'What I say. I go with you to Tyumen. And on from there, too. Comrade Romanov –' and he laid rough emphasis on the 'comrade' – 'is *ours* and we mean to keep him.'

'Ours?'

'You know what I mean – the Urals Soviet.'

'I cannot permit –'

He banged his fist on the desk. 'You cannot *prevent*,' he said. 'I go, or Nicholas doesn't.'

'You have no authority,' I told him, and he laughed sharply.

'Authority? You mean bits of paper from Moscow? Listen to me, Yakovlev. We are letting you go – we are letting you take Nicholas, as a *courtesy* to Moscow! It is not your pretty face or your fancy papers. Oh no, my friend. If I kill Nicholas, here, now – and I would most willingly, believe me – I would be a hero in Ekaterinburg! Be grateful to me.'

'Very well.' I shrugged. 'It makes no difference. Come with us. I fail to comprehend the reason for your rancour, Comrade.'

'And I don't like your airs,' he said. 'Don't force me to doubt your loyalty.' With which, again, he departed.

I dined with Kobylinsky, the two of us alone. He was tired. He had been labouring all day at the packing of the possessions of the Imperial Family but he ate little. Often I sensed his eyes on me, and at last I said, 'It is my belief they will be safe.'

When I looked up, it was to see a tear in his eye. He brushed it away and said with great sadness, 'All my life I have served my country and the Imperial Family, and now I can serve no more.'

'You can serve those who remain here,' I told him. 'Has the choice been made?'

It had. Young Alexei, the former Tsarevitch, whose claim to succeed had been waived a year earlier when Nicholas abdicated and who was therefore merely a sick boy of thirteen instead of a Crown Prince, was to remain in his sick bed. Three of his sisters, all of whom had nursed him devotedly, Anastasia, Tatiana and Olga, were to remain with him. The ex-Tsarina, Alexandra, and the third daughter, Marie, aged nineteen, were to accompany Nicholas.

'What is to happen,' Kobylinsky then asked of me, 'when the boy has recovered? Will you come back for him?'

'If I can.' I could promise no more, but could hardly promise less. The position of this stricken family bore down upon me more heavily with every passing hour. I had made a private resolve that somehow I would contrive to accompany them until the exchanges were made, until Zaharoff accepted a paper and a family and gave in return the means of war.

'Then will you,' Kobylinsky asked me, 'come with me to reassure the Grand Duchesses – I beg your pardon, the Romanov daughters – that it is intended the Family be brought together again.'

Though I had no instructions to that effect, I gladly agreed. It is always better for people to live in hope. Accordingly I accompanied Kobylinsky to an upstairs sitting-room where the Imperial Family was resting preparatory to parting and departure. The feeling of strain among them was obvious, yet so too was a sense of strong unity and affection. The boy's bed was in the room and he lay propped on pillows, his sisters all around him. I noticed particularly that as I entered, both his hands were being held by one sister or another, and their smiles were directed at him.

Seeing me, Nicholas rose and made again the formal motion of the head that was half-nod and half-bow. He was simply-dressed in a plain, belted tunic and his manner *en famille* was also one of simplicity.

There was little to discuss, nor did I wish to take up time he could spend better with his children. I simply asked him to confirm who would go and who would stay and this he did.

It was then I thought of the letter. Nicholas could as well read it here as anywhere, and perhaps if I were to leave it with him and his family so that it could be discussed, less suspicion might attach to it, and to me.

'One word more, your Majesty, if you will?' I moved away from the rest, towards the window, taking the missive from my tunic. He hesitated, then followed me. 'Well?'

I held out the envelope. 'For you to read, sir, and – I believe – to sign.'

'What is it?' He had not yet taken the envelope and his eyes were not upon it, but upon my face.

I shook my head. 'I am the messenger, no more than that. But my instructions are that it is concerned with your release.'

He took it then and placed it on a small table. 'Thank you.'

I turned to leave, and found my wary barred by one of the daughters. Preoccupied as I had been with Nicholas, I had barely so much as glanced at the girls, or at the boy Alexei, but the upraised face before me now fully caught my attention, for it was striking indeed.

'I am Marie,' she said, 'and I am to accompany you, Commissar Yakovlev.'

I saluted.

She was very pale; she had wide, dark eyes. It was a face of symmetry and, one can fairly say, of beauty. She was quite tall and perfectly slim, and I can see her now, as I write this, see her standing between me and the door, looking at me with that composure that bespeaks courage. 'Will you,' she asked me, 'answer the question which most concerns us all?'

99

'If I can.'

'We are to be separated for the first time,' Marie said. 'Is it true we are to be brought together again before long?'

As I said earlier, hope is easier to live with than despair. 'Yes,' I said. 'That is the intention.' It seemed to me impossible that if Nicholas were freed, the girls would not be set free also.

She stood aside at once. 'I thank you for that reassurance.'

I saluted again, and left. As I descended the stair I found she lingered in my mind. From time to time one meets an individual whom one recognizes on the instant to be of superior mettle to the rest of humankind. She was one such, and there was no mistaking it, however brief the encounter.

Downstairs, Ruzsky awaited me. 'Well?' I asked him. 'What now?'

He still wore that smirk of his. How I ached to wipe it from his unpleasant countenance!

'Your horse,' he said. 'I have borrowed it.' He waited for me to say when, or how, or why, or for what? I did not do so and he was therefore obliged to speak. 'To send a man to Ekaterinburg. They will be anxious to learn of this departure.'

'It's a long ride,' I said. And so it was – close to four hundred miles!

'He will go by train from Tyumen,' Ruzsky said, smiling. 'As you will.'

'Very well,' I said, as calmly as I could. But inside I was fuming, knowing what the creature intended. When I put the Imperial Family on the train at Tyumen and started for Moscow, the train would have to pass through Ekaterinburg. Yankel Sverdlov had warned me of the likely conduct of the Soviet leadership in the city and Ruzsky, having underlined the warning, was clearly intent upon mischief.

This matter now required much careful thought, but did not get it at that time, for I became too busy. The excellent

Koznov and his men were doing their best, but to load and organize a substantial convoy of horse-drawn *koshevas* is no light matter, and there was some confusion. It was hard work, bringing order to bear, but gradually it came about, and soon after three o'clock in the morning the baggage was all loaded and I was able to go back indoors to summon the family. They awaited me in the hall, the ex-Tsarina and Marie wrapped in furs, and Nicholas between them, in a top coat that came down no further than mid-thigh.

Seeing that the time for departure had come, they exchanged kisses and goodbyes with those who were to stay behind, and followed me outside into the cold, blowing snow. I saw no tears.

'Commissar!' A woman's voice and I turned. 'I will ride with my husband.'

I saluted the former empress. 'I regret that that is not possible. I must myself accompany him. I have arranged that you occupy a *kosheva* with your daughter.'

She was disposed to argue, but Marie intervened. 'Come, Mama, the arrangements are already made. The commissar can hardly leave Father alone!'

She was German, the Empress, and I saw signs of German truculence then in her face, but such was her daughter's persuasiveness that she gave way quite easily and took her seat as I guided her.

We were ready to go. Yet the cold was bitter, and Nicholas Romanov wore only that light coat. I sent for another.

He said, 'It's what I wear. I'm all right.'

I said it was out of the question. I had been sent to bring him alive from Tobolsk. He gave a quiet chuckle and said he was glad to hear it.

And so, at four o'clock, after a few last frustrating delays as a harness broke and sled runners collided and became locked, we were off on the hundred and thirty miles to Tyumen and the train. We went fast; there had never been time for delay and now, with Ruzsky's messenger ahead of us and bound for Ekaterinburg with his warning, there was less than ever.

The falling snow, this late in the year, was set, and the snow on the ground became slushy during the day; a thaw was upon us, and the journey became accordingly harder. I will not attempt to describe it, save to say that no time was wasted, that changes of horses were waiting for us as I had arranged, and that the entire affair took almost exactly twenty-four hours.

During that time I had little conversation with Nicholas. It may seem strange that two men thrust together at close quarters in enforced companionship should exchange no more than a few words occasionally, but so it was. The back of a running sleigh is no place for idle pleasantries. Inevitably, though, there were moments when we talked, as when Nicholas asked: 'What is the true purpose in moving me?'

It seemed a good moment to ask him about the Zaharoff document.

He smiled. 'My signature still seems in demand. It was wanted at Brest-Litovsk, you know, in March. Having given so much away to the Germans, they wanted my imprimatur upon it. Perhaps to blame me later. I refused, of course.' He glanced across at me. 'This document of yours needs more consideration. You will give me a few hours?'

I nodded. 'Of course.'

So at last we came to Tyumen. Weariness lay heavy upon every man and beast in the sled convoy, but there was no sickness and no injury.

I was naturally exceedingly anxious to know if the instructions I had left with the railway authorities had been carried out, and therefore drove direct to the station to find with satisfaction that they had been obeyed to the letter. The train I had demanded upon Sverdlov's orders had not only been marshalled, but waited in a siding with a full head of steam. Quickly I got the Romanovs aboard. Then I left

Koznov superintending the loading of their possessions into two baggage cars while I went to speak to the station controller to inform him that departure of the train must be delayed until I had received new instructions from Moscow. I went from there immediately to the telegraph office, taking with me one of Koznov's men who, luckily for me, could operate a telegraph. Luckily because I misliked the look of the operator: a shifty, small fellow with a cast in his eye and a furtive air. I sent him from the room and composed my message to Sverdlov.

It was lengthy, for there was much to say. I had to report not only our arrival, but that the Ekaterinburg Soviet would soon be aware of the removal of the ex-Tsar from Tobolsk and might well take action. I badly needed advice now. And support, too, if Sverdlov could provide any.

I spent most of the day and half the night awaiting his answer, and when it came it was in many ways most dispiriting. Sverdlov required me to bring my charges to Moscow right enough, as I had expected. It was clear, though, that Moscow's writ did not run in Ekaterinburg, for he instructed me to make a long and roundabout journey in order to avoid that city. To reach Moscow meant travelling west, but since the rail line west went through Ekaterinburg, I was therefore to begin by heading *east* out of Tyumen, in the direction of Omsk. From Omsk ran a great loop of the Trans-Siberian which passed far to the south of Ekaterinburg as it headed for Moscow and the West.

In the warmth of the telegraph room I sat and smoked and considered this. To Sverdlov, in his Moscow office, it would make good sense. Danger came from the men of Ekaterinburg; therefore avoid the city. But how was I to do so when the man Ruzsky, who could no doubt tell east from west, would be with us on the train?

Kill him? I thought of it and thought hard, and not a day now passes but I wish with all my heart it had been done; but it was impossible then, in that little telegraph office, to know anything of what was to come. My central thought then was the avoidance of bloodshed. If Ruzsky died, I thought, it would not end there: the man was of too much consequence.

I therefore conceived a stratagem. Ruzsky was a drinker, that much I knew. If I could get him befuddled . . .

I ordered the station's liquor store opened to obtain two bottles of vodka: one of lemon flavour, the other of plum. They vanished into the deep pockets of my Guardee great-coat. I walked then to the train in its siding and went at once to the wagon-lit I had reserved for myself, placed the bottles conspicuously upon the cover of the washbasin, and went to look for Ruzsky. He was not difficult to find: the man had installed himself in the attendant's alcove at the end of the special carriage in which the Imperial Family now rested. An empty bottle lay on the floor at his feet.

'Got your orders?' he said thickly.

'Moscow,' I said, and shrugged. Then I stretched. 'God, I'm tired!' I said, and looked at the bottle. 'Anything left in that?'

'No,' he said.

'I need a drink,' I told him. 'How about you? I have some back there.'

He looked at me in a puzzled way, as though to say: why are *you* offering drink to me? But he was half-fuddled already, and he followed me without arguing.

The plum was his; it makes me sick. The cleaner-tasting lemon seems not to affect me greatly. It never did, not even when, as a boy, I occasionally helped myself to my father's. Ruzsky sat on my bed with the bottle in one hand and the glass in another. We drank to Russia, to Marx, to the Revolution, all quick and in succession and he had such a head start on me that by then he wanted only to sleep. As consciousness slid away from him, I put my hands beneath his heels and lifted, lowering and turning him on to the bed. He was already beginning to snore as I left and made my way forward, turning on electric lights as I passed. At last I reached the engine and gave my instructions to the driver. He and I descended together to the track to lean upon the points lever.

A few minutes later, with lights shining the entire length of the train, we headed out of the railway station at Tyumen in the direction of Ekaterinburg.

Does that puzzle you – you who read this history – this departure for Ekaterinburg? Do you say to yourself: but he was intent upon *avoidance* of that place! For I was.

But what I did was to let a few miles pass and then bring the train to a halt. Then in the dark, well outside the town, I went again along the train, turning out every light. Now do you see? So it was a darkened train that began to reverse back towards Tyumen. We went at no great speed. I hoped by this means to present the train to any idle watchers at Tyumen station as a legitimate one. I held my breath as the train entered, then passed through the station. All was quiet as we slid gently on our way; and then Tyumen was falling back behind us and I remember letting a great sigh of relief come from my lips. What lay ahead was three hundred miles to Omsk and then the safe journey by the southern loop to Moscow; what lay behind was the dark menace of Ekaterinburg. So my thoughts ran.

Tired as I was, at that moment I enjoyed a sense of triumph, a feeling that my mission was now on its way to a successful conclusion. Like a fool, I allowed myself the luxury of counting chickens, heard in my mind the thanks and congratulations of my sovereign. But then I did not know, nor could I have known, that already the house of cards I had built was beginning to tumble.

So, still, and deceptively, all seemed to be well. As daylight came I washed myself, presented myself at the sitting-room car occupied by the Imperial Family, and was greeted almost warmly.

Nicholas, having bade me a cheerful good-morning, now asked, 'Are we bound for Omsk?'

I nodded. 'It is a long way round, to go this way to Moscow, but –'

'So Moscow *is* our destination?'

'Yes. I had orders in the night.'

'Good, good.' Like me he was full of optimism; like mine, his was baseless. We were in a land of fantasy, all of us.

I said softly, 'The document, sir. Have you had time to –'

He was looking at me now in a new way, as though trying to read my face. I waited, and at length he said, his manner altogether grave, 'I have signed it.'

'Good,' I said, smiling. 'May I –?'

He was watching my face still. 'But it is not here.'

I frowned. 'Not here, sir? Then where –?'

'Tobolsk,' Nicholas said. 'I signed it before we left.'

'But yesterday,' I reminded him, 'in the sleigh, you told me you still required more time.'

He nodded. 'I'm sorry. I judged the deception necessary.'

I felt anger rising in me and suppressed it. 'Why, sir? *Why* was it necessary? The document is an important factor in your release.'

He put his hand on my arm. 'Commissar, I had no wish to answer your courtesy with discourtesy. But I must keep my family together. The letter is with my son. When he is brought to join us, you will have it.'

I swore, but only to myself. His action was understandable enough and I had told him, with more or less certainty, both that the family would be reunited and that I would myself be returning to Tobolsk for Alexei and the Grand Duchesses. But it was, at the very least, a damned nuisance!

'There is another matter, sir, upon which I must speak to you,' I told him. I moved to the far end of the room and after a moment he joined me. From my pocket, I took another piece of paper and handed it to him. He gave me an enquiring glance as he unfolded it, follow-

106

ed a moment later by a look of sharp surprise and puzzlement.

'My cousin's signature, Commissar?'

I said in English, which Nicholas spoke perfectly, 'It is a
letter sent by your children's tutor, Gibbes, to a woman in
England.'

'So I see. But why did Cousin George sign it?'

'To demonstrate its *bona fides*, sir.'

'I do not understand.'

I said, 'Sir, I am not a Soviet commissar.'

'Then who? And *why*?' He was instantly perturbed.
'Where *are* we going?'

'My name is Dikeston, sir. I am an officer in the Royal
Navy, sent to Russia by your royal cousin upon a mission to
seek your removal and that of your family to England.'

'Thank God,' he said. 'I had been told I was not welcome
in Britain.'

'You must tell nobody,' I said. 'I have a part to play still.'

I left him then and returned to the wagon-lit, where I had
left Ruzsky. It was my intention to change my clothes. But I
was no sooner in through the door than he gave me the first
of several shocks.

He was sitting on the bed, unshaven, a cigarette between
his lips, his eyes were more than a little bloodshot, and he
wore his habitual smirk. The shock, however, lay not in his
appearance, with which I was all too familiar, but in his
utterance. He gave an unpleasant laugh and said, 'You're a
fraud, Yakovlev! And I know exactly what kind of fraud.'

I threw him a haughty look which merely made him
laugh more. 'You were told to look out for a man, were you
not?' he said.

'I was sent to bring the Romanovs,' I said. 'You know
that.'

He waved my answer away with an impatient gesture.
'Before you left London,' he said.

I gaped at him and he laughed again. 'Gave you a
surprise, did I?'

107

'Who are you?'

He gave me a mock salute. 'Henri Bronard. At your service – for the moment.'

'Henri? You're French?'

'*Oui, m'sieu.*'

'Then what are you doing out here in the middle of Siberia?'

'I serve various interests,' he said. 'For the moment I am to help you, when you need help. And you will.'

I blinked at him. 'I don't understand. You are a member of the Urals Soviet.'

He grinned, and it was more than the smirk I knew so well and detested; there was arrogance about him now, a clear pleasure in deceit. 'Not difficult,' he said. 'All you need is to be more rabid than the rest.'

'But you sent a man on my horse to Ekaterinburg!'

'Somebody else said they should know. *I* insisted on sending *your* horse. They liked that.'

I said angrily. 'You're a damned fool, Ruzsky or Bronard, or whatever your damned name is. You've alerted them unnecessarily.'

'What's it matter – you're bound for Omsk, are you not? Has Nicholas signed?'

Once again I gaped. Once again he gave that arrogant grin. 'The paper. Has he signed it?'

'Who is it?' I demanded. 'Who's your master?'

He laid his finger along his nose and said, 'Either nobody is my master – or it's Henri Bronard. Did Nicholas sign?'

I declined to discuss the matter further and turned to leave. Behind me his voice said, 'Make sure of that signature, whatever else you do!'

It was close to noon when the train slowed suddenly, shuddering as the brakes gripped. What could be amiss? I lowered a window to put my head out and saw there were men beside the track ahead, apparently talking to the driver. I jumped down and hurried forward until I reached them.

There were eight or ten of them, railway workers. I called, 'What's wrong?' to the driver.

'Warning not to proceed,' he answered. 'Ask *them*.' Which, of course, I immediately did.

A hastily-erected barrier of tree-trunks and stones blocked the track. I stood looking at it for a moment, wondering, but it was clearly enough to prevent the train's moving forward and the men were amused; so I turned to look at the fellow who was in obvious command of the group, and flourished my paper at him. 'Who are you?' I demanded.

His name I forget but it is of no consequence: though by God his actions were! The man was leader of the railway workers in Omsk, a poor, starved-looking intense fellow with gleaming, fervent eyes.

He read the *laissez-passer* document slowly and carefully, then looked up at me with a slight frown. 'I apologize, Comrade. You cannot take the train through.'

'Why not? As you see, my orders are from the Central Executive, from Comrade Sverdlov. Is this what happens when Moscow sends –'

He interrupted me. He was shaking a little. 'We have to respect *all* our comrades. You bring us orders. We are used to orders. But from the Urals Soviet we have a request. It is not from great men in Moscow, but from our brother workers. Please, they ask us, do not accept the passage of this train. That is their request. *Please* – do you notice the word? Yet your paper threatens death. Such was always Moscow's way. Comrade Commissar, we live in a new world now, where worker heeds the words of worker.'

I surveyed him coldly. 'So you halt the train – what now? We stand here in the snow?'

'No, Comrade. You return along the track to Tyumen and then to Ekaterinburg.'

'If I do that,' I protested, 'I shall be going directly against the orders of the Central Executive Committee. I shall be shot.'

He said he cared, but he didn't. There was no moving him or his men. But they were without authority – merely a group of railway workers. Ahead in the city must be the members of the local Soviet: more moderate men than those of Ekaterinburg if the ones at Tobolsk had been typical.

'You will have no objection if I go on alone into the city?'

'None at all.'

I uncoupled the locomotive and the Omsk men obligingly cleared their barrier to allow it through. On its footplate I reached the dreariness of Omsk, found three members of the local Soviet, including the secretary, and for two hours I argued and cajoled and waved my paper at them. They were adamant. There was no hostility, or not, at any rate, to me; but at the end I knew all about their feelings regarding the Imperial Family. The Omsk men did not care: whatever happened, Bloody Nicholas had brought upon himself. Their attitude was simply that, if Ekaterinburg's Soviet cared enough to make a formal request, the Omsk Soviet must comply with it; to do otherwise would be to strike at the very basis of solidarity.

'But they're extremists,' I said. 'They'll kill them.'

'They are workers like us,' I was told, 'and we are all free now to make decisions.'

They were immovable. Sympathetic to *my* dilemma, yes; pleasant and even polite to *me*, yes. But implacable. The train must go west to Ekaterinburg.

'I must telegraph Moscow.'

'By all means inform Comrade Sverdlov. Give him our greetings. Inform him that the Omsk Soviet grows daily in stability and authority.' This was the secretary speaking.

I did all that, adding these words: 'Therefore returning Ekaterinburg. Your urgent intervention required there. Yakovlev.'

After that there was nothing I could do save leave. I rode back at no great speed, endeavouring with some desperation to work out in my mind some means to avoid the

110

unwelcome requirements of the two Soviets – some way to keep my charges out of the hands of the Ekaterinburg men. Several crossed my thoughts. A return to Tobolsk, for example, and some attempt to travel north from thence up the Ob river to the Arctic.

But it was hopelessly impracticable. There was no boat at Tobolsk, I knew that from Kobylinsky, who must clearly have had the same thoughts. The boats would come with the spring thaw. Soon, but not yet.

What else? Go on foot? Take the Imperial Family and head south? Try walking to meet the White Russian army? It could be tried, but the snow was thick yet, and the distances great. To try was to ask for death in another form.

At last, as the barrier by the track came into my sight, a decision had to be made. I made it. The Moscow leaders, the great names, Lenin, Trotsky and Sverdlov – they wanted arms. Nicholas was part of the price of the arms. *They* must save Nicholas! After all, could it really be true that Lenin and Trotsky could not persuade a rabble of uneducated peasants and workers? No, they *would* do it. For the sake of their Revolution, they *must* do it!

The railway workers' leader strode towards me as the locomotive came to a stop. 'Well, Comrade Commissar?'

Sourly I said, 'Well, what?'

'Where do you go now, eh?'

'Ekaterinburg.'

He nodded with satisfaction. 'I thought you would. Now the Tsar does as *we* say, eh Comrade?' Then as I turned away from him he said, and it must surely have been out of habit, 'Go with God.'

I told him sharply that I had very little doubt some of us would go *to* God as a result of his actions.

So far in this telling, I have referred always to 'Nicholas' or 'the ex-Tsar'. I can do so no longer, for truly he was a king, that one. Faults he certainly had, many of them, and deep. I know what history says: that he was weak, dominated by his wife; that he never grew up; that he was too

111

blind to see where the autocratic road must lead. All true, no doubt. But I am a sailor and we judge a man also by his courage. There I cannot fault the Tsar.

He must have waited for me in the corridor of the train; I could see him standing there as I swung myself up to the carriage; there was a cigarette in his hand and a grave, sad look on his face. As I approached, he threw down the cigarette and ground it beneath his boot.

'They've turned us back?'

I had no need to answer, for he had read it in my face. He gave a little resigned smile. 'It's Ekaterinburg, isn't it?'

'Yes,' I said, and went on: 'I have informed Moscow and the Central Executive.'

'Thank you.' He gave that little inclination of the head. 'If you will excuse me, I must tell my family.'

'Of course, Sir.'

As the door closed behind him, I went angrily in search of Ruzsky to tell him what had happened. To my surprise the man was unconcerned. 'Don't worry about Ekaterinburg,' he said. And then he laid his finger against his nose in the manner of cunning men.

So we set off. There is a town on the track between Omsk and Tuymen, its name Kulomzino: a place of no great size or importance and it figures in this story only as a marker, for we passed its lights at night and the train was perhaps ten miles beyond it when suddenly the air was filled with the sound of gunfire! The driver slammed on the brakes, and the train ground abruptly to the sort of halt that flung people from their seats.

Coming to my feet, I hurled open a window to look out. Soldiers milled around us in great numbers, many of them with sabres drawn. We must have fallen across one of the dangerous small armies that were ravaging the country behind the Urals!

As I stood looking out at them, a mounted officer suddenly lunged at me with his sabre, pinning my coat to the woodwork.

112

'And who the devil are you?' I yelled at him.

He gave a bold grin, and well he could afford to. 'Not so noisy, my friend. We're White Cossacks – don't we look like it?'

'Who is in command?'

The grin widened. 'Fond of questions, aren't you?'

'Who commands?'

He laughed at me. 'What's it matter to a dead man, eh?'

'You must take me to him!'

Something in my voice or my face must have told him there was urgency, for his expression changed. 'Open the door and jump down!'

I did so, and felt his sabre at my back as I was propelled along the track.

'Halt and be still!'

I stood. Ten yards away, mounted upon a milk-white horse, a shako on his head, sat a lean figure with a flowing moustache. My captor called, 'Sir!' and the man's head turned towards me.

'Well?'

I said, 'May I speak to you in private?'

He flung back his head and laughed. 'With a thousand men around us?'

I put my hands in my pockets for paper and pencil, and wrote a message quickly. My captor handed it on. In a second the leader slid off the horse's back and strode over to me. 'Nicholas Alexandrevitch *here* – on board?' he asked incredulously.

I nodded. 'Also the Tsarina and the Grand Duchess Marie.'

'Great God!' He swore and slapped at his thigh. Truly, he was a weird and melodramatic figure there in the night with his hat and his horse and his recklessly extravagant gestures. 'I swore an oath of loyalty to Nicholas once. Never expected to be held to it now, though! Where? Take me to him!'

So I did, still not knowing his name. Nicholas knew him,

though, knew him at once. I knocked upon his door; he opened it a crack, saw our faces and flung it wide. 'General Dutov!'

Dutov fell upon one knee.' Your Majesty, how can this be? Where are you bound.'

'Ekaterinburg,' the Tsar said.

'No, you're *not*! Too damned dangerous,' Dutov roared. 'Come with me. I've men to keep you safe.' He had, too. And nothing in his way. I am certain now that had Nicholas gone with Dutov that night he could have ridden off to safety.

But he would not. 'Thank you, General, but no.'

'Great God, why not? You could go to your death in Ekaterinburg, Sir!'

Nicholas's quiet voice seemed all dignity beside Dutov's roaring. 'My children are in Tobolsk, General. I cannnot depart and leave them.'

'Sir, they won't harm children!' Dutov insisted. 'But you and the Tsarina are another matter. Come with *us*!'

But he would not. Instead he said to Dutov, 'Once my family is united I will be glad of any help you can offer. But as you see – at the moment, General, I am helpless.'

Shortly thereafter Dutov withdrew with his band of marauders. Without robbing us, either! It was a still night, and very dark, and now unutterably lonely in the great spaces of Siberia. I shuddered suddenly in the chill, signed to the driver to restart the train, and climbed aboard.

I was standing in the unlit corridor of the Tsar's carriage when the door opened and a head emerged, said 'Oh!' as though startled and then asked hesitantly, 'Commissar Yakovlev?' I needed no telling whose voice this was. Very quietly she said, 'May I talk to you?'

*   *   *

The second part of Dikeston's narrative ended there. Instructions as to the means of obtaining Part Three were appended in an envelope, paperclipped to the last page. In

114

his panelled office at 6, Athelsgate in the City of London, as Sir Horace Malory picked up a silver paper-knife and slit the envelope, he found his hands were trembling . . .

CHAPTER FIVE

———————◆———————

Deeds and Mr Grace

Everybody who has ever purchased a house is familiar with the airy ways and dilatory habits of lawyers. Most people are aware that it is the profitable practice of those who specialize in the conveyance of property to discover great thickets of difficulty where few truly exist. Even a solicitor who is not trying to cause delay will often do so, out of habit or lethargy, for months at a time. The lawyer with his heart actually set upon spinning out time will make a limpet look as lively as a thoroughbred stallion.

Dikeston's brief instructions began the trouble, and it was perfectly clear to Malory that that was how they had been designed.

'The deeds of Carfax House,' ran Dikeston's relevant sentences, 'are to be presented for inspection to the manager of the Liverpool branch of the Irish Linen Bank together with the sum of fifty thousand pounds. Both are to be passed on to the holder of a special account numbered X253.'

'And in return, what we get is packet three?' Pilgrim asked.

'Yes.'

'Horace, *where* does it say so?'

Malory's lips tightened. 'It says so on the envelope, Laurence. In typescript. It actually reads, if you're interested, "Instructions for obtaining part three of the narrative of –"'

'Yeah, okay. Now, how about these deeds? Tell me the English legal set-up.'

116

'Have you read Dikeston's narrative?'

'Well, I kind of skimmed it. The guy's in a fix, sure. Look, Horace, we all know it's a sad story. When they get to Ekaterinburg, the Romanovs get slaughtered, that's how it ends. You can read it for nothing in the library. You can even see a movie. Tell me about the deeds, huh?'

'I told you about Yakovlev – that he went off with a trainload of treasure and then vanished?'

'Sure you told me.'

'Very well. Now I'll tell you about Dutov. He was a warlord, a law absolutely unto himself on the far side of the Urals.'

Pilgrim held up a hand. 'I've got the picture, Horace. I understand, believe me. There's chaos, and all these people are milling about in the middle. There's a fortune in various kinds of treasure. There's Zaharoff's document. Now we have warlords. Okay, it's exciting. But tell me about the deeds. You get them when you buy a house, right?'

'Well, yes. After the purchase is complete.'

'I thought so. *After!* We have to buy this damned house.'

'Yes.'

'Okay, Horace,' Pilgrim sighed noisily. 'Go right ahead. You don't need my say-so.'

'I'm simply informing you. The house can probably be sold later. That isn't important.'

'How much so far, including the house?'

'Two hundred thousand, I suppose. But as I say, the house can be sold.'

'Better check first,' Pilgrim said, 'that it can be bought.'

'Oh, it can.'

'Sure, at a price.'

Business talk over luncheon was preferable, it seemed to Malory that day, to further discussion with Pilgrim of South London property values. Accordingly he ate his salmon and drank his Mosel with one ear swivelling like a horse's in the direction of whichever of the partners had matters to

117

raise. In the partners' dining-room at Hillyard, Cleef it had long been the custom to discuss openly any matters which might benefit from a general airing. One partner, recently married to an actress half his age, had received what he described as 'an interesting opportunity' to invest in a film. Smirks were exchanged across the table and thumbs turned down. General approval greeted an application from one of the great civil engineering concerns for a six million advance towards its costs in a Saudi building project. And Fergus Huntly's revised bid price for the seed and fertilizer company got a thumbs up. Privately, Malory thought it to be pitched unnecessarily high but was not disposed to say so. His thoughts were anywhere but in the City of London. One moment they would be sweeping like a satellite across the Urals; the next pointing like a finger at a neat, if not authentic, Georgian house some six miles from where he sat.

Mr and Mrs Denis Abrahams, their house in Blackheath by now newly-decorated and repaired, were *not* anxious to sell.

'It's such a sweet house,' Mrs Abrahams told Jacques Graves, gushing extravagantly. 'We're frightfully attached to it. And it's so convenient. All our friends are near by.'

Her husband took a slightly different line. He was prepared to consider a good offer.

But not an independent valuation. 'I am, after all,' he said, 'a creature of the market place. Supply and demand, and all that.'

Graves knew all right: Hillyard, Cleef was bent backward over the barrel, and standing upright again would come expensive.

'The actual worth?' Sir Horace Malory asked him.

'Value to us,' said Graves flatly.

'There must *be* a figure.'

'I got two local estate agents to give me an idea. One said a hundred and five thousand, the other a bit higher.'

'Offer the higher figure.'

'Okay.'

Mr and Mrs Abrahams accepted. The higher figure was one hundred and fifteen thousand pounds. Graves, sitting in their gleaming drawing-room, rising to shake hands on the deal suddenly thought Abrahams's eyes looked shifty.

And so it proved. Abrahams's solicitor was a Mr Thomas Plantagenet Grace, a partner in Holdfast & Grace, of London Wall. He was also Mrs Abrahams's brother-in-law.

'The point is,' Abrahams told Grace, 'that they must want it badly, but I don't know how badly.'

Grace nodded wisely. 'We'll find out – if somebody else comes in with an offer,' he murmured.

Solicitors acting for Hillyard, Cleef, and this was a firm accustomed to enormous fees in recognition of its willing-ness to match its pace to the urgent needs of a banking house, then approached Mr Plantagenet Grace. Their letter was opened and acknowledged by Mr Grace's secretary, and then placed in a folder marked 'Abrahams conveyance' to await his return. Mr Plantagenet Grace was away for a while; it was his custom, at that time of year, to recharge his batteries with a trip to Barbados.

Hillyard, Cleef's solicitors informed Jacques Graves, who consulted Abrahams. Abrahams was surprised and regretful, but having instructed Mr Grace felt unable to do more than wait.

To nobody's surprise, not Graves's and certainly not Sir Horace Malory's, the Barbados hiatus produced a further offer. Mr Thomas Plantagenet Grace discovered it on his desk upon his return. It upped the ante to £130,000.

'This,' said Malory grimly, 'can go on for years. Damn fella will be in Timbuctoo next, and the new offer'll be a million. Offer one hundred and thirty-two conditional upon immediate acceptance.'

But the hostage had by then been given, and it had been examined with pleasure. It was now very clear that Hill-

119

yard, Cleef not only sought to possess Cavendish House, but did so with great ardour. 'And Hillyard, Cleef,' as Thomas Plantagenet Grace observed, 'are rich, rich, rich!'

The riches, however, had not been accumulated by succumbing very often to essentially simple lures. Malory and Graves could play this game, too, and frequently did. The Hillyard, Cleef offer was suddenly lowered. Neither Graves nor Malory was subsequently available when Mr Grace telephoned to enquire if he understood the reduced offer aright. A further and genuine bid then materialized from another source altogether; this for one hundred and fifteen thousand pounds. It was made by an elderly lady who marched up to the white-painted door one evening, said she was from Australia, and would buy the house there and then. 'Here,' she said, 'is my cheque. And *here*, because there are crooks in this world Mr Abrahams – and I'm not saying you're one of them because I don't know whether you are or not – is a document for *you* to sign. In the event you call off the deal, you pay me ten thousand. Fair?'

It was fair, Abrahams thought. But Mr Thomas Plantagenet Grace was privately doubtful. He suspected that the elderly lady was a plant, an agent of Hillyard, Cleef. What is more, he was right. She was herself a director of a Hillyard, Cleef subsidiary in Australia. Mr Grace could prove nothing. What he *could* do was delay matters.

He did.

At Hillyard, Cleef the effects of the delay varied according to the individual. Laurence Pilgrim, with a somewhat irritable Malory haunting the building seven hours a day, began to hope that part three of Dikeston's memoirs would surface soon, if only to get Malory off his back.

Malory passed his day harrying lawyers, Graves, and anybody else within reach. He was, by now, thanks to the historian from Oxford, as well-informed as it is possible to be about the question of what happened to the Romanovs after Yakovlev was compelled to turn back outside Omsk. Evenings at Wilton Place tended to be spent in his study with a volume of Romanov reminiscences, rather than at the bridge table. He read the memoirs of Romanov uncles, cousins, aunts, teachers and friends. In some areas all said much the same thing. In others they differed.

Not one mentioned a meeting with Dutov – nor was there mention anywhere of the possibility that Commissar Vassily Yakovlev was a British agent.

There were other mysteries, too.

When at last Cavendish House changed hands – and it took a full month despite all the pressure exerted by the no-nonsense lady from Australia – Graves heard the news without pleasure. A most useful part of Graves's make-up was a pronounced node of suspicion which probably came from his French ancestry, and which told him that there was a great deal more to Dikeston's story than might be gathered from a first and superficial view. Dikeston, he thought, was obsessive; Dikeston had taken trouble with his arrangements, and had carried his grievances a long time. Dikeston had also liked setting traps and Graves, thinking about all the years Dikeston had had to set them and all the money available for them, viewed his own future involvement with no enthusiasm at all. He had originally accompanied Laurence Pilgrim to London because working for Pilgrim in international financing projects would provide the challenges to which he best responded: locking horns with clever and energetic men on a familiar battlefield and according to rules universally comprehended. But Dikeston's legacy – and Graves by now felt this strongly – was something very different. Had he been able to avoid further involvement, he would have done so, but Pilgrim had made clear his own aversion to what he described to Graves privately as 'Malory's senescent flourish', and had indicated that Graves must bear the load.

The load had been borne quite lightly for several days,

since Hillyard, Cleef's solicitors were taking the weight. Jacques Graves, temporarily freed as a result, had been in Vancouver, British Columbia, tying up a profitable deal involving the building of two ocean-going tugs. He was sitting in the dining-room of the Bayshore Inn, picking with pleasure at a handsomely arranged plate of Crab Louie, when he was paged. There was a telex from Malory. It read: 'Return at once.'

'The deeds.' Malory's smooth hand, brown-spotted with age, manicured throughout a lifetime, patted twice at the manilla envelope which lay upon his desk. He took the gold hunter from his waistcoat pocket and consulted it. 'I don't think,' he added, 'that you should waste too much time.'

Graves, baggy-eyed and dopey with jet-lag after the seven thousand-mile overnight trip, reached for the envelope. 'Where was the address again?'

Malory looked at him reprovingly. 'A good memory,' he said, 'is extremely important in our profession, Mr Graves. Perhaps you'd better write it down.'

As the train travelled north to Liverpool, Graves's tired mind wrestled with images of Dikeston. Graves had never before in his life been subject to the feeling that he was being oppressed, but he felt it now. By some means or other, he thought savagely, anything that had its roots in Dikeston turned out to be uncomfortable, difficult or humiliating. It was evening when the train arrived in Lime Street.

He awoke refreshed in one of the big high beds of the old but comfortable Adelphi Hotel in Liverpool; he breakfasted well and afterwards took a taxi to the premises of the Irish Linen Bank. The morning was bright; Graves felt cheerful; the dark, Dikeston-based delusions had been sloughed off by sleep and he was on his way to a bank to collect papers. What could be simpler?

Yet it happened.

'I have an appointment,' Graves said, presenting his card, 'with Mr O'Hara.'

'One moment, sir.'

The girl who came over to him was O'Hara's secretary. Mr O'Hara would not be in until after luncheon. Yes, she knew Mr Graves had an appointment; yes, she realized he had come from London; indeed an attempt had been made to call his office and warn him. No, it was impossible to get a message to Mr O'Hara. But he *would* be in after lunch.

O'Hara arrived, finally, at a quarter to three and Graves, who had been cooling his heels with growing impatience for four and three-quarter hours was shown in. O'Hara, a big open-faced Irishman, was very apologetic and extremely sorry to hear that the warning message had not reached Graves at Hillyward, Cleef.

'But what is it I can do for you, Mr Graves?'

Graves removed two envelopes from his slender document case. Handing the first, and fatter, envelope to O'Hara, he said, 'We are fulfilling the terms of some old and somewhat, er, *odd* instructions. These are the deeds of a house, which you are to inspect and be sure they are what we say they are. And this –' he offered the second envelope – 'is our cheque for the sum of fifty thousand. Both are to be passed to the holder of an account here.'

'Lucky fella,' said O'Hara. 'Whose account is that?'

'I don't know.'

O'Hara smiled. 'As you say, odd. But if you can't tell me the name –?'

'There's a number. It's a special –'

He was interrupted by the ringing of the telephone on O'Hara's desk.

'Excuse me.' O'Hara picked it up. 'Yes,' he said. Then, 'No.' Then 'Two and one, my dear, a diplomatic defeat.' Then, 'Well, nobody can go round Birkdale without –' He stopped, the open face suddenly flushing. 'I'll call you later, dear.'

123

'Golf?' Graves said, anger almost erupting. 'You were playing *golf*?'

O'Hara's explanation was as full as his apologies were fulsome. 'Called out at the last minute, terribly sorry, but the General Manager . . . and one of our most important customers . . . promotion in the wind, you know . . . no way of refusing . . . Now, you were saying?'

'I was saying there is a special account at this bank. It's number is X253.'

'An X account is it? Well, well. First time I've encountered any business with one of those. So these –' he held up the two envelopes – 'go to the account holder.'

'The cheque does. The deeds are to be inspected by you. And in return there should be some papers.'

'I see.' O'Hara rose. 'You'll excuse me a moment?'

He came back two or three minutes later, a deed box in his hands. 'The old and held file, that's what we call this, Mr Graves. Real mystery stuff. Now –' He found a key on a big ring and turned it in the lock.

There was a fat foolscap-sized envelope in the box. It was sealed with wax, which O'Hara broke. He took out a sheet of paper and read it, then looked across the desk. 'Very well, Mr Graves.' From inside the envelope he took another, its shape familiar by now to Graves. 'I am to give you this. Perhaps you'll sign for it?'

Graves took out his pen. 'Yes. Oh, by the way.'

'Hmmm?' O'Hara glanced across.

'Whose account is it?'

A slow smile spread across the Irishman's features. 'Oh, now, Mr Graves! You know I can't tell you.'

'Then I'll just have to find out,' said Graves.

'Do. If you can.' O'Hara laughed. 'We're as tight as the Swiss here, and twice as difficult!'

'You wouldn't care to make it easier?'

'No.'

Graves put the new packet of papers into his document case, and left the manager's office. Outside, in the main business area, he picked up a copy of the *Financial Times* and took a seat, from which he had a good view of the whole floor. Carefully, he surveyed the staff of the Irish Linen Bank. Quite a number, he knew from experience, would regard an offered chance of a move to Hillyard, Cleef as one of life's great wonders. Few, however would have access to information about secret accounts.

But somebody must – in case, for instance, O'Hara dropped dead on the golf-course. As Graves profoundly wished he would. The question was, who? The assistant manager, the accountant?

O'Hara, meanwhile, was at his desk. The deed box still stood open before him. The foolscap envelope which had held the packet had also held something else: another envelope. His sheet of instructions told him to post it. He looked at the address before placing it in his out-tray.

It was addressed to Coutts & Co., The Strand, London.

All very mysterious, O'Hara thought.

But he was more concerned with another mystery: O'Hara was in line for promotion, that much he knew. The question was: would it be to London or Dublin? It occupied his mind.

Later his eye fell upon the envelope again as it lay waiting for his secretary to take away. Coutts, it occurred to him, were the royal bankers, and O'Hara enjoyed little flights of fantasy.

Could this be a royal mystery?

CHAPTER SIX

─────────◆─────────

Third instalment of the account, written by
Lt Cdr H. G. Dikeston, RN, of his journeyings
in Russia in the spring of 1918

I have observed before in these papers that to set eyes upon
the Grand Duchess Maria Nikolaevna was to be aware on
the instant that here was a human being of the finest.
Something curious was there in the face and one can always
tell; one can look at a man of position and know him at once
for a rascal, at a tramp and know him for a decent fellow.
Some people are incapable of giving importance to words
over which they labour long; there are others whose light-
est remark is worth attention. All this is difficult to convey,
and indeed there is no real need to attempt to do so, for all
of us know the truth of it.

Thus when, in the corridor of the train, moving through
the night between Kulomzino and Tyumen, the door of the
royal compartment opened and the Grand Duchess spoke,
her words, though simple, conveyed much.

'May I talk to you?' was all she said. Yet I at once
understood much more from certain subtleties of emphasis. I understood that she felt disloyal in leaving her
parents even briefly; that such a brief escape was none the
less necessary to her; that she sensed a future in which free
talk would be rare for her. Many things.

'Of course, Your Royal –'

'Oh no!' she protested. 'I'm not a royal anything.' Then
she laughed quietly. 'Except perhaps a royal relic. My
name is Marie.'

I found myself smiling. 'Very well, ma'am.'

'Marie. Say it.'

I said it.

'Good. And you are Henry, I know that. Oh, so English a name! I've been there, you know. To England, I mean.'

'I know.'

'Father says you are a sailor. I met a young English sailor once – Prince Louis of Battenberg. You know him?'

'No. But I know of him.'

'I liked him. I think I like the English. Do you like Russians?'

'Some more than others.'

'Oh *yes*.' She laughed. 'Some *much* more! You know, Henry – this is very wrong.'

'What is?' Though I knew.

She giggled. 'Why – standing in the dark talking to a sailor. Oh, shameful! And unique, I think.'

'Unique. A girl talking to a sailor? Hardly that.'

'Not an opportunity much granted to me,' she said. Then: 'Have you seen the world?'

'Some of it.'

'Tell me. I have seen so little. Have you been to China?'

'Yes.'

'Tell me about China.'

I can remember every second of it, that hour we passed in the Siberian night. In her lay a magical gaiety and attention and time went like the wind. How she could be so disposed, at a moment when only the most dangerous uncertainty lay ahead, is hard to understand, except that it was her nature. She wanted to know: I had seen and could tell. She was full of questions and swift insights following upon my answers. Nor would she allow talk of the present or the future: it was the wider world she wanted to know about; the world and the bright and exciting things in it. And so for a time we chattered and laughed, until she said suddenly. 'I must go,' and spoke my name. 'Good night, Henry.'

'Good night – Marie.'

She paused. There was scarcely any light, but I could dimly see the pale outline of her face.

She said softly, 'Thank you.' And kissed me on the cheek. And was gone.

I stood for a while beside the closed door. Much of the magic of the night had departed with her, and realization that there was a dangerous time ahead came flooding back to me. I went at last to find Ruzsky: if nothing else, he could tell me about the city of Ekaterinburg and so keep from my mind the suddenly-gathering and fearful images which now crowded in. But he was asleep and snoring.

I lay on my bunk and tried also to sleep, but could not. Then, for I must have been more weary than I knew, I did indeed doze for a little while, only to be awakened when the train halted.

Yet I had given orders that it proceed without stopping to Ekaterinburg, and this was only Tyumen! And while I was still rubbing sleep from my eyes, the train was boarded by a dozen or so men and I recognized some of them as part of the Ekaterinburg detachment which had been at Tobolsk.

They recognized me too, and just as quickly. Before I could move from where I stood, there was a pistol in my ribs and a voice snarling at me: 'Commissar Yakovlev, you are under arrest!'

'By whose orders?'

'On the authority of the Urals Soviet.'

I began my ritual protest. I was an emissary of the Central Executive Committee. Death awaited anyone who impeded –

'Keep it for your trial!' I was told.

I was shoved roughly back and the door of the wagon-lit was slammed.

Thus imprisoned, I came to Ekaterinburg. They opened my door as the train halted jerkily, and I was pulled into the corridor. Through the carriage window I could see that there was a jostling crowd around the train; a noisy one too. There were yells of 'Bring him out!' 'Hang the German bitch!' 'Show us Bloody Nicholas!' Truly it was a most frightening sight.

A moment later I was pushed to one side by the bearded lout who was guarding me, and as I turned my head I saw the Imperial Family coming towards me along the corridor, Nicholas first and carrying his own luggage, his face set.

I thought, Damn this rabble! and stood to attention and saluted.

Nicholas stopped and looked at me.

I said. 'I have informed Moscow. They're bound to intervene, sir.'

His face darkened, and he gave me a look filled with hatred. 'We are under arrest, you treacherous pig!' he said, and stepped past me, adding over his shoulder, 'You've killed us all!'

In the end, they changed its name. Ekaterinburg was founded by Peter the Great and named for his wife. Now – and what irony there is in this! – now the city is Sverdlovsk, named for Yankel Sverdlov.

Oh yes – the same. The Sverdlov who had sent me to Tobolsk, the Sverdlov who had christened me Yakovlev, the Sverdlov whose signature lay upon the paper which demanded all men assist me.

They spat upon his signature that day – and laughed openly at mention of his name! When I brandished Lenin at them, and Trotsky, they were no more impressed. Times have changed indeed. . . .

But *then* – well, I was flung in to prison, and a real prison, too, with stone walls and clanging iron door. When the iron door opened again it was to admit two men. I had seen neither before.

I was sitting on the grubby cell floor, for there was no chair and no bed. Scrambling at once to my feet I faced them angrily. 'How dare you imprison me!'

One of them – he looked like a superior clerk: fat, with a dark moustache and a creased suit – stood forward. 'Dare?'

129

he said. 'The Urals Soviet does not *dare*. It *acts* – in full Soviet legality.'

'Doesn't Sverdlov?' I demanded. 'Doesn't Lenin? Are their actions *illegal*? Tell me, whoever you are. And I'll pass the message on!'

He surveyed me angrily. 'I am Alexander Beloborodov, chairman of the Urals Soviet, lawful government of the Urals region. Comrade Goloshchokin here is also a member.'

'I travel on direct orders from the Head of State!' I insisted, and showed my paper.

'To set Bloody Nicholas free!' said Goloshchokin. He was another type, this man: thin and intent. 'You know as well as I do what they're doing. It's a dirty deal with the Germans, made because the damned Tsarina's a German.' He turned on me angrily. 'Isn't it?'

I gave anger for anger. 'How do I know what's in their minds in Moscow? I do as I'm told. Maybe they *have* got one eye on the German army. To them it's too damned dangerous and too damned near. I am under orders to deliver the whole Romanov family to Moscow. When they get there, I don't know if they'll go on trial, if they'll go to the Germans – or if they'll be sent to Timbuctoo, for that matter.'

'Ah, but what do you *want*?' asked Beloborodov softly.

'Want?'

'What should be done?'

I thought for a moment, and thought damned carefully. These two would string me up, as soon as not, I sensed *that* with no difficulty. Their anxiety to demonstrate independence from Moscow was manifest.

'Me?' I said. 'I'd put them on trial before the world. There's evidence enough. But it's not my task to decide.'

'It's mine,' Beloborodov said. His round face glistened, though there was little warmth in the cell.

I shook my head. 'Why? Why you? Upon what basis?

130

Are you Commissar for Foreign Affairs or is Comrade Trotsky? You merely want to kill for vengeance –'

'Yes.' They said it in chorus. 'That damned German woman,' Goloshchokin went on angrily. 'How many deaths can be laid at her door?'

'And you want more?' I demanded. 'She's a German princess! If they want her back as the price of peace, what then? If she can be used to save the lives of *our* soldiers, why not? Because *you* want revenge, eh? And *you* are safe – a thousand miles from the German army.'

He scowled at me, and I turned to Beloborodov. 'You think I'm a traitor, do you?'

'Perhaps.' He said it quietly, threateningly.

'And Sverdlov – he's a traitor too? And Lenin? If they are not, I am not. Look at that signature!'

'How do I know it isn't forged?' Beloborodov said.

'You will know if you telegraph Moscow. There must be a telegraph available here.'

'He's bluffing,' Goloshchokin said.

'Am I? It's easy to find out. Send a telegram to Moscow!'

Whether or not they did, I have no way of knowing. What I do know is that they left me in that malodorous cell and as the iron door clanged behind them, I felt near to despair. All had gone dreadfully wrong. I was in prison, as the Tsar and Tsarina and Marie must now be. And it was I who had allowed them to fall into the hands of men who desired their deaths. No wonder the Tsar thought I had betrayed them.

I spent time staring unseeing at the stone floor before the thoughts came. What of Ruzsky? The prospect of Ekaterinburg had worried *him* not at all – as it would not, since like Goloshchokin and Beloborodov he was actually a member of the Soviet.

Whatever else he was! The man was a riddle: on the one hand a fanatic, on the other some kind of agent. And French, to boot! What was it he had said? After some thought I could even remember his words: 'I serve various interests,' he had said. 'For the moment, I am to help you when you need help.' And also: 'You were told to look out for a man before you left London.'

What could I make of it? It was all true enough. I *had* been told to lookout for a man upon reaching Tobolsk. I had also been told the man would be able to help me. It was in the sheet of instructions given to me by Mr Basil Zaharoff.

And Zaharoff was known, to the Press at any rate, as The Man Who Peddled Death!

'I serve various interests!' So Ruzsky, or Bronard, or whoever he was, was Zaharoff's man, of that much I was now fairly certain. But what was he doing here? How did it come about that Zaharoff, the arch-capitalist, had his own man as a member of a Soviet in the middle of Siberia? I know now that *nothing* was beyond that man. There will be Zaharoff agents among the ranks of angels; yes, and the devils, too. It seems extraordinary enough now, years later, when I know more of him. Then it seemed to be beyond believing.

But of course I got no further with my thoughts, not then. Hours went by before once more that iron cell door was thrown open. Goloshchokin appeared, looking at me grimly. I thought him to be alone, but in a moment it was Ruzsky who slouched into view, that smirk of his much evident.

I came to my feet. 'What did Moscow say?'

Neither answered. 'Personally I'd hang you, Yakovlev,' Ruzsky suddenly said to me. He turned to his companion. 'You should have seen him bow and scrape to the Romanovs.'

'I wish we *could* hang him.' Goloshchokin gave a sigh. 'But the chairman believes him.'

Ruzsky laughed. 'Maybe the chairman has Moscow ambitions. No, Comrade, I don't really mean that. I admire Beloborodov.' He turned to me. 'You should be grateful to him, too.'

132

'Why?'

'Why? Because you're free. Who says there's no Soviet mercy, eh? A Tsarist provocateur, and what do we do? We let you go! We won't let *them* go, though, will we, Comrade Goloshchokin?'

Goloshchokin looked at me sidelong. 'Not even to Moscow. And be careful, Yakovlev, or you'll be back in here.'

He stalked out, Ruzsky slouching after him. I followed, and found myself standing close to Ruzsky, apparently by accident, by the road outside the prison gate. He didn't turn towards me, or even acknowledge he knew I was there. He spoke, though, quietly and clearly. 'Behind the Palais Royal Hotel at nine o'clock,' he said, and slouched away.

It was two hours to nine.

I wandered in the dark, found food and drink in a tavern, and listened to the talk there, anxious for news of the Imperial Family. Nor were tidings long in coming, for talk in the tavern was of nothing else. Every snatch of it seemed to tell more.

'. . . I saw them at the station. Just shoved off the train, they were, like sacks of grain. I thought for a bit the crowd would grab them, but . . .'

'. . . My God, they looked frightened!'

'. . . Wouldn't you? Did you see who drove the car, though? Parfeny, yes. Oh, you know him, yes, 'course you do. Head of the Railwaymen's Punitive Detachment. Real swine, wouldn't want him driving *me*.'

'. . . They say Professor Ipatiev was given only six hours' notice to get out. Six hours, that's all.'

'. . . House is too good for them. It's like a bloody palace! Big white place up on Vosnesensky Avenue – the one with the archway. *And* Nicholas still has servants with him!'

I sat very quietly in a dark corner, absorbing it all, astonished at how easy it was to learn. I heard that the

133

Family was now guarded by detachments of men from two local factories.

I rose when they began to go over it all again; from the excitement in their voices they'd spend the night repeating it all endlessly. In the street outside I stood for a moment, wondering at the whereabouts of the places they had spoken of: Ipatiev's house and Vosnesensky Avenue. But they were not difficult to find. The city of Ekaterinburg buzzed with the knowledge of the Romanov's presence, and I quickly realized many in the streets were sightseers bound for the house. I simply followed.

No one was allowed nearer to the house than the other side of the Avenue: There was a high palisade built of logs before the entrance, close against the building so that nothing could be seen, and a few armed militiamen stood in the roadway moving along the many passers-by.

I looked as long as I could. It had been a house of some style, but was a prison now and unmistakably so. Guards in the streets, guards at the gates, guards no doubt in the house itself. Around me, in the talk of the townspeople, there was nothing but hostility. Why keep the Romanovs alive? Why not shoot them now? It was all talk of that kind. I thought of the quiet courage of the Tsar, of his refusal to go with Dutov when he could so easily have done so. I thought of the marvel of that hour I had spent with the Grand Duchess Maria. No, not Maria. *Marie*.

Then I thought of the paper – Zaharoff's paper – the paper that was supposed to be vital to so many: with a value of millions in money *plus* the weapons for an army; and on top of that, God alone knew how many human lives!

The Tsar *had* signed it, he'd told me so! And everyone was waiting for it; everyone from Ruzsky to Lenin and Trotsky; everyone from my own humble self to Zaharoff and my Sovereign, King George.

Many men's worlds hung upon that piece of paper!

As I trudged along towards my meeting with Ruzsky, my thoughts whirled. Oh yes, everyone wanted it; but only *I* knew where it was, the Tsar and his son excepted. Well, I would keep it so, keep it above all from Ruzsky until I understood his purpose more clearly. For my tumbling thoughts were now presenting me with strange notions and stranger conclusions.

Lenin and Sverdlov had sent me to Siberia to bring the Tsar out. And I had done so, or nearly. If I hadn't been stopped at Omsk, had not been sent back to Ekaterinburg . . *then* both I and the entire Imperial Family would by now be halfway to Moscow.

The questions drummed in my mind: Had I *really* been stopped by the rivalry between provincials and metropolitans? Could it *really* be true that the men of Omsk and Ekaterinburg took no notice of Lenin and Sverdlov?

Or was it something else? Did those devious and clever men in Moscow actually *want* the Romanovs to be held in peril in Ekaterinburg rather than safe in Tobolsk or Moscow? And then I saw it, or thought I did. The Germans were the key; camped as they were, menacingly and in army strength on Moscow's doorstep. Suppose there were negotiations; suppose the Germans were demanding that the Imperial Family be surrendered to them; suppose Lenin and Sverdlov had no alternative but to agree? Yes, suppose all that – what *then* if Moscow did not *want* to hand over the Romanovs? Oh yes, now it was simple enough. Send me to bring them (*and* kill two birds with one stone!) and then *arrange* for the Romanovs to be detained by wild men in far Siberia, and say to the Germans, Oh, we're *trying* to persuade the local Soviet, but they won't even listen.

Was it all conceivable?

Certainly it was. That explanation fitted all the complexities, answered all the questions. Yet I could barely believe a word of it. Too outlandish, I thought. But as I approached the Palais Royal Hotel I was resolved to play matters close in future. And to learn more of Ruzsky.

He was waiting in the shadowed street behind, and was

135

not a sight to give any man hope: drink in him, and bearing and manner scruffy. Yet when he spoke, it seemed his mind was more or less clear – and entirely concerned with the paper.

'Have you got it?' he demanded.

I shook my head. 'It had to be left with the Tsar. Then – when the train was halted – there was no chance to ask him.

'Precious little chance now. But we've got to get it.'

'We?' I said harshly. 'You're the one who must recover it.'

'You imagine he'd give it to me? He knows me, remember. No, you're the only one he'd trust.'

I did not tell Ruzsky the Tsar's view of me now. Instead: 'I could give you a note to him,' I said.

'A note of hand?' Ruzsky laughed sharply. 'If the guards search me and find it, what then? I'll tell you – I'm the bearer of clandestine messages between you, who tried to take the Tsar to safety, and Nicholas himself. And *my* life then would be worth nothing!'

We regarded each other warily. At last I said, 'What will happen to them?'

Ruzsky shrugged. 'Do you care?'

'Yes. I care.'

'My guess is that there is a majority of the Soviet in favour of killing them.'

'Cold-blooded execution?'

'It is a difficult question. There is a lot of discussion. Good Bolsheviks should not molest women and children, some say. But others say this is the German woman, and that's different.'

He knew more of the circumstances of imprisonment than I. 'Is there,' I asked him, 'any chance of freeing them?'

He gave me an amused glance. 'White horses to the rescue, you mean? No, my friend. They're as good as dead, that's my view, unless they have value in bargaining. And yes, that they have, but only with the Germans.'

'So?'

'So they will be there for a long time, unless a rescue *is* attempted. In that case the guards will pull triggers at once. There are White Russian armies loose in Siberia and you may be sure of one thing, my friend: neither Nicholas nor his son will be allowed to fall into White hands. There are still some who would restore the Throne.'

'You have suggestions, then?'

'Yes, wait.'

'And do nothing?'

He gave me a look. 'Be patient. What is there to do? If he'd signed that paper you could have been off to England now, but you didn't force it!'

'I couldn't force it. But it seems to me I might just as well set off for England, anyway. I have no position here. You have, though. Whatever's to be done, you'll have to do it!'

'I told you, be patient! Remember the purpose. It is *not* to save the Tsar's neck, it is to get his signature on the paper. Don't forget that. The paper, signed, and off to Moscow and London.'

'I wish I knew what was in it!'

'You know enough,' Ruzsky said roughly. 'Remember this: the only thing that will save the Romanovs' necks is that paper, signed and on Lenin's desk.'

'If Lenin wants it he can –!'

He shook his head. 'That's not the way of things. Think, man, can you see Lenin coming here, in person, to bicker with men like Beloborodov and Goloshchokin and even be refused? By yokels like that? And then have word spread through the country that Lenin himself betrays the Revolution by talking to the Tsar. No, not in a thousand years. So it comes back to you, whom the Tsar may trust. He'll certainly trust no one else! If you leave now, his death-warrant is signed.'

'I'm helpless,' I said.

Ruzsky made that odious gesture: finger laid along his nose. 'Nobody is ever helpless,' he said. 'Time creates opportunities.'

We parted then, I to return to the train for I had nowhere else to go and it ought to be standing at Ekaterinburg station, still. The arrangement for the future was that we should meet nightly, at the same time, in the same shadowed place behind the Palais Royal Hotel.

But when I reached the train there was a guard on it and I was given instructions to report at once to the office of the station-master. When I got there it was quickly apparent that this was no professional station-master, but a nonentity in unfamiliar shoes too large for him. He had orders for me, though: orders I did not like, that came from the Urals Soviet under Beloborodov's name. I was to take the train forthwith out of Ekaterinburg and return it to Tyumen where the engine and rolling stock rightly belonged. In no circumstances was I to remain in the city. If I did, I would be subject to arrest and trial on suspicion of pro-Tsarist activities.

I found my engine-driver and roused him. He grumbled a little, but it seemed he was not sorry to be going, for in Ekaterinburg he had found himself in an odd position, caught between those who wanted low gossip from the driver of the Imperial Family's train, and those who regarded him as a criminal for even driving it. He had been offered both drinks and threats.

The train had been shunted into a siding after the removal of the royal passengers and my own arrest, and it was there still, guarded in two ways. The Urals Soviet had a couple of men by the engine and two more at the rear: factory workers with rifles, from the look of them. Aboard, there remained several of the cavalrymen who had been with me since my first arrival in Tyumen, including the sergeant, Koznov, who made it abundantly clear he was pleased to see me.

'Where to, sir?' he asked brightly.

'Tyumen. You have no other orders?'

'No.' He looked at me expectantly, in that way every officer in a fighting force knows: he would obey any order,

138

but orders were needed. A good man but without initiative.

It was a characteristic of those chaotic days that nobody believed anybody else, and the next events at Ekaterinburg station proved it. Though I was under direct instruction from the highest local authority – Beloborodov and his Soviet – and their instructions had been transmitted to me via the man in charge of the station, the lone guards did not believe any of it. There was a long debate about which of them should be sent to the station-master to make a check on the matter, and when a man had been chosen and despatched and had at last returned, *he* was not believed either. So, in the finish, all four of them made separate forays to the office.

At last they were all convinced and we could set about getting steam up. I could also ask Koznov the question it had been impossible to ask in their presence.

'The contents of the two locked carriages,' I said anxiously, 'have they been disturbed?'

'No,' Koznov told me. 'One of the guards wanted to look inside and was greatly insistent. For a minute I thought I might have to restrain him by force, but it was his companions who prevented it. The Tsar's property was community property now, they said, and must remain so.'

I thanked God for that, and busied myself as fireman, thrusting wood into the engine's furnace and keeping my eye on the steam pressure gauge. Those two locked carriages, to which I had the keys, must hold things of great value, and I was deeply concerned at having responsibility for them.

It must have been two or three o'clock in the morning when, with a full head of steam and the signal clear, the train hissed and clanked out of the station, and began its journey east from Ekaterinburg, back towards Tyumen.

As the city fell behind and the train came out on to the wide lonely spaces, I found myself standing in the corridor of the

139

royal coach, in the very place where I had stood once before – for that single magical hour with the Grand Duchess Marie. Then the night had been black dark, so that I could barely see her; now there was a trace of moonlight. Oh, had she only been with me now . . .

I was overcome for a little while by melancholy and then by a fearful sense of helplessness. For what could I do? By staying in Ekaterinburg I would be putting myself at risk – and pointlessly, too, for it was already obvious the Tsar was to be sealed away from any outside contact. If I went to Moscow it would be to report complete failure – and where was the sense in that? I must somehow contrive a purpose for remaining in the region: a purpose which would stand up to all examination.

I brought my thoughts back to reality and considered my situation. The paper was in Tobolsk. I had the train. Simple: I must go and get the paper! If the paper was itself a weapon, perhaps *I* could use it, too.

What were the realities? I had been ordered out of Ekaterinburg. Very well, I had obeyed orders. But those orders gave me justification for remaining in the wider region, for they required me to return the train to Tyumen and keep its contents intact. The reason was obvious enough: if I were with the train in Tyumen, I would not be stirring trouble in Ekaterinburg. And further, since the contents of the train were valuable, having Yakovlev stand guard over them in a place as remote as Tyumen was one way to keep them safe. So both ways I was secure. I was armed with Urals Soviet written orders concerning the train and Sverdlov's *laissez-passer* concerning my own person. Anyone who would not accept the one ought to accept the other.

And what, anyway, was I guarding? I had seen it loaded as we prepared to leave Tobolsk, but then it was just boxes and bags, chests and parcels and cases. What lay inside? I decided to find out.

And it was dazzling. Nicholas Romanov had been

monarch of one-sixth of the earth, and Alexandra his queen. Their possessions were bound to be of the grandest. I found the carriages contained not only silks and velvets, china and crystal, not only a number of the most exquisite paintings and icons, but also a great many jewels. A great many? *Boxes* of them! Just how many I do not know, for I opened only a few of dozens of containers of various kinds. One was a chest of wood perhaps eighteen inches long by a foot wide and five to six inches deep: and it was full of gold coins in huge variety: Austrian thalers, English sovereigns, American 50-dollar pieces, Mexican, Spanish. It was too heavy for me even to lift from the floor.

In one suitcase lay a small leather-covered octagonal box which, when I opened it, proved to contain only jewellery of a religious nature: crucifixes, small enamelled icons and the like. But it was all of immense richness, with large precious stones used liberally for decoration.

To find oneself responsible for such a treasure is, I can assure you, an extraordinary and unnerving experience. Soon I realized that something must be done: the treasure had to be hidden or buried or taken to a place of safety if such could be found.

I made haste to close everything up and lock the carriage doors. The first light of dawn was showing as I began to make my way forward towards the locomotive.

And it was at dawn that the ambush must have happened, for only a few minutes afterwards, as I stood beside the driver on the platform of the locomotive, looking ahead along its sleek, steel side as we rounded a bend, a battle came sweeping into view.

A train stood halted on the track ahead, perhaps half a mile away, and was clearly engaged in a furious fight with attacking troops. We had heard nothing of the firing, naturally, for the sound of our own locomotive was more than enough to drown out anything else. The driver's hand flew to the brake and I swung off along the handrails at the side of the tender to warn Koznov and his men. Before I had even reached the first carriage, a bullet clanged upon steel close by and went humming past me; turning my head, I saw horsemen riding hard towards us.

Koznov, it turned out, was already alert and his men stood in the corridor with rifles trained upon the approaching riders. Similar scenes are commonplace in these modern days in cinema films about the West in the United States of America. The difference here was that the attack was not by a tribe of painted savages, but by cavalrymen. Whose were they? I snatched a look through binoculars at them, and at the far larger group surrounding the train ahead. Suddenly I noticed a milk-white horse . . .

Dutov!

'Don't shoot,' I told Koznov, but it was a useless instruction, for even as I spoke we ourselves were under fire, and Koznov's men were firing back.

'Hold your *fire!*' I shouted, and snatched up a white pillow from a compartment and waved it from the window. I had them drop their rifles then, and descend to the track with their hands raised. They were resentful, but this was the only thing to be done: it would have been slaughter otherwise.

We were then made to sit by the track and wait as the battle raged farther ahead. But even at that stage it was clear enough that Dutov's troops must carry the day, for it was a couple of hundred against a thousand or more: revolutionary guards against highly-trained men. Determined resistance was certainly put up, but at last the red flags at either end of the Red train were torn down and the inevitable surrender occurred.

It was a full hour after that that I was prodded to my feet with a cavalry sabre and marched to where Dutov sat, on horseback still, beside the surrendered train.

He glared down at me, the big moustache bristling. 'Where is the Tsar?'

I told him straight: 'Imprisoned in Ekaterinburg.'

142

He struck angrily at his thigh with a gauntleted hand. 'I knew it! Bound to happen. He's alive still?'

'To the best of my knowledge.'

'Alive but abandoned,' Dutov raged. 'You've left him to rot.'

'I was imprisoned, and then turned out of the city,' I protested. 'If I go back they'll arrest me.'

'Where are you bound now?'

I said, 'The other royal children are still at Tobolsk. I said I'd return.'

'Stay by your train,' said he. 'We'll talk when I've done here.' And he wheeled away.

In the next hour or so he mopped up. The survivors from the attacked Bolshevik train were formed up, with their wounded, and set to marching due north, and a dishevel-led-looking crew they were. Dutov's men then swarmed aboard the train and seemed to be taking for themselves anything that was both movable and useful. Then the white horse came cantering towards us and Dutov swung one leg forward over the horse's neck and slid to the ground.

'Got any vodka?' he demanded.

There was perhaps two inches of the lemon remaining. I handed the bottle to him and watched his head tilt back as he drained it. 'None on that damned Bolshevik train!' he said. 'Precious little of anything. All we got was a few rifles and some ammunition boxes. God knows what they live on!'

I told him we had a little food in tins, but he wasn't interested. 'It's arms we want. I could do with money, too – it's a while since my rascals were paid. Not –' and he laughed wickedly – 'that they could spend it anywhere, eh! But it keeps a man loyal, money does, no matter what the Bolsheviks say! Now, tell me about Nicholas.'

So I told him what I knew: of the pressure for assassination, of the place where he was imprisoned. But not, of course, of the paper.

'What forces have the Bolsheviks?'

143

'Impossible to know. There are guards everywhere, men with weapons in the streets.'

'Rabble!' says he. 'You can give a man a gun, it doesn't make him a soldier.'

'You're thinking of attack?'

He gave me a glittering grin. 'No! I'm *not* thinking of anything of the kind. God, I had you for a lily-livered nothing running off with your tail curled down, and what is it you want of me? To attack Ekaterinburg with my little force, no less! But don't worry, it *will* be retaken before too long, that's a promise.'

'I hope it won't be too late,' I said soberly.

He regarded me for a moment, then fished in his tunic pocket, brought out a leather cigar case and lit one carefully. 'Upmann,' he said through wreathing, fragrant smoke, 'and I have seven left. The boy's where?'

'The Tsarevitch?'

'Yes, Alexei.'

'At Tobolsk. Why?'

Dutov drew on the cigar and looked hard at me. 'The succession, man!'

'Nicholas abdicated for himself *and* his son.'

Dutov nodded angrily. 'Damn fool. The boy would have been a rallying point.'

'Probably a dead one,' I said.

'Not necessarily. And he wouldn't be the first son to reclaim a father's throne.' Dutov was tempted, he told me a moment later, to ride for Tobolsk, and secure the Romanov children; and he was angry when I shook my head.

'Why not?'

'There are extremists in Tobolstz who'll kill them at the first sign of an army. You'd never get near enough!'

'But *you* would?'

'They know me, the Bolsheviks there.'

'Maybe, but do they trust you?'

I shrugged. 'The sight of Yakovlev won't set them murdering the youngsters.'

144

'Thinking of a boat, are you – from Tobolsk up the Ob?'

I shook my head, though that was precisely the direction of my thoughts. 'What will *you* do, General?'

He puffed smoke. 'More of the same. Harass these Bolshevik dogs wherever I can. Wait for the rest to arrive: they'll be here in a few weeks!'

'Who will – what others?'

'The Whites. Kolchak's army, the Czech Legion, all of them. It's advance, advance at the moment and the Bolsheviks are falling back. One day soon you'll get your wish. We'll take Ekaterinburg. Meanwhile I need guns and money.'

'Let's hope the Tsar will still be alive when you reach him. Will money buy guns?'

'Takes time,' Dutov said. 'Munitions have a long way to come from the Far East, but yes.'

For some minutes I had been looking at General Dutov with a thoughtful and sceptical eye, for there was a picture in my mind of that chest of gold coins, and a rearing question: should it be handed to Dutov?

My own instinctive answer was that it should; what is a royal treasure *for* if it is not to be spent on the arms necessary to preserve the royal life? But Dutov was a brigand if ever I saw one. He was not a man who, shown the gold, would say at once, 'How generous! A thousand thanks.' Dutov would say, 'Where did it come from?' and 'How much more?'

Therefore I asked him, as great favour, to arrange for the line ahead to be cleared of the standing train. He agreed – 'I like playing with trains' – and departed to arrange it. The task would be a simple one, for there was a spur siding actually in view.

Then, while he was away, I had Koznov assist me to lift the chest from the carriage, bear it forward to my wagon-lit, and stow it beneath the bed. That done, I took up the pillow used earlier to surrender, stepped down to the track and began to wave it. The signal brought a galloper and I said, 'Ask General Dutov if he can ꜱᵣ₋ₗᴄ me a moment.'

The man appeared to regard this as mild effrontery. '*You* should go to the General,' he admonished me.

'Tell him it will be worthwhile.'

I watched him ride off. A minute passed, then the milk-white beast came flying towards me.

'What's this?' barked Dutov. 'A damned summons?'

'Come with me.' I climbed aboard the train.

'What is it, damn you?' All this was an offence to his dignity. He followed me along to the wagon-lit, growling to himself.

I flung open the door and pointed to the handle of the chest where it protruded from beneath my bed. 'Help me pull it out.'

'I'll get one of my men.'

'Better,' I said, 'if this is private.'

He looked at me sharply.

'Entrusted to me by the Tsar,' I said, 'so it wouldn't fall into Bolshevik hands.'

He gave a little roar of eagerness and together we dragged the box out. When I lifted the lid, I thought he would explode with joy.

'A king's ransom, here,' he purred.

'A king's treasure,' I told him. 'To be used, as His Majesty insisted, in the general cause.'

'General damned nonsense,' said Dutov dismissively, his hands in the chest and coins clinking merrily. 'There isn't a general cause.'

'There's an anti-Bolshevik cause,' I said, 'and that will do.'

He was suddenly roaring with laughter. I for one had certainly never seen the like of the fortune in gold which lay in that chest, and I doubt if Dutov had either. Then suddenly the laughter stopped, and he was regarding me with suspicious eyes. 'How much did *you* take?'

'None,' I said.

'None!' he yelled. 'You're a damned liar! I bet you've taken –'

'Close the lid, man,' I said. 'And you'll see that the chest is full to the top. I have this –' and I took from my pocket a crucifix encrusted with sapphires, and lied to him – 'a gift from the Tsarina which I would not exchange for a moment. Not for all of that!'

He didn't know whether to gape at me or at the gold; his eyes were not still for a second. Perhaps a minute passed before he said, with a wonderful air of cunning: 'Think what I can buy with this!'

'Exactly,' I said.

So now my train could push ahead along a clear track, for Dutov did not remain long after the gold came to him. It was an easy and uninterrupted run through empty country that brought us at last back to Tyumen, and by then my mind was made up concerning the treasure. I left the faithful Koznov and his men to guard it at the station and made my way to the river quay. There was ice on the water still, and plenty of it; but it was broken now and the edges smooth as it melted.

There was a building containing an office or two, and behind that, a warehouse of good size. A brass plate on the door of the offices proclaimed this to be premises of the West Siberian Steamship Co. The door was locked, and repeated banging on it produced no answer. It was probable, I thought, that the workers in this place would hibernate in the winter. But the winter was over now. I set out to find the responsible men.

The manager I found without trouble, in a house no distance away. He was a man in some difficulty, for the winter had changed his world. When in October the frosts had rendered the river unnavigable, there had still been a Provisional Government, and the company's owners, though far away in London and Oslo, were at least known. Now he knew only what the local Bolsheviks had told him:

147

that everything belonged to the people. So, with spring upon him and a steamship company to manage, he was looking round for instructions very keenly.

'That steamer over there –' I pointed – 'is she fit to sail?'

'Oh yes. We keep a fire going through the winter months so –'

'How long to get steam up?'

'What are you proposing, Comrade?'

'*Commissar* Yakovlev,' I said, and produced my paper. He goggled at it.

'I intend to requisition that steamer for a journey to Tobolsk.'

'Of course, of course. We can have steam up in three hours.'

'Good. And I shall need horses and wagons.'

There was surprisingly little trouble: Tyumen was once again merely a town along the track, for the men from Ekaterinburg had gone. Carts and horses were rapidly assembled and it was perfectly clear that the relationship between the steamer manager and the carters was both long-standing and amiable. So all was done with fair ease and proper care. I stood by the rail carriages to make sure there was no attempted theft. One might imagine that men like those carters, who could never in their lives have come across such things before, might be at the least curious and at worst fiercely acquisitive; but they were not. In their placidity and capacity for work they much resembled their own horses.

By mid-afternoon all was aboard the *Rus*, for that was the steamer's name, and I was ready to depart. The boat's master, one Meluik, was at the wheel and Koznov's men were below, ready to feed the boiler from the stacks of corded wood.

So we sailed. What I remember from that journey aboard the *Rus* is a sense of peace. Tyumen is itself a small town and Tobolsk hardly bigger and there is little between them save the waters of the river and a few villages along

148

the banks. So the steamer nudged along through the ice, thrusting it aside; and on either bank the farmland was green with the spring thrust of young corn.

There came a point when Captain Meluik pointed to a village as we passed and said, 'That is Pokrovskoe, Commissar.' His tone suggested I should know its name.

'Pokrovskoe?' I repeated, snapping my fingers. 'Ah, that's where –?'

'Rasputin,' he said eagerly. 'The mad monk came from there. Last year when the Tsar and Tsarina made this journey on my ship –' and then he caught himself. 'Your pardon, Commissar, the ex-Tsar and ex-Tsarina, that's what I meant.'

'Tell me.'

'I pointed out the village to the ex-Tsarina. She wept and fell to her knees on the deck and prayed.'

'You knew him?' I asked.

'He travelled on the *Rus*. I spoke to him.' Meluik gave a little shudder. 'A man to fear. Such eyes!'

So I was regaled with stories of Rasputin, the ship and the region, as *Rus* drove steadily north, and came at last, on the next day, to the great bend of the Irtysh River where stands Tobolsk. From the bridge of the steamer the Governor's House was clearly visible, and through my binoculars I could discern that there were figures sitting outdoors on a kind of balcony which caught the afternoon sun. I regarded them with a profoundly guilty feeling.

For it is here that I must make a most dreadful confession. The peace of mind of which I spoke lasted only the first half of the *Rus*'s journey. It happened that I lay that night, so Meluik told me, in the bed occupied the previous year by Nicholas. Somehow that knowledge made me, for a time at least, quite unable to sleep, so that my mind ran hither and yon over the events of the immediate past and possibilities for the future. It was then, listening to the water and the bumps of ice, that I pictured my own King, whose first mysterious summons had set me upon this road,

149

and who was so desperately anxious to save the Imperial Family. And I realized that I must endeavour by all available means to carry out my Sovereign's dearest wish, whatever the risks. But I had almost no money.

You may have guessed already the nature of the temptation to which I succumbed. The truth is that at dead of night I entered the hold of the *Rus* where all the Romanov possessions were stored, and searched among them for small and valuable things, portable and easy to exchange. I came up with a good handful of items, loose jewels, brooches, earrings and the like. Their value cannot possibly be guessed at, but must have been substantial. It was an unforgivable crime: I see that now. But at the time, as I searched among the belongings for suitable items, the thought dominant in my mind was that if the necessity should arise to bribe an official, or purchase services for the Tsar's sake, it would be unthinkable for me to fail to have the wherewithal when the wherewithal was available.

And so, a thief in the night, I stole. Next afternoon, when the *Rus* had been tied up at the West Siberian Steamship Co.'s quay at Tobolsk and I strode off to greet the royal children, my pockets contained *their* things.

At the gate of the Governor's House I put on a bold manner and called for Colonel Kobylinsky. He came quickly, but with the air of a man looking over his shoulder, and led me, without speaking, inside to his quarters. Once there and with the stout door closed, he asked me at once, 'What of the Tsar?'

'You haven't heard?'

'We hear nothing.'

So I told Kobylinsky briefly of the incarceration of Nicholas and Alexandra and their daughter.

'Can anything be done?'

'I'm trying. The situation is very difficult.'

'Are you taking the others?' Kobylinsky then asked me worriedly. 'They very much want to go to their parents, of course. But I don't like the prospect of Ekaterinburg . . . I don't like that at all.'

'No. There's no question of taking them, but I'll talk to the youngsters.'

He nodded. 'Try not to worry them.'

So I made my face as cheerful as possible and adopted a matching tone, but it was a melancholy experience to face the three Grand Duchesses and young Alexei and to tell them the news. That they blamed me was clear in their eyes, but they were all of them too well-mannered to say an accusing word; they simply sat in a little semi-circle round me, listening with great concentration and absorbing every movement of my eyes and lips and facial muscles.

When I had finished, the questions came, and they were heartbreakingly polite and formal: How is Papa? How is Mama? Is Marie well? I told them what I could, but such explanation as I could make satisfied them as little as it satisfied me.

The leader among them, though not the eldest, was clearly Tatiana, a thin-faced girl of twenty. She sat silent for a while, listening as I spoke, and then broke in: 'Commissar Yakovlev, we are of one mind. If our parents and our sister are imprisoned, we wish to be with them. Please take us to Ekaterinburg.'

I had hoped to avoid telling them of my own arrest and expulsion from the city, because to do so must increase their burden of worry, but it became impossible to conceal.

'I cannot take you,' I told her, and explained why.

'Then who *is* responsible?' she demanded. 'We all understood you to represent the highest Bolshevik authority. We understood also that safety, at the very least, was guaranteed.'

'I have informed Moscow by telegraph,' I told them. 'And I feel sure that authority will soon be re-established over the Ekaterinburg Regional Soviet.' I tried to sound convincing, and perhaps the younger ones believed me, but plainly Tatiana did not.

151

'Did you really come on orders from Lenin and Sverd-lov?' she asked me. 'Is it true?'

'Perfectly true.'

'But they are masters of all Russia now! How can this happen, this defiance?'

I told her what I had once thought myself: that the answer lay in a failure of communication, and perhaps in rivalry.

'I', she said, 'think it is all a trick! Commissar, if our request cannot properly be made to you, to whom *can* it be made?'

'I will pass it on to Moscow. That is all I can do. And now I must speak alone to your brother.'

'Why?'

'I have a gift for him, and a message.'

Tatiana blinked distrustfully at me, but of course she was powerless to prevent it. She led the girls from the room and I was alone with Alexei.

He smiled at me, quite cheerfully. 'Tatiana always looks on the black side,' he said. 'I'm sure we'll all be together soon.' And then the smile broadened. 'You said you had a gift and a message. Who from – Papa?'

I took out the sapphire-studded crucifix and held it up by its chain so that it swung.

'A crucifix,' Alexei said confidently, 'must be from Mama. Am I right?'

'Not entirely,' I said. 'The gift and the message go together, and really they're from your father. He told me that he had left something with you, a document –'

I saw the boy's quick frown and made myself smile. 'It is just that he changed his mind, you see. He told you to keep the document safely and to give it to him only when the four of you are taken to join him. I know that's what he said. He told me so. You were to keep it secret and give it to nobody. But now he wants you to give the paper to me.'

'No.' Alexei's lips were clamped together. 'He said I must give it to nobody.'

'I know he did. You heard me say so. Alexei, he sent the crucifix so you would know the message was from him, because you would recognize the crucifix. I'm sure you do.'

He was distressed now, and I hated myself for lying to him. The fact remained that the paper might well be the only means of saving all their lives. He said, on the edge of tears, 'But he *told* me, and made me *promise!*'

I said gently, 'Alexei, did *you* tell me about the paper?'

He shook his head. 'Of course not.'

'Did anybody else know – your sisters, for instance?'

'No.'

'It was between the two of you, between you and your father – a secret between men?'

'Yes.'

'Then how do *I* know?'

He stared at me, blinking.

I said, 'Only he or you could have told me, Alexei, and you didn't, did you? So it must have been your papa, mustn't it? And the crucifix is to show you that's the truth.'

A moment passed, and his brow cleared a little. Then he stretched out a hand for the crucifix. I gave it to him and he examined it.

'You know it, don't you?' I said.

Alexei rose. 'I'll bring you the paper, Commissar,' he said politely.

With the paper safe in my pocket I next sought out Kobylinsky and took up with him the matter of the steamer *Rus* and her contents. Discussion produced the stratagem that I, as emissary of the Central Executive, issue papers to the vessel's master and to the Tobolsk manager of the shipping company commandeering the boat, and then handing control of it to Kobylinsky in the name of the Central Executive committee. He was greatly concerned about the position of himself and his men. Kobylinsky, after all, had no standing at all. In a country increasingly controlled by the Bolsheviks, he was an officer of a former regime and one, furthermore, tainted by personal contact and service with his old master, Nicholas. He could never live it down; he knew that and was accordingly hoping for the advance of the White armies to Tobolsk so he could join them. Kobylinsky's life was difficult. Elements of the guards from both Omsk and Ekaterinburg still remained, and though the good colonel had nominal command, it was in truth beyond his exercising. All in all, I determined, it was better that I leave at once.

I went on horseback. The *Rus* had to stay where she was, and with the spring thaw now powerfully under way, a sled would prove impossible, for its runners would cut through the wet snow and scrape the ground beneath.

So I made the decision to ride, and a foolish choice it was – one that was to cost me dear. But as I rode those first two or three miles, the document given so trustingly to me by young Alexei, and so much wanted by Lenin and by Zaharoff and apparently by half the world, was burning a hole in my pocket. From the beginning, from the very first awed conversation in Lenin's room in Moscow, I had had a notion of what it must contain. Now I found I had to know. And so, in the last of the light, I reined in my horse, took the envelope from my pocket, and broke the seal.

I checked first that it had indeed been signed – and there was his signature: not a simple Nicholas as once it must have been, but 'Nicholas Romanov'. I saw, too, that it had been witnessed by Kobylinsky. Surprising, I thought, that it had been witnessed at all; but then I realized the document was composed in English, a language Kobylinsky did not speak.

It was only then that I read it through. My eyes followed the typewritten lines with growing incredulity, for though something of what I expected was there in the dry, legal language, there was far more. So much more! At stake with this document was so much that my senses reeled. Then the questions flooded in. Who knew? Did King George the

154

Fifth? I couldn't believe *that*! Lenin then? No, the deceit encompassed him too.

But two men had known. Nicholas Romanov, ex-Tsar of all the Russias – *he* knew. And so did Basil Zaharoff, whom many held to be the most sinister figure in Europe.

And now there was a third, for Henry George Dikeston knew . . .

Progress in snow depends upon the condition of the snow, and a horse is as dependent upon it as is a man. Set the animal upon firm, hard-packed snow and a horse is happy and moves well. Set him upon soft slush, which is half-water, half-ice, and all treachery and discomfort, and the horse prefers to pick his way.

It was true of all those I rode and I exchanged horses several times. They would trot, certainly; flog them hard and they'd work up a gallop, but only for a few moments. That ride back to Tyumen began in difficulty and rapidly became more and more unpleasant. On a succession of horses I splashed and slithered my way southward, part of the time through falling sleet. I grew so wet and cold that had I been asked I would have said it was quite impossible to be wetter and colder. But that was wrong. I had more than a hundred miles still to go when the horse fell and threw me and I landed in a pothole in the road, a hole filled with earthy black water, and though neither the horse nor I was hurt, by the time I had remounted and ridden a few minutes in that bitter wind, I was chilled to the marrow. I should have stopped. In a village I could have found fire and food and warmth. But I was alone, and the solitary night-time traveller in remote country had better beware, whether he is in Siberia or Somerset, especially when, as was the case with me, there was wealth in his pockets.

So I pressed on. My teeth chattered and my feet were blocks of ice; gradually the cold crept through my body, so that I shivered uncontrollably. Come morning, I was aware that I was already quite unwell, for alternately I shook and

155

was feverish, and felt increasingly foul. But I came into Tyumen still in place upon my horse's back, just in time to leap direct aboard a train bound west for Ekaterinburg.

That journey, also, was a nightmare. The remnants of my money bought me a place only in a third-class carriage which was impossibly crowded, and not only with people, though there were three for every two places. In addition there was baggage and several animals, including a goat whose stench, I swear, was no greater than that of several of the peasants near me. Probably I stank also; certainly I steamed and in the press of humanity there were many like me: soaked and steaming. I felt increasing hunger and thirst, but there was no means of satisfying either. My health deteriorated by the hour: I was hot, I was shaking; the fever was rising, I sweated like a hog. The last three hours of the journey were spent huddled on the floor, sleeping perhaps, though it was more of a faint.

As the voice yelled 'Ekaterinburg,' I dragged myself to my feet. It was just after eight o'clock by the station clock as I staggered out of the stinking, steamy heat of the railway carriage into the cold night air of the city.

In an hour I must meet Ruzsky.

I would have waited another day to see him, and should have done so. Food and a bed and healthy warmth were what was required, but I had no money for lodging, the last having been spent on the train journey. Only a few kopeks remained and with those I bought tea at the station. It refreshed me a little, as tea does, but I was in a poor way as I set off from the station towards the Palais Royal Hotel. Already I knew, from talk heard in the station, that the Imperial Family remained imprisoned in the Ipatiev House.

Ruzsky was late. It is unimportant, I suppose, but it mattered that night to me, feeling as I did, and leaning against the rear wall of the hotel, miserable as a sick dog. But it is difficult to blame him. In the days since I had left

156

Ekaterinburg he must have kept our rendezvous faithfully, and was keeping it still.

At the sight of me he said wrathfully, 'Where in hell have you been?'

I began to tell him and my teeth were chattering. He pulled a bottle from his pocket. 'Plum brandy. Drink it.'

Then he listened as I told him about the steamer and Tobolsk. The story took little time in the telling, so that soon I could ask him: 'What news of the Romanovs here?'

That, too, was soon told. There were no *events* to record; the Imperial Family remained under guard, that was all. But one change had occurred: and it struck me at once as deeply sinister. Ipatiev's house now had a new name, by proclamation. It must now be known as The House of Special Purpose!

'But what does it mean?' I demanded. 'What special purpose?'

Ruzsky gave a shrug. 'Who knows? A name means nothing. Drink some more.'

The political state of affairs was unchanged, he told me then: the Urals Soviet had been meeting almost daily, and always there was discussion of what to do with the Romanovs. 'General opinion is for execution of Nicholas.'

'He alone?' I asked.

'That depends who speaks. Beloborodov, the chairman, would kill the Tsar and spare the rest, or so I think. Goloshchokin's for butchering them all. With the Whites too near for comfort he thinks their presence is a danger to the city.'

'Is there no opposition?' I demanded. 'Surely there must be – when there is talk of killing children?'

'Hardly children,' he said, 'except for the boy, and he's fourteen now. Yes, there's opposition.'

'How many – what's the balance of the committee?'

'Never tested,' Ruzsky said, 'and some decline even to offer a view, on the grounds that the matter is of no importance. I'm doing what I can, but it's little enough.

Nobody, even of the Soviet, may enter the House of Special Purpose to see the Romanovs except Beloborodov. And the guards, of course. That's the problem.'

'How *much* opposition?' I repeated.

'There's a fellow named Scriabin; he's Regional Commissar for Natural Resources: one of the milk-and-water people who won't shed blood. I make a point of being close to him in spite of disagreement.'

'So is there a chance?'

'There's always a chance,' Ruzsky said.

*   *   *

Pilgrim, despite his impatience and his professed lack of interest, continued to see Dikeston's manuscripts; he merely declined to allow thought of them to dominate his waking hours. That morning the third instalment, thoughtfully Xeroxed for him by Malory, won a small battle for his attention, a battle with the *Financial Times*. Pilgrim, speed-reading, his concentration firm, barely noticed the entrance of Jacques Graves to his office. He murmured, 'Important?'

'Not really.' Graves, from long familiarity knew when not to disturb. 'Later will be okay.'

He laid a single sheet of paper on the left side of Pilgrim's desk, and withdrew.

Pilgrim ignored it for several minutes, then reached out a hand. The note read:

> 'Account no. X253 at the
> Irish Linen Bank
> belongs to . . .

Pilgrim swore to himself, rose and marched down the corridor to Malory's room. Malory, wreathed in expensive cigar smoke, looked up. 'Have you read it?'

'Some of it.' Pilgrim flourished Graves's note. 'Did Jacques tell you?'

'Tell me what?' Malory removed his glasses.

158

'That damned account at the bank,' Pilgrim said. 'Know whose it is?'

'No, he didn't tell me.'

'Then I will. How's UNICEF grab you?'

Malory frowned. 'You know, I'm never too sure which of those things is which – WHO and UNESCO and so on. Which *is* UNICEF?'

'It's the children's fund, Horace – The United Nations Children's Fund.'

'Ah, I see.'

'So do I. My God, fifty thousand – plus the deeds of a house worth another hundred and fifteen – and we've handed the goddam lot to a charity! We'll never see one red cent back. Have you the instructions for the next instalment?'

An envelope lay beside Malory. He patted it with a brown-spotted hand. 'Here,' he said.

'What do they say?'

'I'm waiting to learn. Until I have finished reading.' Malory glanced pointedly at the Act of Parliament clock on the wall. 'Tell me,' he continued, 'are you beginning to find this interesting now?'

'At ten pounds a word, sure it's interesting!' There was irritation in every line of Pilgrim's back as he turned and left.

Malory put on his glasses and resettled himself to read. The temptation to turn to the end and to open the envelope were almost, but not quite, irresistible. Dikeston was clearly in terrible trouble, but equally clearly he had got out of it – with something that was worth £50,000 a year for *ever*.

Deep inside myself, Malory thought with conscious realism, I am now a man torn: I deeply believed in the potential disaster, yet I am perversely beginning to enjoy the game Dikeston has set us all to play.

*   *   *

159

I felt like death by this time. Sweat coursed down my body beneath my clothes, yet at the same time I shivered and burned.

'What I keep pressing upon Scriabin,' Ruzsky told me, as we stood beneath the dark shelter of the hotel wall that night, 'is that the Romanov family should be brought together.'

'Why?' I asked. Though I was awake and standing up, my mind worked barely at all. Yet I recall clearly the sound of a clock chiming near by. Oddly, in that place, it was a Westminster chime.

'Why? Because,' Ruzsky said, 'it is foolish on all counts to separate them. Even for the Bolsheviks it is wrong. So Scriabin tells the Soviet, and I reinforce his argument as much as I dare. So long as Nicholas is here and the son at Tobolsk there will be two potential rallying points: for the Whites *and* for monarchists of all kinds, here in Siberia. It is even an invitation to White armies to a two-pronged attack!'

He gave me a grin then, and tapped his nose. 'Better for us too, eh? – if the Family were together here.'

'Why? We're helpless.'

'Nobody is helpless,' Ruzsky said. 'Least of all you and me. But,' he went on, 'it is true we stand in need of help.'

This was so ludicrous an understatement that I was near to laughing in his face. He looked at me hard, then forced more plum brandy on me. Perhaps he sensed what the future held for me; at all events he would brook no delay and no argument. He took my arm and began to propel me along the dark streets, talking as we went.

'The help we need,' he argued, 'is from someone of position. You have none now; I have standing only in the Soviet and my attitude cannot alter there. We need an outside power.'

'Of what kind?'

160

'British,' Ruzsky said firmly. 'The British have a consul here. His name is Preston. His position is secure; he may even be able to force diplomatic access to the House of Special Purpose. Come along, man, you must stay on your feet an hour or two yet.'

And I did, God alone knows how. I stayed on my feet as we trudged towards the forbidding palisade at the Ipatiev House, as we walked past it, eyed by the guards, along Vosnesensky Avenue. Ruzsky knew where he was going well enough, and when we halted at a big house with a strongly bolted door upon which the lion and the unicorn did their dance, he did not so much speak as issue an order. This was the British Consulate.

'Knock,' he said. Obediently I did so.

We waited. The door was opened at last by a man in a long silken dressing-gown.

I said to him in English, 'I am in urgent need of your assistance!'

And he, in the very best traditions of the British Foreign Service when confronted with a fellow countryman visibly *in extremis*, said, 'I can't help you now. It's far too late. Come back in the morning.'

* * *

The King, thought Malory – it all began with the King, with George V, acting *alone*. No, not alone – through Zaharoff. But acting in a remarkably furtive manner all the same for a King-Emperor. Malory ticked off the steps one by one: the King calls in Zaharoff, who unearths Dikeston from somewhere or other and sends him off to Siberia. And there – surprisingly, if one did *not* know Sir Basil, but unsurprisingly if one did – another Zaharoff man is encountered. At no point, Malory noted, was the British Government involved. Or not, at least, to that point.

But now, it seemed, the Foreign Office was about to be dragged in by its reluctant if elegant lapels.

He stretched out a hand to the letter, broke the seal and

with care extracted the sheet of paper therein.

The first sentence read:

> I did not know that evening, as I spoke to Ruzsky, that on that very day Bolshevik orders had reached Tobolsk from Moscow relieving Colonel Kobylinsky of his command, dispersing his troops and replacing him with one Rodionov. Nor did I know that within a week the steamer *Rus* would again be used – this time to move the Romanov children from Tobolsk. But they did not journey north to the Ob river . . .

Dikeston's instructions followed.

CHAPTER SEVEN

———◆———

'Do I hear <u>one</u> million?'

'I don't care what was agreed!' Laurence Pilgrim's usual manner was one of brisk tolerance leavened by a streetwise New York humour. But as he spoke now he was near to a snarl. 'The idea, Horace, was that *you* were to stop *me* making a goddam fool of myself in an unfamiliar milieu. It's called advice. I agreed with the international board that I would listen, because they all think you're nobody's fool.' He paused. 'That's what I used to think, too!'

'Used to?' said Malory dangerously.

'Yeah, used to. Let me ask you, Horace, who's it making a goddam fool of himself here? Who's buying houses and handing them to the United Nations? Who's paying cheques into 'X' accounts? This is a *bank*, Horace, not a bottomless benevolent society.'

Malory crossed one immaculately creased trouser leg over the other. 'It is a bank I have served for a great many years. I'm entirely ready to re-examine the profit record and the growth under my stewardship. May I say that if you do as well, you will be doing *very* well! I can read profit and loss, I can see prospects and dangers, I can make financial assessments, all of those. But there are times, as now, when –'

'Look, we had all this before. There's a danger and we have to know what it is, that's your case, right? So answer me just one question, Horace.'

'If I can.'

'We've spent two hundred thousands pounds. Okay.

Are we any nearer knowing what this danger is? Are we one single goddam step nearer?'

Malory pursed his lips. 'We know the general source of the danger lies in the relationship between Zaharoff and the Tsar. We are learning more, stage by stage.'

'Oh sure,' Pilgrim said angrily. 'Information is dispensed word by word by Dikeston. Dikeston met the Tsar; Dikeston met Zaharoff; Dikeston met the King, Lenin, Trotsky and Whistler's goddam mother for all I know. Dikeston's in charge of a train loaded with jewels. Dikeston's whizzing round Siberia like a fly with a ginger ass, and we don't even know who Dikeston is!'

'Oh, but we do, Laurence,' Malory said gently. 'We know he represented royalty at the highest level, and business too, also at the highest level. We know when he was born and when he died.'

Pilgrim blinked. 'Do we? Since when?'

'Since I arranged scrutiny of the death register at Somerset House. It showed that Henry George Dikeston died on 20th October, 1968.'

'You're *sure* he's dead, Horace?'

'There is a death certificate. He died at Sainte-Maxime in the South of France. But there was no will and no property.'

'No property! When he had fifty thousand a year for –'

'None in France or England, I meant, Laurence. None that can be traced.'

'What else do we know?'

Malory's eye inspected the shining toe of his hand-lasted shoe. 'I have a tame historian. Consider this, Laurence. It seems that in the first months of the nineteen-fourteen war, the Tsar sent huge amounts of money out of Russia. Much of it was part of his own personal fortune and he was undoubtedly at that time the richest man on earth.'

'Oh, come *on*, Horace. Not that stuff about Romanov millions scattered all over Europe and America and never claimed! You're not going to feed me that one?'

'I fear not,' Malory said. 'I'm going to *feed* you, as you put it, the report of Professor Bernard Pares to the Prime Minister, Lloyd George, and quoted in Lloyd George's War Memoirs, that relations between Britain and Russia were being gravely jeopardized by the failure of Vickers, Maxim & Co. to supply munitions.'

'Who was Pares?'

'A scholar with political ambitions. Lloyd George had sent him to Russia. You know who represented Vickers, Maxim?'

'Zaharoff?'

'Zaharoff indeed.'

Pilgrim passed a weary hand across his brow. 'Okay, I get it. You think Zaharoff fleeced the Tsar.'

'I don't see why not,' Malory said. 'He fleeced thousands, and most of them were a good deal brighter than Nicholas Romanov.'

'And Dikeston – where's Dikeston come in? You worked that out yet?'

'Two things worry me,' said Malory gently. 'The first is the piece of paper. Sir Basil's paper. Did the Tsar sign it, and if so *what* was it?'

'And the second?'

'Is the really serious one. Laurence – you talked about all the people Dikeston had met, but you quite failed to mention one.'

'Who was that?'

Malory gave a small smile. 'We're all human, you know, Dikeston included. He's told us he met the highest and the lowest. Let me ask *you*, Laurence, which individual do you think made the greatest impression on him?'

Pilgrim thought for a moment. 'You mean the girl – the Grand Duchess?'

'Marie. He fell for her.' Malory said. 'Fell like a ton of bricks. They talked for an hour and he never forgot a moment of it. And then what happened?'

'I don't follow you.'

165

'Don't you? She was butchered,' Malory said harshly. 'We really *must* find the painting Dikeston talks about. Don't you agree?'

Dikeston's letter of instructions was, in this instance, hand-written.

> You should keep a weather-eye open for a name. It will appear quite soon in the catalogue of one of the art auction houses – Christie's, Sotheby's or perhaps Phillips'.
> The name is Mallard. I am afraid it will be necessary for you to purchase the painting. The manuscript is in the frame.

'I suppose we have to be grateful it's not a Rembrandt,' Pilgrim said bitterly. 'Name mean anything to you, Horace?'

'Offhand, no. Except that it's a kind of duck. And if I remember, the name was once given to a railway engine.'

'We'll finish by running behind that engine, you want to bet?'

'I think not.' Malory took himself off to his room and there examined the Shorter Oxford English Dictionary, which confirmed that the Mallard was indeed a duck, or at any rate a drake. It was also a festival celebrated on January 14th at All Souls College, Oxford. Of art or artists there was no mention.

He sent for Fergus Huntly. 'There seems to have been an artist, Huntly. His name was Mallard. I want you to find out about him. Oh yes, and get on to the art auctioneers, Christie's, Sotheby's and Phillips. I want their catalogues.'

Huntly nodded. 'You know nothing about this artist?'

'Not a thing,' Malory said briskly. 'Come to think, it may not be an artist at all. Could be a picture, couldn't it?'

'Of a duck?'

'Well, why not! What about Scott? Peter Scott – that's the chap. Painted lots of ducks.'

'Right, Sir Horace.'

Huntly took himself to the London Library in St James's Square, but though he consulted a wide selection of art books, he found no artist named Mallard. Nor, it seemed, from enquiries at the art auction houses, was any painting of wild duck – or not a painting of any consequence – coming up for sale.

He reported sadly back to Sir Horace Malory. 'There's no trace at all.'

'Isn't there?' Malory sat ruminatively over the remains of a tumbler of malt whisky. 'Who do I know in art?'

'Well – I don't know. I mean, you know a lot of people, you must know a lot of –' Huntly got hold of himself, wondering what it was in Malory that gave him verbal dysentery.

'Historian, he is, yes, this fella. You know the one. None too savoury, matter of fact. Traitor and a pansy, nasty combination!'

'Oh, *him*!' said Huntly.

Malory found *him* at a club. Both men were members of several, but had only this one in common. The art historian, who had achieved eminence as a scholar and infamy as a betrayer of his country and had somehow contrived not to be prosecuted, should, Malory thought, have been sitting in a cell. He crossed the large, decaying room, with its vaulted ceiling, its worn leather chairs and its moth-eaten Afghan rugs, reflecting mischievously that the art historian was not the only one in his wide acquaintanceship who might properly be in gaol. Half the City for a start. Why, he himself, observed in a certain light . . .

Malory smiled to himself and tottered towards the man's seat. He wore his doddering old buffer act as comfortably as though it were an old jacket.

'. . . my dear fella, indeed, must be years. Good heavens, yes. All getting old, though, aren't we, eh?'

The art historian, almost eighty and bent with rheumatism, sat crouched in his chair watching warily.

167

'You'll have a whisky, won't you? Yes, good. No, you'd prefer cognac, would you?' He felt the eyes coldly upon him from their depths in the network of wrinkled skin. 'Yes, yes, I could cope with a little Bisquit myself, first today, ha, ha.' He wondered which of them had been a member longer, and by that time the cognac had been brought by the steward and the treacherous art expert had decided in his own favour and relaxed a little. Malory asked his question. 'M'wife really. Asked me to find out about a painter. Tell you the truth, I think she must be doing a crossword puzzle. Moment I saw you, I thought: he'll know in a jiffy. Name Mallard mean anything to you?'

Wrinkles slid about on the ancient and reptilian countenance opposite. There was a small smile. 'I have never heard of a painter so called.'

'Or a subject?'

'Plenty of people paint wildfowl. There's no single celebrated picture, I think. Mallard, you say?'

'Yes, Mallard. Well,' Malory poured the brandy down his throat, 'thanks, old lad. I'll tell my lady.' He had already doddered three or four steps away, when:

'Oh, Malory.'

He turned. 'Yes.'

'You're sure it's Mallard?'

'Well that's what it says. Why?'

'Not Mallord – with an "o"?'

He thought about it for a moment. Dikeston's directions *had* been handwritten. An 'a' for an 'o'? It was hardly impossible.

'Could be, I suppose. There's a Mallord, is there?'

'Well, yes. Not his surname, you know. I mean, you wouldn't find him so listed. It's one of his three Christian names.'

'Whose?'

Again the smile on the wrinkled features. 'Joseph Mallord William, those were his first names.'

'And his surname?'

168

'Turner. You've heard, have you?'

Malory turned a pale face to him. 'Heard what?'

'One's been found.'

'Oh, really. Where?'

'Happens all the time, you know. There are lots and lots of Turner drawings.'

'Any great value?' Malory asked, knowing already.

'Turner drawings? They vary. Depends how good and how big and what period. Even now you might get one for, oh, as little as eight or ten thousand.'

Malory relaxed.

'But this isn't one of *those*. Not from what I hear.'

'Oh,' said Malory politely. 'What is it you hear?'

The tortoise mouth widened in a grin, though whether of pleasure or malice it was hard to tell. 'I hear it's a big one, same size and period as *The Fighting Téméraire*. If it is, God alone knows what it will fetch!'

Vivian Sudbury, for all the expensive simplicity of his Huntsman suit, his Lobb shoes and his Turnbull & Asser haberdashery (Malory guessed there was a thousand pounds on Sudbury's back), still bore with him that peculiar oiliness unmistakable in dealers in fine things. His eye had about it that lambent humility which is ready at once to turn either to obsequiousness or contempt, according to the state of negotiation.

He said, 'Turner,' in a voice like velvet.

'That's the feller,' Sir Horace told him. 'Tell me about him.'

Sudbury glanced round the room, pricing everything in a single swift survey. He lit a cigarette which, Malory's nostrils told him, was Egyptian. 'There are,' said the velvet voice, 'Turners and Turners.'

Malory nodded encouragingly. 'So I'm told.'

'The highest price ever paid at auction,' Sudbury continued, 'was for a Turner: six million four hundred thousand dollars, at Sotheby Parke Bernet.'

169

'In New York City. I remember,' Pilgrim forced the words past wincing lips.

'Beautiful painting, three feet by four. *Juliet and her Nurse.*'

'This one that's coming up,' Pilgrim asked. 'What's known about it?'

'Remarkably little.' Vivian Sudbury spoke with a patent affection for mystery, which he adored because it unfailingly forced prices higher.

'The subject, for example?' Malory asked.

Sudbury smiled. 'They're being rather coy at the moment. Naughty of them, but then' he waved a bejewelled hand in a gesture of tolerance 'it does help to build up interest.'

'How would you like to cut the crap?' said Pilgrim, hating him. 'We want to know about Turner and about this painting. For that you're charging a stiff fee. Tell us.'

Sudbury smiled. 'I'm so sorry. As a rule I find I'm talking with people deeply interested in *art* as such –'

'Not money *as such*, like you and me?' Pilgrim said.

'Oh, very well. What I imagine you want to know is what the painting might be – perhaps because you're considering investing?'

'Perhaps,' said Malory.

Sudbury nodded. Rudeness to him did not pay: he never allowed it to. And he had just thought of a way . . .

'Then if it *is* a major Turner, – well, two, anyway, are known to be missing. They are *The Temple of Jupiter Panellenius Restored*, exhibited first in 1816 at the Royal Academy. Not seen since 1853. If it's still in good condition I'd guess it might fetch two or three million.'

'Dollars?'

'Pounds, I'm afraid. The other, *Fishermen Coming Ashore at Sunset*, was quite possibly Turner's first commissioned painting – done in 1797 when he was twenty-two – and the more interesting for that.'

'Value?'

170

'Perhaps a little less. Up to two million.'

'Any others?'

'A hundred or so sizeable pieces. Many of them are watercolours, but Turner really was quite amazingly prolific: did more than 500 oil paintings and nearly 20,000 pencil and watercolours. So there could be absolutely *anything*!'

'At *any* price?' Pilgrim asked grimly.

'Oh, any price at all.'

A week passed: time used by the fortunate auctioneers with considerable skill. The painting, it gradually emerged, presented a mystery to delight the hearts not only of the Vivian Sudburys of this world but of all Fleet Street. For it had conditions attached. In the course of that first week the revelations came one by one: the Turner was said to be a *new* one, and an oil. More – it was a sea-and-landscape with ships. It was, for the moment, housed in a specially-built packing-case twelve fect square of which TV news and all the papers carried photographs as it was driven on a large truck through central London.

But it had not yet been seen, even by the auctioneers; and for them this might have constituted a grave moral dilemma in that they could scarcely offer for sale a Turner they had never seen, yet one condition of sale was that the packing case remain unopened until one week before the auction. The auctioneers, however, did have a documentary authentication dating from the 1840s. They therefore went ahead happily, and their catalogue described the painting as the 'Mysterious' Turner.

Interest grew, and many questions were asked, not least by Mr Vivian Sudbury on behalf of Hillyard, Cleef. Where had the painting and its packing case *been*? But no answer was forthcoming, for this was the 'Mysterious' Turner. The questions Who is the owner? Who bought it last? Why was it not listed among Turner's much-catalogued works? also remained unanswered.

171

The honour of talking the first photograph of the painting was one for which any photographer in London would have been anxious. Famous names, great photographic artists, offered their services at half or a quarter of their normal fees. At the auction house, however, it was decided that here was an opportunity to give youth a hand, and it so happened that one young member of the Royal Family was currently studying photography with a view to a career. She was miles from the throne, but she was nubile and therefore newsworthy. Pictures of the young princess and her picture of the painting made front pages and centre spreads all over the world.

For by now interest was spreading rapidly. Copy transparencies of the youthful princess's photograph were put aboard jet aircraft at Heathrow and Gatwick and examined a few hours later in air-conditioned galleries in Southern California and Saudi Arabia, in Texas and Johannesburg.

And now the picture found a title, for the setting of the painting was Plymouth, and The Hoe was discernible. *Naval Vessel and Plymouth Hoe*, though not Turner's title, was felt to have a nice restraint about it.

Each of these events caused its little *frisson* in newspapers, television studios, and galleries. But one major surprise was saved for last. The princess's photographs had been cropped to show the picture and only the picture; nothing of the frame was visible. Malory and Pilgrim, placed in the unique position of being far more interested in the frame than the picture, found themselves suffering from a most distressing absence of information. They sought help from Vivian Sudbury who, having spent a lifetime greasing palms in the art world, none the less found himself helpless. The auctioneers kept their door firmly closed to everyone. The bank's name, usually a key to most places, proved valueless, for many large financial institutions were now interested.

And in London many were represented.

But of course it is not strictly necessary to be present in

172

order to bid at an auction. There are always agents bidding on behalf of unnamed clients. But technology has introduced new factors into ancient practice: electronically, and by satellite, an auction can these days can be conducted on a worldwide basis.

And so on that Wednesday at five p.m., when the auctioneer's gavel called an audience of the very rich and the very famous to order, it was in a room bathed in hot light and surveyed by cameras. For in addition to the multi-millionaires present, others – several of them billionaires – were seated in front of TV sets in places as diverse as Riyadh, Rio, Hong Kong, Dallas and Tokyo.

'And now,' said the auctioneer, 'a painting by J. M. W. Turner provisionally titled: *Naval Vessel and Plymouth Hoe.*' He turned his head to watch as a porter in a stuff coat removed the draped cloth which had until that moment concealed the painting. Now he gazed blandly over an audience sitting rigid with surprise.

For the frame in which the picture was displayed was fashioned in dulled stainless steel, with clearly reinforced corners.

The auctioneer spoke gently but persuasively. It was part of the conditions of sale that the painting be offered *in its frame*. There would be absolutely no difficulty in removing the frame later, nor would damage be done to the picture in such removal. He then spoke briefly of the Turner's provenance, citing both the original certificate of authentication and another accorded in the last few days by the custodian of the great Turner Bequest at the British Museum; and he added a few quiet but proud words concerning the self-evident quality of the painting. Then, becoming practical, he further explained that bids would be accepted in steps of fifty thousand pounds.

At that point the auctioneer coughed, just once, as a kind of punctuation. 'Now, ladies and gentlemen,' he said, 'do I hear *one* million?'

173

In fact he *heard* nothing. The first bid was made by a small nod of a silver head. But it came at once . . .

Whatever the state of disagreement which lay in the background, the instructions to Vivian Sudbury had all the clarity of a pool of dew. 'Buy it,' Malory had ordered him boldly.

The boldness evident in Sudbury's demeanour was somewhat less in evidence in Malory's face as the bidding climbed. Pilgrim's face reflected only pain. But Sudbury was a happy man as the price floated upward: for Sudbury was on commission, which reinforced his determination to follow his client's instructions.

At £3,250,000 the painting was knocked down to Mr Sudbury. There was sadness among disappointed buyers round the world that the masterpiece would not now go to America, or South Africa, or Brazil.

But there was great happiness among the cognoscenti in Britain that the Turner would not now go aboard. None of this happiness was apparent among the purchasers.

'We shall sell it again,' Malory murmured as he and Pilgrim walked out into St James's. 'Perhaps even make a profit. Care for a bracer? My club's up the road.'

'Thanks, but not now.' Pilgrim had hailed a taxi that was emerging from King Street into St James's. As it pulled up, he glanced at his watch. Timing's right, he thought.

In his flat a few minutes later, phone in hand, he punched up the three-zero-five of Florida, then the Key Biscayne code and the number of Robizo's private office.

'Hello.'

'Pete?'

'Who is it?' The voice was flat, almost but not quite hostile.

'Pal, how goes it?'

Now the tone changed. They had been brought out of Hungary together as boys in 1956, had gone to school and

174

business school together. Now Pyotr Nagy was private
assistant to Pepe Rabizo.

'Why wasn't Pepe bidding tonight?' Pilgrim demanded.

'For the Turner? Because he bids himself – no middle-
men – and he had business right here.'

'Would he want it?'

'Price?'

'It went for three and a quarter.'

'Dollars?'

'Pounds, Pete. This is England.'

'Hey, that's big, even for Pepe!'

'Pepe could buy fifty, don't snow me. You want it?'

'Can you get it?'

'I think so.'

'Hey, Pal, it's Pepe – for Chrissake don't putz around.
Do him a favour and he's your friend. But foul up, oh boy!'

Pilgrim flushed. The painting now belonged to Hillyard,
Cleef. He was Senior Partner. A quick sale, even a profit
beckoned. He said, 'Plus ten per cent.'

'And you *can* deliver?'

'Right.'

'Pepe'll be very happy. He wanted it. I'll telex his
confirmation.'

Pilgrim hung up. He found he was sweating a little. Pepe
Robizo was big, dangerous and enormously rich: a huge-
scale building contractor with strong connections in
Washington and even stronger ones in the Mafia, now
trying hard to buy social acceptance through his art gallery.

Pilgrim took a shower, and then, as he shaved, regarded
his face in the mirror with satisfaction. Money-back-plus-
ten for the price of a phone call!

Two signatures were always required upon any Hillyard,
Cleef cheque for a sum of more than one hundred pounds.
This was another Zaharoff legacy. Malory, not much relishing the task, took the half-signed cheque to Pilgrim's
office next morning and placed it before him.

175

Pilgrim glanced at it in silence and reached for his pen, then did a double take.

'I remember *exactly*,' he said, 'because it is graven upon my heart, the figure we had to pay for the goddam thing! And it was *not* three million, five hundred and seventy-five thousand pounds! We paid three and a quarter!' His voice had risen.

Malory sighed. 'I'm afraid there's something called a buyer's premium. Ten per cent on the price paid.'

'Oh yeah.' Pilgrim remembered it now. 'That goes to the auctioneer for doing nothing, right? Three hundred and twenty-five thousand! We're in the wrong business, Horace.'

Malory, hatted and coated, went on his way to St James's, accompanied by a security company van and several men armed with clubs and gas sprays, to collect the Turner. He returned less than an hour later and the security men bore the painting, no longer in its twelve-foot-square crate but in a light wooden one more appropriate to its size, up the stairs to the partners' room. The men then adjourned to stand unobstrusively outside 6 Athelsgate.

Malory, meanwhile, approached the crate with a cold chisel and a hammer. It proved not difficult to open. With Pilgrim's assistance the painting, in its steel frame, was lifted out.

Together they examined the frame. In the back there was a small flap, closed and sealed. Malory broke the seal with anxious fingers, and lifted the flap to reveal a key. There was a keyhole in one corner.

When the key was turned part of the frame came open and a small bundle of papers was revealed.

It was all very simple. If rather expensive.

CHAPTER EIGHT

———◆———

Fourth instalment of the account, written by
Lt-Cdr H. G. Dikeston RN, of his journeyings
in Russia in the spring and summer of 1918

I stood swaying in the night, feeling like death, and repeated, in Russian, 'I am in urgent need of your assistance.
It is most important that I speak with Mr Preston, the
Consul.' I could barely stand, so powerfully was the fever
upon me now; but the man stood there in silk, looking
down his nose at me. He said again, 'It is too late,' and
made to close the door.

It was Ruzsky, beside me, who turned matters. He said
in a low and threatening voice, 'Urgent! We are from
the Urals Oblast Soviet. You should have a care, Comrade.'

The man frowned. 'Who are you?'

'Commissar Ruzsky. He is Commissar Yakovlev,' said
Ruzsky. 'Inform Preston at once.'

And so it was done. Preston appeared; I told him I must
speak with him urgently and alone; he took me to an
upstairs room and looked upon me with no great favour.
'What the devil is all this about?'

'It is about the King's business,' I said, and he looked at
me sharply, cocking an eyebrow; he must have wondered if
this were a joke of some kind. 'Have you a Navy List?' I
then demanded.

He had, the Lord knows why, for he stood a thousand
miles from navigable ocean. I said, 'Dikeston, Henry
George, Lieutenant-Commander.'

'Then what's this Yakovlev nonsense?' he demanded,
laying the List to one side.

'I want your word, Preston,' I told him. 'Your word that

177

nothing about me, and nothing of what I tell you, will ever be passed to another soul.'

He frowned at once, reluctant. 'Only if you convince me you are on the King's errand. You'll have to prove it.'

'I can't.' But I told him my tale and showed him my paper from Sverdlov, and I could see he soon began to believe. Mention of Zaharoff made him scowl, though. '*That* man – and with the King!' It was as though he could not believe it.

'And with the King's blessing,' said I. 'Now: your word.'

He gave it, and I then explained our difficulties. Preston had some of his own. He was under pressure from both London and the embassy in Moscow to intercede for the Imperial Family and had been making daily attempts to visit them. All his requests had been refused. 'However,' he went on, 'though I have been unable to have audience of His Majesty, or to speak with him, it *is* possible to see him from a distance. Come with me.'

I accompanied him to the stairs and we climbed to a room on the upper floor, where he drew back a curtain and, as the moonlight entered the room, said, 'You see?'

And indeed I did. The consulate lay beyond the Ipatiev House, with the result that the view that lay before us was a slanting one. But from that upper room the line of sight was of a height to pass over the palisade and see direct into a corner of the courtyard of the House of Special Purpose. The space was deserted now, of course, and no movement was visible in the former Ipatiev House, though in a few places there was light at a dimmed window.

'You *do* see them?' I asked Preston.

'Oh yes.' He was matter-of-fact in his manner of delivery, but it was easy to see that Consul Preston had deep feelings. 'For an hour or so each day the Tsar and Tsarina and their daughter come into the courtyard there, for air and exercise. They walk up and down. Imagine – for the Tsar of all the Russias to be so confined!'

'Could you communicate with them?' I demanded. 'Would it be possible?'

178

He shook his head. 'I dare not.'

'Dare!' I said angrily. 'Surely when the cousin of your Sovereign is in such –'

He interrupted me. 'There is much you do not know. Difficult news.'

'In what way?'

Preston sighed: 'British and American troops have made a landing at Archangel. Accordingly, I am now the representative here of a power engaged in acts of war against Russia.'

'At war with Russia!' I could hardly believe my ears. Russia had so long been Britain's ally.

'Not *at* war,' Preston said. 'Though it is a mere technicality, there has in fact been no declaration. None the less my position here in the Urals must now be considered precarious. For myself it hardly matters, of course, but as senior Consul I represent the interests of many residents here, not only British subjects, and I cannot put them further at risk by provocative acts.'

I eyed him angrily, but he put his hand on my sleeve and went on, 'There is a similar view across the street, perhaps a better, from the Purin house. From there the garden can be seen.'

'Where is this house?' I asked him.

It was close by, and owned by a merchant, one Lev Purin.

'Is he loyal to the Tsar?' I demanded.

'He's a banker,' Preston said wryly. 'What is there for him now but loyalty?'

The hand on my sleeve must at last have sensed my trembling, for he now said, 'You are ill?'

'I shall be,' I replied, for by now I was certain of it.

'Aspirin, hot toddy and lemon,' he said, and took me to a sitting-room where a fire burned, even though the evening was a warm one. He made the toddy with whisky and boiling water and as I drank it, Preston told me more of Purin, and remarkable listening it made. For not only did

179

the Purin house offer a better sight of the House of Special Purpose; it had a secret telephone. Purin's wife had a sister who lived elsewhere in the town and the private line ran between the two houses. 'It could be useful to you,' Preston said.

In that way he was helpful; otherwise he was determined he could offer nothing more. I recall arguing with him heatedly about duty, but I was close to collapse by then, and have no true recollection of the detailed conversation.

Soon I left, staggering, barely able to stay upright. I remember little more, save that Ruzsky had waited outside for me: that I babbled out to him the things told to me by Preston, and that twice he cracked his palm across my cheek when I was in danger of sinking to the ground . . .

I woke in a bare room and for a time lay unmoving, eyes closed more than they were open, for merely to raise my eyelids seemed to require an effort beyond my strength. Then, gradually I came to know my surroundings. A white sheet covered me, the walls were white also; there was a window, small and barred and bare of curtains, and I thought for a moment this must be a cell – as indeed it proved to be, though not in a prison. An hour passed, in which I learned the extent of my weakness. To lift my hand or move my head was an impossibility. To move a finger needed willpower. My body seemed without sensation and my mind afloat in emptiness.

I lay for an hour, unconcerned. I learned later this was a product of weakness, for I was weak indeed, weakened almost to death.

At last I heard a door catch, and the movement of harsh fabric, and a woman's voice said in Russian, 'Can you be awake?' I tried to answer, but my mouth was arid and nothing came but a grunt.

Next I saw her face looking down at me. She was a woman of perhaps fifty, her head and shoulders shrouded in the habit of a nun of the Orthodox Church. 'You *are* awake,' she said, and added when I tried to nod, 'No, be still.' She put her hand on my forehead and it felt cool and dry. 'How do you feel – are you thirsty?' My eyelids, heavy as they were, gave her an affirmative and she filled a glass with water and, lifting my head, held it to my lips.

I drank gratefully, and she said, 'Prayer saved you, you know. We all prayed *so* much.'

I thanked her and asked where I was, and learned that this was a convent and that I was still in the city of Ekaterinburg.

The water had moistened my mouth and lips; now I could speak, but weakness lay also in my voice, which emerged as the barest of whispers. 'How did I get here?'

'Your friend brought you. Monsieur Bronard. Oh, so long ago, m'sieu!' She had slipped into French; like so many educated Russians in those days, she must have preferred that language to her own.

'So long ago?' I asked. 'When does that mean?'

'Almost one month,' she said, smiling. 'For almost one whole month you have had us all worried and praying for you.'

A month! 'What is the date?'

'The fourth of June.'

Yet I had returned to the city on May 10th! 'How can it be – what has happened?'

She gave me a smile of great gentleness. 'Pneumonia: first one lung, then the other. Two bouts of severe illness, m'sieu, two long fevers, two crises. Twice you were all but dead. Now you need food, strength.'

The shock was clearing my head now. My mind was no longer content to drift and was instead engaged in speculation as to what might have happened.

'Tell me, *ma sœur*, who holds the city?'

'The Bolsheviks,' she said with tight lips. It was apparent she had little time for them.

'The Whites have not –?'

181

'They advance,' she answered. 'So it is said. But not yet to Ekaterinburg.'

'And the Tsar? Is he –?'

She shushed me then. 'Too much talk, m'sieu. You must rest.'

'Tell me.'

'We must not speak of such things,' she said.

'Is he *alive*?'

She nodded and moved away, murmuring, 'Sleep now, m'sieu.' And I heard the door latch.

My mind would have had me out of bed at once, but my mind was not in control. A few minutes' wakefulness and a sip of water had given me no vitality and indeed I felt, if anything, still weaker. Willy-nilly, sleep took me and when I woke again it was to a shadowed room lit by candles, to the sight of the good sister – and to the smell of food! It was a broth of meat and she placed a stool beside my bed and fed it to me, spoonful by spoonful, as though I were a baby. There was barley in it, I remember, and onion, and in all my life I remember no food so entirely delicious. And more, for as I ate it was possible to feel something positive in my body, an awakening of strength, a movement in the blood. When it was done the nun smiled again and said, 'Soon now you will be strong,' and departed.

Bronard came an hour later, and now I was slipping into sleep, but he would have none of it and pinched my cheek until my eyes opened. Even so, I begged him to leave me, but it could only have been weakness that spoke, for in fact I was desperate for news.

He whispered, 'Don't you want to know?'

'Yes, yes.'

'They're here. The whole family.'

'Where?'

'The Ipatiev House. Still under guard. The others were brought from Tobolsk – the boy and the three Grand Duchesses. Now they're all together.'

'But alive?'

182

'So far,' he said. 'Some of their entourage have been returned to Tobolsk.'

I felt a great sense of relief: the family was together and unharmed. An entire month gone and they remained safe. 'What other news?' I asked.

'One of the servants has been shot,' Bronard said harshly.

'The paper – what of that?' But my strength was ebbing.

'I can hardly hear you,' he said irritably.

'Paper,' I muttered.

'No,' he said impatiently. 'I haven't got it! But we *must* find a way – understand!'

CHAPTER NINE

———————◆———————

The Boy on the
Talking Motor-Cycle

It was not Sir Horace Malory's habit to attend the quarterly dinners of the organization known as UKUS, a society whose members, as the name indicated, came equally from United Kingdom and United States business and banking houses in the City of London. The society's twin purposes were to ease the flow of business between the two nations, and to enable Americans resident in Britain to become acquainted in congenial surroundings with one another and with well-disposed Brits.

By tradition the evenings were boozy: bread rolls were thrown about, speakers hissed, practical jokes played, wagers won and lost.

Malory felt he was a little old for that kind of thing, but he went, for Pilgrim's sake. The man might enjoy it . . .

He didn't though; nor did Malory. A florid actuary sitting across from them at the long table began the trouble.

'Saw you at the Turner auction the other night,' he said jovially to Malory. 'Any idea who bought it?'

'No,' said Malory shortly.

'Lot of cash for a yard of canvas and a smear or two of paint, wouldn't you say?' the actuary went on cheerfully. 'People really do toss their money around. Don't believe in it myself.'

'Nor I.' Malory, disliking this talk, wished the man would shut up. He put on his bumbling-old-duffer manner, 'Lot of damned nonsense. That's what I say. Waste of good money! I say, I was hearing about the Chancellor –'

184

'Funny,' said the actuary with determination. 'I *did* hear Hillyard, Cleef were the buyers.'

'Got more damned sense,' Malory bumbled. 'Hillyard, Cleef! Dear, oh dear. Hear that, Pilgrim?'

Pilgrim laughed harshly. 'Where'd that pile of horseshit come from?'

'And,' added the actuary cheerfully, raising his voice a little and looking around for additional attention, 'that wasn't *all* I heard!'

'If the rest is as puerile as *that*, I should concentrate on the soup,' Malory said. He sipped his own. It was scalding hot.

But the thing was started now. 'The way I heard the story,' said the actuary happily, 'it started very close to the dealer who did the bidding. He said the buyer had to remain anonymous, but it was an Anglo-American banking house –'

'Stuff and nonsense!' said Malory.

'– with a guilty conscience.' The circle of laughter round the actuary widened.

The doddering-old-buffer-manner slid away from Malory's shoulders like a snake's sloughed skin. He could sense now what was coming. He reached across the table, placed his forefinger beneath the rim of the actuary's soup plate, and tipped it into the actuary's lap.

As he said later to an astonished Pilgrim, 'Really it was the only gratifying moment in the whole evening. Nice to see the fella hopping about clutching his trousers, what? You do know what he was going to say, don't you?'

'No.'

Malory gave him a warning glance. 'I'm not going to let the words even pass my lips, my dear chap. Let things like that get out and they take wing.'

They were taking wing even as he spoke. The actuary had a smallish but painful scald in a thoroughly inconvenient place and he was not the kind of man to allow Malory's grey hairs to offer protection against retribution.

From his bathroom, where he sat with a bag of ice in one hand and a telephone in the other, he set about discovering the name of the current Art Critic of *The Times*. This established, he managed finally to reach the man and pass on what he described as 'a rumour, but from well-informed circles'. The man from *The Times* said he was most interested, and certainly he sounded it.

'The City Editor of *The Times* would be grateful for a word with you,' Pilgrim's secretary said brightly, early the following morning.

Pilgrim picked up the telephone. 'What can I do for you, George?'

It turned out not to be George, the City Editor, whom he knew, but one Valentine, the mumble-mumble, whom he didn't.

'Just one question, Mr Pilgrim, really.'

'Go ahead.'

'Is it true you bought the Turner to present it to the nation?'

Pilgrim proceeded to think very rapidly. If his answer were no, the next question would be, 'Then why *did* you buy it?' A 'yes' would cost Hillyard, Cleef three and a half million-plus. 'No comment?' No comment indicated slippery men in dark corners. Pilgrim disliked being rude to reporters. Fashionable theory at the Harvard Business School in his time had dictated that the Press was a friend.

So what he said was: 'You're out of your skull.'

'You mean you didn't buy it to add it to the Turner Bequest?'

'I mean,' Pilgrim lied crossly, 'that *we* didn't buy it. That clear?'

'Perfectly,' said Valentine, 'and thank you. Oh, Mr Pilgrim –'

'You said one question.'

'I thought you'd like to know that this story has very wide

186

currency. They were even talking about it in the bar at the House of Commons last night.'

'I see.' Pilgrim ground out a laugh. 'Wonder who's spreading this junk around? Thanks for the tip.'

'So you'll get a lot of enquiries. I should be careful with your answers.'

Pilgrim hung up. On the blotter before him lay the telex from Pepe Robizo confirming that purchase-plus-ten was acceptable.

Pilgrim winced: He now appreciated the truth of Malory's observation of the previous evening: the idea *was* out and was indeed taking wing. As a result, forces would be gathering. Hillyard, Cleef might be compelled to give away the Turner. And he, Pilgrim, *had* promised it to Pepe Robizo of all people. The thought made his back feel chill with sweat. That was like snatching its dinner away from a tiger.

Time for confession, then. Malory was the adviser; let him advise.

To his surprise, Malory appeared quite unconcerned about Robizo but was grimly angry that the story was all over London. 'It's plain malice,' he muttered. 'That oily little mongrel Sudbury's behind it – can't be anybody else.'

'We can't prove it.'

'Of course we can't. Whole point, isn't it! Fault's yours, Laurence, if I may say so. Fellas like that, they think they have a licence to bore you to death, as well as rob you. But you told him to get a move on. It's wounded vanity.'

'It's going to be all over the papers.'

'Flat denials. It's the only way,' said Malory firmly. 'If we answer no long enough, it will all go away.'

But it stayed. A photograph had somehow been taken on the pavement outside the auction room as Malory and his security men placed the crate in the armoured van. That night the picture was all over the front page of the *Standard*, the remaining London evening paper, along with a report of Pilgrim's denial.

'It's a *lovely* likeness! Sir Horace,' Mrs Frobisher re-

marked as she brought the newspaper into Malory's office.
And it was.

Malory, knowing now what was coming, diverted himself for a while by playing a game he rather thought he
could win. If Pilgrim's dangerous millionaire Robizo really
was a man of strong social ambition, then Robizo was
vulnerable; such people always were. It was, after all,
simple enough: Robizo was not currently acceptable to a
few people whose society he craved. Not the rich: Robizo
was rich, so the rich *would* accept him. It was therefore the
aristocratic, the old money. And in Florida that meant . . .
Malory smiled. There was always someone. And in this
case there was old Digby's daughter, wasn't there – Ran-
dolph's first wife! Pretty thing, too: Malory remembered
the wartime wedding at Admiralty House, even the little
silk Persian prayer rug he'd given them. Daughter of one
aristo, bearer of the great name of the century, and now
married to God! All he needed was somebody in regular
touch. After all, it wasn't a question of inviting this Robizo
creature to dinner; just some charity reception or other and
a large donation plus a shake of the Harriman hand. Yes,
she could certainly be asked. Malory was quite busy for a
while on the telephone. At last a lady promised to talk to
Clarissa, who'd talk to Digby's daughter. Something would
certainly be arranged.

In spite of this pleasing little triumph, however, the next
few days were not happy ones for anyone except the Press.
They, however, loved it! Some targets are far more satisfying to strike at than others, and very high on that list are
banks. Then come greedy oil companies, profligate local
authorities and corrupt clergymen. The Bank with the
Golden Hoard got it very firmly in the neck. The louder the
denials, the less they were heeded:–

'Sir Horace Malory' [wrote a gentleman in the *Sunday
Express*], 'has spent most of his seventy-eight years

making mountains of money. He has a mansion in Gloucestershire, a town house in Mayfair and several million in the bank. Wouldn't it be nice if he devoted some of his filthy lucre to a good clean purpose and added the Turner masterpiece to Britain's great heritage of art treasures!'

'You can't take it with you, Sir Horace . . .'

'I'm not going,' Malory muttered savagely. 'Not yet, anyway.' He and Pilgrim, both by now feeling somewhat beleaguered, sat in Pilgrim's teak and steel office.

'Can't be Dikeston doing it,' Pilgrim said. 'You can't play Press campaigns from the grave.'

'No, no, no. It's the Sudbury chap,' Malory said.

'It's so damned *unfair*!' Pilgrim went on. 'We buy a painting – what the hell's wrong with buying a painting? Now we have to give it away – we can't even sell it!'

'Clever, though,' said Malory. 'You'll admit it's clever.'

Pilgrim gave him a long, hard look. He thumped both hands palm down on the desk and said with new determination, 'We're going to fight back, Horace. We have to. We start off with hundreds, it goes to thousands, then to hundreds of thousands – and now it's goddam *millions*! The next stage is tens of millions and after *that* it's hundreds and we're wiped out! How in hell did Dikeston get this thing going?'

'He had fifty thousand a year and a lot of time to think and plan,' Malory said. 'And at the moment, if I may remind you, we have no idea *at all* where the next packet of Dikeston's papers will be coming from. There were no instructions with the last batch.'

Pilgrim said, 'Look, we don't need the papers. We *know* what happened to the Romanovs. They were shot in a cellar in Ekaterinburg, right?'

'So it's said,' Malory said, scepticism in his voice.

'You don't believe it.'

189

'It's problematical, Laurence. Some would disagree. There's a book I'll lend you –'

'I've read the damn books. The Reds shot the whole family.'

'And so?'

'So what's to worry about?'

'We worry about the paper,' Malory said. 'To Zaharoff the secret of that paper was worth a fortune. Remember his choice of word. He warns of calamity.'

Again Pilgrim's flat hand thumped the desk. 'Calamity! The only calamity I see lies in carrying on round this obstacle course Dikeston set. He's got us paying on a geometrical progression. It'll ruin us!' He stood straight and fixed Malory with a hard eye. 'We come back to Zaharoff, don't we? Always back to him. Why does he matter so much? You knew him, Horace; you held him in high regard. You –'

'No.' Malory held up a hand to stop him. 'You're wrong, quite wrong.'

'What do you mean?'

'I held him in *awe*. I was terrified of him, Laurence!'

'I thought you liked the guy.'

'Like?' Malory gave what might have been a snort of amusement. 'I do not believe there was a man on earth who liked Basil Zaharoff. Not one. And only one woman. Respected, oh *yes*! – he was respected! He was feared, and with reason. He was listened to, he was courted as an ally. But not as a friend, I think.'

'Yet *you* still think his word is holy writ?'

'If you like.' Malory paused and pursed his lips. 'Tell me, have you ever played a ball game of any kind against a really good player?'

'A little squash once,' Pilgrim said, with a touch of pride. 'I had a knock-up once at the New York Racquet Club with Hashim Khan.'

'Then let me tell you what it was you noticed. First, he hit the ball both much harder and much straighter than you.

190

Secondly, he did not make mistakes. Thirdly, he could keep going at a very high level of performance far longer than you could. Agreed?'

'Oh, sure.' Pilgrim was smiling now at the recollection. 'But you left one out.'

'What's that?'

'Positional play. Anticipation, if you like. He was there and ready with the answer while you were still trying to set the question –' Pilgrim broke off, abruptly comprehending.

Malory said, 'Precisely. All these things are games. Zaharoff's game was power, and he played it supremely well.'

Pilgrim crossed to the window and stood looking out. 'I realize you're convinced of it all, Horace. You know I'm not. Could you convince *me*?'

'Yes, I think I could.'

'I'm going to ask you to do it right now,' Pilgrim said. 'But first . . .' He pressed a button on his intercom and said, 'Come in, would you, Jacques.'

Graves came in immediately. 'What I want, Jacques,' Pilgrim said, 'and I'm afraid it will probably be one hell of a job, is a complete list of all regular payments made by Hillyard, Cleef which are or even *may be* pension payments. Up to and including – what year did Zaharoff die, Horace?'

'Nineteen thirty-six.'

'Okay, from, say, nineteen-fourteen to nineteen-thirty-six. Right?'

'Right.'

As Graves departed, Pilgrim settled into his chair. 'Convince me.'

'Have you ever been to Monte?' Malory enquired.

'Monte Carlo? Yes.'

'Did you visit the Casino?'

'Yes.'

'And play?'

'No, not me.'

191

'Nowadays, of course,' Malory said musingly, 'it's not what it was. There are casinos everywhere, even –' and his lip bent in distaste – 'here in London. But there was a time, Laurence, when Las Vegas did not exist, nor casinos in London and other cities. Rich men and women who wanted to play chemin de fer or roulette had to go to Monte. Know anything, do you, about Monaco's status?'

'It's a principality, isn't it? – What's the guy's name? Rainier?'

'The family name is Grimaldi. Hereditary rulers. Have been for centuries. Keep them in mind, will you, my dear chap, while I tell you something of Sir Basil. Oh – and the lady I believe I mentioned – she *must* have liked him. She waited forty years to marry him.

'Zaharoff was born in any number of places, and born poor in all of them, or so he said at different times. But effectively he started off in Constantinople as a fireman, of all things – this is the eighteen-sixties, mind, when fire brigades were perhaps a little less, er, technically minded than they are these days. Those chappies used to start a fire, then run round with their axes and chop their way into the surrounding property and see what was portable. You understand?

'He was Greek, Zaharoff was, and this was Turkey, with scrapping going on all over the place. He began to sell arms. Sold more and more. Worked for Nordenfelt, then heard about Maxim's new machine-gun, forced a merger between 'em and became the salesman for Maxim, Nordenfelt. And when I say salesman, as I'm sure you understand, Laurence, I do *not* mean that he drove a little Ford motor-car and made fifteen calls per day.'

Pilgrim smiled. 'What did he drive?'

Malory smiled back. 'Hard bargains. Took his commission, of course. Then came the day he sold a submarine for Vickers, I *think* it was to Queen Marie of Roumania, and rumour had it the deal was done *à deux*. Heard of Queen Marie, have you? Quite a lady *she* was! Well, never mind.

192

Zaharoff quickly became Vickers' top figure. He was only a director, one among many, not chairman or anything, but his will determined everything. He started wars, armed both sides, that kind of thing. Kept the Balkans boiling for decades. When you talk about anticipation, mark this – no sooner had the Wright Brothers flown at Kittyhawk than Zaharoff set up chairs in aviation at three universities: Oxford, Paris and St Petersburg. There was a fella called Constantinescu who devised the gear which enabled machine-guns to fire through rotating propellers. He was Basil's, I seem to remember.

'But meantime, he fell in love. Oh yes, Zaharoff fell. Here comes the lady: Spanish grandee, Duchess of Villafranca and much else besides. Married to a madman, the Duchess was, and powerfully Papist into the bargain, so – well, there couldn't be a divorce. Had to wait for the Grim Reaper. So they waited: forty-three years, I think it was. Then the Duke died and they got married. Are you still listening?'

'You have my attention, Horace, believe me.'

'So here's our poor boy from the slums of Constantinople. He's now among the richest men in the world and his wife is a duchess. Lloyd George, meantime, has given Basil a knighthood. He's quite the grandee himself. All he lacks is a kingdom to lay at the feet of his bride.

'Now, consider Monaco. For three hundred years, from the time of the Treaty of Peronne in 1641 Monaco has been part of France. The Grimaldi prince has no true sovereignty and what's more, he has a French garrison quartered on him just in case he turns ambitious. But there were one or two things he could still do, and in 1862 he granted to a man named Blanc a concession to open a casino in Monte Carlo. Blanc was clever and also had a son who was *very* clever; so, before you could say Athelsgate, the place was coining money. So much that the whole of Monaco lived on it, from the prince downward. No taxes. Police, judges, public works, all were paid for. As an arrangement,' Malory said admiringly, 'it was quite lovely! But then came the war.'

'Which war?'

'Ah. Nineteen-fourteen. Am I boring you, Laurence?'

'Not yet.'

'Well, with the war going strong, business dwindled. For poor Monsieur Blanc, that is, not for Zaharoff – as you might imagine. *He* had a small commission on many of the bullets, most of the shells and almost all the guns. But with business going down in the casino, down went the income of the current Grimaldi prince, who didn't much like it, and therefore made an approach – quietly, of course, to Zaharoff. What it amounted to was that in due course, given a secret option to purchase, Zaharoff would be able to throw out Blanc and his sons and sons-in-law, one of whom was a Buonoparte, by the way, and the other a Radziwill. Sure you're not getting *lost* in all this, Laurence?'

'I'm waiting for the fish hook.'

Malory smiled. 'Soon, soon. One further point to remember is the long relationship that existed, on the very closest terms, between the French premier Georges Clemenceau and Zaharoff. Forgive me if I sound like a schoolmaster, will you?'

'Go *on*, Horace!'

'What happened – and this in the middle of the greatest war in history – was that Clemenceau suddenly concluded a treaty – a treaty which was kept absolutely secret! – with Monaco's Prince. Under its terms Monaco was to be a sovereign principality again. The treaty was never published, I might tell you, not as such. But the terms did turn up eventually, in the small print of the Versailles Treaty, where it was damned hard to find.

'After that,' said Malory, 'it was easy. Zaharoff paid a million for the Casino and so he became the true ruler of Monaco.'

'Smart,' said Pilgrim.

'Yes, that's a fair word.'

'He was quite an operator.'

'He was indeed. Are you conv – *Good gracious me*!'
Malory sat as though pole-axed, mouth agape, eyes staring.

Pilgrim came quickly out of his chair, wondering if the old man might not be having some kind of seizure. 'You okay, Horace?'

Malory frowned at him. 'Eh?'

'You all right?'

'All right? Oh yes. But damned puzzled.'

'By what?'

'The date of the Treaty between France and Monaco – between Clemenceau and Grimaldi. I've just realized what it was!'

'And?'

'Basil got his kingdom on July 17th, 1918.'

'Christ,' Pilgrim breathed. 'I know that date, too. That's the day they shot the Tsar!'

The cheque, signed by Pilgrim and by Malory, and delivered by Malory when he made his well-documented visit to collect the painting, had now been paid into the auctioneer's bank. Another cheque, drawn by the financial director of the auction house, was sent to Coutts & Co., bankers to Royalty – and to the anonymous seller of the Turner. This cheque was for £2,925,000, a sum arrived at by deducting ten per cent from the auction price of three and a quarter million. The ten per cent represented what was termed 'Seller's Premium'. Hillyard, Cleef had already paid a ten per cent *Buyer's* Premium. The auctioneers had therefore cleared £650,000 and were pleased to act with reasonable expedition. They did not, as was their normal practice, keep the money for a month to earn interest at money market terms; the cheque was sent in a very few days.

Mr Everard Polly, the official at Coutts & Co. entrusted with all matters concerned with removal of the Turner from its vault and its subsequent sale, now proceeded to ensure rapid clearance of the auctioneers' cheque, and then consulted the instructions deposited at the bank by their deceased client. The final passage read:

> . . . upon receipt of the monies raised at sale by auction, Envelope Five shall be forwarded to Messrs Dazey, Cheyne & Co., solicitors, of 199 Chancery Lane, London.

Mr Polly was enormously intrigued. He had been with Coutts & Co., for more than forty years and this was infinitely the most . . . he had difficulty finding the word . . . *flavoursome* transaction he had been involved with. Yes, flavoursome. A great painting in the vaults, a price of millions, everything done in great secrecy. Oh yes, *flavoursome!* It was with some regret that he summoned one of the bank's messengers and told him to deliver Envelope Three at once, because Mr Polly knew that with that action his own involvement ended. It was a shame that he would never know . . .

The messenger from Coutts took a taxi. It was not very far from the Strand to Chancery Lane, and as it was a pleasant morning he could easily have walked, but he had gathered from Mr Polly's expression and manner that there must be something rather special about the wax-sealed manilla envelope with the large Roman V upon it which now rested in his document case. He decided that, having delivered the envelope, he would walk back through Lincoln's Inn Fields. With luck the girls would be playing netball, and he could pause at the new wine bar . . .

He handed the envelope to Mr Redvers Pratt, chief clerk of Dazey, Cheyne, who said, 'Right, thanks, who's it from?'

''Fraid I can't tell you.'

Mr Pratt frowned. 'Don't be daft. It must be from somebody.'

'Bound to be,' said the messenger, 'but I don't know who. My job to deliver, that's all.'

'Oh.' Mr Pratt looked at it and smiled. 'Bomb, could it be, d'you reckon?'

'Too thin.'

'Hope you're right. Thanks.'

As the messenger left Mr Pratt broke the seal. Inside lay a further envelope and, paperclipped to it, a single sheet of paper upon which was written, 'To be delivered at once to the Senior Partner, Hillyard, Cleef, at 6, Athelsgate, E. C.'

Unlike Mr Polly, Mr Pratt was only mildly and momentarily interested. The passing on of papers was part of his job, and he simply took a small pride in doing it efficiently. As the postal service declined, Mr Pratt had searched for replacement means and had recently taken to using a firm which had given itself an extremely unlikely name.

'Suzuki Highway,' said the girl's Cockney voice on the telephone, when he rang up.

Said Redvers Pratt: 'This is Dazey, Cheyne, solicitors, of 199 Chancery –'

'Piss orf, darlin, why doncha?' The girl said amiably. 'Don't waste me bloody time –'

'We're customers,' said Pratt patiently. 'Look up the account like a good girl. We all know it's a funny name. Dazey, –'

'Cheyne. Yer, Gorrit. Orl right, I'll have a Crimson Suzuki with you in a minute, okay? Who's he ask for?'

'Mr Pratt.'

She laughed. 'By name if not by nature, eh?' And hung up. Pratt, too, was smiling. He was an East Ender himself and enjoyed his occasional contacts with the native sharpness.

Several Crimson Suzuki motor-cycles were at that moment delivering packages and letters in various parts of the metropolis. Several more, parked in assorted places, awaited the call. It came always by radio.

197

Crimson Suzuki 7 stood at that moment outside a Macdonald's Hamburger palace in Shaftesbury Avenue. Its driver-owner, one Dave Legg, dressed in leathers of surpassing griminess, had just purchased a Big Mac and a large Coca-Cola and was settling himself comfortably on the saddle when the loudspeaker behind him squawked suddenly.

He swore, bent, placed the Coke on the pavement, and picked up the hand-microphone in his gauntleted free hand. 'Yer?' he said.

'Where are you?'

He told her.

'Outside MacDonald's again, aincher,' she said. 'Listen, go to 199 Chancery Lane, right? 'Ere you'll get fat, you will.'

Dave Legg, in replacing the mike, kicked over the Coke. He swore again. Goo from the Big Mac was dribbling down his leather gauntlet. He licked it off, crammed half the hamburger into his capacious mouth, kicked the starter, and carved up an approaching taxi as he roared through the traffic stream.

Redvers Pratt greeted him pleasantly a few minutes later. Mr Pratt liked to think of himself as a student of contrasting human behaviour, and it was fascinating to think of this grubby thug entering the refined portals of 6 Athelsgate.

'This envelope is for the Senior Partner,' Mr Pratt told Dave Legg. 'Don't give it to anyone else, okay? No secretaries – him personally.'

''Sis 'andle?' said Legg.

'What? Oh, his *name*? He's Mr Pilgrim, you got that? Pilgrim. Six Athelsgate, that's in the City.'

'Do me a fiver, mate?' said Dave Legg mysteriously. He pulled a Mars bar from his jacket and departed, leaving the wrapper on the floor.

Seven minutes later he faced Sir Horace Malory. Already he had defied the doorkeeper, two junior employees more than willing to accept the envelope, and Pilgrim's secretary.

'It's only for this Senior Partner geezer,' Dave Legg insisted. 'Swarree said. No secketries, nobody!'

Malory smiled. 'I'm the *other* Senior Partner, Sir Horace Malory. You may safely leave it with me.' He could recognize the envelope, even with most of it half-concealed in Dave Legg's greasy gauntlet.

'Pilgrim, swarree sed. Mr Pilgrim, nobody else!'

'Oh, *really!*' Mrs Frobisher came close to stamping her foot. 'Sir Horace is –'

"E ain't this geezer Pilgrim,' Dave Legg said stoutly, and turned to Malory. 'Are you, squire?'

'Er, no.' Malory held up his hand. 'Where have you come from?'

'199 Chancery Lane.'

'Oh, I see. Dazey, Cheyne.'

'Dunno what they play, squire,' said Legg with a grin.

Malory, possessed by now of twin ambitions: to strangle this ghastly lout, and to get his hands on Dikeston's narrative, more or less in that order, was still able to force a smile. 'Perhaps if we telephone them and explain that Mr Pilgrim is out – perhaps from *them* you would accept different instructions?'

'Yus, mate,' said Dave Legg.

Mrs Frobisher telephoned Mr Redvers Pratt and then handed the receiver to Dave Legg with her fingertips. She rather thought he wasn't very *clean*.

'Geezer ere says 'e's – worrizit?'

'Malory,' Sir Horace said softly.

'Yer, Malory. Okay is it? Right, squire.'

He hung up, turned to Malory and held out the envelope. 'All yours, mate.'

'Thank you,' said Malory. 'Very much.'

CHAPTER TEN

———————◆———————

Fifth instalment of the account, written by
Lt-Cdr H. G. Dikeston RN, of his journeyings
in Russia in the spring and summer of 1918.

I mend quickly, or at any rate my body does. As my mother used to say, there is a good healing flesh in the family. But in 1918 in Ekaterinburg it seemed too slow. On the second day on which I woke I thought with a sharp pang of the precious paper I had brought from Tobolsk and became desperate as, too weak to move, I lay wondering what might have become of it.

When the nun appeared again in the whitewashed chamber, and as she fed me more of some nourishing broth, I asked, 'Where are my clothes?' and heard the weak whisper of my voice.

She smiled. 'Safe. And clean, moreover, which they were *not* when you arrived.'

I whispered. 'Sister, this is important –'

She interrupted me. 'First the broth. It is that which is important.' And she refused to listen until the bowl was empty. 'Now?'

'In my pocket,' I told her weakly, 'are papers which matter greatly to me. Tell me, please, if –'

She raised a hand. 'Save your strength. I will go and see.'

She was back two or three minutes later. She carried a paper bag and as she sat beside my bed, I saw she was frowning with some severity.

'Here are your things.'

'Paper,' I muttered. 'In a stiff white envelope. Is it –?'

She peered into the bag, then put her hand inside. 'This?' she asked, drawing it forth.

It was no longer so white, nor so pristine. In my immersion, water had reached and stained it, but I would have known that envelope anywhere. I let out a sigh of relief.

The sister now said, 'You are a wealthy man?'

'No!'

The frown remained on her face, despite the gentleness of her tone and manner.

I whispered, 'Why do you ask?'

'Because there are jewels here, and trinkets. They must be valuable, and they must have been in your pockets when you were brought here.'

I had not remembered until that moment, but I remembered now, at once, my shameful behaviour on steamer *Rus*. Oh God, I thought, how can I explain?'

But one forgets that true goodness lies in simplicity. Even as I was about to tell her the matter was secret, she said, 'I am so afraid they may be mislaid.'

'Place the envelope beneath my pillow, please, Sister.'

So she did, and it was there when Bronard came again. I had strengthened a little in the course of the day and listened to him with interest. The essence of what he had to say was that little had changed in the long month of my illness. The Imperial Family was reunited, but imprisoned together in the Ipatiev House and impossible of access. On the Urals Soviet there were some, possibly a majority, in favour of a violent end to all the Romanovs. 'It's not enough just to have them off the Russian throne,' Bronard quoted Goloshchokin as saying. 'We must have them under the Russian ground!'

Bronard, with his catspaw Scriabin, was engaged with the opposite view. Scriabin was, it seemed, having the same difficulty experienced by so many in dealing with the Soviets since. For even then they were men who spoke with a lofty moral tone and sought only blood. Scriabin, arguing for the justice of a properly-conducted trial, a man making a genuinely moral stand, found his was a very lonely voice.

Bronard, meanwhile, was weaseling. He was *for* blood, he told them. Nicholas must pay with his life; furthermore,

201

the entire family shared his guilt and they too must pay. 'But *not*, I keep telling them,' he said, 'unless it can be presented as Socialist justice.' He grinned that loathsome grin of his. 'You should hear me, Comrade! I yell for blood, and then I say that we must not besmirch the name of Socialism with murder, however justified. I say that Scriabin is right, but right for the wrong reasons. That what we must show is not mercy but determination and we must show it to the world! How can we contemplate, I ask them, emulating the despotic lawlessness of Imperial Russia?'

When he had gone I lay flexing my wasted muscles in an endeavour to exercise them, conscious all the time of the paper beneath the pillow, of the jewellery I had stolen which lay with it, and of the rightful owners, who slept no more than a mile or two away and over whom the shadow of doom now stretched. It was clear that, for whatever reason, the new leaders of the Russian nation had made no move in the last month to extend mercy to the Romanovs.

I said: 'My clothes, Sister, if you please.'

'Nonsense! You're far too weak.'

'I have the most urgent business. I insist – my clothes! And if you can get one, a taxi, or a cart even, to the station!'

'But you can't travel. Not in your –'

'I must!'

I browbeat her at last into aiding me – for dressing took more strength than I had imagined. My head was light and I had little sense of balance. When I stood upright I wavered and almost fell several times, but in the end I was walking slowly, leaning upon a stick the sister gave me, out to a cart which waited in the yard of the convent. The back was filled with clean straw, upon which I reclined in no little comfort and directed the driver to take me to the house of Preston, the British Consul, in Vosnesensky Avenue. On the way, I naturally had to pass the so-called House of Special Purpose where the Imperial Family was incarcerated, and the mere sight of it, allied to the thought of the humble

202

circumstances to which a great monarch had been reduced, made me yet more determined upon my journey, foolish or no.

Preston, in the miserable manner of British diplomats abroad, made endless fuss about the advance of funds. Though he knew who I was and my purpose in the city, when the matter was raised of handing cash to me, I might have been the direst criminal. At last, losing patience, I said, 'Your trade, Preston?'

He gave me a vinegary look. 'I am not *in* trade, sir!'

'Your work, then? Your qualification, if such you have?'

He was in Ekaterinburg for the mining, like everyone else. It was silver and copper and platinum that had brought Preston to the Urals, and on that basis, I handed him an item taken from the *Rus*: a single ruby close to half an inch across in a platinum setting. 'Hold that against two hundred pounds,' I said.

'Is it yours?'

'Damn your impudence,' I said, 'and damn your caution, too. There are more important things afoot than provenance and collateral. You want a signature?'

He did, of course. His kind always do. But fortunately his kind always have money about somewhere and at last he advanced me sovereigns, a hundred and fifty of them.

The cart now took me to the station, and that place must not be omitted from any narrative concerning Ekaterinburg, for there was nothing there of equality, nothing of to-each-according-to-his-need. If you could pay you could feast, otherwise you starved. I went to the old first-class restaurant, expecting some cloth-capped commissar to deny me entry and preach me a sermon into the bargain; instead I found a head waiter in tails, a string trio and a menu two feet long. It was an extraordinary sight. Here were rough-looking men eating with their hats on, drinking spirits until they fell off their chairs. And shrieking women, too. I saw Beloboradov, even, the chairman of the Soviet, snapping his fingers for a waiter and shouting for champagne. It remained a luxury restaurant. Missing now was *ton*.

I ate quietly, my back turned to the room. I needed but had no appetite for food and left as soon as I had finished to seek accommodation on the next westbound train, only to discover that, as in the restaurant, gold spoke authoritatively. No third-class this time: I had a room for two to myself *and* assurances of privacy!

The journey took three days and there could hardly have been a better convalescence. I started out weak as a kitten, and came finally into Moscow rested and revived, as nearly filled with strength as I was with determination. And in the ensuing days I was to need a plentiful supply of both, for I was entering into a period of the most intense frustration, which indeed began at once!

All I needed was sealing wax and matches and matches I had already; but sealing wax was impossible to find. I tramped Moscow from shop to shop, asked in post offices, stationers, anywhere I could think of, but it was near nightfall before a counter clerk in the Finland Bank said he was sure they had some somewhere, went away, and came back not with a stick of the stuff, but with an unopened box of a gross! I almost fell upon his neck in gratitude. Instead I sealed my precious letter with copious quantities of wax, marked it with my initials in several places, and asked the fellow:

'Are you a Finn?'

'We all are, sir.'

Well, I thought, there would be no guaranteeing Lenin's behaviour, or Trotsky's – they'd eat Finland for breakfast if they felt like it. But perhaps they wouldn't and you can usually trust a Finn. They can be wild men, but they're pretty honest, too. I held up the envelope. 'This must be kept secure. You have a vault?'

'Yes, sir.'

'And how much interference from the authorities?'

'Very little, sir.'

'You could keep it for me?'

'With pleasure, sir.'

It was done without receipt, but upon a signature – Henry George was the name I used – a sovereign changed hands by way of fee in advance, and I took myself off to the Kremlin in a taxi. As I alighted at the tunnel arch that led through the wall beneath the Spassky Tower, it was immediately apparent that much had changed in the weeks since last I came to the ancient fortress. Then, a levelled machine-gun had greeted me: now it was two Red Army soldiers in smart uniforms, rigid at attention. Neither took the smallest notice of me, but none the less it was only a moment before a corporal was barking at me, yelling to know my business.

'Is Comrade Sverdlov still in the Kavalersky Building?' I demanded of him.

'Who wishes to know?'

'Convey to him,' I said, 'that Dikeston the Englishman has returned to Moscow and wishes to see him.'

'Many people wish to see him.'

'Convey it. And quickly.'

But nothing was quick. That was another thing much changed; for a cold formality had fallen here, and an army of clerks ruled. I was passed from t'other to each quick enough, but made no apparent progress towards my objective; the universal notion was to be rid of me, rather than to assist, but where in the modern world is it not?

I was back next morning, having spent the night in a rooming-house that had, until recently, been a lavish private dwelling. It had also been looted, so that though the heavy bed itself was of elaborate gilt, there was no linen and the single blanket was of the roughest. Still, it was clean and free of bugs. I returned early to the Kremlin and began again the curious quadrille with endless petty officials. By two in the afternoon I had reached a waiting-room. It was crowded; a clerk sat at a desk inside the

205

doorway and examined the chit which had brought me thus far; he scowled up at me.

'What does this concern?'

'Comrade Sverdlov knows.'

'He's very busy.'

'He sent me upon a task of some importance. Do not prevent my giving my report!'

He scowled further. Prevention was his chosen career. 'You may give your report to me!'

'Have a care,' I told him, 'or my report will be *about* you!'

He gestured angrily towards the waiting people, indicating that I should take my place among them, and I did so. The chairs were hard, the atmosphere sticky with heat, and there was no refreshment. It was hardly a pleasant wait, but at seven in the evening a door was opened with great obsequiousness, and one of the clerks said, 'Comrade Minister, please to receive Commander Dikeston.'

I entered and he fixed me with a fierce eye. 'What the devil do *you* want?'

I was angry, no doubt of it, and spoke too sharply for one in my position addressing one in his. 'Sense,' I said. 'That's what I want! Do you know where it's to be found?'

He was taken aback, no mistake, and we glowered at each other for a moment or two. It would have surprised me not at all to be arrested then and there, but after a moment he laughed and shouted suddenly, 'There's damned little of it here, you're right!' He gave me a tight grin then, and said, 'Could you stand a drink?'

I nodded and a second later had a half-tumbler of slivovitz thrust into my hand. Sverdlov lifted his glass in a silent toast, and drained it. I followed suit as is required in courtesy and, feeling the spirit bite at my innards, decided I must take my chance quickly before my senses began to reel. I said, 'You gave me a job and stopped me doing it.'

'You didn't do it then? The Zaharoff paper's unsigned?'

206

'That's right – it's unsigned.'

'Why? You had plenty of time.'

'Why!' I said. 'Because you arrested me and locked up Nicholas! That's *why*!'

'The Regional Soviet did it.'

'On whose orders?' I demanded. 'On whose orders was I turned back at Omsk? Tell me that!'

He frowned at me, then again gave that tight grin. 'Where is your paper?'

'With Nicholas. If he's still alive.'

'What do you mean – still alive?'

'There's a majority in Ekaterinburg in favour of killing him.'

Sverdlov gave a tiny shake of the head. 'Don't worry,' he's safe.'

'Is he?' I said. 'Among the wild men you can't control? You gave me a pass, remember. They spat on the pass. Spat at your name. Spat at Lenin's, even!'

'Nevertheless, they are safe – the Romanovs.'

'How do you know?'

'Because I know.' He spoke softly now, his tone intense. I had gone too far and he was making it clear.

I said, 'I'm relieved to hear it.'

He gave me a glare. 'Relieved! Why are you relieved?'

'Because the thought of the murder of children is offensive to any man.'

'They are Romanovs. Their history is of blood. You wouldn't understand!'

'There are four girls, a sick boy –'

'And Nicholas the Bloody and his German bitch!'

I said, 'Are the arms still important?'

He stared across the desk at me, picked up the bottle. 'More?'

'Thank you, no, if you will excuse me. I have been ill.'

Sverdlov poured into his own glass, said, 'To your health,' and drained it. 'Arms are important if you need them.'

207

'And do you not need them,' I asked, 'against the Whites and the Czechs in Siberia?'

'Perhaps more here.' he said. Then he rose and stretched. 'I'm tired, Englishman. Come and see me tomorrow, eh? At noon.'

'If your clerks will let me,' I said sourly.

He laughed then, and scribbled quickly upon a slip of paper. 'My name may not count for much in Siberia,' he said, and laughed again. 'But here it should be effective.'

I left him, feeling somewhat puzzled. In many ways the things he had said had confirmed my own hypothesis: that the Romanovs were imprisoned in Ekaterinburg for the very good reason that that was where the Moscow Bolshevik leadership wanted them. That reason and no other. But why then was Sverdlov treating me with reasonable courtesy? I knew of his involvement, and of Lenin's. If aught were to go awry, that knowledge would besmirch both their names. I was better out of the way, yet he was taking trouble to reassure me, and to give me his time . . .

And it continued next day. When I was shown in, Sverdlov waved me to a seat beside his desk and pushed a paper across to me. It was headed 'Signal' and addressed to one General Jan Berzin, Ekaterinburg Military HQ. It read:

Report at once condition of Romanov family now confined your district. Your personal assurance of their well-being urgently required.

V. I. Lenin.

'Yesterday's date, you'll notice,' Sverdlov said.

'And the answer?'

'Is awaited. Sit and drink some tea.'

I stepped to the samovar to prepare my glass of tea, and was required to make one also for him. As I placed it before him, he held up a newspaper. 'This is why.'

The paper was *Trud*, I remember, and the item said

208

Nicholas Romanov had been shot by Red Army men in a train as he was leaving Ekaterinburg.

'You're sure it's untrue?' I asked.

'We'll know soon for certain,' he said. 'The papers are full of these irresponsibilities. We'll have to learn to control the Press.'

An hour and a half later a message was brought in and placed upon his desk. Sverdlov read it and laughed. 'Here you are.' He handed it to me.

Military Telegram, to Moscow CEC from Ekaterinburg HQ.

Have visited Romanov family in detention this city. All are in good health. Premises secure, medical supervision available, rations more than adequate.

Jan Berzin, general, Red Army

'Satisfied?' said Sverdlov.

'They're not my affair. All I want is my document.'

'You should have made him sign it, my friend.'

'Made him?'

'A pistol at the head achieves miracles, I assure you.'

I said, 'Is that how you made him endorse the Brest-Litovsk treaty?'

'Nicholas didn't endorse –' he glanced at me, and then laughed yet again. 'All right, all right. But I have no time, not now. Just be assured: nothing will change for a while. If the Romanovs are brought to Moscow, you will be given access. Fair?'

I nodded and he picked up a bell on his desk and rang it. A secretary entered, a woman, attractive and dressed in sober black. He told her: 'This is an Englishman, Nadezhda. I can't even pronounce his name. Make arrangements to keep him informed on the Romanov question.'

'Yes, Comrade Minister.'

He rose and offered me his land. 'Why did Nicholas not sign?'

'I think he is wary,' I said.

209

'Not soon enough,' said Yankel Sverdlov. 'He should have been wary long ago. Of Kaiser Wilhelm, of Rasputin, of his wife. Goodbye, Comrade.' He held out his hand.

'Goodbye, sir.'

'Not "sir". Say "comrade".'

'I'm English. We address our superiors as "sir".'

'Superior?' he said. 'To an Englishman! None of you will ever believe it!' He gave me an amiable clap on the shoulder and I left.

'Now,' the woman's voice said crisply beside me, 'as to the arrangements. Do you require a report daily?'

'I don't require it, though it would be useful.'

She nodded. 'Very well. Here is my office. You should come to it as necessary.'

I thanked her and left. It was an extraordinary situation. If the Tsar had the paper, then from Sverdlov's own point of view, all that was necessary was to send me back to the Urals with instructions to General Berzin that I was to be admitted to the royal presence. Berzin apparently did not have difficulties.

That way, assuming the recommended pistol-at-the-head method to be successful, I could be back in Moscow in a week with the key to releasing to the Soviets a vast quantity of arms, all of which must be sorely needed.

Why, then, was I being held in waiting? Personal kindness and daily information from one of his secretaries – it appeared to be generous, but in reality gave nothing. If his aim was to keep me quietly in Moscow, he would achieve it – and lose the chance of the arms. Didn't they want them? Could a new regime, embattled on many fronts, really afford to ignore a mountain of available war material?

Or, I thought suddenly, was something else more important?

The Germans, for instance. For their army was in easy striking distance of Moscow!

CHAPTER ELEVEN

❖

Visit to a Black Widow

Malory's tame Oxford historian had produced, at Sir Horace's request, and upon two sheets of foolscap, a kind of timetable of known events concerning the Romanov family and the city of Ekaterinburg in May, June and July of 1918. Coming to the end of Dikeston's narrative, with its reference to the Germans, Malory reached for the foolscap list and ran his eye down it. 'Germans, bloody Germans . . .?' he murmured quietly to himself. They'd be there, they always were. What was it Churchill had said: They're either at your feet or at your throat. He smiled in quiet private malice and then saw the reference: 'Throughout the months of May and June a German train is reported to have been standing, with all blinds drawn, at the station in Ekaterinburg. Source of information: Baroness Buxhoeveden, the Tsarina's lady-in-waiting, who was in the city throughout this period, in her book *Left Behind*.'

Dikeston, thought Malory as he pushed the list aside, was a fox. The narrative showed him to be something of a clown, and a pompous one at that, but he yet contrived to be everywhere of importance; not an easy matter to achieve, as Malory well knew. A fox then. A fox with a secret he had kept for six decades. A fox who knew where everything and everybody was, during one of the century's more mysterious episodes. He asked Mrs Frobisher to take Dikeston's narrative to Pilgrim's office.

It was an hour before Pilgrim responded. Then the intercom buzzed beside Malory. 'Got a minute, Horace?'

Entering the room, Malory noted the satisfaction that

was in Pilgrim's expression. It was well-contained, even suppressed, but *there*.

'Interesting about the Germans, wouldn't you say?' Malory mumbled. ''Morning, Graves,' he added, for Graves stood at Pilgrim's shoulder. 'Been busy, have you?'

'At work in the vaults, Sir Horace.'

'Oh?'

'And,' said Pilgrim, 'old Jacques has found pay dirt.'

'Pay dirt, eh?'

'I got the idea,' Pilgrim said, 'of going through the old books to see if there were any references to Zaharoff's pensioners. Jacques has been down there hunting for three days. He found one or two things.'

'Do go on, dear boy.'

Pilgrim was smiling. 'Actually he found three. All dated from the First World War, or from the very early 'twenties. The way Zaharoff did it was to deposit enough straight cash to buy an annuity and cross-refer it back to Senior Partner's notes.'

'He would. Done it myself,' said Malory. 'Which company?'

'Condor Planet Mutual. In Senior Partner's Notes it simply says "Authorized, ZZ."'

'Who was he paying?'

'Widow of a French politician.'

'Briand?'

'That's the one. Then there was some guy in the Balkans.'

'In Bulgaria,' said Graves.

'Who's dead,' Pilgrim said.

'Which leaves one, I think?' Malory's eyebrows lifted interrogatively. '*Who* is that?'

Pilgrim grinned. 'You're right about the "is", Horace. It's an old lady. Lives in Nice. Name of Bronard.'

'Bronard, eh?'

'Yup. Paid since – guess, Horace.'

'I would suspect nineteen-eighteen.'

212

'You'd be wrong. Nineteen-twenty.'

'And is the lady unfortunate enough to be a widow?' Malory asked.

'I don't know.'

Malory looked at Graves, who said, 'I don't know, either. But I'm on my way to Nice on the afternoon plane to find out.'

Pilgrim rubbed his hands. 'We're really gonna crack it, Horace! That name Bronard – it has to be the same one, huh?'

'I would imagine so.'

'Sure it does. We're gonna get the whole thing. No more Turners, no more goddam Georgian houses. The whole thing, Horace!'

Malory smiled. 'I do hope so,' he said.

'Oh, sure, Horace. Dikeston's had his fun. Here's where we get the answers he keeps holding back from us.

It was hot in the town of Nice, and had been so for weeks. So, as always in the summer there, the day's heat came not only from the sun overhead: it came from stones which had long been absorbing it, from paving baking beneath the feet, from asphalt cracking like dermatitic skin to reveal tar shiny beneath. Graves toiled up the steep narrow alleyways of the old town. His jacket was off and slung by a finger over his shoulder, his tie loose at his throat, and sweat made wide wet patches on his back and beneath his arms. He was where the taxi-drivers would not go, for the narrow alleys with their rough projecting stones unfailingly made expensive scrapes on bodywork.

Graves swore as he climbed. The rule still held, that apparently inalienable rule he had noted after Dikeston's first appearance in his life: the rule that said – you will encounter discomfort. *You.* Not Pilgrim, not that old bastard Malory, but *you*, Graves.

If he turned and looked back, the blue Mediterranean glittered with invitation no great distance away. In a quarter of an hour he could be in the water, all this behind him, encompassed by a profound feeling of comfort. Pretty girls to look at, long drinks to sip.

He cursed again, and climbed on.

The square was tiny, barely meriting the name; really it was no more than a place where alleys met. In it there was nothing of what the world understands when the name of Nice is mentioned: there was no sunshine, no palms, no sand, no beauty, no self-indulgent luxury. But then, the richest cities always have places for the poor.

Graves, glancing round him, understood that at once. A few feet above, an ancient olive tree thrust its gnarled trunk from a wall and darker shade lay in an inviting pool beneath it. He stepped into its comfort and lit a cigarette, and he stood very still as sweat ran down his body. Five minutes passed. He saw a tin sign half-fastened to a wall opposite. *Byrrh* it said. An open doorway stood beside it, the room beyond very dark. He levered his moist body off the wall and took the few paces that were enough to cross the little square. It was cool inside the tiny bar. There was a zinc counter, a sink, a few bottles, and water dripping. The woman was in black and her face was much lined from the sun.

'Une bière, madame, s'il vous plaît.'

'Pas de bière.'

Anything cold would do.

'Pas de glace.'

In Nice! he thought. No ice, in Nice.

He took a glass of white wine, far from cold, and it was sour on his palate. The woman kept her eyes on him.

He finished the wine in a gulp. 'I am looking for Madame Bronard.'

No answer.

'She lives close by?'

Just the black eyes on him. He tried again. Once. 'She must be very old now, Madame Bronard. You know her, madame?'

214

A shake of the head.

He walked out into the heat. A man sat on a rock that jutted from a wall. Graves went over to him. 'I am looking –'

'For Madame Bronard. *Oui*. I heard.'

'You know her?'

'Oh yes.' The man looked at him with a strange expression. 'But do *you*?'

'No. But I want to see her.'

The man began to roll a cigarette in thick, stiff fingers. After a moment of concentration he looked up again. 'She is very old.'

'I know.'

'Also hostile to strangers.'

'Nevertheless . . .'

A shrug. A thick finger pointing. There was a doorway at the mouth of the second alley; its door stood open to admit air. 'The house there, m'sieu. Third floor. She's – she's not easy, well, to . . .'

'Thank you.' Grave's smile was answered with another shrug.

He found stairs of worn stone, uncarpeted, and began to climb. It was refreshingly cool in the house, and there was a draught of sorts down the stairway. Poor old soul, Graves thought, all these stairs to climb!

The door was old, oaken and blackened. Spidery handwriting on a grubby card said 'Bronard'. He knocked, and something scraped at the far side of the door. An ancient voice said, 'Who knocks?'

He saw that a little grille had moved, and tried to look through it. 'My name is Graves, madame, Jacques Graves.'

'What do you want?' A harsh tone now in the weak voice.

'To talk to you. On business.'

'Business?' Shrill and surprised. 'I have no business.'

'I'm from London.'

215

Silence. He said it again, slowly. 'Did you hear, madame? I'm from London. From England.'

'Oh, I heard. My pension. It's about my pension?'

'Well, yes.' He heard movements inside, beyond the door; the click of a bolt withdrawn. A full minute passed, then the cracked voice said, 'You can come forward.'

Graves raised the iron lever and stepped inside. There was no hall, no passage. He was at once in the little room, and it was clear this was where she lived. A bed stood against one wall; there was one small table, one chair, a small chipped stone sink.

Madame Bronard sat in a wheelchair on the far side of the room. Behind her were narrow floor-to-ceiling french windows, flung wide, and a tiny iron-railed balcony. She was little more than a silhouette against the shadowed light outside, and moreover was dressed head to foot in black. On her knee was a bag of black canvas which Graves's imagination first told him must be a black cat. *Macbeth*, he thought: Act One, Scene One. You can find a blasted heath anywhere.

She said, 'My pension. You are from the company, *hein*?'

'From *a* company, madame.'

'Pffft. The people who pay. With the so foolish name.'

'Condor Planet Mutual. No, madame, I am not.'

'Then who?'

'I must explain. May I sit down?' He took a step towards the solitary chair.

'No.' Her hands moved incessantly, like big trembling white insects on the black bag. She said, 'Three pounds English, you understand? Enough when it began.'

He suddenly understood the bitterness.

'But not for years. I have had half a century of grinding poverty. You hear me, m'sieu from Londres?'

Graves said. 'It was never increased?' and cursed himself for failing to think about how much interest the principal

216

would produce, for not asking Condor Planet Mutual for details.

'Increased? *Never!* I wrote. I begged. They stopped answering. Just the few sous, every month. Who are you from?'

Graves made his tone emollient. It was a weapon in his armoury: his voice could be made very soothing, and it rarely failed.

'A bank,' he said. 'I may be able to help you.'

'Bank?' she said. The cracked voice had an edge like a saw. 'Which bank?'

'I doubt if you'd know –'

'Which bank, m'sieu?' She was the secret, black and midnight hag incarnate, every inch, and growing more agitated by the instant.

'Hillyard, Cleef,' Graves said gently. 'It's a kind of private –'

She said, 'Zaharoff's – it's Zaharoff's bank?'

Graves smiled. 'Not for a very long time, madame. Sir Basil Zaharoff died in nineteen-thirty-six. I believe your late husband worked for Sir B-'

She said, 'I have been waiting.' The hands never stopped moving on the bag. 'All these years I have waited. So you, m'sieu, are Zaharoff's man?'

Graves laughed gently. 'Well, no, madame. As I told you, he died long ago.'

'Like my pension,' she said, and cackled.

Something made a shiver run down Graves's back – the cool after the heat, he thought.

'Well, we can try –'

She interrupted again, head shaking. 'It's too late. Fifty years too late. If my man had been dead it would be three times more, but there was no *proof* that he was dead, *hein*? So old Zaharoff didn't pay me, *hein*?'

'I'm sure –'

'So am I, m'sieu. Very sure.' He now saw that the apparently aimless movement of the old hands had

217

achieved something. The bag was open at the neck and her hand was inside. 'But I saved *something*, m'sieu,' she said, 'as you will see –' and there was an ancient pistol in her hand, a massive, monstrous thing; her hands shook with its weight – 'for Zaharoff. He is dead, so – for his agent.'

Graves said, in astonishment, 'But –' Her forefinger was tightening, and the wavering pistol was enormous.

She fired.

'Just there,' said the man in the square to the agent-de-ville. 'I was sitting on that stone, smoking a cigarette. Heard this loud bang and looked up, and she came flying backwards over the balcony, wheelchair and all. My wife went to her and I ran upstairs, but the man was dead. My God, but there was a hell of a hole in him, did you see it?'

'I'm not surprised. Kill an elephant with that gun – God knows where she got it. They're rare, guns like that,' said the agent-de-ville. 'You'll come down and make a statement?'

'Naturally.'

'What a way to go, eh? Surprising, isn't it,' said the agent, musing, 'what fate has in store? An old lady – what was she? Eighty-six – an old lady actually flying off to Heaven!'

The man chuckled. 'To Hell,' he said. 'And I never doubted she'd fly there.'

The agent looked puzzled. 'No?'

'Yes – on her broomstick!'

In the height of the dog days, it made a very pleasing story: Mystery of the Banker and the Crone – that was the way most of the English papers played it. The French press had more fun: 'Was it an assignation?' asked *Nice-Matin*. There was an inside page feature on the celebrated strange tastes of the British. Zaharoff was not mentioned, of course, since Mme Bronard, who would gladly have yelled curses on his name from the rooftops, was silent in refrigeration,

218

and nobody else who was willing to talk knew about him. But Hillyard, Cleef were in the papers again. Senior executives of private banks are not shot every day by old ladies wielding revolvers so powerful that the recoil hurled the firer to her death! And this was, in any case, one of the men, and certainly the banking house, which had figured so recently and so much in the still-extant controversy over Turner's great painting.

'Lousy goddam jokes!' Pilgrim complained. 'They have this great reputation for wit, the English, but there are no laughs, just sniggers.'

'Usually,' Malory agreed.

'I was at a Bank of England lunch.'

'Luncheon, yes.'

'It was the Governor, too. Some discussion on spelling. He said –' Pilgrim attempted an Old Etonian languor – 'he believed everybody at Hillyard's could spell necrophilia.'

Malory frowned. 'Naughty.' He paused. 'We *will* live it down, Laurence.'

'I'm not so sure. You may. I won't.'

'Rubbish.'

'Rubbish it's not, Horace. Maybe it's something in the air here. I never goofed in my life before. Here I goof all the time. Who set this ball rolling? I did. Who got Graves shot? Who had to be saved from Pepe Robizo? Every time, the answer's Pilgrim.'

Malory said with a kind of gruffness: 'My fault really, m'dear boy. I insisted on following through.'

Pilgrim shook his head. 'So I'm going,' he said harshly.

'Where to?'

'Back to the States. I tell you, Horace, on Wall Street I feel safe, my feet are on rock, my head's clear. Here I make mistakes. I don't feel I have a foothold. I'm going back where I can operate!'

'You're wrong.'

'No. We can't have a joke running this place and I'm turning into a joke. Every time we look at each other,

Horace, every time we talk, Pepe Robizo'll be there with us. No thanks.'

'I repeat, you're wrong. The joke who ran this bank was me. That's why you came in and I moved over. In any case, the joke's on me, too.'

'The difference,' Pilgrim said, 'is that you're an old, respected City figure. I'm Johnny-come-lately and all those bastards are enjoying it!'

Malory pursed his lips. 'You'll go back and do what?'

'What I did before. It's no problem.'

'It is for me, dear boy. Lady Malory intended that I retire. Now Lady Malory is likely to be severely displeased and I tell you that is no small matter. In any case, there's the Grim Reaper – I hear the scythe swish occasionally. It's not on, you know.'

'It's on,' Pilgrim said. 'I see two scenarios here. The first is where I go and you take hold again and everything slides nicely into place. The second is where I go back to Wall Street and some other guy comes over here and runs things. Neither way should the names of Pilgrim and Hillyard, Cleef be bracketed in this City again!'

Sir Horace spread his hands. 'It must, of course, be up to you.'

'And I've decided. Naturally, I'll send my apologies to Lady Malory –'

'She collects amethysts,' Malory murmured.

'She does? I'll be sure to remember that. Anyway, you won't have to hold the baby long, Horace. Wall Street's full of bright young –'

'Yes, *isn't* it!' said Malory.

Within days Pilgrim was in New York, Harrods were packing his impedimenta, and Horace Malory, once again in control at 6 Athelsgate, was spending another fraught hour in contemplation of the most recent instructions from Dikeston.

In order to obtain the next – the sixth, and penultimate

instalment of the narrative, certain conditions were to be fulfilled. Sir Horace frowned as he read and re-read the typed sheet, sniffing for hidden snags but unable to detect them. That there would be snags he did not doubt, and he was reasonably sure the Turner painting must be involved, because:

Six large copies, photographic or otherwise, of the painting *Naval Vessel and Plymouth Hoe* now in your possession, are to be despatched, one copy each to the following institutions, together with the number appropriate thereto.

There followed a list of six United States banks. Opposite each name appeared what looked like an account number, consisting of two or three letters and up to a dozen digits.

The consequent happenings were not described but it was clear to Malory that, where Dikeston was concerned, nothing came cheap. The copies had been made, for speed's sake photographically, on 10 × 8 inch transparencies.

He buzzed for Mrs Frobisher. 'Will you send one of these to each of these.'

'Yes, Sir Horace.'

'Air freight them. And get them off today.'

'Yes, Sir Horace.'

Six American banks, Malory noted, his thumb stroking idly at the numeral which hung upon his watch-chain.

Next day he was taking tea in mid-afternoon when the call came. 'A Mr Ed Sochaki is on the line,' Mrs Frobisher reported, 'from the Custerbank in Santa Barbara, California.'

Malory glanced at his watch. Mr Sochaki, he reflected, must be one of those tiresome people who went to his desk at seven in the morning. He picked up the phone. 'Hello, Mr Sochaki?'

'Sir Malory?'

'Horace Malory speaking, yes.' Curious how often people got it wrong.

'I got your picture.'

'Must be a little puzzling to you,' Malory said. 'Matter of fact it puzzles us, too. Eccentric client, just following his instruction. Haw, haw.'

'Yeah, well we got something for you. Deposited years ago, along with the instructions.'

'Oh? Well, good,' Malory said. 'What is it?'

'Looks like some papers. In a packet.'

'That's fine, Mr Sochaki. I'd be grateful if you could send them – express if you would.'

'Why, sure. Be glad to. There's just one thing.'

'What's that?'

Sochaki said, 'Well, it sounds kinda crazy, but this packet only gets sent to you after we read something in the newspapers. You understand that, Sir Malory?'

'At the moment, no. What is it you are required to read?'

'That you people have given something to your country.'

'We do it all the time,' Malory said. 'It's called income tax.' But he knew what was coming.

And it came. 'A painting. By a guy called Turner.'

'When you read that,' Malory said sadly, '*then* you send the packet. Not before?'

'Why, no. Our client's instructions –'

'Cannot be varied?'

'Certainly not, Sir Malory. This is the Custerbank of California.'

Malory thanked him and hung up.

Later in the day something drew him to the boardroom. It was an old-fashioned place, not often used, furnished in heavy Victorian mahogany. The long table shone with polish; the hide upholstery remained soft from much waxing over the years. For Horace Malory the place was full of people and memories. Half-close his eyes and he could see his father again, frock-coated at the side table, pouring one

222

of the brandies that finally felled him at eighty-eight. His grandfather, too, had sat in this boardroom, though Malory, hardly surprisingly, had never met him. Few people, in fact, actually believed in Malory's grandfather, who had been born before the French Revolution (i.e. in 1786), had served as a lieutenant in Collingwood's flagship *Royal Sovereign* at Trafalgar, had fathered his only son at the age of 68 in 1854, and had lived to ninety on a diet of lobster and Mosel wine. At Malory's birth, his own father had been fifty years of age, and the three of them therefore spanned better than two centuries.

Years of increasing prosperity, too, Malory thought. Until now. There were cigars in the humidor, and as he stood selecting one, his eye fell upon the chair that was the only piece of oak in the room; it was dark and very old, and of a design that was probably Greek. A tiny silver plate affixed to the side of one arm bore the initials ZZ.

Malory lit the cigar with care, and in the wreathing fumes had little difficulty in picturing Sir Basil seated in the chair.

'What would *you* have done?' he murmured. 'Would *you* have given away three million and more in money?'

On this day, it was as though he heard the answer in his head: 'I did, I did.' Malory smiled. 'Yes, but with a purpose. Always that.'

It was extraordinary how clear the image was: the blazing eyes, the little Second Empire beard and moustache, the authority. Malory daydreamed infrequently, but his visual memory was powerful, and as a young man he had conversed often with the great man, and always in this interrogatory style; somehow, under the influence of Zaharoff's personality, people discovered answers to their own questions.

Three million and more to find out – what? That the Tsar was dead, had been murdered in Ekaterinburg? At least I'd *know*, then, he thought. Hell of a price, but I'd know. A long echo seemed to float down the years, of a light voice, faintly accented: 'It is necessary always to know.'

223

Malory smiled to himself. He'd tell his wife tonight, and she'd be impatient, but then she believed in ghosts. He didn't: but his memories were powerful and could be used.

He reached for the telephone on the side table beside the chairman's place. 'I should like to talk to whoever administers The Turner Bequest,' he told Mrs Frobisher. 'And then to the Press Association, Reuters, and – no, make it the Associated Press *first*!'

Mr Sochaki's expressed packet arrived two days later, bearing Pan American stickers.

CHAPTER TWELVE

———◆———

Sixth instalment of the account, written by
Lt-Cdr H. G. Dikeston RN, of his journeyings
in Russia in the spring and summer of 1918

The Germans it was, right enough, though if I'd had to rely on Nadezhda the secretary or her master, Sverdlov, for information, I'd never have known. I've wondered often, since, what became of that woman, for she had the makings of power if ever a woman had. A real bluestocking, with one of those cold and superior brains: she was the kind that makes grown men feel like small boys, with all the snap of the scrubbed schoolroom about her.

Daily I went to see Nadezhda, and daily she told me nothing. But no – that's not entirely true, though it might as well have been. Every afternoon I went through the same drill, showing Sverdlov's pass at the Spassky gate and proceeding to her office, there to be told that the Romanov family remained in good health in the hands of the Urals Oblast Soviet. Thereafter I was virtually obliged to leave. After many days of this, and with time on my hands, I began to cast about for other sources. I went to see Robert Bruce Lockhart in his room at the Elite Hotel and had short shrift. At the time I had the impression he was strongly pro-Bolshevik, but it was untrue, though certainly he and Trotsky liked and admired each other. All Bruce Lockhart did was treat me courteously for a minute or two and then throw me out with the advice to make my way to Murmansk and take a British ship home. There were others I tried of the scattered Britons in Moscow. Arthur Ransome, for one, then a reporter for the *Manchester Guardian*, and a naval man named Le Page who had some strange liaison assignment. But mention of the Tsar to any of them

225

produced at the very least impatience, if not outright boredom.

And so it went on, until one day when I was in the corridor after leaving Nadezhda's office, I saw a group of men walking confidently towards me and stood aside to let them pass. Suddenly I believed I heard my name spoken. I turned to see one of this approaching band had halted and was repeating my name:

'It *is* Dikeston – yes, I knew it!'

I blinked at him, and from him to his companions, two of whom were in *German* uniform!

'Come now, you recognize me!'

'Oh yes,' I said, goggling.

'What are you doing here?' he demanded. He was jovial, but looking at me sidelong all the same; for this was Graf Wilhelm von Mirbach, German ambassador, since the treaty was signed at Brest-Litovsk, to the Bolshevik Government.

It was a difficult question, but fortunately I did not have to answer; or not at that moment. He said, 'Can you wait? I shall not be more than twenty minutes.'

I nodded and he and his group strode off, I noted where they went, for it was through a familiar door: the German Ambassador was now closeted with Sverdlov. As for me, I felt myself to be in a dilemma. As a serving officer of the Royal Navy, I had no business to be greeting Germans on terms of friendship, even on neutral soil. Yet it was at once clear that my acquaintance with Willi von Mirbach might be of great value. Remembering the man Le Page and his naval liaison work, I decided quickly to pretend his role was my own, at least for Willi's ears, and then stood smoking a cigarette and awaiting the promised return.

And he was as good as his word. Within fifteen minutes he was striding towards me, smiling, and demanding, 'Have you found a tennis court in Moscow, Harry?'

Tennis was the last thought in my head. I smiled and said, 'No.'

226

'Pity.' He took my arm. 'I haven't played since nineteen-fourteen. And you and I – when was that?'

'Biarritz,' I said, 'in nineteen-eleven.'

'No, no, in London!' He came sometimes for Wimbledon, before the war. 'The year the Doherty brothers won!'

'They won *every* year,' I protested.

'No, the last time. Must have been nineteen-five. Will you dine with me?'

'A little improper, is it not, Willi?'

'The war, you mean – or the dinner? Yes, it's improper. But we'll meet as Russians, eh? There's a gipsy restaurant, the *Streilna*. Tomorrow, if you're free.' He turned to one of his aides. 'I'm clear, am I not?' And upon being assured he was: 'At nine, Harry! *And* I'll set about finding a court.'

And then they were gone.

Were we friends? I suppose not – friendly acquaintances was more like it. But our paths had crossed several times: in St Petersburg when I was first posted there, in Berlin, in Wimbledon, in Biarritz. I used to beat him at tennis, though not by any great margin, and he was forever demanding the return match.

And now Willi was Ambassador of His Imperial German Majesty in Moscow!

I had only the clothes in which I stood, and by now they were far from fresh. How, then, could I dine with an Ambassador? But then I remembered my first arrival in Moscow, and being taken to choose a naval uniform suited to Yakovlev. I had had a suitcase with me then, and had left it in that malodorous hall of uniforms. I returned, and found the bag untouched, still in the care of the custodian.

So it was a different Dikeston who went next night to the *Streilna* restaurant. *Tsiganer* music reached gaily out into the street as I arrived and I thought then that this was a strange place indeed to find still extant in Bolshevik Moscow. By the time I was inside and being seated at Mirbach's table, the music had saddened, and a woman with a grave, dark beauty was singing 'Black Eyes'. I felt then that here

227

was a last stirring of days that were almost gone, and I was right, for the restaurant closed soon after.

Willi von Mirbach arrived intent upon enjoyment. 'We'll speak only Russian, Harry. No German, no English. All right?'

'All right.'

'And we'll get drunk!'

I grinned and said, 'Good!' though I had no such intention. Already, looking round the smoky room, I had caught sight of Bruce Lockhart, the British Consul-General, with a noisy group at another table. If *he* saw me with Willi and told the Admiralty, there was a fair chance of my being shot!

We drank *charochki* – toasts in vodka – to everything we could think of, and made pigs of ourselves, on caviare of course, and became, both of us, gradually less discreet. It was an absurd conversation we had, considering our respective positions, for he was charged with preventing the intervention in the war of the Allied troops which had already landed in northern Russia, and those forces were in part British! Furthermore, I was the enemy. For enemies, though, we got along well. We talked of places and acquaintances, of tennis-players and old times, and of summers and scenes gone by. And then abruptly, as we spoke of such matters, my head was filled with an image of that Family now beleaguered in Ekaterinburg and I said to Willi, 'Can *you* help the Tsar?'

My tone must have told him that I took the matter seriously for he became quiet and looked carefully around him before replying.

Then he said, 'He's quite safe.'

'You're sure?'

'I have assurances that the whole family is well-treated –'

'From whom do these assurances come?'

He frowned. 'From Sverdlov. Also from Lenin. The Romanovs are held in Ekaterinburg, but it is temporary.'

'You believe they will be released?' I demanded.

228

He put a hand on my shoulder. 'Not so fierce, Harry, this is not your affair.'

'It's yours, then?'

'The Tsarina is German, Harry, and her daughters are German princesses. Yes, it *is* ours. And it is well in hand, please believe it.'

'What would you say,' I asked, 'if I told you there was a majority on the Urals Oblast Soviet for murdering the lot of them? Would you still say it was well in hand?'

He looked hard at me. 'No. But I would ask where you got your story. How you know.'

'Because I came to Moscow from Ekaterinburg, Willi. Because I have seen their prison, because I have met their captors.'

He laughed. 'What nonsense! Too much vodka, Harry. How could it be so?'

'You don't believe me!' I was stung.

'Another drink, Harry. Come –'

But I had the pass from my pocket now and pushed it beneath his nose. 'Read that!'

He bent his nose over it, and from the time he took, must have read it three or four times.

'You are *Yakovlev*?'

'Your humble servant.'

He looked at me in astonishment. 'How did all this happen? You *must* tell me.'

And tell him I did. Everything from Tobolsk to Ekaterinburg and back again – I told it all, and watched his face as I did so, and for all that Willi von Mirbach had the still mien of the professional diplomat, I saw the emotions at play upon his face. He was keen on every detail. He wanted to know the demeanour of those who turned me back at Omsk, the attitudes of officials and populace at Ekaterinburg. I told all I knew, and then I too asked a question: 'It was for you, was it not, that they were to be brought to Moscow?'

He blinked at me, and sighed. 'Harry, I'm responsible,

here in Moscow. I cannot speak freely to you, much as I trust you, for your plain duty is to your country, as mine is to mine!'

'My duty,' I said, 'as I see it, is to seek to save their lives – the Romanovs. You have my word nothing you say will go farther.'

'Very well, then. It *was* a promise. The Romanovs would be brought to Moscow – I agreed it in early May with Sverdlov and Trotsky. Trotsky demanded the right to put the Tsar on public trial with himself as prosecutor; he envisaged such a trial broadcast by wireless throughout the country. But the women and the boy would go to Germany. That was agreed. We have had a train at Ekaterinburg station, waiting for them.'

'You've been tricked, Willi!'

He nodded, and his jaw tightened. 'I can trust all you say?'

'Every word.'

'Tomorrow,' he said grimly, 'I am to attend again at the Fifth All-Russian Congress at Moscow Opera House. I'll see Trotsky there, never fear. And Lenin, too. And I'll frighten the life out of them, Harry, my friend! I'll have the Romanovs here in days!'

And so we left matters. I had no doubt, that night, that freedom for the Tsar and his family lay a day or two away, or that Mirbach's talk with Trotsky on the morrow would be sufficient to guarantee safety for the Romanovs. Was not a German army at Moscow's gates!

But it was not to be. The fifth congress became a brawl, through the penultimate attempt of the Left Social-Revolutionary opposition to retain a hold on power, and it took all Lenin's powers of persuasion to prevent mass fist-fighting. Mirbach was there, I know he was, because both sides jeered him from the floor, and when finally he left it was with soldiers protecting him.

Next day, towards evening, I was seized in the street by Cheka agents, and taken in a truck to one of the Kremlin fortresses. There I was flung into a cell and joined shortly after by three brutal-looking men who demanded to know why I had been with Count von Mirbach. I told them we were old friends, and was punched and kicked for my pains, but when I spat out Sverdlov's name, along with a loose tooth, they looked at me with different eyes. They searched me then, and discovered two papers bearing the Chairman's name and became remarkably polite.

'We apologize,' said their leader. 'But when a tragic murder is under investigation, it is sometimes unavoidable –'

'Murder!' I said. 'Whose murder?'

'The assassination of Count von Mirbach.'

When next day I went to see Nadezkhda, she showed me direct into Sverdlov's office. The Chairman was not alone: standing at the window, his back to me as he looked out, stood a man whose posture struck some faint chord of memory, though I could not immediately place it. Nor did I, at that moment, have either interest or time to look more closely, for Sverdlov was staring up at me, black beard bristling.

'He told you, did he?'

'What do you mean?'

'Mirbach. He told you we have agreed to release the Romanovs?'

'Yes,' I answered, thinking; if I'm the only one who knows, my life isn't worth a hair!

He nodded. 'Are you ready for another journey?'

'To what end?' I asked. 'And where?'

'To conduct the Romanovs out of Ekaterinburg.'

'Me?'

'Of course, *you*! Nicholas has your paper, has he not? You will meet him and his family. You will conduct them to the German train that waits at the station in Ekaterinburg. And on the way you will obtain your paper from him. Clear?'

231

'Perfectly.'

He nodded. 'And here's your companion for the journey.'

The man at the window turned, and I nearly dropped with surprise, for I had seen him last in the prison at Ekaterinburg the day the Tsar was taken to the Ipatiev house, and this man had stared at me malevolently and expressed his strong desire to hang me!

'I believe,' said Sverdlov, 'that you have already met Comrade Goloshchokin?'

We did not shake hands; he did not offer and nor did I. Cool nods were exchanged, no more. I thought to myself that no man looking for a travelling companion would readily look in Goloshchokin's direction, but there was clearly nothing to be done.

'When do we go?' I asked.

'When I tell you. But soon,' Sverdlov said.

We left on the ninth. There was trouble on the rail line east, so we were warned to anticipate delays, and we encountered them, too, but there was no great discomfort. As princes had travelled in former times, so commissars journeyed now: Goloshchokin and I had a first-class carriage for just the two of us, bathroom, dining-room, bedrooms and all, so that it was barely necessary for us to meet, though we did of course, driven into each other's company by an absence of reading matter and a surfeit of flat country beyond the window glass.

I had thought him poisonous on first meeting nad nothing I heard from him then changed that impression. For a start, the man was, though a revolutionary by disposition, a dentist by training, and I have never for the life of me understood the impulse that drives a man to pass years in study in order to spend the rest of his life peering into reeking mouths filled with rotting teeth.

He could talk though. Maybe it was the cry of his profession, 'Open wide,' ringing forever in his ears, but his

232

mouth barely closed. He was a boozer too, which helped. They are, you know, these politicians – they're all talkers and all fond of the bottle. And braggarts, too. Aside from Lenin and Trotsky, Sverdlov was the top man in Russia then, so I got Sverdlov by the earful. Hearing him blether on about Sverdlov's house (he'd been staying there in Moscow) was like hearing women talk about dresses; he remembered every stitch, colour and texture: odd for a Red revolutionary, if you ask me.

But I learned other things too, and they had a nasty significance, some of them. For one thing, he didn't *want* the Romanovs released, no matter what advantage to the state. 'Yet I must obey,' he said. 'Obedience is the lesson all Russia must learn.'

'Obedience to whom?' I asked.

'To the Party.'

'That means Lenin,' I said. 'Why not say so?'

But he wouldn't have it. He was an intelligent man, but he parroted and distorted as they all do. His orders were from the Party, not from Sverdlov – even though I knew the opposite. Still, they were clear enough and sounded simple, but as Goloshchokin talked I realized they weren't.

'There'll be no snags this time?' I asked.

'How can there be,' he wanted to know, 'when it is all arranged within the Party? A procedure has been set out, Comrade Yakovlev –' he persisted in calling me Yakovlev, though his English was good and he knew my name – 'and it will be followed.'

Then he got into his cups and the braggart floated up through the vodka. So I asked about conditions inside the House of Special Purpose.

'Better, much better now.' Goloshchokin said, and belched.

'Now – why now?'

He fumbled in his pocket and produced a page from a signal pad. 'Read it.'

So I read:

Beloborodov to Sverdlov and Goloshchokin – Moscow

SYROMOLOTOV HAS GONE TO REORGANIZE ACCORDING
CENTRE'S INSTRUCTION. NO CAUSE FOR ALARM. AVDEYEV
REMOVED. MOSKHIN ARRESTED. YUROVSKY REPLACES
AVDEYEV. INTERNAL GUARD REPLACED.   – July 4

'You see?' he demanded thickly.

'Who are these people? Who's this Avdeyev? Why has Moskhin been arrested?'

'Avdeyev commanded the guard inside the House of Special Purpose. He's been removed.'

'Go on.'

'The man's a thief. Barbarous anyway. Couldn't keep his men in order. There were complaints.'

I poured vodka into his glass. 'Complaints?'

'Behaviour towards the prisoners, especially the young girls. Can't have it. The new society must be –' and he belched again – 'must be better.'

Bit by bit I got it out of him. Moshkin was Avdeyev's deputy and as bad as his master.

'Yurovsky – what about him?'

Goloshchokin grunted. 'Jewish,' he said, as if that explained much.

'So?' I asked.

'He's bitter. We're all bitter, but he was in the army in the Ukraine. Cossack trouble.'

'So?' I asked again.

'Pogrom – you need to ask?'

'Not in the army, surely?'

'Some village,' Goloshchokin said. 'When we made him Regional Commissar for Justice he thanked us with tears in his eyes. The Tsar controlled the Cossacks, that's what he said, and it would be a privilege –' he smiled – 'to sentence him to death. And to carry it out personally!'

I said incredulously, 'And *he's* in charge at the house?'

234

Goloshchokin giggled. 'Don't worry. Yurovsky's a good Communist.'

He was slipping into sleep and I let him go over. But I disliked deeply the sound of what I had heard. Avdeyev's toughs making free of the Imperial Family's possessions and insulting the Grand Duchesses was bad enough; but now they were all in the hands of a man who not only had a lust for vengeance but, as Commissar for Justice, had the power to sentence. And, as gaoler, the opportunity to carry it out.

Yet I slept soundly enough, and next day we continued our journey across the great flat plain. Once when the train stopped, at Kazan, Goloshchokin said, 'The holy city.'

'This is?' I said, looking out of the window. 'Why?'

'Because here Lenin was a student.' He was perfectly serious. 'In years to come it will be a place of pilgrimage.'

'Really,' I said, and he gave me a look and jumped down from the train and went to the telegraph office.

A message awaited him and he came back to the carriage frowning over it.

I said, 'Trouble?'

'The Whites have Omsk and are approaching Ekaterinburg. It doesn't look as though they can be held.'

'What's the Red strength?'

He looked at me grimly. 'Not enough. It's not just the Whites we fight – the Czech Legion is there.'

'So withdraw,' I said.

He smiled faintly. 'Oh, we shall – until they're dog-tired of advancing. And then –' He drew his finger across his throat. 'But in the meantime, Yakovlev, there'll be those who'll want to kill the Romanovs to stop them falling into White hands.'

In truth, Goloshchokin's mind was concentrated less upon the Imperial Family than upon the defence of the entire region which was now governed by the Urals Oblast Soviet; he served upon that body as Commissar for War, and war

235

was certainly moving steadily and remorselessly towards him. When we arrived at the station at Ekaterinburg on July 12th, the chairman himself stood, fat and impatient, upon the platform as the train steamed in.

'It's good you're back,' Beloborodov told Goloshchokin. 'The military situation is causing great anxiety!' His eyes rested but briefly upon me, and though recognition showed, he did not speak to me. Moments later, by which time all three of us were in a Mercedes car, driving away from the station towards the Hotel Americana, Beloborodov returned to military affairs. It was clear he was a worried man, and with reason, for the Bolsheviks had a wild beast loose in their midst that was like to devour them. It was a beast moreover of their own creation. For when the treaty at Brest-Litovsk produced peace between Germany and Russia, all the Czech forces fighting on the Allied side in Russia were withdrawn and put on trains to journey to Vladivostock and thence home. But they objected when attempts were made to disarm them. The Czechs then overpowered their guards, reformed themselves into the Czech Legion, joined up with the Bolsheviks' White Russian enemies, and set to fighting with a will against the Reds.

Arriving at the Hotel Americana, we went direct to a small meeting-room on the mezzanine floor where several members of the Urals Soviet were gathered. An easel held a large-scale map of the area, and beside it stood a man in uniform khaki, seemingly explaining.

Upon Goloshchokin's appearance, this man came to attention and saluted. As the meeting progressed I discovered him to be the General Berzin whose signal giving assurances of the good health of the Imperial Family had been shown to me in Moscow by Sverdlov.

For those present, his news was anything but reassuring. The map bore tapes and arrows, setting out a complex picture of positions and advances. But its message was crushingly simple.

236

Goloshchokin looked at it grimly, turned to General Berzin and asked his question in a single word: 'Encirclement?'

Berzin nodded.

'It is inevitable?'

'There is no possibility of halting the advance,' Berzin said, and his hands made a gesture of weariness. 'We are fighting two full divisions of Czechs, together with the Whites. We simply have not the strength!'

'How long?' Goloshchokin demanded.

'A week, if we're lucky. Probably less. Our men are fighting like tigers, Commissar, believe me. But we are fewer in number, less well-trained, less well-armed –'

'I understand. In the end,' Goloshchokin said, 'we shall win. But meantime withdrawal . . .'

The discussions began, with me quiet in a corner, looking at faces and wondering whose they were. Bronard/Ruzsky was there, and I identified one Chutskayev whom Preston had mentioned to me. But it was Yurovksy, Commissar for Justice and commander of the guard at the Ipatiev House, whom I sought. I concluded finally that he could not be present, and when the meeting was concluded, asked Goloshchokin.

It was Beloborodov, however, who answered. 'He barely leaves the Ipatiev House now.'

I asked why, and he shrugged. 'Yurovsky is obsessed with the Romanovs.' Beloborodov then turned and began shaking hands as the others departed. I noticed one or two lingered, though – or perhaps he detained them. When the door closed, there were six of us: Beloborodov himself, Goloshchokin, Chutskayev, Berzin, Ruzsky and myself. Goloshchokin wasted no time.

'The Romanovs are to be released to their German relatives,' he said. 'If you wonder why Moscow has so decided, it is because we have harsher priorities than dealing with *them*. The chairman has had a further telegram today reporting that Germany is seeking the right to

237

station a battalion of troops in Moscow – yes, in *Moscow!* – to protect her embassy. We cannot allow that, yet we cannot stop them if they choose to move. It is vital at this moment that the Germans be placated, however much we hate it! So – we will placate them with the useless Romanovs they want so much!'

'Spare them after all?' yelled Ruzsky angrily. 'When they should be punished according to the people's justice!'

'It is necessary,' Beloborodov told him harshly. 'And it is agreed at the highest level.'

Ruzsky subsided, muttering, while I watched him and wondered at his purpose in going through this play-acting. He had a place – and no doubt a reputation – to keep up. It must have been that.

'One thing more,' Goloshchokin said, indicating me with a wave of his hand. 'This is Yakovlev. Some of you know him or know of him. He has the task, given him by Comrade Sverdlov personally, of delivering the Romanovs to the Germans. That means getting them out of the House of Special Purpose. So – *it is vital Yurovsky be not told!*'

'It will be difficult to get them out,' General Berzin said. 'The last time I saw him, Yurovsky swore to me not one of them would ever leave the house alive.'

'What if we were to *order* it – as a Soviet?' Beloborodov asked, with more than a little of pomposity.

Berzin said, 'I asked him much the same thing. I said, "Trotsky wants to put them on trial before the world, in Moscow." Yurovsky said that in that case Trotsky would have to come and fetch them personally and *promise* they'd die for their crimes against the people. Only then might he let them leave the Ipatiev.'

'Then means will just have to be found,' Goloshchokin said. 'Yakovlev and I will discuss the matter. But I repeat – *Yurovsky must not know.*'

'It must also be quick,' Beloborodov said then. 'If the Whites and the Czechs overrun us, they may try to restore

238

Bloody Nicholas to the throne. He must be out of here, if he is not dead. But he must *not* fall into their hands.'

And so it was left, but as we broke up and went our ways Ruzsky nudged my arm and muttered that he must talk to me later. We arranged to meet in the familiar place, at the rear wall, of the Palais Royal at eleven. When we did, he gave me news which sounded sinister indeed.

'You should know,' said he, 'that Yurovsky has been asking Scriabin for his maps and charts.'

I'd forgotten about Ruzsky's friend Scriabin, and certainly knew nothing of maps or charts. 'What maps?'

'Scriabin is Commissar for Natural Resources,' Ruzsky told me then. 'He knows all about the mining in this region.'

'Why is that important?'

Ruzsky said, 'Because it means he also has records of mine shafts. Yurovsky's looking for one that's disused and remote.'

'My God!'

'And there's more,' Ruzsky said, and when he spoke of matters like this there was an unpleasant, low relish about the man. We were supposed to be serving the same cause, yet I could hardly bear to be with him. I waited uneasily for his next revelation. It was delivered with a smile.

'He's ordered petrol,' Ruzsky said, 'barrels of it. And a massive amount of sulphuric acid.'

As he spoke, there was a low rumble in the distance, which some might have thought to be a summer evening's thunder, but I knew it for guns – the Whites and the Czechs were forcing the Red Army back.

Next morning I was up at six and down to the station – and there I halted, sniffing, as I passed the station restaurant. Fresh ground coffee, unmistakable; and new-baked pastry! I breakfasted, guiltily but fully, in no more than ten minutes and began looking round for the German train, which was hardly difficult to find, standing as it did on

239

a marshalling spur no more than a furlong from the restaurant.

I looked at it in speculation. Six carriages, two engines, Red Cross markings and drawn blinds. No German flag; indeed nothing to indicate its origins – and there was no lack of wisdom in such anonymity considering the Russian opinion of things German. I stopped for a moment beside the big driving wheel and felt the boiler casing for heat. It was cold, and there was no glimpse of fire when I hoisted myself half up to the footplate.

I walked to the nearest carriage, swung half up and tried the door. Locked. Damned Hun stayabeds, I thought, and banged at the door with my fist until a baggy-eyed orderly swung it open, looked irritably down at me and demanded to know my business.

'I must see the commander of the train.'

'Who are you?' Then he added a tentative, '*mein Herr*,' in case I held rank.

'From Goloshchokin, Commissar for War,' I snapped. 'Is the commander asleep?'

'I don't –'

It was all plain enough. They'd been here for weeks and were bored stupid. I sent the orderly to rout out his master, found the saloon, and took a seat.

The commander came in his dressing-gown – and a great ornate affair it was in figured brocade. The fat crest on his left breast pocket had enough gold and silver wire in it for a Bulgarian admiral and he was screwing a monocle into his right eye. There was a duelling scar from the eye to the lip. If you were caricaturing a German general for *Punch*, here was your model.

All the same, he'd heard of me. When I told him I was Yakovlev, he gave me a level look and said: 'You came close, my friend, so I hear.'

'And this time we'll do it,' I said.

He gave me a glare that was all surprise. 'We?'

'You haven't been told – from Moscow?'

240

'Nothing.' He regarded me warily.

'Then I'll tell you. You have complete command here, do you?'

'I do.' He snapped his heels together, and by God his slippers clicked! He was General Baron von Kleber, at my service.

'Right,' I told him. 'First, you'd better get the boiler lit, keep steam up at all times and be ready to move. I have been instructed to deliver the entire Imperial Family, and such members of their court as are with them, to this train. As soon as it is done, you will move westward.'

His eyes gleamed. 'It will be an honour. When will their Imperial Majesties arrive?'

'At night,' I said. 'One night very soon. There is too much hostility in the town to act by day and it must be clandestine, anyway.'

'Why so, when Moscow agrees?'

'Because it's all deviousness here,' I said. 'And because there's more than one in this town who'd be only too willing to ignore instructions from the Central Executive and shoot all of them out of hand.'

Van Kleber said angrily, 'They wouldn't dare!' But I judged it was just noise; he must know very well they'd do it. Then he gave me a hard look. 'Your task is to deliver them. *How* will it be done?'

'I'll get them out of the house in the small hours.'

He said, 'Will you? And how will you deal with Yurovsky?'

'My business, General.'

He lit a monogrammed Turkish cigarette with a lucifer from a small gold pocketbox. 'Yurovsky is a fanatic. Do you need assistance?'

I shook my head.

'I have a dozen army veterans here, by friend. Experienced fighters. Yours if you need men. Think about it. And think of the numbers of Yurovsky's Letts!'

'Letts?' I said.

241

'Oh yes. Reliable fellows for dirty work, our Lithuanian friends.' Then he added unexpectedly, 'Good luck.' He spoke in English and I must have reacted and looked at him in surprise, for he laughed shortly. 'You *are* British, aren't you?'

I disdained the remark and turned to leave. Von Kleber followed me to the carriage door and there said quietly, 'Don't worry, my British friend. I'm here at the Kaiser's own request. To succeed in this task I'd make an ally of Satan himself!'

Now time began to be lost more than I liked, but there was much to arrange with many people, all of them too busy to be free with their time. First Goloshchokin and Beloborodov went off together to the Ipatiev House to talk to Yurovsky. For ammunition they had with them a telegraph message received that day from a plainly-worried Sverdlov to the effect that if anything happened to Nicholas, then Beloborodov, Goloshchokin and Yurovsky would answer with their necks.

I was waiting at the Hotel American when they returned. My fingers were crossed, for if they had succeeded in conveying to Yurovsky the wider issues involved, then perhaps the Family would be released, and my delivering of them to von Kleber's train would be no more difficult a task than ordering a cab or two.

But I knew at once that they had failed, for Goloshchokin came slowly into the room and stood shaking his head. His hands lifted from his sides, then fell again helplessly and he said, 'Yurovsky's alerted.'

'*What?* How can he be?'

'Or maybe he guesses, I don't know,' Goloshchokin said. 'I think the man's gone mad. He was talking of waiting until the Whites march in, then summoning the White generals and executing the whole Romanov family before their eyes.'

'And what of Sverdlov's message – doesn't Yurovsky value his own life?'

242

'I'll tell you what I think,' Beloborodov said. 'I think that now he's living only for the thought of killing them. And relishing the how and when of it!'

So that was that. If the Imperial Family was to be brought out of the Ipatiev House it seemed it must be done *despite* the guard.

Which meant – by force.

And by me . . .

I went next to Berzin, seeking a soldier's eye and memory, and spent a whole day racing on a thin, scraggy pony from one distant defensive enplacement to the next before I ran him to earth at last, seated on a wooden stool outside a smallish tent which was his present headquarters. He looked tired to the point of collapse, but yet had the soldier's way of sloughing off weariness in a second. Then, in ten minutes' work with a sketch-pad, Berzin produced for me a plan of the interior of the House of Special Purpose – and it was one, furthermore, which showed the positions occupied by guards. The outside I had seen for myself, with its double stockade fronting the arched entrance. When we were finished I tucked the drawing into my pocket and swung into the saddle of my sinewy pony, and then Berzin called and I wheeled to face him again.

'Make a close inspection of that aspect of the house which shows itself from the side alley,' he advised. 'That alley's name is Voznesensky Street, I think.'

'Go on,' I said.

'There's a stair there, rising from the garden to a verandah up above. It's not guarded, or wasn't when I saw it. Good luck.'

'Thank you,' I said, and waved and wished him the same with a hypocritical tongue.

He smiled tiredly. 'Luck won't help me. I need ten thousand men and five hundred guns.'

I rode away then, with the rumbling sound of White gunfire ringing me on both sides and to the rear. Only ahead, to the north where the city lay, was there no threatening firing.

Next morning I was ordered to see Goloshchokin, who demanded to know if I yet had a plan. I told him I had.

'Explain it.'

'No,' said I. 'I will not explain. Once it's told, even to you, then it's out and somebody could carry the tale to Yurovsky. I'm not risking it!'

He glowered at me, but he was no fool.

'When?' he demanded.

'When I am ready. There are things still to be done.'

'Then do them,' Goloshchokin said.

When I reached the German train in its siding at the station, General Baron von Kleber was about to take a comfortable breakfast and invited me to join him. When I declined, he insisted it was the merest *Imbiss* and I must at the very least take a cup of coffee. His breakfast table groaned: cheeses and cold meats, a variety of breads and pastries and fruit – and four soldier servants to heap his plate. The coffee was quite excellent.

Clearly first things came first with von Kleber: the filling of his plate he watched hawk-like, and only when all was to his satisfaction did he look across at me. 'Go on.'

I said, 'Tonight, probably.'

He gave a slow nod. 'You want my Swabian veterans?'

'Yes.'

'Your plan?'

'Is secret.'

'The best way, always.' Von Kleber compressed his lips. 'Tell me what you can.'

'I intend to bring the Imperial Family to you, here, in the early hours of tomorrow. You should have steam up on the engine and be ready to leave.'

'Certainly.'

'Your men, your Swabians – I would prefer they be

244

dressed in the same drill khaki worn by the Bolshevik forces, but –'

'No buts,' said von Kleber. 'We *have* khaki.' He must have seen my surprise, for he added, '*and* sailor suits, my friend, and field grey. We came prepared.'

'Good. Have you arms?'

'Of course. Good German – or poor Russian?'

'German will suffice. You said twelve men. Arm ten with pistols, two with rifles.'

Von Kleber nodded and placed a morsel of game pie in his mouth. Speaking round it he said, 'Paraded where?'

'Paraded nowhere. They are to walk, one by one and from different directions, to Ascension Square. In front of the church, which stands opposite the British consulate, I shall meet them.'

'You'll be conspicuous, my friend.'

'No,' I said. 'There are no street lights at that point. And they'll be there only a moment.'

He picked up his glass. 'Think you can succeed?'

'I can try.'

Despite the early hour, von Kleber now called for cognac. When it was poured, he raised his glass formally. 'To your success, my friend. And to *their* freedom.'

We drank to it and I departed.

At noon, at my request, Beloborodov took himself to the House of Special Purpose to sample the atmosphere.

He came back with a pale and hunted look about him and as he entered the room at the Americana, his first words were: 'The barrage is getting very near. This –' and he gestured at the double windows of the room – 'this muffles the noise. It's loud in the street.'

'What of Yurovsky?' I demanded. By now I was beginning to know Beloborodov, and understood that with the city about to fall and much to be done, he wished only to get on with it. The Romanovs were merely a burden to him. Already now he was bending over a map.

'Yurovsky?' I said again.

He raised his head. 'Determination. Nothing is changed, except that Yurovsky's grip is tighter.'

It was difficult to see how it could be made tighter. 'How?'

Beloborodov said, 'I went to the stairs, intending to go to the upper rooms to inspect the prisoners. He stopped me.'

I frowned. 'How far does his authority stretch?'

'There was a revolver in his hand. *That* stretches authority.' Beloborodov smiled grimly. 'I was in no danger. But if I had insisted I doubt if Yurovsky would have hesitated. He has the Romanovs marked for his own killing. Nobody else goes near to them.'

'Then why does he keep them alive?'

Beloborodov shrugged. 'I asked him, don't imagine I didn't! He said to me "I hold them only in trust for the people, until the enemy arrives. At that moment, when it is clear I cannot hold them – *then* as the people's Commissar for Justice, I shall *dispense* justice."'

I said to Beloborodov, 'I'm the enemy. Even with you behind me, even with Sverdlov and Lenin himself behind me. I'm still the enemy – to Yurovsky!'

Beloborodov game the ghost of a smile and said 'Then move softly and discreetly.'

I had one more question for him and asked it despite his obvious impatience. 'Did you notice anything changed there?'

He flicked me a glance. 'In what way?'

'In any way.'

He gave a small nod. 'I should have mentioned it. There was hammering from above – from the floor where the Romanovs live.'

'Did you ask what it was?'

Beloborodov nodded. 'Yurovsky said he was reinforcing his prison. I told you he's obsessive to the point of madness! He's boarding up all the windows on the side overlooking the garden.'

246

'What!' This was shattering to me.

He repeated: 'Boarding up the windows. He says he fears an attack.'

I said, 'Does he guess – about us?'

He shook his head. 'It's the Whites he fears – a raid into the city.'

But now my plan was in ruins! I had intended to decoy the guards at the south entrance, and then to lead von Kleber's Swabians up the stairs from the garden to the balcony. Once there, and in the house, there would be a dozen men to guard the family, to hold the interior stairs if Yurovsky's men attacked, and to take the Romanovs to safety down the garden stairs to where Ruzsky would be waiting with a truck at the south entrance in Voznesensky Street.

Angrily I told Beloborodov the rescue was now impossible.

'You mean *your* plan is impossible.'

'Yes.'

'Then find another!'

And against the odds, I did, though it was not a plan as the other had been. That had been based upon calculation of the dispositions, and the proper use of strength and surprise. It was a military plan. Now talk would count more and action less. And Bronard was involved . . .

CHAPTER THIRTEEN

Out of the myths of time . . .

Gossips were apt to say in the pubs of the City of London that to rattle Gibraltar would be a good deal easier than to rattle Sir Horace Malory. Even so, he became rattled on occasion, but he was good at concealing it and only those who knew him most closely were aware of the infallible sign: when upset, Malory had a tendency to sibilance.

Lady Malory, to whom after fifty-five years of marriage his mind was an open book, had asked sharply at breakfast: 'What on earth's the matter, Horace? You're hissing like a snake!'

He had mumbled an answer. Something of a problem at the office, m'dear, nothing to worry about.

At which she spoke his name in a peremptory way. Busily scavenging in the obituary column of *The Times*, he did not look up, but she continued to repeat his name, each time more loudly, until he did.

'Yes, m'dear.'

'You should finish it quickly, Horace, whatever it is.'

'What, *The Times* obituary . . . ?'

'I mean the problem at the *office*. Finish with it – or it will finish with you. You will, *won't* you?' Lady Malory was at her most commanding.

'Yes, m'dear,' said Malory.

But it was easier said than accomplished. About as simple as trying to finish with gout, thought Malory (who occasionally suffered from it) as his chauffeur Horsfall and his Bentley car made velvet of the morning traffic. Of late, and not without cause, the Siberian adventures of Henry

George Dikeston had been intruders in his mind at all sorts of unlooked-for times. He found himself unable to take luncheon, or a walk, or even a nap, without Dikeston and his unlovely and disturbing story tapping rhythms in his head like so many demented drummers. It was no wonder he was hissing!

Yesterday he'd attacked the matter with quite a bit of determination, summoning Felix Aston from Oxford and then spending the entire day in what the historian had described as analysis. Aston had arrived staggering under the weight of no fewer than three large briefcases, all of them filled with books. Sir Horace had then proceeded to ask him straight questions, beginning with the straightest.

'*Were* the Romanovs slaughtered at Ekaterinburg?'

'Er – well, Sir Horace. The general opinion has always *been*, you see, that they, er – were. But there's a certain amount of doubt, more recently. Mangold and Summers, for instance –'

'Who are they?'

'Two BBC reporters, Sir Horace. They produced a book, *The File on the Tsar* –'*

'I read that one. Nicholas shot and the rest survived, eh?'

'I'm not sure they'd like that summary. But they reviewed all the evidence most carefully.'

'Nobody knows then, is that so?'

'Yes, Sir Horace.'

'Any ideas about why it's all so mysterious?'

'Well, if they *were* killed, it was to the Bolsheviks' advantage if nobody knew. They were very worried at the time about the Germans.'

'I know.'

'And if the Germans didn't know –'

'I understand. But tell me about their money.' Malory now listened with all the riveted attention he gave to matters monetary. The Romanovs at the time of their

* Victor Gollancz, Ltd, 1976

disappearances had money, or so it was said, in half the banks of France, Britain and America. Banks tended, naturally, to say nothing. The Tsar was the richest man on earth in those days, and the Romanovs the richest family.

Which raised another pertinent and very straight question: 'Who inherited?'

'Well – nobody, apparently,' said Aston.

Malory was now sitting a trifle straighter. Lady Malory would have noticed. 'It has all been sitting there, untouched, since 1918!'

'Or before, Sir Horace. This is the point, so some would say, about Anastasia, if she is Anastasia, who has spent half a century proclaiming that she is the Tsar's youngest daughter.'

'And failing to establish it, eh?'

'So far.'

'Any other lawsuits from frustrated heirs?'

'None of significance.'

Malory brooded for a moment. 'Would that be because Anastasia's claim made others impossible?'

'Well, my own discipline is history rather than jurisprudence, Sir Horace, but inevitably, yes. While the case was *sub judice* no others could be determined.'

'Let me get this entirely clear,' Malory said. 'There's a great deal of money –'

The historian interrupted him. 'There *may* be money, Sir Horace. It's not proven.'

'All right, all right. And if there is, then the surviving Romanovs couldn't go after it while Anastasia's case was *sub judice*?'

'True.'

'And moreover, the case was *sub judice* for –?'

'Decades. There were two verdicts – in 1967 and 1970. Of course,' the historian went on, 'neither accepted her as the Tsar's surviving daughter. If they had –'

'She'd have taken the lot!'

'If she wanted the lot, yes.'

250

The conversation became lengthy. References to particular points were sought (by Malory) and produced (by Aston). That, however, was the nub of the long talk. Still, before he left 6 Athelsgate for Paddington and the Oxford train, the historian produced two further nuggets of information. The first came in the form of a lengthy extract from *The War Memoirs of David Lloyd George*.

'Met the old rascal a time or two,' said Malory reminiscently. 'After he was done, of course. He was PM when?'

'From 1916 on. Until 1922, that is.'

'The point is what?'

Aston passed him the book. It was Volume One of the memoirs, open at page 82, and the wartime Prime Minister, in discussing the ordering of armaments, criticized very severely the practice of some major arms companies of accepting orders 'far beyond their capacity to execute'.

And Lloyd George went on: '. . . some of them had undertaken orders on a gigantic scale *from the Russian Government*. When they accepted these Russian contracts they must have known that they had not the faintest chance of executing them in time . . . Their failure to execute these orders was largely responsible for the disasters which befell the Russian armies in the campaign of 1914–15.'

Malory looked up. 'Could he mean Vickers?' he asked.

'Among others. Everybody feels the lash, but Vickers in particular. Read the best bit – about Professor Pares.'

Lloyd George went on: 'A careful and considered report on the situation came from the pen of Professor Bernard Pares, a distinguished scholar who knew Russia and Russian thoroughly. He visited Petrograd in 1915 . . . and on his return presented . . . a very remarkable account of the state of things in Russia . . . a forecast of the wrath to come . . .

'See what Pares said about Vickers?' asked the historian.

'Coming to it now,' said Malory, and read: 'I have to submit that the unfortunate failure of Messrs Vickers, Maxim & Co. to supply Russia with munitions . . . is

251

gravely jeopardizing the relations of the two countries.

'The Russians have so far put in line seven million men. Their losses when I left Petrograd had reached the enormous figure of three million, eight hundred thousand.

'I am definitely told that so far no supplies of munitions have reached Russia from England.'

Malory's eye hurried on: '. . . failure which all Russians . . . associate intimately with the crushing losses . . . and the obvious necessity of almost indefinite retreat . . .'

And then a paragraph which jolted even Malory. 'It has also led to threatened signs of resentment against the Russian authorities, which in my judgement must lead if continued to grave internal complications. Momentous developments . . . inevitable.'

Malory placed the book on his desk. 'Authoritative, that,' he said.

'Pares rather more so than that old rascal Lloyd George – in my view.' The historian grinned. 'But it can be summed up very simply. One, Russia places big orders with Vickers. Two, Vickers don't deliver as promised. Three, Russia has nearly four million dead. Four, the Russian Revolution follows. Five – if I may say so – Ekaterinburg, July 1918. All in a dead straight line.'

'Yes.' Malory sighed. 'As you say, a straight line. Thank you for your time.'

'Thank you for your fee, Sir Horace,' Felix Aston said. 'I'll leave the books if you like.'

'Please do,' Malory said, 'and good day.' His mind was already focused on Vickers, for it was Zaharoff's company: Vickers, Maxim & Co.

He turned suddenly. The historian was still slipping on a light raincoat. 'I say! Before you go . . .'

'Yes, Sir Horace?'

'Care for a swift whisky?' Malory rose and poured. 'One thing: how would the munitions be paid for?'

'You'd know more about that than I, Sir Horace, surely? Credits and things, I expect.'

252

'Perhaps, perhaps. But I'm thinking of all those Romanov holdings in overseas banks.'

'That's private money, of course.'

'Yes? I wondered about that.'

'The Tsar would hardly have spent his own money on arms, though, would he?'

'Indeed not,' said Malory. 'Er – what time's your train?'

'In forty minutes, Sir Horace, and I'm afraid I daren't miss it. I have an American guest at High Table tonight and –'Aston smiled modestly – 'there's a visiting professorship at stake.'

'It's money, you see,' Malory said. 'What about tomorrow?'

'Tomorrow is fine.'

And now it *was* tomorrow, and Lady Malory's instruction echoed in his mind as he waited and savoured (though not as much as usual) a Romeo No.3 with Blue Mountain coffee. David Lloyd George, he reflected, had been a wicked old devil. None wickeder.

None? What about Zaharoff?

And what a *pair* they made!

'Tell me,' Malory said before the historian had so much as added sugar to his coffee, 'about the relations between Lloyd George and Zaharoff.'

'Well, it's a bit mysterious.'

'I imagined it might be,' said Sir Horace. 'Do go on.'

'Not much known, actually. But there's a fascinating point. Zaharoff was – well, whatever he was: who knows if he was Greek, Turk, Anatolian, even Russian. Lot of covering-up went on in the matter of his birth. Records burned. Impossible statements sworn by a bench of bishops. *You* know.'

'Yes, I do. Born in Mughla in Anatolia, that's what he always said.'

'Usually said,' Aston corrected. 'But the point is he was a naturalized Frenchman. French domicile too.'

'Agreed. What about Lloyd George?'

'The old Welsh Wizard slipped Zaharoff a big gong in nineteen-eighteen. Made him a Knight of the Order of the British Empire.'

'Yes, I know.'

'And ever afterwards, Zaharoff called himself Sir Basil.'

'Doesn't fit, does it? Can't do it, can you?'

'*He* did, Sir Horace, all his life. Lloyd George gave him a step up in 1921: Knight of the Most Honourable Order of the Bath. Still called himself *Sir* Basil but still a French citizen. Now – how could that come about?'

'I suppose,' said Malory, 'that people just *assumed* –'

'What, the College of Heralds? Just assumed? No, my guess is he wanted a title, a British one, and Lloyd George *fixed* things.'

'It would take a little doing,' Sir Horace murmured.

'There never was a fixer like him.'

Malory brooded for a moment. 'Why then did Lloyd George turn savage in his memoirs?'

'He didn't. Not to Zaharoff. To Vickers, yes, but Zaharoff was long retired.'

'Friends, were they – or useful to each other?'

'Useful, I'd guess.' Once more the historian produced his grin. 'Or how about partners?'

'Partners?' echoed Malory.

'Partners,' said the historian. 'Think about it.'

'Oh, it has my attention. *Partners*, indeed! But in what, do you suggest?'

Felix Aston hesitated. 'I'm near my limit, Sir Horace.'

'What do you mean – what limit?'

'You'll perhaps think I am ridiculously cautious, but people have come to sticky ends in chasing Zaharoff.'

'Sticky ends – what *do* you mean?'

'I mean they have died, Sir Horace. Two to my knowledge. One found dead in a hotel, the other drowned in the lake at his French estate. So I repeat, sir, that I'm near my limit. I'm enormously discreet, you see. Always. And I can see the general direction of your interest, though not, *of course*, the precise nature of it. But there *is* one more thing. Are you aware of the story – I hesitate to describe it as fact, though it was reported quite widely – that soon after Russia entered the war in 1914, and just before ice closed the port of Archangel for the winter, two British warships dropped anchor there?'

'No,' said Malory. 'I'm not aware of it. Is there more?'

'The *New York Times* then, and a lot of historians since, reported that the ships were met by barges loaded with gold from the Tsar's own mines. The warships took it to Britain. It was to buy armaments. The Tsar's private contribution, you might call it, to the war effort.'

'How much?' Malory asked.

'The story is,' and Aston enunciated with care, 'that it was two point seven billion. That's dollars. But you *could* say about five hundred million in sterling. At 1914 values.'

'I'll be damned!' said Malory. And though there was no letter S in the epithet, it emerged as a longish hiss.

It was so clear! No mistaking *this*, Malory thought. The historian had gone by now and his books with him, and Malory paced slowly up and down the room at 6 Athelsgate, while the ingredients boiled together in the cauldron of his brain.

What a pity it was that Sir Basil had burned his papers (he'd also damned near burned down his own house, at 45 Avenue Hoche in Paris, at the same time, Malory recalled). Because it was a safe bet that Zaharoff was in Russia touting for business as soon as war was declared. God, he thought – the whole thing *stank* of Sir Basil. The richest man on earth, Tsar of All the Russias, who had a million a day in private income, setting up a war chest with his own gold. To buy arms, from Vickers!

Who could send warships? Not Zaharoff. But Lloyd George was Minister of Munitions, then.

Five hundred million! But brought out of Russia *fairly* secretly. Distant press reports, no more.

And no arms were delivered.

And revolution followed.

And the murder of Nicholas *and his entire family* followed too!

So no heirs? . . . No, no heirs.

Or were there?

Malory stopped pacing and glanced down. His highly-polished shoes gleamed black against the deep red of the carpet. But the gleam, he thought, savagely, was as nothing to the gleam of the gold bars three floors below, in Hillyard Cleef's celebrated vault.

As *nothing*!

Oh yes, he knew the details. One hundred million in what are known as 'good delivery bars' each of 400 troy ounces. Placed in the vaults on January 1st, year of Our Lord, 1915. One hundred million kept permanently on display, by agreement with Her Majesty's Government. *And* the Bank of England. Because for many years after 1915 there were tight and difficult restrictions on gold holdings . . .

But it was a simple enough proposition, so hallowed by time that Malory had barely thought of it in years. By agreement, the hundred million was a constant. If the gold price rose, a number of bars were taken from 6 Athelsgate to the Bank of England. If the gold price fell, the process was reversed. It was a simple thing. The Government and the national reserve benefited inevitably, in the long run, because the price of gold rose with equal inevitability over the years. Hillyard, Cleef benefited because its gold reserve was always there to maintain confidence.

Malory thought about gold. He had touched one of the bars, once only and with his fingertips, when he was quite young. It had had a slightly greasy feel, he remembered. Remarkably easy material to work, though, and salted away under mattresses all over the world in bars of various weights. The firm of Johnson Mathey, here in London, made bars of all sizes, from the 3.75 troy ounces of the ten-tola bar upward. No difficulty in finding a way to put new markings on a gold bar, either: you melted it down, re-moulded it, and put another stamp on it. You might remove a South African stamp and replace it with, for instance, that of the Banque de France or Credit Suisse.

Five hundred million. At 1914 values.

God!

The Tsar's war chest. That's what it was.

But Lloyd George needed a war chest, too.

'Despite repeated promises, the munitions were not delivered,' reported Pares.

They got their hands on the gold – Zaharoff and Lloyd George – and used it: one to stuff his exchequer, and the other to underwrite his business.

Brilliant – absolutely brilliant! Malory thought. Zaharoff's idea, of course . . .

But he did not linger on the delights of so ineffable a stroke. It was necessary to think it through.

There was no surviving heir. Hillyard, Cleef and the British Government had in effect inherited.

There was no heir because there was no proof. The Tsar, who would by now have been a hundred and ten years old, was not even legally assumed to be dead.

The Grand Duchess Anastasia had failed in her claim, and for no sensible reason that Malory could see, the rest of the Romanov family had never tried with any show of determination to get their hands on Nicholas Romanov's huge assets abroad.

Why not? Because they knew something? Because lawsuits were expensive and the Romanov cousins knew they would fail? Yes, all that was possible.

So – a single survivor *or* proof of death. Either would suffice. Either was the key to enormous wealth.

257

And Dikeston was in Ekaterinburg in July 1918, at Zaharoff's insistence!

At dinner that night, though he was already thinking of the means to have the Hillyard, Cleef ingots recast, Sir Horace Malory was not himself. He punished the malt whisky beforehand, and opened a second bottle of claret.

'You're getting worse,' said Lady Malory disparagingly, 'you sound like a pit full of vipers.'

CHAPTER FOURTEEN

———————◆◆———————

*Seventh and final instalment of the account,
written by Lt Cdr H. G. Dikeston, RN, of
his journeyings in Russia in the spring
and summer of 1918*

When first I encountered it, I was much struck by the
degree of mutual distrust common to the Bolsheviks. Here,
after all, were men who had fought a long-established auto-
cracy and overthrown it. They claimed their victory in the
name of the People and proclaimed Brotherhood and Equality. Trust, though, was not to be their way, as history shows.

Bronard first explained it to me, grinning in contempt.
Within the Urals Soviet were a dozen shifting alliances, he
said. A pair of Commissars might agree on one matter and
disagree on three more. Factions proliferated, as did en-
mities. 'Friendships,' said Bronard, after I used the word,'
'do not exist. Too dangerous.'

'But Sverdlov and Goloshchokin are old friends, surely?'
I said.

'Old acquaintances and old allies, but *not* friends,' said
Bronard. 'Does one friend threaten another with death?'

I had not sought Bronard out; rather he had come to me,
having learned from Goloshchokin that my plan must
perforce be abandoned.

We were sitting in a room at the Americana, Bronard
nursing half a tumbler of vodka. A great pity that we don't
know where Nicholas keeps the paper,' he said thoughtfully.

To tell the truth, I had forgotten, until that moment,
about the document. After all, it was safe in the Finnish
Bank in Moscow. And for many days my mind had been
concentrated entirely upon the hope of rescuing the Romanov family.

259

'Why?' I said. 'Even if we knew, we couldn't get to it.'

He gave me a look. 'Yurovsky, you mean?'

I nodded. It was then he began to talk about alliances and about the way he had insinuated himself into the Urals Oblast Soviet.

'Every man, if he's a politician, has an *idée fixe*,' he said with a smug chuckle. 'With Scriabin it's gold, God alone knows why. Agree with him that all gold belongs to the workers, and he's on your side in everything else. I support Berzin and Goloshchokin in demanding more arms for the working class: that's what *they* care about.'

'Are you saying Yurovsky trusts *you*?' I asked in surprise.

He shook his head. 'You don't listen, do you? Yurovsky doesn't trust *me*. He doesn't trust, really *trust*, anybody. Nor do any of them. But Yurovsky knows I'm on his side where the Romanovs are concerned. He's heard me ranting about them and I always ranted loudly. He trusts my views about his own *idée fixe*, because they are his own views. But it's my opinion he trusts, not me – you understand?'

'Oh yes. I understand. Tell me – would he let you in to the Ipatiev House?'

Bronard took a long swallow of vodka. 'He might.'

'But not Goloshchokin?'

'I'm not Goloshchokin, am I? *He's* Sverdlov's man. Yurovsky'll have guessed a lot of what Sverdlov's doing; and why the Germans are here, too. He's not a fool.'

'Could *you* enter the house?' I persisted.

'Not much point, is there?' Bronard said. 'I yelled for Nicholas's blood often enough, and at Tobolsk he heard me do it. Nicholas wouldn't trust *me* with any paper he thought important. We'd have to get you in to him.'

I said, 'To get them all out would be better.'

He gave me a curious smile. 'Oh, I'm not being reluctant, don't imagine that. The moment has come and I can recognize it. But it's taken time and trouble to make a place

260

here.' He gave a shrug. 'So I'll abandon it, if I have to. What do you want?'

'Answers to questions.'

He stretched like an animal. And somehow, like a cat stretching on a hearthrug, he seemed at the same time to be indolent, comfortable and fully alert. He said, 'You – you neither like nor trust me. It's true, eh?'

'We have a common purpose,' I told him.

And he laughed. 'That's right! You and I – we're like the Bolsheviks, you see. It's unity of interests. To get the paper we must get the Romanovs out. Lucky, is it not, that I'm the one Yurovsky might listen to!'

I said, 'It's damned useful!'

'They'll all talk to me. Yurovsky, Goloshchokin, Beloborodov, Berzin – all of them. It takes *work*, my friend, and preparation. That's why Zaharoff pays me well. In two years the Urals Soviet will be buying their arms from Zaharoff, and I'll be rich and in retirement!'

'Yurovsky's Letts – what of them?' I said.

'What do you mean?'

'If he were romoved, what then?'

Bronard frowned. 'Will you never understand that there *is* no personal loyalty here.'

'They're not his men, then?'

'They're soldiers of the revolutionary army. And yes, it *can* be done!'

I must have looked puzzled. 'What can be done?'

He sighed. And then, to my amazement, he told me precisely what my own thoughts had been a mere moment earlier. The whole stratagem made good, practical sense, Bronard said, and should, furthermore, be put into operation at the earliest feasible moment. We agreed on that, at least. And shook hands on it . . .

Three men and a single vehicle: the required resources for rescuing an emperor, his consort, his heirs. The truck was an almost new American Dodge ('abandoned by a fleeing capitalist,' said Bronard with a truly wicked laugh) and the men were our two selves and Goloshchokin, who had agreed to drive the truck.

Why Goloshchokin? Because above all the need would be for confidence and authority: the first Bronard's with Yurovsky, the other Goloshchokin's with the Letts.

And so, a few minutes after midnight – it was, accordingly, July 17th – the truck drove along Voznesensky Avenue to the House of Special Purpose. As we approached I saw the new-piled sandbags of what was obviously a machine-gun emplacement at the north end of the stockade. Here was Yurovsky preparing his defences!

One of his Letts stamped over to us as Goloshchokin turned the truck round and then reversed it until its rear entered the gap in the stockade. The guard's rifle was in his hands rather than at his shoulder – another sign the whole place was alert.

'Who are you?' the Lett demanded.

'Ruzsky,' responded Bronard cheerfully, 'with Commissar Goloshchokin. Here's my pass. Tell me – do you like fish?'

'Fish?' repeated the guard, made uncertain by this joviality on the part of a high official. He took the pass. 'Well . . .'

'Because we've found a barrel of pickled herring. Thank you –' he took his pass back – 'found it at the Americana Hotel and it's Baltic herring, my friend, and I said, those Balts in Comrade Yurovsky's guard would enjoy eating those. Am I right?'

'Yes, sir.'

'Yes, *Comrade*,' cried Bronard. 'Come on, let's get it unloaded!'

So we left Goloshchokin at the wheel and Bronard and I unloaded the herring barrel and a bottle or two of chilled vodka and a jar of pickled cucumbers. Gaining entry to the Ipatiev House, the gaol of a king, was as easy as that. The guard stood and watched as the two of us walked through the high stockade with our little hoard of food.

I had thought Yurovsky might be asleep, but he stood waiting as we entered the first hallway: a thin man of medium height, with sparse sand-coloured hair. He wore, as I had been told he usually did, a short white jacket of the kind often worn by doctors and dentists. His glance rested briefly upon me and he frowned, but then he turned at once to Bronard and said, 'What *is* this nonsense?' Over his shoulder I could see, through the open doorway, that two Lettish guards were standing, at ease but watchful.

'Brought something for your men,' Bronard said loudly. Whether he actually was a little drunk I do not know, but I doubt it. Still, he gave the impression of one with over-much liquor in him. He explained the discovery of the herring barrel in the hotel's cold-room. 'Thought straight-away, Yurovsky's men would like 'em, that's what I thought. Brought something to go with 'em, too!' He waved a vodka bottle in each hand.

I watched Yurovsky carefully. So much depended upon how he received this farrago of nonsense. But all seemed well. Where he had been frowning, his face now relaxed into a faint smile, one almost of indulgence.

'How kind of you – come along through here.' He gestured at the doorway in an almost courtly way. We followed and placed our load upon the table that apparent-ly served as his desk, and he now made a great fuss: 'Herrings from the Baltic, yes, my Letts will be delighted,' and 'Hasn't it been *hot* today!' and so on. I could almost have been at tea with a maiden aunt.

We had agreed, Bronard and I, that we must take him prisoner at the first good opportunity. Both of us were armed with pistols and I know that when I put the heavy pickle jar on the table, I turned, with my hand ready by the pistol, only to see that for the moment it was impossible: two guards with rifles occupied the doorway. We would have to wait.

Yurovsky gestured towards me. 'Who is this?'

'Yakovlev.'

Now the frown returned with a vengeance. 'But he was expelled from the city!'

'He came back from Moscow with a personal despatch from Trotsky to General Berzin,' Bronard said. 'He's a messenger, that's all. But he can drive a truck, so I put him to work, eh Yakovlev?'

'A pleasure,' I said.

Yurovsky's eye was still hard upon me. 'Are you Trotsky's man, then? You were Sverdlov's once.'

I said, 'Neither, Comrade. I am a pair of hands and a pair of feet. I do as I'm told.'

'But by whom?'

'The Party. If you make me choose a man, then I'm always Lenin's, like all of us.'

'Hmmm.' His hand ran across his chin as he looked at me, and I could hear the rasp of his beard. 'When did you leave Moscow and have you heard Trotsky's intentions about the Romanovs?'

'A week ago. There's talk of a trial in Moscow to be broadcast to all of Russia.'

'Whose idea is it – Trotsky's?'

I said, 'Characteristic of him. Good propaganda, perhaps.'

'Will it happen?'

'I doubt it,' I said. 'I don't think, apart from Trotsky, that anybody else cares.'

That sentence has echoed in my brain all down the years. I have examined it a thousand times for shades of meaning, for hidden subtleties. But I am not a subtle man, neither in speaking nor in examining words. I can see nothing there.

All that happened was that Yurovsky said, 'It's so hot in here. The heat gets into the stones by day and comes out again at night.' He produced a handkerchief and mopped his brow. Then, 'For refreshment – your own vodka, Comrades? Or –' and he became chatty; I repeat, there

264

was a most marked resemblance between Yurovsky and my maiden aunts – 'the capitalists know how to look after themselves, I can tell you, Comrades. Why, in this house there's a huge refrigerator, made by Westinghouse and brought all the way from America! So we have ice – think of *that*, in a private house! – and tonight I made lemonade!'

I remember smiling at the thought of lemonade; that too was a link with my aunts.

'You'd like some?' Yurovksy asked almost eagerly.

'Very much.'

He slipped out then, past the two in the doorway, and closed the door behind him. I turned to Bronard and said, 'When he returns.'

He nodded urgently. 'The instant he returns!'

I loosened the pistol in my pocket, ensuring that I could produce it swiftly and without entanglement, then I rose and stood by the curtained window. From somewhere in the house I heard footsteps on a wooden floor. One of the Imperial Family, perhaps, so near to freedom now. Then there was silence, interrupted after a few seconds by a sudden sharp cracking sound.

I glanced at Bronard and saw his head had cocked to one side and he was listening.

And then it came: that single crack was followed by a rapid volley of gunfire. Unmistakably it was a barrage of shots, and close at hand! I sprang to the door and jerked it open. Silence now and the corridor outside was deserted. As I looked anxiously first one way and then the other I heard first a cry of pain, then a thump, repeated, and then a further shot.

I raced along the corridor, pistol in hand, entered a hallway with a wide stair. I plunged through the open door opposite, across another room and into a square hall, the air of which was grey blue with reeking gunsmoke. Yurovsky stood facing me and I halted, gaping, at the sight of him. He wore a strange smile and in his hand was a revolver

265

from whose barrel a thin trace of smoke ascended. And he said in a high, mad, cracked voice, 'Lemonade you wanted, eh? Not this –'

I knew by then, of course – had known from the instant of the first shot. I flung myself past him while the shots still echoed and saw to my left open double doors and a wall of men's backs. And still there were shots.

Then a ghastly quiet fell and there came a whimper and a thud and a last crack.

I forced myself through the wall of backs and saw . . . a charnel house.

I will *not* describe that scene. In the room eleven people, fine people who had been *alive* a single minute earlier, now lay slaughtered. Dazed with horror, I recognized Tsar Nicholas, his Tsarina, his son, his daughters – and oh *God!* . . . there Marie, my beautiful Marie, lay dead in a pool of her own blood! Gaping round, through rage and a stream of hot tears, I recognized only Botkin, the royal doctor. The remaining four must have been servants.

And then I saw a movement . . . one of the Letts . . . kneeling beside her, beside *Marie!* . . . and searching . . . robbing her body!

I stepped close, shot him in the neck and then swung round, with Yurovsky next in my mind. Yurovsky *must* die! But he was not there, must be outside the room. I stepped forward, and now saw Bronard, saw his foot swinging quickly up, kicking my revolver from my fist.

I was seized by the Letts, dragged from that room to Yurovsky's, flung inside. Goloshchokin stood there, ashen-faced, holding a pistol pointed at Yurovsky who still wore that sickening grin of triumph.

'Kill him!' I yelled, and Yurovsky leered at me and said, 'Too late, isn't it?'

I flung myself at him, but somehow Bronard had interposed himself, and he, too, was armed. I stood raging, helpless as they forced me back. Of the four of us, probably only Bronard was sane at that moment.

And *he* was more than sane: for he was actually thinking! The first words then spoken were his, and I shall never forget their cold calculation. He directed them at Goloshchokin, who stood trembling visibly with fear. He said, 'There will be a way all this can be turned to advantage . . .'

Advantage! With the whole Imperial Family lying butchered a few yards away *he* was looking for advantage. Yes, and quickly finding it! He walked to Goloshchokin and cracked his flat hand across the man's cheek, and snarled 'Think – and listen, damn you! Or we're dead!'

'Sverdlov!' Goloshchokin kept muttering. 'He'll shoot us all!'

'Not if he doesn't *know*!' Bronard said.

'How can he not know?'

'I'll tell you how.' Words tumbled from Bronard, and he turned quickly to Yurovsky. 'That mine on the Koptyaki road. Did you –?'

Yurovsky nodded, still smiling. 'Petrol and oil of vitriol. All there.'

'How much?'

'Enough.'

Bronard stood blinking for a moment. Then he picked the telephone from Yurovsky's desk and thrust it at Goloshchokin. 'We need another truck. Arrange it – quickly!'

There was something totally compelling about the fellow. Goloschchokin, a man of greater authority and influence, deferred unhesitatingly and did as Bronard bade.

Bronard, meanwhile, was still talking, half to himself. 'Mystery,' I heard him say, 'is to everyone's advantage if we can create it.'

Goloshchokin replaced the telephone. 'A second truck is coming.'

'Then here's what we must do,' Bronard said. 'We must

267

take them all away – the Romanovs, the servants, everybody!'

I found my voice now, and began to protest and he levelled his revolver at me and said, 'A word – one *word* – and I shoot you! Just listen, damn you.'

He said Yurovsky had already planned the last resting-place of the Romanov Dynasty – at this mine he referred to as the Four Brothers shaft. 'Now,' he hurried on, 'we also have the four servants and there is the dead Lett and the doctor. *Six* bodies. Take *them* to the mine, Yurovsky. The Whites will be in the city in a week but it will be an age before the mine is found. Scatter Romanov clothing, and a few possessions there.'

'But they'll know!' Goloshchokin protested. 'Everybody will know. There are forensic tests that will identify –'

'Shut up!' Bronard said. 'I told you to listen. The Whites will say we Bolsheviks killed the Romanovs – oh yes, they'll *say* it. But how can they *prove* it when they are the *wrong* bodies?'

'Where will the other bodies be?'

'We'll take them,' Bronard said, pointing at me. 'He and I will take them, and bury them. Yakovlev's a man for a Christian burial I've no doubt!'

'What of the Letts?' cried Goloshchokin. '*They* know.'

'Send them to the front!' offered Bronard brutally. 'You're Commissar for War. Make sure they're killed in action. Or shoot them yourself. But wait until they have scrubbed this place clean!'

And so, at dead of night, when as legend says the blackest deeds are done, it *was* done; the bodies of the royal servants and the doctor were placed in a truck and driven away by Yurovsky and Goloshchokin. Bronard and I then set to the melancholy task of bringing the remains of the Imperial Family from the room in which Yurovksy had murdered them all.

You may wonder why I did nothing to take revenge for them but there was, in truth, nothing I *could* do. All were dead! Had there been the smallest chance of aiding them, I should not have hesitated to act at whatever risk, but of course there was not.

Furthermore Bronard's words rang in my mind. The Imperial Family had been deeply devout. A good Christian burial they must have – and only I cared enough to ensure it. That service, the last possible service to them on this earth, must be done for all the Romanovs, and especially for Marie.

We wrapped each in a blanket brought from the sleeping quarters upstairs, and one by one they were placed in the truck and by me, at least, with reverence. No one saw us, of that I am certain. When all was done, Bronard summoned the Lettish corporal and ordered that he and his men remain in the Ipatiev house until orders came from Commissar Goloshchokin. They were forbidden to venture out, or to speak to anyone. At last Bronard turned to me and said, 'Get in. We take the road east, and then we turn on to small tracks.'

'The paper,' I reminded him, because I was curious. 'Are you not going to seek it out?'

He looked at me grimly. 'It doesn't matter now. And we must be away.'

We came strangely, and while there was still dark, to a place a dozen miles or so to the east of the city. It was uncanny because abruptly the carbide lamps of the truck picked out a small shrine beside the track and beyond it what seemed to be a great black cross silhouetted against the night sky. Mystified, I stopped the truck and went to look, treading carefully, for I soon found this was marshland. And there was the cross, true enough, though a far from perfect one: made by a big, symmetrical tree, half-destroyed by lightning, but with two great boughs forming the crosspiece. What more could I do, I thought, than see that the Imperial Family be buried, all together, at the foot of a great cross!

Spades we had brought, and as the first of the light began to grow across the sky, Bronard and I bent our backs to the digging. Though the surrounding earth was wet, a little knoll lay beneath the tree, and it was there, in spongy soil, that we made the grave. It was a hard task, and Bronard dug little, but I worked violently, glad of a fierce spell of activity to direct my mind, however momentarily, away from the hates and the horrors of the night. And I swore two vows. Swore them to myself, and swore them upon the grave I dug. I swore to kill Yurovsky, and I swore to kill Sverdlov. The machinations of the one had delivered the whole family to the executioners of the other. They merited death, and more.

And then, came a dreadful task; for the bodies had to be carried, one at a time, from the truck to the tree. I fashioned a rough stretcher from birch branches and rope, and we began, working in the same oppressive silence we had maintained ever since leaving the Ipatiev House. When at last all seven lay side by side in the grave, Bronard sank to his haunches beside it and produced cigarettes.

I said, 'Not here, man!' He shrugged and moved off a little, and lit up. As he did so he inhaled deeply and with evident satisfaction. Then he gave me that detestable grin of his and said, 'Well, it's over! And we did well, eh?'

I exploded. 'Well?' I said. 'With a dozen deaths! With regicide and assassination! *Well?*'

'I never have understood,' he interjected, 'how Zaharoff came to send *you*.'

'What do you mean?' I demanded. 'Damn you – this is a wretched moment for –'

'Calm down,' he said. 'We've worked hard. We need a rest. I do, anyway.'

I could bear him no longer. I turned away and returned to the truck, for I too had need of tobacco and mine was there. With a cigarette lit, I looked down at the trembling of my hands, felt the pounding of my heart and the pressure in my head. Yet *he* was so calm! Glancing towards him, I saw he was standing now, with both hands against his face. Mystified, I stared harder, trying to work out what he was doing.

And then I realized – he had a camera and was taking a photograph!

But why?

I ran to him, and found he had done yet more. The blankets in which each of the royal corpses had been wrapped had been opened, so that faces and clothes were plainly visible!

As I whirled on him, he was taking yet another picture. I dashed the camera from his hands and he swore at me. 'You damn fool!' His hand was at his pocket, and I saw the butt of a revolver emerging and flung myself at him. Though he was quick, I was quicker and filled now, moreover, with a wild and vengeful fury. In a second, I had him by the throat . . .

Yet even then his nerve held. As I tightened my grip, Bronard used the breath that could have been his last, to croak: 'Don't you want to know why?'

Even then he lied. Had I not seen the Tsar's signature and read the document that now rested in the Finnish Bank in Moscow, I might have believed him, for he was plausible as the devil. He told me the tale as I had understood it first, on my arrival in Moscow from England, as I had gathered it in listening to that conversation in Lenin's office: the money deposited in London for the purchase of arms for the Imperial forces; the promise by Zaharoff that arms worth fifty million would be available to the Bolsheviks provided the Tsar would sign the document.

'What was in the paper?' I demanded. 'And why did you say, this morning, that it didn't matter?'

'It is a disclaimer,' he said. 'But the Tsar is dead. It has no value now.'

That was when I knew he lied; and knew also that he must have lied about many things. To me as to others. To Goloshchokin, for one. 'It was you,' I said.

271

He looked at me in insolent enquiry. 'Me? What about me?'

I said, 'You told Yurovsky!'

Bronard looked me in the eye. 'Don't be stupid! Why would I do that?'

I said, 'So that all of them would die. As they did. So that even if the Tsar's disclaimer could not be obtained, or could not be taken to London, there would be no Nicholas, and no Tsarina, and no children.'

Even as I spoke it was becoming clearer. I knew why, at that moment, the corpses of the doctor and the servants were being destroyed at the mine.

I said, How much was it? How much had the Tsar sent?'

He stared at me. I said angrily, 'Zaharoff volunteered fifty million to the Bolshevik leaders. Half, was it? Half of the hundred million Nicholas sent to London. If they're dead, it can't be claimed. If they've disappeared –' And then it hit me like a blinding light!

Oh, they'd been clever. So damned murderously clever. Zaharoff more than Bronard, as you would imagine – you who read this now.

I killed him with my own hands. I completed the burial of the Imperial Family, and made a rough sketch-map of where the grave lay. Bronard's body I dragged into the marsh and left to be devoured by predators less evil than himself.

There is little left to tell. I left the forest bearing with me the map and the camera – and a new vow. Yurovsky was to be first to die; and he died, within a month, at my hands in Moscow, where he had fled with many royal valuables.

That done, I concerned myself for a time with opposition to the Bolsheviks. The Romanov treasure aboard the steamer *Rus*, still at Tobolsk and still guarded, was captured by White Russian forces, guided by myself, a few days after the fall of Ekaterinburg and went into the war chest of Admiral Kolchak's anti-Bolshevik armies. I fought with Kolchak for a while, but became spirit-weary of war and killing and at last contrived a way to Moscow where, when I had recovered the document, I learned that Sverdlov had died already of some natural ailment.

Is there more? Yes, there is Zaharoff: he was already Sir Basil by the time I returned to England; honoured everywhere, trusted nowhere and rich as Crœsus.

God, *how* he deserved to die! – he who all his life had profited by the deaths of others. But somehow I could not kill him though it would, ironically, have been supremely simple. For many times I watched him sit, often alone, at a café in Monte Carlo. But killing was now beyond me. I had seen enough of death.

So I decided in the end that a truer justice should be done. Zaharoff's empire must be toppled by the greed that built it. And this I have arranged.

Did he know? Yes, he knew. For years he had me hunted; paid me a pension of fifty thousand pounds a year because he had no alternative. And had me hunted. Not successfully. The money I sent to children, always: principally to those damaged (and always there are plenty) by weapons of war.

He would have had me killed, but he never found me. I could have killed *him*, but I left him to age and the knowledge of his mortality.

We are both gone, now. But in my old age I have drawn comfort from the knowledge that though I failed so many, I shall not fail in the end. Greed will pull down what was built.

You – whoever you may be – you began the process by questioning the payment. That was the trigger. I knew that some day, a greedy man would seek to prevent the payment. And so would begin to bring down the Temple. For, once the process was begun, nothing would stop it.

What, then, have I done? I have simply provided others

273

with the means of litigation. There are three papers, three pieces of evidence.

1. The document signed by Nicholas Romanov disclaiming not fifty but *five hundred* million in gold sent to London and to Zaharoff.

2. My own sworn statement that Tsar Nicholas II signed the disclaimer under duress.

3. Several photographs – those taken outside Ekaterinburg on 17th July, 1918. Bronard was as clever at photography as at treachery, for they are all clear and very recognizable. Their authenticity I have also attested in a sworn statement.

As you read this, copies of all these documents are on their way to you, but also to the present head of the House of Romanov, and to the Soviet Government, both of whom will, I feel sure, be keen to acquire the sum which five hundred million has grown into after more than half a century in the hands of a fine and reputable bank.

I remain,

Yours faithfully,
H.G. Dikeston.

CHAPTER FIFTEEN

————— ◆ —————

The Zaharoff Defence

Malory sat white-faced, the final packet of Dikeston's story on the desk in front of him.

It was all before his time, yet it was no puzzled; he knew enough of the times to make sense of it, and what he was not sure of, could guess. The Tsar had sent the gold: there was very strong evidence for that. Dikeston's narrative was true, too: it squared too closely with history to be anything else.

The hundred million in Hillyard, Cleef's vault could only be a part of the Romanov bullion. But where was the rest? Covered by the Arrangement, the ever-mysterious Arrangement? That Arrangement of Sir Basil's with the Chancellor of the Exchequer and the Bank of England, and known only to the Chancellor, the Governor, and the Senior Partner of Hillyard, Cleef: the Arrangement that there be *always one hundred million in the vault.*

All the rest went to the Bank of England. As gold prices rose, the Bank took more. It had done so for half a century.

The Arrangement made by Zaharoff and Lloyd George, Malory thought. Made by cunning men: the one with war businesses to feed, the other with a war to be paid for.

Five hundred million! Four hundred taken into Lloyd George's – no, into the *nation's* – coffers to pay for a war. And one hundred to Zaharoff's care. But not for spending, not for conversion, not for transfer; no, something worth more than any of them. Here was the provision of eternal stability.

Clever, cunning men . . . Malory sat up suddenly.

275

Eternal?
Apparently not.

All through the day Malory sat; a stooped and elderly version of Rodin's *Thinker*, he was brooding and almost motionless. Beside him lay the papers which step by step had brought Hillyard, Cleef to the edge of the calamity promised by Zaharoff in that first Senior Partner's note.

Malory had no doubt that if it could be shown that enough bullion to make up the justly-famous Hillyard, Cleef hoard had come originally from Imperial Russia, from the private treasure store of Tsar Nicholas II, then serious legal battle would unquestionably be joined. Romanov survivors would lay claim to Romanov gold; the Russian Government would demand the return of Russian gold. Hillyard, Cleef would have to defend against both.

The golden foundation upon which Hillyard, Cleef had been based so proudly for so long, would be ripped away . . .

Not only that; the British Government, having mis-appropriated four-fifths of the Tsar's gold in 1915, would find itself paying interest *compound*! Malory informed the office of the Governor of the Bank of England of a prob-able and large liability and quite soon the Governor came round in person to 6 Athelsgate to hear the story and left, moaning softly to himself, to calculate compound interest at assorted rates on four hundred million for sixty-odd years.

All this left Malory still plunged in thought and deeply unhappy. Though he had suspected from the very start that Dikeston's threat was anything but a joke, the realization that ruin now faced Hillyard, Cleef was a single and continuing nasty surprise, recurring minute by minute. He was naturally much troubled at the thought of the bank's ruin but he was baffled and angry at the prospect of defeat by a man like Dikeston who had been not only less than clever, but was *dead*!

But most of all he was unhappy with Zaharoff. The old villain had known the danger and had even paid out a fortune over the years to ward it off; but he appeared to have erected no actual defence. Zaharoff must have guessed, presumably, at Dikeston's hatred, but he who foresaw everything had not foreseen the attack upon the bank itself.

Why not – when he knew the hazards?

Surely, Malory kept muttering to himself, Zaharoff must have taken further measures to protect the gold. He had done so once – by sending Dikeston to Russia. But then nothing more? Ridiculous! Malory suddenly sat up straight and busied himself with a fresh and aromatic Romeo No.3. Yes, ridiculous: Sir Basil would have done *something* . . .

He lit the Romeo with particular care and searched the wreathing smoke for Zaharoff's likeness, wanting to peer even into the phantom brain. The image was elusive. He sent for the oaken box of Senior Partner's Notes and went through the many envelopes. No luck again. By now, however, Malory was convinced that Sir Basil *had* done something, *must* have done something. It had not been in the nature of the man to leave his castles undefended. Somewhere there would have been a drawbridge to raise.

Would have been? The virtue of gold was that it was indestructible, more or less, short of a nuclear bomb. So – there *would* be!

Soon, in the boardroom – he had been hunting through the building for traces of Zaharoff's remaining spoor – he sat looking at the oaken chair, wishing the old man were seated in it. He contemplated the ancient wood fruitlessly for a long time and actually rose to go before noticing in the decorative carving that curious continuous line which keeps turning back upon itself: the pattern known as the Greek Key.

Scenting the trail, he went over the chair from top to bottom, and could see nothing. He tapped with a paper-knife for hollowed places; there were none. Any knobs and

277

cracks in the wood were prised and pressed: hidden compartments were not revealed.

As Horsfall drove him home, Malory glowered out of the Bentley's window, seeking inspiration in the streets. Twice in as many miles he saw the Greek Key pattern again: once on the canopy above a restaurant, and again in gold on the window of an antique shop.

Lady Malory awaited him in the library, as she always did; she stood, again as she always did, beside a silver tray upon which decanters rested. He kissed her cheek, and she began to pour whisky. He said, 'Not now, thankee, m'dear.'

She stared at him. She had poured his evening whisky for half a century, failing to do so only when he was abroad. 'You're not *ill*, Horace?'

'Puzzled.' He lowered himself into a chair, rather heavily, she thought.

'Is it serious?'

He nodded.

Lady Malory, too, had known Zaharoff. Her interest immediately quickened at his name, and a smile began to flicker on her lips. She had been a famous beauty as a girl and Sir Basil, even in old age, had had an eye for beautiful girls. She had once told Malory of a contemporary, a lovely debutante of the same year, who had an enormous fondness for the city of Venice. Zaharoff invited her to dinner at his Paris home in the Avenue Hoche and in the course of the evening took her to see the cellars. One had been flooded. On the water floated a gondola. It contained a double bed.

Lady Malory was in no doubt at all that her husband must be right. 'It will be simple,' she said, 'and really rather clever. And it will be nothing whatever to do with the Greek Key design. That simply informs you there *is* a key.'

Unusually, Malory had no appetite, but his thirst returned after an hour or so. Lady Malory also sipped malt whisky and as the hours went on they became obsessed with a possibility.

Upon Sir Horace's thin watch-chain hung a gold numeral. The number was 6, and he had inherited it from his father; the numeral represented 6 Athelsgate, and had been given to Malory's father by Zaharoff.

It was quite possible that the 6 could serve as a key. But where was the lock?

Six Athelsgate being very much a place of small rituals, the telephone on Malory's desk rang next morning at five minutes to eleven. Since the day was a Tuesday, he knew why.

He lifted the receiver and said, 'Good morning, Griffin.'

'Five minutes, Sir Horace, if you're coming down.' Griffin was the keeper of the gold, a once-massive Cockney now rather shrunken by advanced years, and responsible not only for the machinery of protection, but for showing the gold to inspecting parties.

'I don't think so. Any visitors?'

'Party of kids from Wapping, that's all. Just the five minutes, then?'

'Yes.'

Malory replaced the telephone. The thought and the disconnection came simultaneously and he hurried out of his office and down the stairs, to stand glowing with a patient benevolence he was far from feeling as a dozen or so twelve-years-olds made noises of astonishment at the sight of the gold.

'Hold it open,' he said to Griffin as the last of the youngsters filed out.

Griffin, old as he was, made haste. An electronic code linked 6 Athelsgate to the safe-makers, Messrs Chubb, whose technicians alone could override the time lock which would shortly come into play. If the door closed, it would not open again for a week.

'**HOW LONG?**' asked the computer screen.

'Tell them several hours,' Malory replied. He looked at the gold stack and calculated there must be roughly fifteen hundred bars; he then decided, and typed, 'Vault to remain open until further notice.'

They apparently had collective hysterics at Chubb & Co., but Malory's signature number showed his authority. He was warned that he must bear responsibility.

'What's going on, Sir Horace?' Griffin asked in surprise. Nothing like this had ever happened before.

'I have just realized,' Malory said, 'that I know far too little about your work, Griffin. Please describe it.'

'Well, sir.' Griffin turned to look at the stack of ingots he had spent a lifetime tending. 'It's less than it used to be. Time was when the gold just about filled the vault. Inflation, that is, sir. Pound's worth nuthin'.'

Malory nodded and otherwise kept silent. Somewhere in this place, he had become convinced, the answer must lie. Even if Griffin was a chatterbox, Malory was very ready to listen.

'Most of it's never even been moved,' Griffin went on, 'Not since the gold came here. One or two bars on the top may get moved about, but not the rest.'

'Why's that?'

'Orders, Sir Horace.'

'Whose?'

'Blessed if I know, sir. Come from before my time, but they've always been followed. When the bars are moved it's always from the top layer. Never touch the next till that layer's gone.'

'So the bottom ones have been there since –?'

'Well, since the vault was built, sir. Nineteen-fifteen, wasn't it?'

'Do you have the orders actually written down?' Malory enquired.

'Well, they're typed out, sir, nowadays.'

'Nowadays?'

'They weren't always, sir. They were in Indian ink on vellum for years. But the vellum got wore through.'

'And thrown away, Mr Griffin?'

'No, sir. I kept it. Would you like a look?'

'Oh yes!' said Malory fervently.

How marvellous! he thought. The handwriting was quite unmistakable, influenced as it was by the graceful, flowing Turkish/Arabic script of Zaharoff's Constantinople youth. Further, there stood at the foot of the sheet of instructions the letters ZZ. The sheet of vellum was certainly worn – and grubby too – but it was perfectly clear. Malory fumbled for his spectacles and began to read.

As Griffin had said, the instructions were precise, but they concerned only the moving of the gold by mechanical hand on to the tiny trolley beneath the vault which connected directly with the bullion vaults of the Bank of England. They specified the order in which bars were to be removed from each layer (Zaharoff had envisaged roaring inflation; that was clear).

And then: 'If at any time the second lowest layer of ingots be breached, such breach may only take place in the presence of the Senior Partner of Hillyard, Cleef. He must be alone in the vault at the time.'

Malory gazed at the rows of ingots stacked like bricks on the floor of the vault. 'Something's hidden in there,' he murmured to himself.

'Beg pardon, Sir Horace?'

Malory began to take off his jacket. 'How old are you, Griffin?'

'Seventy-four, sir.'

'Well, I'm seventy-eight. If I can, you can!'

'Can what, sir?'

'Shift these bars.'

It would have been hard labour for two fit young men. With the gold price that day at $ 350 per troy ounce (give or

281

take a cent or two) Hillyard, Cleef's one hundred million
was represented by something a little short of fifteen
hundred 'good delivery' bars, each bar being of four hundred troy ounces. Each weighed, accordingly, close to
twenty-eight pounds.

Moving the first two was accomplished with enthusiasm
accompanied by rapid diminution of energy. 'Half a
hundredweight, that is, sir,' Griffin muttered. 'And there's
only eighteen tons to go.'

'My God!'

'Yes, and I *was* wondering, sir . . .'

'Go on,' Malory gasped.

'Well, if you *want* to do it all by hand, Sir Horace? 'Cos
we have got the mechanical hand.'

Malory smiled at him. 'Chairs, too?' he enquired.

They sat and watched. Griffin showed him how to control the hand as it picked up an ingot, pivoted, placed it as
required, and returned for another. Malory found the
movement pleasant to watch: soothing, almost – but he was
too on edge to be soothed.

In two hours the stack had been reduced to two layers,
and all the bars, Malory was delighted to see, still bore as a
'chop', or imprint, not the Imperial Russian Eagle, but the
oval of the Credit Suisse. How the devil *that* had been
achieved, with war raging in Europe, he did not care to
speculate.

The soft whirr of the mechanical hand ceased now, and
Griffin rose. 'Leave you to it, Sir Horace.'

'Yes. Thank you.' Now alone, Malory began to move the
bars . . .

The object was of so similar a colour, and Malory's eyes
had been half-dazzled for so long by the glow of the
overhead lighting reflected by the surfaces of the ingots,
that it must have lain exposed for some moments before he
saw it and switched off the hand.

He leaned over, picked up the object, and could not

suppress a chuckle; for Zaharoff's secret (and he was certain now that this *must* be Zaharoff's secret) was contained in a vessel entirely appropriate to the man: a brass shell-case. He frowned, though, as he turned it in his hands and saw that it was stamped with the name of its maker.

Not Vickers of Sheffield, though. The familiar stamp 'Kpz' was the mark of Krupp, of Essen.

It took time to summon Griffin, to communicate with Chubb's, to close the vault door. Inside the vault the bars were not replaced in a single neat stack. That could wait . . .

Sir Horace Malory, a long brown envelope in his hand concealing the shell-case, was on his way to his own office, where he quickly discovered that the 'Kpz' of Krupp was not the only peculiarity of the shell-case. Further lettering had been punched into the brass and it read: 'Do not attempt to open without correct key.' Malory looked for the keyhole and found it without difficulty. Where the percussion cap would normally have been, a barrel lock had been fitted.

His hands trembled a little as he removed the gold number 6 from his watch-chain and examined the small key opening of the lock. This was a moment – and he was keenly aware of it – of no little danger. The shell-case itself was warning enough, and everything he knew of Zaharoff underlined the warning. To use the wrong key would probably activate some explosive or incendiary device; Zaharoff had fabricated not toys, but arms. And if the shell-case contained protection for Hillyard, Cleef, then Malory was sure it would also contain the means of its own destruction.

He looked at the lock.

He looked at the key, noting the exactly-fashioned curve of the descender, which must presumably act upon the lock's spring.

I am, perhaps, about to die, he thought. He lit a cigar and

283

poured a small measure of Cardhu, and relished both. After a while he put the key into the lock: and heard the spring inside give. So far so good.

All the same, Malory removed the contents of the shell-case with considerable care. They were papers, rolled up, and had to be straightened before they could properly be examined. He performed the little task patiently, and found himself at last looking at a number of documents.

There were eighteen or twenty sheets altogether. Most were in either German or Russian; some were handwritten, others typed. They appeared, in the main, to be lists of names, though some seemed to be organizational charts. Only one was in English and that, like the instructions in the vault, was in the familiar cursive hand of Basil Zaharoff. Malory, sitting as he now felt he was, in a castle under siege, hoped this was the drawbridge, or even the boiling oil, which would keep the enemy out.

'In April of 1918 I made a visit to Germany,' Zaharoff wrote. 'Because of the war it was not made without difficulty, and for it I adopted a Bulgarian persona.'

Malory nodded to himself. Historians had already unearthed the strange fact of Zaharoff's trip – and the disguise he had used: that of a Bulgarian doctor – but had never fathomed its purpose, such purpose being largely unimaginable, considering that Britain and Germany had been four years at war and Zaharoff supplied many of the means of Britain's making that war.

I went to see Krupp, and Generals Ludendorff and Hindenburg to discuss the effect of the Treaty of Brest-Litovsk upon the future of the European conflict.

In February the previous year, because pressure upon me from the Imperial Russian Government had become too intense, I conceived the idea that Lenin be at once sent back to Russia to further foment the

Bolshevik Revolution and I conveyed this idea to Ludendorff and Hindenburg.

It was not done until March, because the German General Staff required safeguards. But then they agreed to the provision of the sealed train in which Lenin travelled, and the necessary safe-conduct through German lines, only upon Lenin's agreement to give, in exchange, the means of acting against the existing Communist organization inside Germany and Austria if it became necessary to do so.

Lenin agreed to this! The papers enclosed are lists of local members and cells of the German and Austrian Communist parties. The lists are Lenin's own, supplied by him, many in his own hand. They are the originals (Ludendorff and Hindenburg retained and required only copies) and several bear Lenin's signature.

Also among the papers is a letter from Lenin to General Ludendorff, confirming the authenticity of the documents.

All these were supplied to me in April of 1918 as a gesture of thanks after the establishment of peace the previous month between Lenin's Bolshevik regime and Germany.

They were, at that time, merely a means of applying pressure, if necessary, upon Lenin himself. With Lenin's death, and his subsequent steady elevation to something approaching sainthood, it seems to me now that these papers, (proving as they do that Lenin was willing, even eager, to betray all his political friends for personal advantage) could be used to strike at the very root of the Lenin legend. I feel sure any Soviet Government, now or in the future, would be deeply anxious to avoid their publication.

As to other potential contenders for our metallic assets: they may seek to prove many things, and some they may succeed in; but unless they are able to prove that our metal is their metal, they will be wasting their time.

Not notional sums: The metal itself.

ZZ

An hour later, the intervening time having been spent in reflection, Malory telephoned the Governor of the Bank of England. 'Thought I'd put you out of your misery, old feller. I've found it.'

'Found what?'

'The Zaharoff Defence,' said Malory.

'Oh, nicely put,' said the Governor. 'But will it work? How watertight is it?'

'Imagine you're Stalin,' Malory said, 'or Khruschev, or Brezhnev, or this feller Andropov whoever. Imagine that, eh? You've already got half the world and you want the other half. All of it on Leninist principles.'

'Go on.'

'And then somebody turned up who could show the idol's feet of clay?'

'And Zaharoff could?'

'You can forget Zaharoff,' said Malory. 'I rather believe I can do it myself!'